Home is

Where the

Heartburn is…

Home is Where the Heartburn is...

Kathleen
Kole

Sublime Coyote Media

This is a work of fiction. Names, characters, places and incidents are either the product of the author's imagination or are used fictitiously, and any resemblance to actual persons, living or dead, business establishments, events or locales is entirely coincidental.

HOME IS WHERE THE HEARTBURN IS...

Copyright © 2017 by Kathleen Kole

ISBN-13: 978-1927791-04-2
ISBN-10: 1-927791-04-9

This book is published by Sublime Coyote Media.

As always, for my Peter.

Thank you for believing.

Chapter 1

Paula winced when a sharp gust of wind blew across her face, tiny needles of cold pricking the skin on her cheeks as they passed. "Gadzooks," she muttered to herself, tugging at the green, knitted cap on her head and hunching her shoulders against the chill. If only she'd opted to dig out a heavier jacket, instead of donning her black trench coat when she'd left the house earlier that morning, she would have been better dressed for the elements.

Granted, it *should* have been warmer outside - it was only the top of October after all - but it seemed the sudden drop in temperature was holding fast; as though nature was sending a warning to the residents of Boxwood Hills that autumn was going to be swiftly danced out the door by winter in snow-covered boots.

It was probably high time she left anyway, if she was to be honest. She'd been stationed on the sidewalk for the last hour staring at the empty Craftsman-style home in front of her, the *SOLD* sign on the lawn swaying back and forth in the wind. After so much time, it seemed reasonable she'd been spotted by the residents in the neighboring houses and, more than likely, they were growing concerned about her presence. Heck, depending upon their natures, it was even possible they were fretting she was a potential squatter, scouting out the place.

Paula grinned at the idea of herself as a squatter and lifted the cardboard takeaway cup clutched in her right hand toward her mouth, only to discover it nearly weightless in her grasp.

"Well, hell," she said, her breath forming a small vapor cloud in front of her face as she gave the cup a shake.

Yup, empty.

Apparently, she'd been so focused on the slate grey and white trimmed house, she'd finished the last of her coffee without noticing.

"Time to go," she said, just before another blast of chilling wind rushed up against her, sending a shiver up her spine, and the fallen leaves from the neighbor's towering Red Maple tree scattered across the yard with abandon.

Paula watched them swirl in hypnotic circles of gold, ruby and eggplant across the shorn blades of grass on the lawn in front of her, until she was distracted by a section of branches on the tall, densely packed cedars along the perimeter of the yard: they were vibrating.

"Hello?" she called out, frowning at the hedge. "Is someone there?"

Before she could offer a second inquiry, a flash of black and white in the form of a cat burst from beneath the foliage, making her jump and yelp, "Oh!" while pressing one hand to her chest, over her heart.

The cat, meanwhile, paid her no mind. Instead, it gave itself a brisk shake then sauntered across the remaining expanse of lawn to spring soundlessly onto the bottom step of the house's whitewashed, wooden front porch.

Paula coughed, her esophagus stinging from the cold air she'd inadvertently swallowed when she'd gasped, then bent forward to rest the empty coffee cup on the pavement between her boots. Hands now free, she tugged off one of her green mittens and rummaged in her jacket pocket for a tissue to blot her running nose: all the while eyeballing the cat with distain as it sat regally on the step as though it owned the place.

Which it didn't.

And how did she know that? Easy. *She* owned the place. Okay, fine, *almost* owned it. In just a few more days the final subjects would be removed and it would officially become hers - well, hers and Declan's.

Paula wiped her nose with the rumpled tissue she'd liberated from her pocket and shifted her gaze to the house, recalling the feeling she'd had when she'd first set eyes on it from the backseat of their realtor's car as they'd pulled into the driveway two months ago.

Awestruck. Yes, that was the perfect word.

It was a beautiful place, simply beautiful. From the gabled roof and handcrafted stone accents, to the double-hung windows and sweeping front porch just waiting for summertime's return, she'd known their search was over the moment she'd crossed the threshold.

"Enjoy yourself while you can," Paula instructed, speaking directly to the cat. Well, to be fair, as directly as one *can* to a cat: felines being famous for indirect eye contact. "And don't think because you're cute I'm going to be any less adamant."

The cat yawned, displaying its white teeth and pink tongue.

"I don't care if I'm boring you," she went on, despite feeling certain that the neighbors who might have worried about her squatter potential had now added the concern she was batty as well, speaking loudly to a cat.

"We may not be able to move *ourselves* in right away because of the renovations," she continued, waving her mitten at the house, "but all of our *stuff* will be here. *And,* as soon as they're done we'll be here is a shot, so don't get too comfy."

A car pulled up to the curb behind her, interrupting her monologue, and Paula tugged her mitten back onto her hand while turning to see who'd arrived. The black and white cat took that moment to move with stealth-like precision further up the steps and disappear into the shadows.

Declan, her husband and soon-to-be co-house-owner, stepped from the vehicle and she regarded him - tall, broad-shouldered and so kind-hearted it practically lit him up from the inside. They'd only been married six months and their courtship had been fast: just four months dating before they'd gotten engaged and immediately eloped.

Prior to their meeting and subsequent whirlwind romance, Paula's life had been going in a completely different direction. It had been a no-nonsense road made up of work and more work, with the unfortunate addition of a man who had been fast proving himself unworthy of her time and attention.

Then, suddenly, there was Declan.

He'd stepped onto the scene and everything had spun around so fast, Paula had found herself able to consider the idea of miracles. The unworthy man who had been causing nothing but chaos had been smartly erased from the picture and she'd only had eyes for her now-husband. Even now, gazing upon him, her heart gave a flutter and she found herself thinking she was one lucky woman.

Declan grinned as he closed his car door, the crinkles at the edges of his hazel eyes warm and inviting, then joined her on the pavement. "I thought I'd find you here," he said, holding out her phone.

"Sorry," she apologized, taking it from his hand then pressing the button on the screen to check the time: 12:30 pm. No wonder her stomach had begun to rumble. "I didn't realize I'd left it behind until I'd gone too far to turn back."

"How long have you been out here, anyway?" He swept his gaze across her pink nose and cheeks, before looking into her brown eyes.

"Not long, I'm fine." She averted his knowing stare and tucked the phone into her jacket pocket. "Just been chatting with the cat."

Declan fastened the buttons on his navy blue, wool coat then turned his head back and forth. "Cat?"

Paula looked back toward the house. Nothing. "It must have left."

"Probably had the good sense to go inside where it's warm." He pulled his grey, hand-knit cotton scarf from around his neck and draped it around her shoulders. "You, on the other hand, look like you're nearly frozen and need to get out of this wind."

She smiled gratefully and swaddled the scarf's softness around her face. "I needed to get some fresh air. I stopped in at my parent's place to drop off a few things and Mom was cooking something with so much spice my eyes started burning."

He straightened the collar on his coat to cut the wind sliding down the back of his neck.

"I told her it was too much but, *as usual*, it fell on deaf ears. She's never understood that flavor and spice are two different things." She wrapped her arms around herself in a half-hug. "I remember this one time, when I was about eight and had a bowling party with my best girlfriends … have I told you this story?"

He shook his head. Even if he had, he'd let her tell it again. It was cathartic.

"Okay, so there I was, eight years old and my parents had just finished taking me and all my little girlfriends bowling. We went back home for snacks and everything was going along just fine … until the parents all started arriving for pickup time."

Declan nodded. He remembered the story. The last time it had been told was by Donna, Paula's mother, and her version was told with much hilarity.

"My mother had made up a batch of oatmeal, chocolate chewies for the parents, but failed to divulge she'd spiced them to - as she explained it - *'give them some kick'*."

"Right," he agreed.

Paula nodded at him. "So you do remember the story?"

"Uh-huh."

"Okay, so that would mean you *also* remember the ending, where we had eight parents whose mouths were nearly scalded by the addition of ghost peppers to the chewies. I mean, seriously, who the hell does that? I wanted to run away, I was so humiliated."

Declan regarded her fondly as she hunched her shoulders against the wind and tucked herself more deeply into his scarf.

"It won't be that long, you know," he soothed, smiling gently, then picking up the empty takeaway cup still nestled between her boots on the sidewalk.

"Long enough," was her reply as she reached to tug on the edge of her knit cap before wiping her nose again with the tissue still clutched in her other hand.

"The time will go by in a blink," he insisted, walking the cup over to his car and placing it on the hood.

"I wouldn't leave it there. The wind will take it."

He picked the cup up a second time, opened his car door and leaned in to put it in the holder in the center console. "It will be like we were never even there," he further assured her, straightening up and closing the car door.

"Said the guy who's not moving back into HIS parent's house for the next month."

"Two weeks, technically."

Paula rolled her eyes. "Right. So they *said*. But they were also super speedy to clarify that the timeline was an *estimate* and, let's be honest, they're contractors and timelines always shift. You, of all people, should know this."

She had a point.

Declan's work as an IT manager was all about estimates and, more often than not, they shifted when new problems appeared that hadn't been evident when the job began.

"Well, we'll have to stay optimistic then." He tucked his hands into his pockets and strolled back over to stand beside her, facing the house. "We'll work from the premise that their estimate is spot-on and keep our eyes on the prize."

Paula blotted her nose. "What I don't get is, why they won't let us move in while they're working."

"Well, it's not so much a matter of not *letting* us, as it is about the fact that we'd be trying to live in a house without a functioning kitchen," he reminded her. "And, come on, people have to have a kitchen…."

"I mean, they can't *legally* keep us out, right?" She put her hands on her hips, superhero style.

"Well, *no*. But —"

"Exactly. Obviously they can *advise* us about the risks of moving in while they're working, but legally keep us out? No dice."

"Well, of course, that's true," he agreed, "but—"

"BUT, it still comes down to the fact we can do whatever the heck we want," she stated, turning to face him head on. "Just like that cat."

"Sure." Declan still hadn't seen a cat and, besides, it really was the least of his concerns. "So what, then? What are you saying? You want to forget staying at your parent's while the work is being done and move in here, instead?"

The righteous expression slipped from Paula's face and she shook her head. Her hands followed, dropping from her hips to hang limply at her sides; a defeated superhero.

They both knew the lay of the land. It was an older home and, like it or not, the kitchen had been left to deteriorate. From the rotting cabinets to the peeling floors to the terrifyingly outdated stove, (how the former owners had avoided a grease fire, Paula would never know), it needed a complete overhaul. Truth be told, they'd thanked their lucky stars the rest of the house had been maintained, otherwise they would have had to forget it - no matter how great its potential - and keep searching.

"No. Of course not," she sighed. "I'm just having a moment of self-pity. In my ideal scenario, we'd be able to afford the overlap of the rent payment at the apartment *and* the mortgage payment at the house, *and* have money for the renos as well."

Declan grinned. "Now there's a scenario I like."

"Me, too," she said, then pointed sharply at the house when she caught a movement out of the corner of her eye. "Ah-ha! See? There? The cat."

Declan turned to look and, sure enough, the black and white cat she'd been talking about slunk from the house's shadow and seemed to ooze down the front porch steps.

"Told you. Not crazy." She raised an eyebrow and threw him a pointed look.

His eyes widened. "What? I never said a thing."

"Mmm-hmm," she murmured, tucking the used tissue in her hand back into her jacket pocket.

The cat paused in the middle of the lawn and turned its head to look at them.

Declan raised a hand in greeting, and the feline assumed the same wide-eyed expression he'd just worn.

Paula chuckled as it sprinted back into the hedge cover.

"Apparently, it thought it was invisible," Declan observed.

"Apparently," she agreed, before the smile dropped from her face as an image of her parents, and living back at their house, flitted across her thoughts. "I know how it feels."

"What?" Declan asked, keeping his voice playful as he attempted to lighten the suddenly shifting mood. "Don't I shower you with enough adoration?"

"She didn't even hesitate, you know," Paula stated, referring to her mother. "When I asked if we could move in for a couple of weeks, she just said she'd have clean sheets for us in my old room - my old room!" She exhaled sharply.

"That seems nice," Declan offered, before she cut him off.

"No." She pointed a finger at him. "Not in this case."

Declan waited, he knew she had more to add. Again, it was cathartic.

"This isn't a situation of her keeping my room because she can't part with the memories."

"No?"

"No. It's a situation of her being so bloody self-involved that my moving out, *a freaking decade ago*, didn't even register on her radar."

"Come on, Hon," he tried, again. "You know she noticed."

"You'd think so, wouldn't you?" she asked, frowning. "But the damning evidence of not one thing changing in that room since then seems to indicate otherwise. We should just be grateful they vacuum it."

Declan shook his head, not following her logic.

"Of course *you* don't get what I mean," she said, throwing her hands up in the air. "*Your* Mom has kept your and your brother's rooms exactly the same since you moved out: like shrines to your childhoods. That's the norm in *that* house. Very different from my parents."

Declan had the good grace to shrug his shoulders in agreement. It was true, after all: his mother *had* kept his and his four brother's bedrooms exactly as they'd left them after each one of them moved out. He wouldn't have been all that surprised if she went the full gambit and roped them off for viewings.

Paula gave herself a small shake, then said, "Anyway, it doesn't matter now. It's all water under the bridge."

Declan reached out and gentle touched her cheek. "It does matter. Finish your thought. You'll feel better."

She picked up the length of scarf draped across the front of her jacket and fiddled with the edging. "I don't know, maybe I'm just being a cliché; twenty nine years old and still bothered by my mother and her nuttiness. I should stop such nonsense, my habit of romanticizing things, and learn to see my invisibility as a blessing in disguise."

"Trust me, you are anything BUT invisible," he said, placing his hands on her shoulders and looking directly into her eyes. "And, if it makes you feel any better, if you were invisible I'd trade you for some of it. You get *my* Mom's radar and I get some of your cloaking. Win, win."

She chuckled and let the scarf drop back across the front of her jacket. "I used to ask if I was adopted, much to their great amusement."

Declan slid his hands from her shoulders and gave her a quick kiss on the lips. "Listen, if you can just remember that *that* was a long time ago and us living there is only for two weeks, it will be fine. We'll focus on how great everything is going to be here at the house when the kitchen is done and forget the rest."

"Fat lot of good that'll do me when I'm in custody for assaulting my mother. You'll have to bring me actual *physical* photos of the reno, because they will have confiscated my phone when I was dragged away kicking and screaming."

Declan laughed. "I can do that."

"And why isn't even one of your brothers a contractor?" She threw her hands up in mock-exasperation. "I mean, seriously, just one. You have four of them, for god's sake, you'd think at least one of them would have gone into a trade."

Declan smirked and ran his fingers through his hair. "Hey, be grateful Liam didn't insist on proving he could do the work or we might have been sorry."

Liam, thirty one years old, two years younger than Declan and the baby of the five Dempsey brothers, was a landscape designer. When he'd gotten wind of the need for the kitchen renovation in the new house, he'd gone to great lengths to argue he was fully qualified to do the job. (Based, apparently, on the fact that he'd once helped their Dad replace a toilet.)

Paula remembered the daily texts Declan had received from his brother stating he could do it and grimaced at the thought.

"Uh-huh," he said, watching her face. "In fact, I think we should be *thanking* Angus, Cian and Emmet for busting his chops about it to the point he finally revoked the offer. Can you imagine the drama that would have happened if they hadn't and we would have had to say no?"

Paula nodded. It was true, there would have been drama. His Mom, Bonnie, would have gotten involved and tried to guilt them into letting Liam do the work and then they would have had to deal with *that*…. Ugg. "Point taken."

"Okay!" He clapped his hands together. "I think we've said and seen enough, don't you?"

"And given the neighbors enough of a show."

"Exactly, let's get outta here."

Paula reached out to wrap her arms around his waist and he pulled her close, the scratchy texture of his blue wool coat familiar against her cheek. She closed her eyes and leaned into his warmth, inhaling the scent of him: soap and cologne mingled with the crisp autumn air. Home. She opened her eyes to look, again, at the house and tried to muster up some optimism for the two weeks ahead. Two weeks spent living at her parents place. Two weeks of she and Declan sleeping in her childhood bedroom. Two weeks of trying her damnedest to keep a level head when her mother drove her to distraction.

Declan released her and gestured to the car, waiting curb-side. "After you, Darlin'."

Paula followed him to the vehicle and looked up at the grey-white, overcast sky. "It feels like it could snow."

"God, I hope not," he said, opening the passenger side door for her. "It's too soon."

Paula slipped past him and settled into the soft leather seat with a sigh. Maybe they could just live in the car until the renovations were done. It sounded like less work and at least they'd be in the driveway of the new house; instead of down the hall from her parent's bedroom.

Declan walked around the other side of the car, got in and started the engine. "Okay, so we only have a few more boxes to pack before tomorrow morning when the movers arrive. The plan is, we'll get those done then open a bottle of wine to celebrate the new chapter beginning."

She grinned at him, enjoying his enthusiasm.

He turned to gaze up at the house. "Nothing but good times ahead. Our future begins here."

Excitement flickered in Paula's chest. Yes, that was what she was going to focus upon: their future. Holding the bright glow of it in her thoughts would illuminate what mattered most while effectively banishing, once and for all, the dread of staying with her parents. It was only two weeks, after all. A brief detour, nothing more. It would pass in a blink of an eye.

She reached over to squeeze his hand in solidarity. "Let's get those boxes packed and start pouring the wine. Our future is calling."

Douglas, sitting at the butcher-block table in his kitchen, looked up from the newspaper crossword puzzle he was working on when the back door opened and a blast of chilled air rushed inside, pushing Paula and Declan along with it into the house.

"Jeez," Paula complained, her face scrunched as she scooted behind Declan. "If I wasn't sure before, I am today. Autumn has definitely arrived."

"Hey! There you two are!" Douglas cheered, all smiles as he pulled his black-rimmed, rectangular reading glasses from his face and set them on a pile of white paper napkins on the tabletop.

Declan grinned at his father-in-law then pushed the door closed behind them, banishing the elements from the house. "Hey, Doug, what's shakin'?"

"Just my fist at this darned puzzle," he remarked, chuckling good-naturedly as he put his pencil down on the newspaper.

"Hey, Dad," Paula said, warmly. "You're smart to be wearing your flannel."

Douglas pushed the drooping left sleeve on his red-plaid flannel shirt up to his elbow and nodded. "Mom ordered me a bunch of new ones online, so I'm set. So, how'd everything go? Your stuff all ready to be moved into the new house tomorrow morning?"

"You bet," Declan replied, while Paula took a deep breath then started coughing and waving her hand in front of her face.

"Good god, Dad," she gasped. "What on Earth is that smell?"

Douglas' eyebrows arched in surprise. "Smell?"

"Oh, come on," Paula insisted, tugging the knit cap from her head and unwinding Declan's scarf from around her neck. "Are you seriously telling me you can't smell that? As soon as Declan closed the door it hit me in the face. It's like you've opened a can of gasoline in here." She looked at her husband. "You can smell that, too, right?"

Declan bent to remove his shoes, staying silent and keeping out of it.

"Mom *has* been cooking this afternoon...," Douglas offered, rubbing the salt and pepper stubble on his chin as Donna rounded the doorway from the family room into the kitchen.

Paula braced herself, as she so often did, for her mother's ... *exuberance*. The woman could be a force of nature.

"Oh, WONDERFUL! You're home!" she effused, straightening the front of the green apron she had wrapped around her flowing, brown and yellow tie-dyed ankle-length skirt.

Paula flinched at the word *home*, she'd long stopped referring to her parent's house as that, but instead of correcting her mother she turned around to open the rectangular window next to the kitchen door.

Declan shucked his coat from his shoulders and hung it on one of the mismatched hooks on the wall adjacent to the backdoor, then smiled at his mother-in-law. "Hey, Donna. Something certainly smells interesting in here."

Paula snorted at his choice of the word *'interesting'* and raked her fingers through her short, red hair.

Declan pretended he didn't hear her.

"Funny you should mention that," Donna remarked, pulling at her unkempt, copper-colored waves; giving the impression of urgency. "Because we need your help."

Paula unbuttoned her coat and asked, "What kind of help? Airing out the house?"

She waved her hand, dismissively. "Not *you*. Declan."

Paula rolled her eyes and hung her coat on an empty hook next to Declan's jacket.

"I'm all ears," he said, straightening his burgundy sweater and stepping around Paula to join Douglas at the kitchen table.

"'Cause your sense of smell is shot," Paula quipped, flicking her shoes off with sharp jerks of her feet.

Donna continued, as though she hadn't heard her daughter's comment. "We've been having a debate about the potatoes."

Douglas gave Declan a pat on the shoulder when he sat down in the neighboring chair. "Good to have you kids around for a bit."

Declan replied, "We really appreciate you letting us stay," to his father-in-law, while Paula simultaneously gaped at her mother and said, "Did you say *potatoes*? Is *that* what we're smelling in here? *Potatoes*?"

"Of *course* not," Donna retorted, pulling off her apron and tossing it onto the table with a flourish.

Paula stared, waiting for more. Nothing. Her mother stared back at her as though *she* was waiting for more as well.

Declan's cellphone trilled, breaking the silence and, thankfully, the staring contest. "Hang on a sec," he said, pulling the phone from his pocket to check the incoming text.

"Who is it?" Paula asked, walking over to the cupboard beside the sink to get a water glass.

"My Mom. Checking in." He quickly typed a reply on the screen.

Douglas, his attention back on his crossword, mumbled 'potatoes' under his breath while he picked up his pencil and peered at the page in front of him.

"Right," Declan said, hitting send on his phone then putting it on the tabletop. "So, you were saying you were debating about potatoes. How can I help?"

Donna clapped her hands together and began pacing the floor, gesturing wildly as she spoke. "Yes! Potatoes! We keep going back and forth, and back and forth, on which type of potatoes to pair with the roast I'm making for dinner."

"So, you're saying that's the *roast* we're smelling then?" Paula asked, pouring a glass of water from the tap and wrinkling her nose.

Donna shook her head and pulled out a chair opposite Declan at the table to sit down. "And we just can't decide between boiled, baked or mashed."

Declan's phone trilled again, but he ignored it.

Douglas picked up his reading glasses and put them back on. "Your phone beeped."

"It's fine," Declan said, then nodded encouragingly at Donna. "So, you can't decide *and…?*"

"Right," she agreed, then started to frown when he said nothing more. "Well, it's obvious, isn't it?"

Declan looked at Douglas, in case he'd missed something. He shrugged his shoulders in a 'beat's me' manner.

"Oh, for pity's sake, you're going to make me spell it out, are you?" she chided, gently, her annoyance turning into amusement when she realized he wasn't connecting the dots. "Fine. *You're* the Irishman in the family, which type goes best with the roast?"

Paula, drinking her water, nearly choked. Between coughs she managed to blurt, "Are you kidding me?"

Donna lifted her eyebrows in surprise at her vehemence. "What?"

"*Really?*" Paula demanded, placing her glass on the countertop with a solid thump then grabbing a dish towel to blot the water that had dripped onto her black blouse. "You don't think there's anything off-putting about that statement?"

"Off-putting? How was I off-putting?" Donna raised her hands in the air, looking from Declan to Douglas.

Declan's phone trilled yet again, but this time no one said a word about it.

"It's a perfectly legitimate question," Donna insisted, righteously, while a gust of wind charged through the window Paula had opened, scattering the pile of napkins on the table.

"It's fine, Sweetie," Declan placated, reaching out to retrieve the strays and re-stack them.

"No, it's not," Paula shot back, tossing the towel onto the countertop.

Donna gave Douglas a *look* and pursed her lips. "For goodness sake, Paula, no need to get so up-in-arms. All I did was ask his opinion about potatoes."

"Because he's *Irish*," Paula practically spat, irritated even further by the *look* her mother had sent to her father. She was married, she knew what was happening there.

"Well, yes, but I didn't mean anything bad by it," she defended, folding her arms across her chest. "I meant it as a compliment."

"A compliment!" Paula repeated, throwing her hands in the air while another gust of wind sent the blue curtains on either side of the window dancing. "How on Earth is that a compliment?"

"Whoa," Douglas said, when the breeze proceeded to upset the napkin pile for a second time, flinging them across the tabletop. "Might want to close that window now."

Donna reached out to pat Declan's arm affectionately. "Because he's our resident expert on potatoes. And perhaps also green beer."

Declan chuckled, earning himself a disgruntled glare from his wife.

"See?" Donna seized upon his good humor. "He doesn't mind. You're not offended, right Declan?"

Declan glanced in Douglas' direction. His father-in-law met his eye, but reserved comment as he collected the napkins. He, too, was well aware of the rock-and-a-hard-place situation at hand.

"Tell you what," Donna declared, releasing Declan's arm. "I'll just go ahead and chose, okay? That way, we can forget this little misunderstanding ever happened. After all, it's only potatoes, for goodness sake. No reason to make it such a big deal and let it sully the celebration of you two moving your things into the new house."

"That sounds perfect," Douglas enthused. "Good plan, Hon."

Paula clenched her teeth. As always, her mother started something then spun it around and, suddenly, it was everyone *else* 'making a big deal out of nothing'. Paula took a levelling breath and distracted herself from her rising irritation by looking around the kitchen: it had been a least a month since they'd visited, but nothing had changed. Heck, nothing had changed since she'd last lived there.

Not that that was a surprise.

Her parents had remodeled when they'd first moved into the house - six years before she was born - and it had stayed that way ever since. The room was a salute to nineteen-eighties style, sporting oak cabinets and red Formica countertops, green and orange checker-patterned wallpaper and matching curtains. It was like something out of an outdated movie set.

"Is that window open?" Donna demanded, changing tracks. "If you don't watch it, the wind is going to start blowing things around."

Paula glanced at Declan while her mother got up from her seat and charged over to the window, closed it, then began darting around the kitchen like a bird with nowhere to settle. She even looked the part, with her tie-dyed skirt and yellow peasant blouse. Declan, however, was shoulder to shoulder with her Dad, studying the crossword puzzle, oblivious to everything else. Finally, when Donna stopped flitting and pulled out a cabinet drawer to rummage through the items inside, Paula sidled back across the floor and reopened the window a crack; determined to get rid of the last remnants of the acrid smell.

"Need any help there, Hon?" Douglas asked, handing the pencil to Declan.

"No." She continued to root through the drawer until she pulled out a quarter. She grinned as though she'd found gold and held it up with a flourish. "Ah-haaa!"

Douglas peered intently at the crossword puzzle while Declan filled in a blank space with '*origami*'.

"We should get our things from the car and take them upstairs," Paula announced, pointedly ignoring her mother's dramatics. If her Dad and Declan weren't taking the bait, she certainly wasn't going to be the one to do so.

Declan looked up from the newspaper, but instead of rising to follow her as she exited the kitchen, he focused on his mother-in-law. She was rubbing the quarter she'd found in the drawer back and forth in her palms. He was about to inquire as to what she was doing, but then she flipped the coin into the air with a grand flourish and said, "Tails!" when it landed in her palm.

Douglas lifted his gaze from the crossword. "Tails?"

She nodded, a satisfied expression on her face. "Yup. Mashed potatoes, it is!"

Declan laughed and shook his head. No question, it was going to be an interesting two weeks.

Declan reclined on the queen-sized bed in Paula's childhood bedroom and watched as she darted back and forth from their suitcases to the dresser: like an overactive honeybee from flower to hive. Under other circumstances he might have commented that she reminded him of her mother when she did that, but her sense of humor was not in residence to appreciate the teasing.

"Want a bite?" he offered, hoping to distract her with a crabapple Donna had foisted upon him as he was leaving the kitchen.

"No, thanks."

"You can have all of it," he invited, holding the fruit out. "I can get another one from downstairs."

She shook her head while ferrying a pile of his t-shirts over to the dresser.

He sighed and ran his free hand back and forth across the cottony surface of the quilt. It was a patchwork of large, multicolored squares and no matter how many times he saw it, he marveled at how both it and the rest of the room's decor gave him the feeling of stepping back in time: circa nineteen ninety seven.

"You *know* that can wait until later, right? It's okay if we don't get everything put away this minute."

"Yes," she agreed, "but if I get it done now we can get on with other things and not have to feel like charity cases, our meager belongings in suitcases."

"Do you want help?"

She shook her head. "No. It's a good distraction from my thoughts."

Declan reserved comment and, instead, settled further back into the pillow beneath his head and ate the rest of the crabapple. While he chewed, he studied the *NSYNC* posters taped to the cathedral ceiling above his head, amused at the idea of a young, girlish Paula standing on her bed to affix them there. "Baby, bye, bye, bye," he sang, under his breath, further entertaining himself.

"And yes, I realize it's family not charity," she went on, opening another drawer in the dresser, "but either way, it feels ridiculous to be living back in my old room when I'm twenty nine years old and a married woman."

"*Visiting* your old room," Declan clarified.

Paula grimaced and waved a hand in front of her face when the repugnant smell of lavender wafted from the open drawer. "Phew! That is strong!" She put the stack of shirts onto the dresser top and yanked a satchel of dried flowers out of the drawer. "And here's the culprit," she verified, before closing it and proceeding to pull out the other two beneath it. "My god, we're inundated," she announced, making mock-retching sounds as she lifted more satchels from the drawer's depths.

"So, tell me," Declan teased, while she dropped the offending potpourri into the waste paper basket next to the dresser and walked over to the window. "Were you a *Joey Fatone* fan, or maybe *Justin Timberlake*?"

Paula smirked at the blatant amusement in his tone and cracked open the window: the sheer yellow curtains on either side of the frame lifted and flapped in the breeze that started blowing through the screen. He could never resist ribbing her about her boy-band phase.

"Ha, ha," she began, before being stopped short by a pounding on the bedroom door that shook the walls of the room. "Jeez!" she snapped, marching across the purple area rug to yank the door open.

Declan shifted himself up onto his elbows to see who was on the other side then grinned when he saw Amber, Paula's younger sister, standing in the hallway.

"What the hell?" Paula accused, while Amber brushed past her into the room.

"Well, *hello* to you, too," she replied, flipping her long dark hair over her shoulder.

"Can't you knock like a normal person?" Paula shot back. "You nearly gave me a heart attack."

Amber eyed the black blouse she was wearing then reached out to feel the smooth material. "Is this new? Can I borrow it?"

Paula slapped her hand away. "Seriously? Where on Earth would *you* wear this? It's not exactly nightclub fashion. And, for the record, no, you can't."

Amber wrinkled her nose. "God, don't take this personally, but it smells like old lady in here."

Paula glared at her, to no avail. From the time she could walk, Amber had been completely oblivious to either of her older sister's irritation. Nothing had changed.

"Blame Mom," she said, pointing to the garbage can.

Amber peeked inside then made a gag-face.

"I know, right? I was going to toss the lot out the window, until I saw the screens are still on. Can you take it downstairs with you?"

"Declan, my brother," Amber responded in a singsong voice, already moving on from the lavender, an easy grin decorating her face as she raised a hand for a high-five. "Welcome to the funny farm."

Paula shook her head, apparently her invisibility cloak had activated without her awareness. She took a breath, winced at the lavender smell, and picked up the garbage can to carry out to the hallway.

Declan slapped her outstretched hand with his own. ""Amber, my sister, good to be here."

Paula snorted derisively, while stepping around her sister. "Said the man who's never spent an entire day under this roof, let alone *fourteen* of them. Your tune is about to change, *my brother*. Mark my words, two weeks from now you'll be singing an entirely different song."

"Pshtt," Amber exhaled and sat down on the corner of the bed. "Don't listen to her. She's always exaggerating things. Such a drama queen—"

"Don't!" Paula interrupted, dropping the trash can in the doorway, outraged. Her mother was the drama queen, not her, and any suggestion of them being remotely the same was a serious attack in her books.

Declan scooted off the bed and pulled her into a bear hug. Then, before she could say anything further, he dipped her backward and planted a kiss on her lips.

Amber whooped and laughed at the pair of them. "Smart move," she offered, while he set Paula back on her feet, her expression slightly dazed from the suddenness of the gesture.

"Okay, now can we call a truce?" he asked. "Because that roast downstairs is smelling seriously fabulous and I'm hoping it's nearly time to eat."

Paula took a breath, eyed her sister, then nodded. "You taste like crabapple, where did you put the core?"

"Ate it."

Paula wrinkled her nose at him. "Seriously?"

"Hey, I said I was hungry," he replied, grinning. "Waste not, want not."

"That's why I came up, actually," Amber said, twisting strands of her hair around her fingers. "It's time for supper. Mom sent me to tell you."

Declan reached for the burgundy sweater he'd tossed onto the other side of the bed when he'd arrived in the room. "Perfect. Exactly what I wanted to hear."

Paula watched as he pulled the shaker-knit over his head. "What are you doing?"

"Getting ready to go back downstairs." He shot her a funny look while he straightened the pullover across his shoulders. "Why? Is there something else I should be doing first?"

"No, but what's *this* all about?" she elaborated, pointing to his sweater.

He looked at his chest then back at her. "What? You mean my sweater?"

She nodded.

"I'm not going to your parent's dinner table in just a t-shirt. My mother raised me better than that."

Amber rose from the bed and slipped past them, her charcoal grey, maxi skirt giving her a floating quality as she stepped gracefully around the wastepaper basket in the doorway and into the hallway. "I'd wear it to work, by the way," she announced, cocking her hip to the left.

Paula shook her head, not following.

"Your blouse." She pointed at Paula's top. "You asked where I'd wear it."

"And that would be the flower shop?" Paula stated, incredulous.

Amber shrugged. "Well, they don't like me wearing *nightclub fashion*, so…."

"Do NOT touch my clothes while we're here." Paula pointed a finger at her. "Understand?"

Amber turned and started down the staircase. "Oh, and Mom said I should tell you we're having mashed potatoes. She said Declan already knows, but to tell you because you'd probably want to know, too."

Paula rolled her eyes, while Declan laughed.

Douglas looked at his family seated comfortably around the large, oak dining room table and sighed contentedly. *This* was what it was all about. He may not have been a multimillionaire, but he was a business owner and *Hayes Happy Zone*, an amusement complex that offered a wide variety of activities, from arcade games to bowling, laser tag, rock climbing and so on, was going from strength to strength. Families, school groups and visitors all frequented the establishment, as well as the local bowling league had their game nights and tournaments - and not only did he love his work, but it let him take care of his family with good food, a warm home and....

"Ohmygod!" Donna blurted, then dropped her fork onto her plate as she leaped up from her chair at the opposite end of the table and dashed out of the room.

Declan turned to look at Paula, who gazed across the table at Amber, who stared at Douglas at the top of the table, who jumped up to follow his wife.

"What the hell?" Paula demanded, pushing out her chair to stand up.

Amber and Declan did the same and the three of them charged out of the room behind Douglas.

"I can't believe I did it again!" Donna lamented, pulling a baking sheet from the oven with, what looked like, large black lumps of charcoal evenly spaced on the surface.

Amber started coughing when acrid smoke filled the air and, before Declan could pose the question, "what are those?" the smoke alarm began its shrill beeping and drowned out any possibility of conversation.

Douglas, used to the drill - it wasn't the first time Donna had forgotten something in the oven - went first to the window and opened it wide to let in the fresh air, then grabbed a dish towel and backtracked to the alarm in the hallway to wave away the smoke that was causing it to ring in the first place.

"Jeezus murphy!" Paula exclaimed, when the alarm finally went silent and all that was left was the ringing in her ears and the sharp smell of burned flour.

"I keep telling you to set the timer, Mom, gawd," Amber grumbled, squinting. "My eyes are burning."

"What does that mean, 'keep telling you'?" Paula rubbed her left ear and looked back and forth between her sister and mother. "Is this a regular occurrence around here?"

Douglas walked back into the kitchen. "There, that's better."

Donna opened the lid on the garbage can and said, "That's more than I can say for the biscuits," then dumped the entire lot.

"I don't know why you don't just *buy* dinner rolls, like normal people," Amber further groused, shaking her head. "How many times do we have to go through this before our hearing is shot altogether?"

Douglas chuckled then caught Declan's eye. "First night here and already dinner and a show. Not sure how we're going to top ourselves now."

Declan laughed, while Paula continued trying to get answers. "Seriously, though, is this a regular thing? Do we have to be worried you're going to burn the house down or something?"

"Oh, *please*, of course not." Donna put the charred pan into the sink and started running the tap to let it soak. "Such a dramatic reaction."

"Said the woman who leaped out of her chair like she'd been electrocuted," Paula swiftly retorted.

Amber snorted. "Good one."

"So should we all retire to the family room?" Douglas asked, smiling. "Declan? I have a new bottle of wine I'm eager to open. My buddy, Bert, recommended it, are you game?"

"Sounds good," he agreed, grateful to his father-in-law for trying so hard to make him feel welcome. He was a kind soul.

"I'm in for wine," Amber stated, reaching into the front pocket of her jeans to pull out her cellphone. "Oh, hang on, maybe not...." She started texting, her fingers flying speedily across the screen.

Declan's phone was on the credenza in the dining room and began to trill loudly. He, Paula, Douglas and Donna all turned to stare at Amber.

She felt their gaze and looked up. "What?" she said, before registering the sound of Declan's phone and catching on. "That's not *me*," she said, rolling her eyes and going back to texting.

"It's probably my Mom," Declan offered, "checking in."

"Why don't you call her back while I help clean up in the dining room," Paula encouraged. "Then you and Dad can have his wine."

He shook his head. "I can do it later. I'll help clean up."

"No, you deserve a break," she insisted.

"I second that," Douglas pressed, smiling at Paula before heading out of the kitchen. "Back in a jiff."

"See?" She pointed at her father's retreating back. "Dad's going downstairs to get the wine from his wine room."

Amber tucked her phone back into her pocket. "What'd I miss?"

"Nothing. Declan is going to calling his Mom, and Dad is getting the wine."

"Cool. I'll get the glasses."

"Okay, fine," Declan relented, while Amber went over to the cupboard and began retrieving the wine goblets from the top shelf. "But I'll only be a couple of minutes."

Donna waved him off. "Go. Paula's right, your mother comes first. That's how it should *always* be."

Paula bit her lip and said nothing. She'd been hearing that statement for as long as she could remember. It covered all manner of sins ... *of the mother.*

Declan nodded and walked out of the kitchen to retrieve his phone.

"Paula, are you having wine?" Amber asked.

"No, I have an early meeting tomorrow."

"I'll have yours then." She grinned cheekily as she lined up the glasses on the countertop.

"I wonder if Bonnie's like that with all five of her boys?" Donna queried, eyebrows waggling, the moment Declan was out of earshot.

Amber closed the cupboard door then moved the wine glasses over to the island. "Like what?"

"You *know*, calling all the time, or *checking in* as he calls it."

Paula narrowed her eyes at her mother's usage of air quotes when she said '*checking in*'.

Amber wrinkled her nose. "Does she call a lot? I hadn't noticed."

"No, she doesn't," Paula assured her. "She keeps in touch, that's all. And it's a normal amount of time, not *all the time*."

"I don't knowww," Donna said while shrugging her shoulders. "Sure seems like it from over here. How does she get anything done for herself?"

"And, besides," Paula continued, levelly, "there's nothing wrong with a mother holding an interest in her children's lives. In fact, some would even go so far as to say it's normal."

"Oh, *please*." Donna shook her head, chuckling. "No grown child wants their mother in their business all the time."

"Well, okay, not all the time, but a normal amount of time like Bonnie does is fine," Paula pushed back. "Which is a good thing, wouldn't you think? So your kids know that you notice them as people, not just an audience."

"That's true," Amber agreed, nodding.

"That's why I've always made sure to have a life of my own," Donna expounded, arms waving about as though she was speaking to a crowd, oblivious to what either of her daughter's had said. "So you three girls would feel free to live your own lives as you see fit and not feel pressured to spend your time focusing on me."

Paula pressed her lips together to quell herself from offering a counter argument while she followed her mother into the dining room to start gathering up the dishes. There was no use attempting to offer an alternate conversational path; the woman believed the story she was selling and that was that. History had proven that when Donna told something as truth, that was the way it was going to be forevermore. It was pointless to suggest otherwise.

"And, by the way," Donna said, turning around to pat Paula on her arm. "Before you feel you have to say it, *you're welcome*."

Paula's brow furrowed and she shook her head. "I'm not following."

Donna dimpled and repeated, "You're welcome."

Paula shook her head a second time. "Still not following. For *what?*"

Donna frowned, making her dimples disappear. "For having my own life, of course. What I've been talking about all this time, for goodness sake."

Paula stared at her mother blankly. What the hell was she supposed to say to *that?* Thankfully, Declan chose that moment to walk into the room, saving her from having to attempt a reply.

"All done," he announced. "Let me help you with this."

"Aren't you a doll, your mother raised you right," Donna flattered, as though she hadn't been, just moments ago, questioning the woman's actions.

"Is everything okay with your Mom?" Paula asked.

"Yup. Just checking in, as I said, to make sure everything went well with the last of the packing."

"Well, that was nice of her, very *thoughtful*," Paula complimented, pointedly, hoping to clue her mother in as to what was consideration actually looked like.

Donna, absorbed in her own thoughts, yawned.

Okay, so much for *that*, Paula thought, while Declan began stacking the sky blue, ceramic dinner plates. "No, no," she insisted, trying to wave him away. "Now that you're done, Dad should be in the kitchen with the wine. You go ahead, we've got this."

Declan grinned and continued picking up the dishes. "This won't take long and, besides, your Mom cooked. She should go put her feet up."

Donna patted his shoulder then started out of the room, throwing, "You picked a good one, Daughter," over her shoulder as she walked away.

Paula took a deep breath then released it. "Yes, Mother."

Chapter 2

Paula shut off her hair dryer and placed it on the white vanity table in front of her, a feeling of déjà vu washing over her as she reenacted the things she'd done a decade ago in the frozen-in-time bedroom of her youth. If it wasn't for the fact she could see her twenty nine year old self reflected in the mirror, she could almost believe she had travelled back through the years to her teenage self, getting ready for high school instead of the workday.

She grimaced, remembering those days with an utter lack of fondness. Despite the insistence at the time of many adults and teachers, they had NOT been the best days of her life. Instead, they'd been more a test of her inner fortitude: could she stick it out to the end, or would she bail out and run for the hills? Thankfully, she'd stuck it out, graduated and moved on and look at her now ... back in her old bedroom.

Paula snorted in amusement at the irony of things. Life was an odd and unexpected pile of experiences and, yes, while she knew full well her presence in her parent's house could not be called an actual return, more like a lay-over, it was still going to be more than enough time to remind her of why she'd moved out the moment she could when she was just nineteen.

She scooped a small amount of styling paste from a jar on the vanity top and raked the product through her choppy auburn hair, expertly creating an artfully messy style. What would she tell her former teenage self, she wondered, if she was able to travel back in time to this very spot in her childhood bedroom.

"Probably," she said, talking to her reflection as though it was her younger self, "something like: *Trust me, life gets way better. Way, way better.*"

Paula grinned, amused by her self-talk, and turned her head back and forth to check her hair in the mirror. Done. Now, all that was left was heading downstairs to the kitchen and getting on with her day.

"You can do this, pretend you're on vacation," she said, encouragingly, to her reflection in the mirror. "T minus thirteen days and counting."

She reached around to wipe her hands on the towel she'd hung across the back of her chair then stood up, walked purposefully across the bedroom, opened the door and stepped into the hallway. Laughter floated upwards from the lower level into the top of the stairwell, it sounded like Declan and her Dad, and she felt better about venturing forward.

"Once more into the breach," she said, squaring her shoulders beneath her cream colored blouse and starting down the stairs.

Declan, sitting comfortably at the kitchen table next to Douglas, a green oversized mug of coffee in front of him, smiled around a mouthful of chocolate glazed pastry when Paula entered the room. He'd risen earlier than her and had snuck quietly from the bedroom so as not to disturb her sleep. A bit of a feat, actually, as it had been dark and he'd almost tripped over the faded, purple-shag rug on the floor.

"Morning, sweetheart," Douglas said, his grin as welcoming as Declan's. "Sleep well?"

Paula walked over to the coffee maker sitting next to the toaster on the countertop and replied, "Fine, you?" while choosing a cup that matched Declan's from the mug-tree adjacent to the coffeepot.

"Always do," he stated. "Your Mom left those mugs out for you and Declan, she said she thought you'd be fans of big cups."

Declan lifted his to his lips, took a gulp of his coffee then said, "And she was right, wasn't she, Hon?"

"Spot on," Paula agreed, while pouring herself a half serving of coffee. While she appreciated the gesture, she didn't have time to drink a full mug.

"And, of course, there's donut holes," Douglas added, pointing out the plateful of freshly baked pastries on the table.

Donna had made them in the early hours of the morning - or maybe the late hour of the previous evening? When did night become morning, anyway?

"And they are out of this world," Declan declared, choosing another one of the confections and popping it into his mouth.

Paula smiled at her husband's enthusiasm. "I thought I smelled fried vegetable oil sometime last night. Some things never change."

Declan reached for a napkin from the stack beside the plate then turned to Douglas. "So, where *is* Donna, anyway? I have to thank her for these before I head out."

Paula put the coffeepot back on its base and waited to hear what her Dad would say. Clearly, Declan had forgotten what she'd told him about her mother never being up in the morning. He'd had a hard time believing her when she'd first informed him she didn't hold one recollection of her mother being present at breakfast. As far back as she could remember, the mornings had been made up of her, Amber, their older sister Jaimie and their Dad. Then, when she'd told him Jaimie had always been in charge of making sure they were dressed, their hair and teeth brushed, while Douglas made school lunches, he'd been rendered speechless. Not really a surprise he'd been gob smacked by the information as Bonnie had not only been awake every morning before everyone else his entire childhood, but had made breakfast to order. Heck, she was probably doing it right then, making breakfast for his Dad.

Paula sighed and sipped her coffee, wondering what that would have been like. Not that she hadn't enjoyed her mornings with her sisters and her Dad, not to mention appreciated how hard he'd worked to make it seem normal for their Mom to never show her face until noon, but it might have been nice to have had the chance to experience the other side of the coin.

"Oh, well…," Douglas offered now, clearing his throat. "Donna's always been a bit of a … well, one would call her a … *later riser.* That seems about right, wouldn't you say, Paula?"

Before she could reply, he added, "I always used to tease her when the girls were little and say she was born in the wrong time zone, didn't I Paula?"

"You did." She nodded and smiled. No need to lament the past and punish him for his wife's quirks.

Declan, meanwhile, shot her a wide-eyed look as she walked around the island and joined them at the table, suddenly remembering what she'd told him. She gave him the same kind smile she had her Dad.

"So, what's on tap for you kids for the day?" Douglas asked, moving things along.

Paula cocked an eyebrow at the question while she put down her coffee mug and chose a glazed vanilla donut hole from the plate. "Work."

"Right, *of course*." He chuckled at himself for posing the query.

It was just that it had become his norm to inquire of Donna the same question when he got home from work for his lunch break, as her day-to-day schedule could be made up of just about anything. And, of course, Amber's shift work at the flower shop was erratic, so that didn't help either. He couldn't remember the last time he'd had people in the house with actual defined schedules. It might have been when his daughters were still in school.

He tried a different direction. "Any new clients on the books?"

Paula took a bite of her pastry and nodded. "We've just acquired a very wealthy client, Bazzano is the last name, and...," she waggled her eyebrows suggestively, "suffice it to say, money is no object."

Douglas leaned in, all ears. "What does he want you to do?"

"A huge, blow-out bash for he and his recent wife's daughter's sixteenth birthday."

"Recent wife?" Declan repeated, a wry smile on his face.

Paula ate the remainder of the donut hole. "Yup," she said, speaking around the pastry, "and you didn't hear it from me, but I believe this is wife number *three*."

"Wow. A sixteenth birthday for his kid by his *third* wife," Declan marveled, before asking, "How old is this guy, anyway?"

Paula shrugged and borrowed his napkin to wipe her fingertips. "No idea."

"You could Google him," he suggested, while she gave the napkin back.

"Oh, but that would be cheating," she said, eyes dancing. "Erin and I have a bet going and we've agreed we won't try to find out once the contract is done."

Declan and Douglas both laughed. Erin was Paula's right-hand woman and, together, they had a lot of fun.

Douglas sat back and shook his head. "Third wife. He's a brave man, that's all I've got to say."

Declan and Paula exchanged a look while she picked up her cup and drank the last of her coffee. They knew *exactly* what her Dad was thinking: having one wife, especially when that spouse was Donna, was enough of a whirlwind. Not that he'd ever admit it out loud, of course. No matter how many challenges she offered, there was no question her Dad adored her Mom.

"So, how are things at *Hayes*?" Declan asked, changing the subject. "Any new games I should be coming over to check out?"

"Yes!" Douglas enthused, slapping his palm on the table.

Paula jumped. "Sorry, dear." He reached out to pat her hand. "Didn't mean to startle you."

"No, no." She shook her head. "It's my fault, I should be ready when the topic comes up. I know how much you love it when you get a new game."

Douglas chuckled. It was true. He never tired of it.

"So, the game?" Declan prompted.

"Right." Douglas' eyes lit up like a child's as he turned in his seat to better face Declan. "It's a two person racing game. Full seats, surround sound, the whole deal. It's getting a lot of positive feedback. You should bring your brothers in to try it out. On the house, of course."

"I'll tell Liam," Declan confirmed. "He'll be there in a shot."

Paula got up from her chair, that was her cue. She carried her empty coffee cup to the dishwasher and placed it inside then chose a few crabapples from the bowl on the island for the road.

"Oh, hey, before you leave," Douglas said, while she retrieved her black satchel from where she'd left it the night before, sitting on the floor next to the china cabinet. "Mom wanted me to ask if you kids will be around for dinner tonight?"

Paula glanced at Declan and he nodded.

"Looks like it," she confirmed, tucking the crab apples into the bag's side pocket. "Do you want me to pick up anything on my way back from work?"

He shrugged his shoulders. "Don't think so. At least, Mom didn't indicate as such."

"Okay. If she thinks of something, tell her to text me."

Her words fell on deaf ears. He'd already gone back to expounding to Declan, a rapt audience, about the new arcade game. She couldn't blame him. After so many years of solo mornings, it must have been a real treat to have company to start the day.

"T-minus thirteen days," she reminded herself, then dashed upstairs to brush her teeth.

Declan pulled into his parking space at work and turned off the car. He couldn't stop thinking about that new game Douglas had been telling him about at *Hayes* and was seriously considering an office team-building day as an excuse to go and play for an afternoon.

He gathered up his messenger bag and the extra paper bag next to it: filled with a club sandwich, juice box and a handful of crabapples that Douglas had given to him before he'd left the house. Apparently, Donna had made not just the donut holes in the wee hours of the morning, but also the bag lunch, and had left a large note instructing Douglas to pass it along. Too bad Paula had managed to slip away before she was given hers.

Declan reached for the door handle when his phone, tucked into the side of his messenger bag, trilled. He paused to consider: did he put everything down to check the message, or did he wait until he got into the office? A second text message pinged then a third, inspiring him to make the decision to check, and he put his things back down on the passenger seat to dig out his phone.

The first message was from his mother: "*Hey, Honey! Do me a favor and give me a call when you're free this morning. It's almost Angus' birthday, as I'm sure you know, and Linda wants to make arrangements for a party with the family.*"

The second message, also from his mother: "*Me, again! Forgot to mention, whatever you do, don't say a word to your brother! Linda is still deciding about whether or not she wants to make it a surprise party.*"

And finally, the third, again from his mother: "*Love you!*"

Declan frowned at his phone, wondering why his sister-in-law couldn't just text him directly. What compelled her to go through his mother every time she needed to deliver information? She and Angus had been married for … well, he couldn't remember exactly how long, but their boys, Finn and Ethan, were eight and ten years old! You'd think, after more than a decade, the woman would be able to make direct contact with her husband's brothers.

Declan tucked the phone back into his bag, regathered his things and exited the car, bracing himself against the cool morning wind that swept across him as he made his way around the side of the office building to the front entrance. He pushed open the door and was greeted by the smiling face of his receptionist, Tammy.

"Morning!" she trilled, her pink, lip-glossed mouth glistening in the overhead lights. "Nippy out there, today! Had to wear a scarf."

Declan returned her smile and noted the blue and brown scarf draped around her neck. "Yeah, I'm thinking I should have done the same, but I was distracted and forgot."

She got up from her desk, smoothed her short, green and black tartan skirt and trailed him into his office. "That's right, you're at the in-laws now. How's that going?"

Declan set his messenger bag down on the brown, suede couch beneath the window and held up the paper bag for her to see. "My mother-in-law made me lunch."

"Sweet," she giggled. "Do you think this is going to be an everyday sort of thing, or just because you're the new kid?"

Declan chuckled and put the lunch inside the mini-fridge in the corner of his office. "Not sure. The way that things function in that house, it could be more of a political statement than anything else."

She furrowed her brow. "How so?"

"Never mind, long story," he reported, removing his coat and hanging it across the back of his desk chair. "How was your weekend?"

Tammy fiddled with the ends of her scarf while she exhaled and shook her head. "Blake nearly gave me heart failure. That kid is too fearless and he's going to give me grey hair before my time."

Declan turned on the computer sitting on his large walnut desk and lifted his eyebrows questioningly. Blake was her five year old son and had a leap-first, think-second, temperament. "What now? Is he okay?"

"Yes, he's fine," she admitted, perching on the padded arm of the sofa. "He just decided he was skilled enough on his mountain bike to ride down a flight of stairs at the park."

"Jeez." Declan winced at the thought.

"I know, right? I'd turned away from him for a half-second and when I turned back there he was, riding down those damned steps, easing his wheels down one at a time: clunk, clunk, clunk."

Declan shook his head at the picture in his head. "So, what did you do?"

"Nothing! I didn't want to distract him and make him fall, so I basically held my breath until he'd made it to the bottom."

"Which he did without hurting himself?"

"Yes, thank god."

Declan smiled at that. Blake was such a cute kid and despite his penchant for daredevil activities, Tammy was a pushover for her son.

"Then," she went on, standing back up, "he was so darned proud of himself, what could I do? I gave him a lecture of course about safety, but I couldn't bring myself to be too hard on him."

"Yeah, can't say I blame you. It's obviously in his nature to push the boundaries. Some kids are just like that. God knows my brother was."

"Emmet?" she asked, referring to the third in line of the Dempsey boys.

Declan nodded. "Yup. Made our Mom nuts. After raising responsible Angus and, after that, Cian, who apparently was constantly pretending he lived in *Fraggle Rock*—"

"*Fraggle Rock*? Which show was that?" Tammy interrupted.

"Okay, are you *trying* to make me feel old?"

She snickered and insisted, "No!"

He laughed at her vehemence then explained, "*Fraggle Rock* was a kid's show and it had *Muppets* and—"

"Oh, like *Sesame Street*?"

"Yeah, no. Well, okay, sort-of," he agreed, giving up trying to expand further. "Anyway, Google it. Blake might like it."

Tammy nodded. "I will, sounds cute."

"What were we talking about?" Declan frowned, trying to remember how they'd gotten to *Fraggle Rock*.

She sat back down on the arm of the sofa. "You were saying that Emmet was like Blake."

"Right." He nodded. "Anyway, all I was saying was that some kids seem programmed to push the boundaries. Emmet definitely made our Mom threaten more than a few times to lock him in his room."

"I'm surprised she went on to have you and Liam."

Declan chuckled at that. "She's a glutton for punishment."

She stood up again and smoothed her skirt. "Well, while I don't have all of your Mom's challenges, you'll still have to promise me you'll give me a raise to pay for the hair dye I'm obviously going to need as the years go on."

Declan shot her a wry grin. "I think you'll be fine."

At twenty-seven, with her makeup-less face and boyish build, Tammy didn't look old enough to be anyone's mother. A few grey hairs wasn't about to change that.

She twirled a strand of her brown curls around her finger, her voice wistful as she sighed, "Maybe, but think how nice it would be to have a sweet little girl, instead of my holy terror of a son."

Declan typed his password into his computer. "You trying to tell me something? Should I be expecting a mat-leave notice?"

"Good god, no," she protested and gave a mock shudder. "That boy only just turned five and Tim and I still feel like we're catching up on lost sleep."

"Good to know, I'd hate to have to start calling temp agencies," he teased, clicking on his appointment calendar. "So, I've got a meeting this afternoon, right?"

Tammy brushed her hair back from her face, switching gears, all business again. "Right."

"Okay, so I've got a few calls to make off the top, then we'll get the team together in about an hour to discuss what's on tap for the week."

"Roger that," she said, striding from the room; her black ankle boots clomping on the tile floor as she disappeared from sight.

Declan settled back into his desk chair and checked the notes he'd left himself at end of day on Friday.

"First call coming up on line two," Tammy called out, then giggled, "*Peabody Accounting.*"

Declan smirked. For whatever reason, the name *Peabody* struck her as hysterical. So much so that on one occasion when he was on the line with the owner, he'd had to close his door because her giggles were so loud in the background.

"Thanks. Think you can keep it together?"

"Lord knows I'll try," she shot back, humor lacing her words.

"That's all I can ask," he said, while lifting the receiver from the phone on his desk and pressing the button to connect the call.

"Of course, no problem at all," Paula assured, speaking into the headset clasped to her ear while simultaneously typing on the keyboard in front of her on her desk. "Pale yellow will be gorgeous. You've made a great decision."

It was a day like any other in her world: soothing clients - this time an overly anxious bride - and assuring them she would get the job done and they would be thrilled with how seamlessly everything came together.

"Please, don't thank me," she insisted, while clicking on her email icon to send a note to the florist in charge of the flowers. "This is what I'm here for and all I care about is that your day is perfect. And it will be, trust me."

And the client on the other end of the line, along with countless others before her, did trust her. Implicitly.

Paula had earned herself an untarnished reputation in her field, as had her assistant, Erin. Paula had brought her on just a few months after launching *Certain Events* and together they'd applied themselves with unwavering dedication to the task of making the company synonymous with reliability. If they promised it, they delivered it; end of story. Now, five years after setting up shop, they were a well-oiled machine.

"Alright, then," she said, ending the call. "I'm on it and I'll send you an email with the new flower details before the morning is done. Talk soon, bye!"

"Wow, you are seriously on fire this morning," Erin commented, carrying two cups of coffee from the small office kitchen and setting one of them down on Paula's desk. "I'm waiting for sparks to start flying off that keyboard."

Paula grinned. "I think moving into my parent's place has infused me with so much pent up energy from squelching my thoughts, it's being channeled into my work."

"After just one day?"

"Yup. My Mom started things off by asking Declan his advice on potatoes, because he's Irish and should know such things."

Erin snorted while she walked over to her desk, adjacent to Paula's, and sat down. "Did she really say that was the reason? He's Irish."

"Yup, almost as soon as we walked in the door."

"Wow."

"It's anyone's guess as to what she might come up with tonight."

Erin sipped her coffee then put her cup down on her desk. "So, what you're telling me is, after two weeks, who knows where things will be at?"

"Pretty much," Paula confirmed, then said, "Love your top, by the way," while admiring the raspberry colored peasant blouse she was wearing with her tan, slim fitting trousers.

While basically the same age - Erin was twenty eight, just one year younger than Paula - the two of them were a visual study in opposites: Erin, tall and willowy - just shy of six feet - whereas Paula was curvy and barely made it to five foot three.

Erin pushed her waterfall of mahogany colored curls away from her shoulders to coil down her back and smiled. "Thanks. Got it at half price."

"Score."

"So, even though it's just been the one day, how's Declan feeling about everything?"

Paula picked up her mug and sipped her coffee while she thought of her husband. The truth was, he was so easygoing it would take something far beyond her parent's nutty household to throw him off his game.

"I'd say right now he's riding the wave. Ask me again in two weeks and we'll see where he's at, at that point."

"Got it," Erin stated, as the phone rang.

Paula glanced at the call display. "Speak of the devil," she said, putting down her cup and connecting the call. "Hey, you. What's the good news?"

"Cool, but no snow in the forecast," Declan, on the other end of the line, replied.

Paula laughed. His weather report was always his standard opener.

"In other news," he continued, "my Mom is sending me texts about Angus' birthday. Apparently, Linda might be going with a surprise party, so we're supposed to keep quiet about it."

Paula frowned. "Isn't he turning thirty-nine?"

"Uh-huh," he said, following her train of thought. "I thought the same thing, but maybe she's purposely making *this* birthday a surprise because she knows he'd be more likely to suspect it for his fortieth?"

"Mmm, maybe."

"Anyway, that aside, I just got a phone call from Vince and something has turned up at the house."

Paula's stomach clutched. Vince was their contractor and, if she was going to go by Declan's tone, she had a feeling the *something* that had turned up was not a good thing.

"Turned up?" she echoed, leaning forward into the call. "What does that mean?"

"It's nothing major, just a pipe that needs to be replaced."

"And?" she pressed. There was always an *and*.

"It's possible it might set back our move-in date by a smidgen."

Paula tensed, unsure if she even wanted the answer to her question, "How *much* of a smidgen?"

"Nothing concrete, yet, most likely just a day or two."

She sighed and closed her eyes.

"I know, I know," he soothed. "But we're both busy, we won't even notice the extra bit of time."

"What's wrong?" Erin queried, alarmed by the grim expression on Paula's face. "What's happened? Is it bad? Oh, god."

"Hang on, Dec," she said, into her headset, before turning to Erin. "It's fine. Just a bit of a bump at the new house that might mean we stay at my parent's a touch longer."

"Oh, thank goodness." She laid a hand across her heart. "Your face really had me worried."

"Hey, Hon," Declan said, into Paula's ear. "I've gotta run."

"Yeah, me too," she acknowledged, trying to keep her voice light.

"Tell Erin I said 'hi' and I'll see you at home tonight. Love you," he finished, before the line went silent.

Paula clicked off and a shudder crawled up her spine. He'd said *home* just as her mother had done when they'd first arrived and, while it should have warmed her heart he felt so at ease at her parent's house … it just made her want to buy a tent.

Chapter 3

Donna lifted her eyebrows in surprise when the kitchen door opened and Amber walked inside.

"What are you doing here?" she demanded, stirring a pot of vegetable soup on the stovetop.

"Hello to you, too," Amber shot back.

"You *know* what I mean. Why aren't you at work?"

Amber unwound the black scarf from around her neck and hung it up on one of the hooks on the wall. "Because I started at five thirty this morning and it's now two in the afternoon."

Donna put the large wooden spoon she was using onto the countertop next to the stove. "Yikes. That's too early for my blood."

Amber slouched out of her jacket and hung it up with her scarf then pointed at her mother's peach and brown, paisley floor-length skirt. "Is that new?"

"I'm thinking beans," Donna stated. "What do you think?"

Amber stared at her. "What?"

"Beans."

"Yeah, I got that part," she said, unzipping her burgundy colored ankle boots and slipping them from her feet, before padding across the room to the fridge. "But what does that have to do with your skirt?"

Donna frowned. "Nothing. Should it?"

Amber retrieved a can of Ginger Ale from the fridge and shook her head. "No. Never mind. What about beans?"

"For the soup." Donna gestured to the pot on the stove.

"Okay," she said, popping open the tab on the can and lifting it to her lips. She'd lost the thread of the conversation, if she'd ever actually had it, so it seemed best to just go with the flow.

"I know," Donna sighed, shaking her head, "I can't decide either. And your Dad isn't answering his cellphone." She snapped her fingers then pointed at Amber. "Wait, I do know! Paula! *Of course*, I'll ask her! This is just her sort of thing, making these kinds of decisions."

"*Is* it?" Amber cocked her head.

Donna, however, was already off and running and didn't hear her. She dashed from the room to find her cellphone with Paula's work number.

Amber continued to sip her soda and enjoy the momentary silence. She'd quite liked the skirt, maybe she'd ask about it again later and see if she could borrow it. It seemed just the sort of clothing that would be perfect for the flower shop.

"Right, okay, hang on a moment," Erin instructed, before putting Donna on hold and waving her hand wildly to attract Paula's attention across the desk.

Paula held up a finger to ask her to wait as she finished with the client she was speaking to on the other line.

Normally, Erin would have taken a message. However, Donna was insistent and she didn't want to make light of things in case they were just the opposite. She waved a second time then made pointing gestures at the phone.

Paula said, "Sorry to interrupt, but could you hang on for just a quick moment?" into her headset, then pressed the hold button on the phone base.

"Sorry," Erin apologized. "It's just that it's your Mom and she sounds a bit on the frantic side."

Paula nodded and connected the call. "Mom? What's happened?"

Erin watched her listen to her mother on the other end of the line and hoped everything was alright. However, when her face began to display annoyance, then subsequently morphed into full-on pissed-off, Erin's stomach lurched. Oh boy. Not okay. Not okay at all.

"Mom!" Paula snapped. "Stop talking and take a breath. I have a client on the other line and I don't have time for this. Make a blasted decision, for goodness sake. Good-bye."

She didn't wait to see if her mother registered what she'd said, instead she disconnected the call, took a deep cleansing breath, then pressed the flashing red hold button to reconnect her with her previous call.

"Hi, thanks so much for waiting!" she said, cheerfully, revealing nothing of the last few minutes. "Let's revisit what we'd just decided."

Erin leaned forward to catch her eye and mouth 'sorry'. She couldn't believe she'd been suckered *again* by Donna. Damn, the woman was good. She'd been breathless and carried on like there was a three alarm fire and only Paula could put out the flames.

Paula smiled and shook her head to signal everything was okay and Erin exhaled a sigh of relief. Perhaps a fresh cup of coffee for the both of them would be a good idea, she thought, getting up from her desk.

"Perfect, I'll get right on it," Paula stated, while Erin went into the kitchenette. "I'll email you as soon as I have things arranged."

Erin poured coffee from a carafe into two clean cups. She added cream to hers and left Paula's black.

Paula hung up the phone then sat back and groaned.

"God, sooo sorry," Erin repeated, the frustrated flush on her face nearly matching her blouse.

Paula shook her head. "No, don't apologize, it's not your fault."

Erin ferried the cups to their desks while adding, "She sounded so frantic. And she insisted you were the only one who could make the decision she needed made, so I didn't want to take a chance that—"

"About beans," Paula cut in.

Erin frowned and sat down at her desk. "What?"

"The big decision she needed me for? It was about beans," she reiterated, reaching to pick up the mug Erin had set on her desk. "More specifically, whether or not she should put beans in the soup she's making for tonight's dinner."

Erin stared at her blankly. "Are you kidding me?"

"My sentiments exactly," Paula said, dryly, holding her cup between her hands and sipping from its rim. "And thanks for the coffee, just what I needed."

"My god," Erin exhaled, her blue eyes wide. "If you could have heard her...."

"I did, believe me." Paula placed her coffee back down on the desk beside her framed photo of Declan. "And that's why I cut her off and hung up so abruptly. Otherwise, it would have gone on and on. Yesterday it was potatoes, today beans. Who knows what tomorrow will bring."

"She's getting more crafty," Erin stated, nodding thoughtfully as she reached out for her mug then leaned back in her chair. "She knows I've gotten wise to her, so she's changing up her game."

Paula smirked. Her face was so earnest and she sounded so indignant, it was amusing.

"What was it about, the last time she got me?"

Paula paused to think, then snapped her fingers. "She thought the neighbor's house was being broken into."

"Right." Erin drank some of her coffee. "And it turned out to be one of the neighbor's friend's boyfriend's—"

"Husband," Paula corrected.

"Yes!" She pointed her finger in the air.

"Darryl," Paula continued, "I've met him. A nice guy."

"Exactly! And yet, somehow she'd convinced herself he was a prowler." Erin shook her head, remembering. "Thank god you were here and not out on a client call, or I would have had the police at her front door. How embarrassing would that have been?"

"For her, or you?"

Erin drank more of her coffee then raised a groomed eyebrow. "For *her*. I wouldn't have been there."

"Oh, well," Paula said, waving her hand. "For her, not at all. My mother doesn't get embarrassed. She *improvises*. And, when life gets a bit mundane, she creates *issues* to entertain herself. If only she would watch some sort of soap opera to distract herself, it would be a lot easier on the rest of us."

"Well, whatever the case, I'm ready now," Erin affirmed, setting her mug soundly on her desk. "I've got her number. Next time, no more gullible Erin to fool."

Paula bit her lip to try and keep her grin at bay in the face of her vehemence. "Excellent. Now I have some calls to make, so I'll leave the phones in your sharp-eyed, or rather sharp-*eared*, care."

Erin cut her eyes at her and said, "I *see* you," making Paula's smile deepen. "And I don't care if you're amused. It's a matter of principle now."

Paula held her hands up in surrender. "Okay, okay, I get it, sorry. It's just that I've been dealing with this for so long, I've had to train myself to become numb to it."

"I know and I'm not exactly new here." She shook her head. "But yet, she still got me."

"Don't worry about it. Sometimes she still gets to me, too."

"From now on, consider me your human shield: at least at the office anyway."

Paula lifted her mug and reached across their desks to clink it against hers. "Cheers to that."

Declan pulled his car into Donna and Douglas' driveway and cut the engine. It was dark, the last threads of daylight had disappeared an hour ago, and he was grateful for the warm and welcoming glow being cast by the copper lamps on either side of the garage door.

He shifted his gaze from the garage to the adjacent house - a rambling Victorian, pale blue, two stories and a large front porch - and felt eager to get inside and greet the family. Not that he'd share such thoughts with Paula. For her, *the family* meant something entirely different than for him. Not that he didn't understand. Of course he did. He had four brothers, didn't he? And his mother was pretty hands-on, all things considered … but he knew they couldn't hold a candle to Donna. She was in a class all her own.

"Just a couple of weeks, no big deal," he said, rehearsing what he'd say in the event Paula needed reassurance; then nearly jumped out of his skin when his cellphone trilled loudly from inside his leather messenger bag. "Jeez," he muttered, catching his breath as his pulse raced from the unexpected rush of adrenalin flooding his body. He reached into the bag for the phone and read the screen: it was a text from his brother, Liam.

"Hey, Dec! What time are you guys going over to Angus' and Linda's tonight?"

Declan paused, wracking his brain for a memory of being invited to his brother and sister-in-law's. He couldn't find one, so he typed: *"We're not going over."*

"Why not?" came the response.

Declan wrote: *"Weren't invited"* then waited: certain that, when Liam put two and two together, his reply was going to be that of displeasure. The phone pinged: the message confirming he was right.

"Fuck."

Declan laughed. He'd nailed it. If he could have wagered a bet, it would have been that Liam's girlfriend, Trina, had arranged with their sister-in-law to have some sort of get together so that Liam would be encouraged to move their relationship along into more serious waters. They'd been dating for a year and Trina's biological clock was starting to tick pretty loudly; or so Liam said.

Declan, still chuckling, wrote: *"Good luck."*

Liam's reply was a thumbs-down emoji.

Declan stuffed the phone into the left pocket of his wool coat, picked up his bag and exited the car. The cold evening wind rushed at him, inspiring swift movements as he locked up then sped along the cobblestone path toward the house. He took the porch steps two at a time and just as his foot hit the landing, the solid oak front door flew open and Amber charged out at him, dark hair flying behind her like a cape.

"THERE you are!"

"Jeez!" he blurted, taken off guard, barely managing to grip the railing to keep from tumbling backward off the porch. "Where the fire?"

"Where's the fire?" she echoed, grabbing his sleeve and tugging him forward. "I'll tell you where the fire is. Inside. And the only way it's going to be put out is if *you* convince your wife that it would be fun to have games night."

"Games night?" he repeated, straightening his messenger bag over his shoulder.

"Uh-huh," she said, still pulling at him. "At least, that's what Mom keeps saying. I honestly couldn't care less: the only reason I'm even remotely involved is because my date cancelled."

Declan let himself be dragged across the porch and into the foyer, trying to get his bearings amidst the sudden cacophony of raised voices accosting his ears.

"See?" Amber said, matter-of-fact, releasing him and closing the door. "They've been squabbling back and forth since Mom first said it was games night."

Declan slipped his bag from his shoulder and placed it on the floor next to the wall. "Is this a usual thing around here? Do you have a set night to play games?"

Amber flipped her hair back from her shoulders. "No. Not really. Mom will get the idea in her head, now and again, and it's just easier to go along with it than argue. Who's it hurting, really? It's just a few games."

Declan removed his coat and hung it up in the hall closet, considering what she'd said. She was right, of course, who was it hurting? However, judging from the irritated sound of his wife's voice coming from the kitchen, he knew he'd be wise to tread carefully and keep his thoughts to himself. No need to add any fuel to that fire.

His cellphone trilled from his jacket pocket and Declan said, "Hang on, gotta see who that is. Could be a client."

Amber shrugged her shoulders and leaned up against the front door. "Take your time. I'm not going back in there alone."

Declan retrieved the phone and read the text from his brother, Angus: *"Are you and Paula coming here tonight for dinner?"*

He shucked his shoes from his feet while he replied: *"Nope"*, and refrained from typing that he would be better off asking his wife what was going on.

"So, it's just Liam and Trina?"

Declan sighed and typed: *"Possibly. I don't know anything more than you, probably less."*

"Hell," Angus wrote back.

Declan chuckled and sent: *"Gotta run. Family situation here. Have fun."*

"Good luck," Angus stated.

"Right back at ya," he replied, then ended the conversation and stuck the phone into the back pocket of his dress pants.

"Everything okay?" Amber asked, over the din of the still-raised-voices coming from the kitchen.

"Yup, fine." He stepped aside and extended his arm for her to go ahead of him. "Lead the way."

She shot him an amused look. "Chicken," she teased, before padding down the hallway.

Declan smirked. She wasn't wrong

Chapter 4

Paula sat stiffly on the couch in her parent's family room, Declan beside her. She grimaced at the cloth pattern - teal with beige conch shells - finding it as off-putting now as she had the day her mother had brought it into the house, twenty years earlier. What had possessed her? Maybe the hope that it would one day win a contest for ugliest sofa ever made? And the fact that she had the cushions re-stuffed yearly, instead of purchasing something new, well that just made it worse.

"Come on," Declan coaxed, reaching for her hand when he saw her face. "It won't be *that* bad."

Paula looked up at him and couldn't help but smile at his misunderstanding. Normally, she'd share what she'd been thinking, but history had proven that offering the slightest comment about the furniture started a discussion that seemed to never, ever end. Her mother would begin by firing off a reel of famous people she claimed owned the same stuff; all of them either dead or off the grid, off course. Then she'd move onto the adage that new things aren't made to last like the old things were and once they'd started down that path, it was a debate that could never be won.

Declan returned her grin and said, "Better," while gently squeezing her hand.

"All right, you lovebirds, enough whispering," Donna chided, sweeping into the room, Douglas trailing behind. "Are you ready for some fun?"

Paula raised an eyebrow, but said nothing.

Douglas settled himself into his brown, leather recliner with a contented sigh. "Those lima beans were delicious, dear. Really hit the spot."

Paula stretched her neck back and forth at the mention of the beans and tried to mentally remove herself from the situation.

"Amber!" Donna shouted, making Declan start. "We're all waiting on you!"

"We should have them more often," Douglas remarked. "They make a nice change from the usual kidney beans."

"That girl, honestly," Donna muttered, shaking her head and sitting down on the love seat that matched the couch. "Should we start without her?"

"Or, we could forget it all together," Paula suggested.

Donna opened the game box she'd carried in with her, ignoring the comment. "I'll get things set up and if she hasn't come down by the time I'm done, we'll go ahead and start."

"You see me, right?" Paula said, looking at Declan. "I *am* in the room?"

Declan snickered and was saved from having to offer a reply when Amber strolled in through the doorway carrying two large yellow bowls filled with potato chips.

"It's about time," Donna quipped.

Amber placed the plastic bowls on the coffee table, settled herself on the other side of Declan on the sofa and began twisting her hair up into a makeshift bun. If she'd heard her mother, you'd never know.

Paula's mouth curved into a wry smile as she thought, the nut doesn't fall far from the tree.

"Chips, Daddy?" Amber offered, pointing at one of the bowls.

"Thanks love," he said, then asked, "What's this game called, again?"

"Dilemmas," Donna stated, shuffling a stack of cards while Amber gave a solid nudge to Declan's shoulder.

"What?" he said, turning his head to look at her.

"Pass the chips to Dad."

"Right." He picked up one of the bowls and extended it toward Douglas across the table.

"There are *smaller* bowls for everyone right there, Douglas," Donna instructed, indicating with a jerk of her chin toward a stack of plastic bowls - miniature versions of the larger, yellow ones - on the coffee table. "Don't hog. Use one of those."

Declan quickly put the large bowl back down on the table and Douglas did as he was told: chose a smaller bowl and doled out a serving of the chips for himself.

"I've heard of this game, by the way," Declan said, as his father-in-law settled back into his chair, bowl in hand and a satisfied expression on his face. "A client of mine was telling me about it."

Paula shifted on the couch, tucking her legs beneath her. She's changed from her work clothes into a pair of black leggings and a baggy grey sweatshirt. If she was going to have to endure games night, she was at least going to be comfortable while doing so.

"And the verdict?" she asked.

Declan leaned back into the couch cushions. "He said it was interesting."

Donna stopped shuffling the cards, her eyes lit up. "I *knew* it would be! In fact, I told Dad when I ordered it online, *this* game is going to change things up."

Amber cocked her head. "What *things*?"

"Didn't I tell you that, Douglas?" Donna insisted, turning to her husband. "Right after I ordered it?"

"You did," he agreed, munching his chips and nodding.

"I *said*, what things will be *changed up*?" Amber pestered.

Donna tutted and waved her hand. "Oh, you know…."

Amber leaned forward around Declan to catch Paula's eye. She raised an eyebrow in return and the two of them giggled. They'd heard *oh you know* their entire lives.

Declan, bookended, looked back and forth between them, uncertain as to what was funny. Amber wore a shit-eating grin, so he focused his questioning look at Paula.

"I'll tell you later," she said, quietly, biting her lip to keep her giggles at bay.

"Okay!" Donna clapped her hands. "Everyone ready to get started?"

"Wait," Amber said, when her cellphone trilled.

Donna pressed her lips together and exhaled loudly through her nose like an irritated bull.

Amber pulled the phone from her hoodie's left pocket, read the text, tittered, shot back a speedy reply, then stuffed the phone back into her pocket.

Donna cleared her throat. "*Now* can we get started?"

"Can we at least get a drink first?" Amber proposed.

"Seconded," Paula declared, lifting her hand.

Donna threw her hands up, but nodded. "Fine. But be quick about it."

Amber was up and out of the room before her mother had finished her sentence.

"That is a bald-faced lie!" Paula insisted, her face pink from frustration.

Donna folded her arms across her chest and shook her head. "No, it is not!"

"Who cares!" Amber barked, lifting her glass of red wine from the table and swallowing the last of it with a flourish.

Paula cut her eyes at her sister. "What, so that's how we're playing the game now? We'll just lie to win? Huh? Does that mean *your* answers have been like Mom's? Nothing but fabrication?"

Amber groaned, shoved the empty glass at Declan and covered her face with an orange throw pillow.

"Excuse me, I *said* I'm not lying," Donna protested, picking at microscopic pieces of lint on her brown, peasant blouse.

Paula slumped back into the sofa cushions while Declan placed the wineglass Amber had foisted on him onto the coffee table, next to the empty chip bowls. "Whatever. I give up. Amber's right, who cares."

"Exactly," she agreed, her voice muffled by the pillow still pressed against her face. "Everyone have another drink and calm the hell down."

Declan blinked at the suggestion: the last thing they needed, in his opinion, was more alcohol added into the mix.

Paula rubbed her eyes, leaving raccoon circles from her mascara behind, as she offered, tersely, "Unfortunately, s*ome* of us have to work in the morning."

"Hey," Amber countered, pulling the pillow away from her face to frown at her sister.

"What?" she challenged.

"I *know* what you're implying. And just because I'm not all nine-to-five like you, doesn't mean the flower shop isn't work."

Douglas yawned, then rested his head back against the soft leather of his recliner and closed his eyes.

"See?" Paula ignored her sister's claim to point at their father. "Even Dad has given up on this absurd game and waste of an evening."

Douglas didn't so much as flinch, Declan noticed, when Paula called him out.

"I don't know *why* you're making such a drama of it," Donna commented, bypassing the accusation toward Douglas. More often than not her husband was in some state of repose; this was nothing different.

"I am not making a *drama* of anything," Paula shot back, through gritted teeth. "A *drama* would be doing something like, I don't know, turning a simple decision about *beans* for soup into a full scale issue!"

Declan suppressed the desire to groan. He'd heard all about Donna's phone call earlier that afternoon.

Donna's lips set into a thin line. "Still no excuse for hanging up in my ear."

"OHMYGOD, you're *both* being serious pains in the ass," Amber cut in.

Declan twisted his neck back and forth, watching the three of them go round and round. It was a foreign dynamic to him, growing up in a household of brothers, and he couldn't profess to understand it whatsoever. His cellphone, on the coffee table, trilled and he had to stop himself from snatching it up like a lifeline. He casually reached for the phone and read the screen: it was his Mom, asking if he'd heard from Liam about the dinner at Angus and Linda's.

Amber pointed at him, hoping the text might offer an excuse to bail out. "Does this mean we're done with the game?"

"You mean done with the *lying*?" Paula retorted.

"Oh, for goodness sake," Donna huffed. "I already said I'm not lying and my answer is still the same. If a woman made advances toward your father, it wouldn't bother me—"

"Which might be half-way believable if that very situation hadn't actually happened before and, if I remember correctly, it DID bother you. A LOT." Paula turned to Amber. "Do you remember that time? Or were you too young?"

"Don't know, don't care," Amber stated, dropping her head back against the sofa and closing her eyes.

Declan debated on using the text message as an excuse to leave the room. Amber would be right behind him, no question. However, when Douglas opened his eyes, sat up and cleared his throat, he waited to see what would happen next.

"Alright then," Douglas announced, making all three women look at him expectantly. "It seems we've hit a bit of a stalemate, wouldn't you say?"

"More like a state of bored-out-of-our-minds," Amber groused, rubbing her face with her hands.

"Right. Well then, maybe it's time to call it a night." He sat further forward and closed the footstool beneath his feet back into his recliner.

Paula tossed her cards into the pile on the pinewood coffee-table. "Gladly."

"Thank god." Amber dropped her cards onto the table and made an unsteady break for it.

"Careful on those stairs," Paula called after her.

"I'm fine," she assured, over her shoulder. "I've climbed them in way worse condition."

"Classy," Paula muttered, smirking.

Declan stretched his arms above his head, stifling a yawn. "Want some help cleaning up?" he asked, looking at Donna.

She began gathering up the cards, her mouth set in a rigid line. "No, thank you, dear. I'll be fine."

"You sure?"

"Perfectly."

He watched her, then watched his wife, neither of them making eye contact with the other, and felt unsure as to what to do next. Paula made his decision for him.

"We're heading up," she declared, standing up.

Declan followed her lead and got up from the couch. "Right, well, thanks for the game. I'll have to tell my client he was right, it was interesting."

Donna smiled sweetly, just at him. "Thank *you*, dear. Have a good rest."

Paula was already out the door and halfway up the stairs by the time he took his first steps to exit the living room.

Declan fluffed the down-filled pillow on his side of the bed then let himself drop onto the soft mattress with a sigh. Paula was still washing up in the bathroom down the hall, allowing him a few moments of solitude to reflect upon the evening they'd just experienced. Or, perhaps, a better word would have been: *survived*. He'd actually had a moment of wishing they'd been invited to Angus and Linda's. *That* kind of awkwardness, he could handle. Heck, it could have even been entertaining, watching Liam trying to dodge the point of the dinner.

The second biggest surprise, after the shock of witnessing their strained interaction, was that he'd been totally unprepared for it. Any time they'd spent with Paula's family, previously, had been civil; albeit in rather short bursts. Suddenly, he had the thought that that had not been by accident, but design. Clearly, his wife had carefully crafted things that way. It was an eye-opener, that's for sure.

Declan's cellphone trilled and he picked it up from the nightstand. It was Liam, texting to ask how the evening had gone. He pulled himself up to lean against the headboard and wrote: *"It was interesting."*

Liam replied: *"Yeah, I heard."*

Declan's brow furrowed in confusion. Had he said something to their mom in his text? He didn't think so. *"From who?"* he asked.

"Amber," came Liam's reply.

Declan's eyebrows did a reversal and shot up on his forehead. He remembered her texting throughout the evening, but had no idea she'd been talking to Liam. It was complete news to him they were close enough to be texting. Especially when, he thought, his brother was supposed to be on a dinner date at Angus and Linda's *with his girlfriend.*

"I thought you were at Angus and Linda's," he sent back, straight to the point.

"I was."

"Oh, for Christ sake," Declan muttered. It was like pulling teeth to get to the point and he wasn't sure if Liam was deliberately being obtuse, or not.

Liam added: *"Sounds like your night was more action packed"* with a laughing face emoji.

Declan debated on what to reply when Paula entered the room, cutting him off. He didn't want her to know what Liam was texting about her sister: especially when it was probably of no consequence.

"God, what a waste of a night," she complained, shutting the door firmly behind her.

Her face had been scrubbed clean, the raccoon eyes gone, and her short hair slicked back by a black headband. Wearing one of Declan's baggy blue t-shirts, a pair of blue and red checked flannel shorts and white ankle socks, she looked eighteen.

Declan quickly typed: *"Gotta run. Talk tomorrow."*

Liam send a thumbs-up emoji and Declan turned off his phone and put it back on the nightstand.

"Who was that?" Paula asked, reaching into her makeup bag on the dresser.

"Just Liam," he told her, while she pulled out a lip balm then slathered it across her lips.

"How did their dinner go at your brother's?"

"Fine," he said, then changed the subject. "Lips dry?"

She nodded and put the lip balm back into the makeup bag. "I swear I ate that entire second bowl of chips to myself. My lips are chapped from the salt. I wish you'd intervened and told me to step away from the bowl."

"No way. I've tried that before and learned my lesson."

"When?"

"Christmas, last year. You and your Mom were at odds about when we'd get together, and you ate that bag of cookies and—"

"Oh, god, yeah." Paula grimaced and held up her hand to stop him reminiscing further. "That was so gross."

Declan yawned broadly and pulled back the blanket and sheets to settle himself underneath. "So, tonight was interesting."

Paula crossed the room and crawled into the bed beside him. "I'm just glad it's over. God willing we'll be long gone to the new house before she suggests it again."

"Yeah, about that…."

She stiffened. She knew that tone: measured and calm, it meant trouble. She shifted onto her side to look him in the eye. "Tell me."

He cleared his throat then took a breath. "Okay, so you know that pipe I told you about?"

She nodded. "It needed to be replaced."

"Right. Well, it's turned into a *bit* more than that."

"Oh, god," she moaned, pulling the covers up over her face.

Normally, she could handle just about anything unexpected, it happened so often in her line of work she'd learned to ride the wave. But the idea of something - *anything* - shifting their timeline to move into their new house was seriously shaking her calm.

She took a breath, forcing herself to keep her voice controlled, then said, "Say it."

Declan looked at her - well, her *shape* beneath the duvet - and braced himself for her reaction. "It's a leak."

Paula pulled the comforter away from her face and snapped her head toward him. "Pardon me? WHAT did you say? Did you say a *leak*?"

"They have it under control," he quickly soothed. "It's just that it caused a bit of water damage, so they have to repair that before they can move forward with the other stuff."

"Ohmygod!" She began thrashing her legs around beneath the covers. "It's happening! It's actually happening! We're going to be trapped here forever! We're only one day in and, already, the noose is tightening!"

"No, it's not," he began, before a loud thump vibrated the wall behind their bed.

"Hey!" Amber shouted, from the next room. "Keep it down! *Some* of us are trying to get some sleep and, besides, that's gross in your old room!"

"Eww, y*ou're* gross!" Paula bellowed back. "We're just *talking*!"

"Then do it quieter!"

Paula raised her middle finger toward the wall and muttered, "How's this?"

"I'll be talking to the guys tomorrow," Declan continued, pretending the shouting match hadn't happened. Clearly, being back under the same roof was causing his wife and sister-in-law to revert to their childhood relationship and he was quickly coming to the understanding that sisters communicated differently than brothers. "I'll stop by the house and take a look for myself and we'll have a clearer picture then."

Paula groaned and pulled the bedclothes back up over her head. That tent idea was sounding more and more appealing.

Chapter 5

Donna stood next to the kitchen sink and scrubbed at a purple stain on her blouse above her right breast. She was sure she'd read somewhere that olive oil would do the trick, but the stain was still there, mocking her efforts.

"Oh, dear," she muttered, while Douglas wandered into the kitchen holding a newspaper out in front of himself in his usual manner of reading and walking at the same time.

He dropped the paper onto the table. "Problem?"

"Maybe. I'm not sure yet." Donna stopped blotting and turned toward him. "When did you get home? What time is it?"

He glanced at the clock on the microwave. "It's twelve thirty."

"Right, lunch time," she said, then pointed at the stain. "Is this really all that noticeable, or am I being overly sensitive?"

Before he could offer a response, Amber rounded the corner and gasped so loudly it was sharp in their ears.

"What are *you* doing home?" Donna demanded. "Is it your lunch break, too?"

Amber ignored the question and pushed past her father to get a closer look at the smeared, greasy purple blotch marring the, otherwise pristine, blue silk blouse her mother was wearing. "Wow, that looks bad, what did you *do*?"

Douglas decided he was out of the conversation and went to pour a cup of coffee.

"I had a craving for grape jelly on toast. Unfortunately, I just didn't eat it…." Donna made a sweeping gesture with her hand to indicate the front of her blouse. "I'm also wearing it."

"What the hell *else* is all over it?" Amber frowned at the spot then noticed the open bottle of olive oil on the countertop. "Olive oil? Are you putting *olive oil* on it? *Why* are you putting olive oil on it?"

"I read somewhere that it can remove stains."

"On *silk*?"

"Maybe." Donna cocked her head as she tried to remember. "Although, now that I think of it, it might have been vinegar."

"Where did you get it, anyway?" Amber asked, before suddenly recognizing the blouse and bringing her hands to either side of her face in an impressive imitation of *The Scream*. "Oh, my, god."

Donna went wide-eyed and looked around the kitchen. "What?"

She pulled her hands from her face and pointed an accusing finger. "That isn't even *yours*."

Donna flushed, her eyes flitting back and forth, avoiding direct contact with Amber's penetrating stare.

"You're dressed pretty casually for work," she countered, in an attempt to shift the focus. "Black yoga pants, a white t-shirt and a yellow hoodie. Is that what passes for work wear now?"

"That's *Paula's* top," Amber continued, her voice now a harsh whisper as she calculated the ramifications of the situation in her head. "You spilled grape jelly, which is bad enough, and now you've made it even worse by slathering the stain in olive oil ... on *Paula's* shirt."

Donna shrugged. "Well, I guess so, but...."

Amber took two sharp steps away from her mother, as though she'd been suddenly contaminated.

Douglas, leaning up against the island, sipped his coffee then shook his head. "This isn't going to end well, is it?"

Amber grimaced and shook her head as well.

"Oh, come on now," Donna cajoled, waving her hand and trying to rally. "It will be fine. It was an accident, she'll understand that."

Amber and Douglas shared another look. It had been a tense week since Declan had told Paula that the kitchen pipe leak at their new house was more serious than originally thought and repairing it was going to push their renovation timeline back another week. Paula had been just barely livable at the beginning of their stay, but when she'd had to face up to the fact that they would be spending three weeks, instead of two, in her childhood bedroom ... well, it was on-point to say her mood had been reflecting the grim status.

"I just need to give it a bit more attention," Donna declared, dropping the olive oil saturated cloth into the sink. "I'll go and change into something else, so I can really get to work on it. Before we know it, you'll never know it was temporarily soiled."

Amber opened her mouth to speak, but shut it immediately when her mother pointed a stern finger at her then at Douglas.

"And if it doesn't work," she warned, waving her finger back and forth between them, "you saw *nothing*. Agreed? *Nothing*."

Douglas lifted his mug in salute, while Amber nodded and remained silent.

Declan yawned widely then rubbed his face to try and wake himself up. It wasn't working. He was beat. No ifs, ands or buts, he was starting to feel the drain of living at his in-laws.

He pushed his chair back from his desk, stood up, and carried his mug over to the coffee pot on the corner console in his office. It felt like it was going to be a three cup, or four or five cup, sort of day.

"Wow, you look seriously like crap. Are you trying out your Halloween costume early, or is this just all you?"

Declan couldn't help himself and snickered. Trust his little brother to throw solid punches. He turned toward the doorway where Liam leaned comfortably against the jam; a smart-ass grin decorating his face.

"So? Which is it, bro?" he asked, loosening the green plaid scarf around his neck and sauntering into the room. "Costume, or just old age?"

"Piss off," Declan replied, then yelled, "Tammy! How did this riffraff get by you?"

Her laughter floated into the room from the reception area, before she called back, "He knows my weakness. Sorry, boss."

"Bribing my staff, again," Declan chided, amusement softening his words. "Have you no shame?"

"No." Liam settled himself comfortably into the brown suede sofa cushions. "She likes Gladiolus and I happen to have a source who can supply them. What kind of boss are you, anyway, denying her such a simple pleasure?"

"Yeah," Tammy agreed, poking her head around the door frame. "*Why* would you do that?"

Declan smiled and raised his hands in surrender. "I'm a monster."

She giggled. "Not quite, but listen *monster* and monster's brother, I'm doing a donut run. Any requests?"

"Oh, man," Liam groaned. "I'd love to, but I can't. Trina has me drinking wheatgrass smoothies and I'm sure she'd smell the sugar on me."

Declan grimaced.

"Yeah," he acknowledged, when he saw his brother's face. "It tastes as good as it sounds."

Both Tammy and Declan laughed, then she said, "Okay, so just the usual then, *monster*?"

He grinned. "Thanks."

She waved and left the room. "Back in a bit, the machine is on."

Declan joined Liam on the couch, coffee cup clutched in his hand. "So, what brings you to this neck of the woods? Got a job nearby?"

Liam spent at least half his work day in his vehicle, driving to his client's sites to check in on landscaping projects being done.

"No. Just thought I'd stop in and see how you're holding up. He ran his hand across his ginger colored beard - a trait all five of the Dempsey sons had inherited from their father: brunette hair and ginger beards all around. Liam was the only one who wore his longer than a five-o'clock shadow. "Word on the family grapevine is there's been some hiccups at the new house and…," he moved his arm in a large, circular gesture at Declan, "judging by this whole ghoulish, death warmed over look you've got going on, I'd say the rumor's correct."

Declan set his cup on the end table next to the couch. "Jeez, who'd you hear that from?"

"Angus," Liam revealed, referring to their oldest brother. "Who heard it from Linda, of course, and she heard it from Cian—"

"Who heard it from Michael," Declan cut in and leaned his head back against the couch.

His family's ability to pass information was impressive.

"Exactly," he agreed, before wrapping up with, "because according to Michael, '*Nothing stays a secret for long amidst the chatter in the hair salon*'.

Declan laughed out loud at Liam's imitation of their brother-in-law. Michael, a hairstylist at *A Cut Above* on Main Street, always affected an over-the-top, camp voice when he was sharing the salon gossip and Liam had matched it perfectly.

"Okay, so who did Michael hear it from in the first place?" Declan demanded. "Other than our contractor who, since he's bald, I can't see going into *A Cut Above* any reason, who else would talk about it?"

Liam shrugged. "*That* I don't know. However, what I *do* know is that after he shared the info with Cian, he was swift to tell Linda and—"

"She immediately told Angus."

He nodded and mimicked their sister-in-law's mantra, "*Because husbands and wives should never have any secrets.*"

Declan chuckled. They'd all heard her say it at one point or another.

"Did I ever tell you she actually took Paula aside to tell her that not long after we got together?"

Liam's eyebrows shot up. "Seriously? What did Paula say?"

"She thought it was both a strange and hysterical thing to do."

He shook his head. "Wow. Noted."

"Hey, that's right." Declan's smile broadened as he nudged Liam's shoulder with his own. "Trina's pushing for the next step. Maybe Linda told *her* that mantra when you were at the dinner party."

"Speaking of which, let me ask you this question," Liam said, shifting in his seat so he was facing Declan straight on. "How did you know that Paula was *the one*?"

"Seriously?" Declan replied, taken off guard by the question.

"Yup."

"Wow, okay. Well, I guess off the top of my head, I'd say it was a feeling, you know?"

"No. I don't. That's why I'm asking."

Declan ran a hand through his hair then elaborated. "What I mean is, there was this feeling I had when I was with her. Like I couldn't imagine my life without her. It felt like I was home. It still does."

Liam said nothing, just shifted himself back to sit facing forward.

Declan tried to read his expression, but couldn't. "What? Does that not make sense?"

"No," he said, levelly. "Just the opposite. It makes total sense."

"So, is that what you came by for? To quiz me about Paula?"

Liam's phone trilled from inside his jacket pocket. "Hang on," he said, reaching for it.

Declan watched him look at the screen, smile, type something back, then put the phone back in his jacket.

"Sorry. What was the question?"

Declan narrowed his eyes. He had a pretty good feeling he knew who that was. "So, tell me, since when do you and Amber talk?"

Liam shrugged. "I don't know."

Declan cocked his right eyebrow, not buying the shrug.

"What?"

Declan stared at him, debating on whether or not he wanted to find out if he was correct and ask if that had been her texting.

Liam took advantage of the silence and changed the subject. "So, what's the problem at the house, anyway?"

Declan decided to leave it. If his brother didn't want to share, so be it. With everything else on his plate, he didn't need another thing to feel he had to fix.

"Which house?"

"*Your* house. As in, your new house."

Declan sighed and got up from the couch.

"Wow, seriously? That bad?"

Declan reached over and picked up his cooling cup of coffee from the table. "One of the workers found a pipe behind the sink area that needed replacing. Straight forward stuff, until he discovered it was leaking."

"Shit." Liam shook his head. "Bad luck. How serious of a leak are we talking?"

"Drywall has to be replaced, subfloor needs to be dried out."

Liam frowned. "Have they at least completed the tear-out stage?"

"I'd assume so, by now. I was there on Tuesday to check out the pipe situation and there was just one section of countertop left to pull out."

"You haven't been back?"

"No, there's nothing I can do but be in the way. And Vince has been keeping me updated every day. Fixing the piping and the leak has been priority one, go figure, and has put the brakes on anything else getting done."

"Vince is your general contractor?"

"Uh-huh." Declan placed his mug on the edge of his desk.

Liam sat forward. "So it's been what now, a week since they started?"

"I know, I know," Declan exhaled, frustrated. "And Paula's been a wreck about us having to spend three weeks, instead of two, at her parent's place."

"And you?"

He shrugged. "Let's just say, while I appreciate Donna and Douglas letting us stay, even I'm starting to find her family's *charms* a bit of a challenge."

Liam shook his head. "Hey, man, you have my sympathy. I can't imagine what it would be like, living with Trina's parents. I mean, don't get me wrong, they're great people; just in small dosages, you know?"

"Yeah, believe me, I know," Declan stated, as his cellphone rang on his desk. He reached for it, looked at the display and held up his hand. "Hang on a sec, I have to take this."

Liam stood up, straightened his leather jacket and pulled his cellphone out of his inside pocket.

"Right. Okay," Declan said, pinching the bridge of his nose as he listened. "I'll come over now while I've got a gap in my schedule. Bye."

"What's up?" Liam asked, finishing a text.

Declan hung up the phone and noted the same expression on his brother's face as the last time he'd been texting, but left it again. He had other issues that needed his attention.

"That was Vince, I've gotta stop by the house."

"Good news?"

Declan went around his desk to log off of his computer. "He didn't say, just indicated he thought it would be good for me to see how things are now that the new piping is been installed."

Liam put his cellphone back in his jacket. "Wait, so you're saying it was so bad it's taken them the better part of a week to fix it?"

Declan looked up and met his eye, just as they heard the sound of Tammy returning through the front door. "Yup."

"Shit," Liam said, grimacing, while Tammy called out, "Donuts!" from reception.

A wry smile curved Declan's mouth when the juxtaposition of their tandem statements offered a moment of amusement. He pulled his coat from the back of his chair, grabbed his cellphone and tucked it into his pocket.

"Need backup?" Liam offered, retightening his green plaid scarf as he accompanied him out the office.

Declan patted him on the shoulder. "If you've got time, that'd be great."

"Leaving?" Tammy asked, while the rest of the staff filtered out of their offices at the promise of treats.

"Quick stop at the new house." Declan opened the door and held it for Liam to pass through. "I have my phone on me if anything's urgent."

"It's cold out there, take these for warmth," she urged, grabbing two fresh apple fritters in a napkin and darting over to him.

Declan took the pastries. "I only need one."

"The other one is for your brother," she told him, grinning. "He's weak and he knows it."

Declan laughed and exited the building.

Declan parked at the curb in front of the new house while Liam pulled up behind him in his grey SUV. It was quite the scene before them: contractor trucks and plumbing vans queued in the driveway, the garage doors open and displaying the abundance of detritus piled up from the renovation.

"Wow," Liam called out, as he exited his vehicle and met Declan at the curb. "I'm guessing this is setting you back a few bucks."

Declan straightened his coat collar to shield the back of his neck from the wind and shot him a grim look. "Tell me about it. The sooner things get back on track, the better. Let's find Vince."

"Wonder what the neighbors think," Liam pondered, as they walked along the front path toward the house.

"They aren't surprised." Declan paused to turn around and look at the houses along the street. "Most of them had already checked out the place online, so they know what needs to be done. If anything, judging by the few I've already met, they're hoping to see it after it's completed."

Liam laughed. "Sounds like they're fishing for an open house party."

"That's exactly what I told Paula," Declan chuckled, as they resumed walking, only to be met by one of the men on Vince's team striding toward them.

"Hey, Mister Dempsey," he said, stopping in front of them on the path, the wide grin on his face matching his broad shoulders. "Good to see you."

"You too and please, call me Declan," Declan insisted, extending his hand. "You're Mitch, right?"

He shook the hand offered. "You bet. Good memory."

Declan gestured to Liam. "And this is my brother, Liam."

Liam said, "Nice to meet you," and shook his hand as well.

Declan looked up at the house. "So, do you know where Vince is?"

Mitch ran his fingers through his hair to slick back the blond waves that were spilling across his forehead. He looked like a burly surfer. "Last time I saw him, he was in the kitchen."

Declan nodded. "Right. Thanks."

"Oh, hey," Mitch said, snapping his fingers. "Before you go in, just wanted to let you know I shared a bit of the tuna from my lunch today with your cat. Hope that's okay."

Liam looked at Declan. "You have a cat? When did you guys get a cat?"

He shook his head. "No, we don't."

"You don't?" Mitch repeated, his face surprised. "Are you sure?"

"Yup," he stated.

"Huh," Mitch said, rubbing his fingers across the blonde stubble on his chin. "'Cause it sure seemed right at home in the house, so...."

Declan, out of the corner of his eye, registered the shadow of amusement crossing Liam's face at the exchange. The interaction was the exact sort he lived for. Declan knew, without a doubt, it was going to become a story told many times: pulled out at family gatherings to be retold again and again. He wouldn't be surprised if the one cat in the story eventually became a litter, the way things were shared in his family.

"You're loving this, aren't you?" he remarked, to his brother.

Liam grinned widely, his hazel eyes practically dancing. "I really am. So, so much."

Declan sighed and said, "Well then, in advance, you're welcome," then turned back to Mitch. "Are you saying the cat was actually *inside*?"

Liam had to restrain himself from hooting with delight when Mitch nodded in agreement.

"Absolutely," he confirmed. "It was waiting on the porch when we arrived and followed us inside. Cute little thing, black and white."

"Uh-huh." Declan remembered it from when Paula had pointed it out. "And then what?"

"Oh," Mitch said, clearly not expecting to offer further information. "Well, then I guess we got to work."

Declan shook his head. "No, sorry, I meant *then what did the cat do?*"

"Oh, right. Okay, well, I'm pretty sure it went into the family room and took a nap on the sofa. You can understand why we assumed it was yours."

"And the lunchtime tuna?" Liam piped up, knowing full well that the query would earn him no brownie points with his brother.

"Right." Mitch grinned. "Smart cat, that one. As soon as we took our break it was right there, up on the window ledge. You know the one, right? The wide one in the kitchen?"

"The bay window," Declan clarified.

"Right," he agreed. "That one. Anyway, it waited as politely as you please, so I had to share. It would have been cruel not to."

"Of course," Declan said, while Liam nodded vehemently beside him. "And do you happen to know where the cat is now?"

He scratched his cheek, his brow furrowed. "Umm, not too sure. Could have left through the cat door in the back."

Declan clenched his jaw to suppress a groan then said, "Pretty sure that was a *dog* door, and also pretty sure it was locked."

"Oh, it was," Mitch assured, "but don't worry, we unlocked it so the cat could come and go as it pleases."

Liam snickered at that then quickly coughed to cover it up when Declan cut his eyes at him.

"So, you guys have a dog then? 'Cause you'll definitely want a fence in the back. We can probably get that done for you. Just set it up with Vince."

Declan shook his head. "No. No dog and no cat."

"Well, if you change your mind, just let us know. We can have a fence built in a couple of days, no problem."

"Alrighty then." Declan hunched his shoulders when the wind suddenly picked up and sent a blast of chilled air down the back of his coat collar. "Good talk. I should get inside and get the lay of the land from Vince."

"Yeah, I gotta get outta here, too." Mitch started down the path then called back, over his shoulder, "Remember, Vince is probably in the kitchen."

Declan lifted a hand in acknowledgement. "Thanks, again."

And then it started.

The moment Mitch got into his van and closed the door, Liam began laughing so hard he was practically choking.

Declan waited a beat, but when it was clear he was going to be a while led the way to the house.

"Oh, man," Liam sputtered, between wheezes, "that just about killed me."

Declan ascended the white-washed, wooden porch steps to the chocolate brown front door then stopped and turned around. "Are you done?"

Liam wiped his eyes, he'd been laughing so hard it had made him tear up, and insisted, "Oh, *come on*. Don't tell me you didn't find any of that even the slightest bit funny. I mean, seriously, if that had been reversed and had been me, you'd be on the ground right now."

Declan's mouth twitched. "Okay, fine," he admitted, chuckling. "It had its moments."

Liam took a steadying breath. "About bloody time. I was starting to worry about you."

Declan shook his head. "I'm sure I'll appreciate it more, later, when I'm not distracted by what's going on, on the other side of this door."

Liam patted his shoulder and took another breath to get himself together. His brother needed his support. "Okay, you're right. I'm good now. Ready?"

Declan twisted the knob and pushed open the door. "Let's get this over with."

Declan and Liam stood shoulder to shoulder in the kitchen, or what was little was left of it, the two of them staring at the large hole where wall should have been. Instead of wall; however, was exposed piping, and beneath *that* was raw sub-floor and … well … you get the drift. The house was quiet, the workmen on their break, and Vince was bringing them up to speed on how things were progressing.

"So," he said, clapping Declan on the back with his large hand. "I know things might not look much different than when you were here on Tuesday, but they are. And while that pipe turned out to be a lot more work than we'd originally thought it was going to be, the good news is we got it handled and there's no way it's going to give you any more trouble."

"Excellent news," Declan stated, before his cellphone sounded, alerting him to a text message.

"Sorry, hold that thought for a sec," he said, pulling the phone out of his coat pocket to check the screen.

It was Bonnie, so he put it back in his pocket.

"Okay, so the pipe," he started to say, before the phone pinged again, cutting him off.

"Sorry," he apologized, while he pulled the phone out of his pocket a second time to check the screen.

It was Bonnie, again.

"Busy," Vince remarked, chuckling. "Everything okay?"

Before Declan could offer a reply, the phone pinged for a third time as it sat in his hand.

He took a deep breath and said, tightly, "Fine," before switching the phone to silent and stuffing it back into his pocket.

Liam shot him a questioning look and Declan gave a small shake of his head and mouthed the word 'Mom" to indicate it wasn't worth discussing. Liam rolled his eyes in return.

"Okay, so the pipe is done," Declan said, to Vince, diving back into the conversation. "And now things are moving ahead?"

"Almost. We just have to get the area checked over to make sure there's no mold lurking, then we can get to work replacing the dry wall, then get the flooring guys in and so on."

"Right," Declan acknowledged, still staring at the hole. "And the timeline on *that*, roughly?"

Vince rubbed his fingers across his closely cropped, black beard: the only hair besides his eyebrows on his smooth dark head. "Pretty good, actually."

Declan brightened and tore his eyes away from the hole, those were encouraging words.

"I'd say a week, no more, and we'll be back at it."

Liam furrowed his brow. "Wait, what do you mean a week? Do you mean *another* week?"

Vince nodded.

"As in, another week *plus* the two weeks already scheduled?"

"Exactly," Vince concurred.

Declan and Liam shared a look. *Not* encouraging words.

"So, you're saying it's going to take an *entire week* to get this dry-walled?" Liam posed the question Declan was thinking.

Vince chuckled. "No, of course not. An entire week for drywall? Come on. No, we gotta get the mold guy in first, *then* the drywall will get done right away."

"Seriously? The mold guy is so booked up, it's going to push things back by a week?" Declan asked.

Vince shook his head. "No, but our floor guys are that booked up. They have time in their schedule to start Monday, or a week from Monday, nothing in-between. Once they start a job, they gotta stick with it until it's finished."

"And they can't start *our* job until the mold guy gives the go ahead, so…." Declan stated, putting the pieces together.

"They'll move onto their next job," Vince confirmed. "Time is money."

"And what happens if that one runs long?" Liam asked.

"Then, we wait," Vince said, matter-of-fact.

Declan ran his fingers through his hair, digesting the information. It sat in his gut like a rock.

Vince's cellphone started ringing and he said, "Hang on a sec, I gotta take this," while he pulled the phone from the back pocket of his jeans.

Declan and Liam both nodded while he stepped away and walked into the adjacent dining room.

"What about the rest of it?" Liam queried. "Won't that start a domino effect for the cabinet installation? Will that crew have to reschedule their date as well?"

"I don't know," Declan replied. "You'll have to ask Vince."

"Ask Vince what?"

The two of them whipped around, startled by the question.

He grinned, his chocolate brown eyes filled with amusement. "Sorry, I thought you heard me come back in."

Declan cleared his throat. "No, we didn't, but listen, Liam has a valid question about the flooring guys affecting everything else."

Vince leaned his broad shoulder up against the wall. "Shoot."

Declan lifted his eyebrows encouragingly at Liam.

"Right, okay," Liam agreed, then reiterated his inquiry. "I was just wondering if the flooring guys delay could end up starting a sort-of domino effect, you know? They're delayed, then the cabinet guys are delayed and have to be rescheduled and so on."

"No, no, that won't happen," Vince assured them. "I'll get them on a job with the same timeline as the floor guys. They'll be ready to get back to this job once the flooring's been laid."

Liam's face grew skeptical.

Vince laughed. "Believe me, it'll be fine. I do this for a living, remember? We'll be right back on track before you know it."

"Except for the extra week, of course," Liam muttered.

Declan took a breath, rallying. "Okay, so you'll keep me updated, right?"

"Absolutely." Vince picked up his stainless steel, coffee thermos from the window ledge. "And hey, before I forget, a couple of the guys were feeding your cat today. Hope that's okay."

Declan exchanged a look with Liam. "It's fine."

"Good. It's friendly, for a cat."

"His name is Sylvester," Liam volunteered.

Declan gave him an incredulous look while Vince chuckled at the information.

"Good name for a black and white cat."

"I know, right?" Liam agreed. "Paula named it."

"I'll let the guys know, the next time it shows up."

"Okay, then," Declan interjected, putting the brakes on the make-believe tale being spun. "Now that we've got that cleared up, I should get back to work."

Vince tipped his thermos to his lips and drank the last of the coffee inside then placed it back on the ledge. "And I'll wait on a call back from the mold guy to schedule him in next week. Once that's done, we'll wait on the flooring guys to finish their job and come back here to get things done. Sound like a plan?"

Declan looked past him through the bay window and thought: what was he going to say, no? Of course not.

Instead he nodded and echoed, "Sounds like a plan."

"No, it will be fine," Declan said, into his cellphone, hoping to convince himself as well as his mother on the other end of the line. "I'm sure we can handle living at Doug and Donna's a little while longer."

Regardless of him not responding to her texts during the time he was with Liam and Vince, Bonnie had kept on sending messages. He knew she wouldn't let up until he replied in some way, so instead of going straight back to work he was sitting in his car, still parked outside the new house, doing exactly that.

"How does Paula feel about it?" Bonnie pressed. "Because she *does* know you two can come here, right?"

"Of course," Declan assured her, fudging the truth.

It was either that or revealing to her that, while Paula did adore her, her over-the-top fawning on a daily basis stood the chance of being almost as bad as Donna's indifference. Better to deal with the devil you knew and all that.

"Okay, well, tell her again," Bonnie insisted, before divulging, "it would be nice to have another woman living in the house for a change."

Declan smiled at that. After a life spent under the same roof with five sons and a husband, she had legitimate reason to feel that way.

"I will," he promised, turning down the heat on the console. "But, listen, I really do need to get going back to the office and I don't have you on Bluetooth."

"Okay, just one more thing. Did you get the family email from Linda about Angus' party?"

"Yup," he said, hoping short answers would help wrap things up more speedily.

"Good. Did Liam? 'Cause he doesn't always check his email."

"That I don't know. It didn't come up."

"Okay," she said, her voice firm. "I'll call him and make sure."

"Really gotta run, Mum."

"Right. Give my love to Paula."

Declan smiled again. While she could be cloying, they could never accuse her of not caring. "Love you," he said, "talk soon."

"Love you, too. Bye, dear."

Declan pressed "End" on his phone and dropped it onto the passenger seat. He took one more look at the house, just in time to witness the black and white cat emerging from between the branches of the nearby bushes that separated their yard from the neighbor's property. He watched it amble across the lawn, pad up the front porch steps, then slip inside the house when the front door opened and one of the workers let it pass before exiting and closing the door behind him.

"Well, son-of-a-bitch," he muttered, while the worker continued walking to his truck without a backward glance.

Declan imagined, when the guy returned to the house, Vince would be informing him the cat's name was Sylvester. He took a deep breath then released it.

"One issue at a time," he counselled himself, before starting the car and pulling away from the curb.

Amber was sitting cross-legged on the floor of her bedroom closet, cellphone pressed tightly to her left ear. Murmurs and the rumbling of voices were traveling through the venting system of the house and she was doing her damnedest to stay out of the line of fire.

"I'm not exaggerating," she insisted, twisting a lock of her dark hair around her finger while she spoke into the phone to her sister, Jaimie.

"I believe you," Jaimie stated.

She was the oldest of the three sisters - two years older than Paula and six years older than Amber - and knew firsthand what Paula could be like when stressed. Living back at home, even temporarily, had to be pushing her levels to the limit.

"Every day that's passed this week has gotten more and more tense," Amber continued to lament, picking at some white lint on her black yoga pants. "I don't know how long I can take it. I think it's even affecting my looks."

Jaimie bit her lip and tried not to snort into the phone. "How so?"

"When I stopped for a bottle of wine after work yesterday, I didn't get ID'ed!" Amber flinched when the sound of her raised voice echoed off the closet walls, she didn't want to give away her hiding spot.

"I'm sure it was a fluke," Jaimie soothed, glad she couldn't see her smirk.

"I don't know," she whispered, hunching her shoulders beneath her baggy, tangerine colored cardigan sweater. "The tension around here might get to me even further and everyone might start thinking I'm in my mid-twenties."

"You *are* in your mid-twenties."

"Or, god forbid, older than that." Her voice was harsh with horror. "Maybe I should come and live with you and Trent."

"Sure."

"Really?" she said, straightening her hunched shoulders. "'Cause, I could—"

"As long as you're okay with sleeping in the baby's room."

Amber stopped talking and pressed her lips together. Right. The baby. Hazel, four months old. She'd forgotten about her.

"Hello?" Jaimie said, into the silence. "Don't tell me you *forgot* about your niece?"

"Of *course* not," Amber protested, glad she wasn't there to see her guilty face. "I was just … *thinking* and it's probably best I tough it out and stay put, to avoid confusing sweet, little Hazel."

"*Right*," Jaime agreed, letting her off the hook. "What's happening now?"

Amber paused to listen, then cringed at the sound of a door slamming. "Sounds like Paula's still on the warpath to find that damned silk blouse. God, Mom can really make a mess of things." She yawned and added, "The real mystery to me is how she thought it would be okay to wear Paula's clothes in the first place. It's like she doesn't even know her."

"Mmm," Jaimie murmured her agreement.

From her vantage point of being the oldest, she'd observed their mother through different eyes than her sisters had while growing up. The fact was, their mother lived in her own world and reality was often a tale spun to serve her best interests.

She had come to terms with it.

Amber seemed oblivious to it.

And Paula found it infuriating.

Thus, situations like what was happening right that moment were born. Their mother had spun a reality where it was perfectly fine to wear Paula's clothes, regardless of whether or not it was true.

"And she has no idea Mom's the reason it's missing?"

Amber stretched her legs and flexed her sock-clad feet. "From the sounds of her tearing through the house, doesn't seem like it."

"Do you know where she hid it?"

"God, no." Amber pulled her legs back up against her chest, reflexively bracing herself against whatever might happen next. "And I don't want to know."

"In case she interrogates you?" Jaimie queried, a knowing tone in her voice. She knew their sister's dog-with-a-bone inclinations.

"Exactly! It's bad enough I saw the stain in the first place. Paula's sharp as a tack and when she's in this mode, well, you know what she can be like."

"Oh, yeah," Jaimie concurred. As far as she was concerned, it was only a matter of time before she sniffed out the truth.

"Oh, hell," Amber hissed, pulling further into herself and shuffling backward to tuck herself behind her clothes basket. "I think she's upstairs."

"Couldn't you have gone and bought a new blouse before she got home and passed it off as the one she's looking for?"

"Ohmygod," Amber whispered, "why didn't *I* think of that? You're a *genius*, Jaimie. An absolute *genius*."

"Seriously?" she shot back. "Is there really a need for sarcasm? I'm just trying to help."

Amber huffed and switched her phone to her other ear. "Well, come on, you don't think I didn't think of that? But you know Paula, she buys so many of her clothes online I wouldn't even know where to start to find it."

"Yeah, okay, that's true," she conceded. "So, what are you going to do? Hide out forever?"

Amber looked up at the four walls of her closet. "Maybe. It's either that or … OH!"

"What? What's going on? Are you still there?"

"Yes, yes. Shhhh. I just heard a loud bang…." she began explaining, before a shrill shriek cut her off.

"Oh, boy." Jaimie's voice was filled with as much dread as Amber had coursing through her stomach. "That didn't sound good at all."

"Wait, maybe it's not so bad," Amber suggested, listening.

More banging and raised voices echoed through the house and she grimaced. Or, maybe it was.

"Wow," Jaimie exhaled, hearing the commotion. "She sounds really pissed off."

Amber groaned. "And if I was to offer a guess as to *why* she sounds so pissed, it would be that Mom wasn't bright enough to take the evidence off site and it's just been found."

"Hey, the baby's crying, I have to go," Jaimie announced. "Good luck and keep me posted."

"I will," Amber agreed, then ended the call.

She looked around her at the closet again and thought: to leave or not to leave, that is the question. She reached for a pillow on one of the shelves above her and tucked it behind her head. She wasn't going to stay forever, but, for now, staying put and out of sight had its merits; at least until the worst of the storm blew over.

Paula's footsteps thundered through the house as she charged from the upstairs bathroom and down the main staircase, the ruined blue silk blouse clutched in her hand. She wanted answers and she wanted them NOW. She rounded the doorway to the kitchen and found … nothing. Her mother, her father, and even her sister: all of them were glaringly absent.

Paula scanned the room, looking for clues. She knew where her father was: work. Her sister, probably in her room. Her mother … well, *that* was the million dollar question that needed to be answered. Paula was sure she was nearby, she rarely ever ventured further than the end of the crescent, but where….

Wait.

Paula's gaze fell on a teacup sitting behind an orange bowl filled with crabapples on the kitchen island. She walked over to it, noted its contents had barely been touched, then reached a hand forward to press a finger against its side: still warm, almost hot.

"Mother!" she bellowed, certain now that Donna was within hearing range.

She waited a beat and, sure enough, heard the audible click of the door latch on the sunporch her Dad had built off the dining room when they were kids. Busted.

Paula dashed from the kitchen and down the hallway, beetling through the dining room in time to see Donna outside, speed-walking away from the sunporch toward the depths of the backyard.

"I SEE YOU!" she yelled, striding through the sunporch and flinging open the door.

Donna, startled by the sound of her daughter's raised voice, slowed her pace. There was no way she was going to get to the back of the garden and out through the gate before Paula was on top of her.

Paula slammed out of the house, shaking the blue blouse in the air and shouting, "WHAT THE HELL IS THIS?"

Donna turned around, her hair and ankle length, purple skirt blowing in the late afternoon breeze. "Goodness, keep your voice down, the neighbors."

"Seriously, mother," Paula said, her jaw set and teeth clenched as she arrived to stand in front of Donna. "I need an explanation and I need it now."

"About?" she asked, wide-eyed, then flinched when Paula released an audible growl.

Paula held the blouse out by the corners, like a flag. "I am completely flummoxed. What the hell happened to my top and, more importantly, *why* did it happen?"

Donna began to fidget with the ruffled fringe on her white cotton shirt, a classic sign she was guilty but trying to find a way to avoid being caught out. Paula had seen it too many times before when she was growing up and it did nothing but incense her further.

"*So?*" she pressed, dropping the blouse onto the grass between them.

"Oh, dear," Donna tutted, shaking her head at the garment. "Is that any way to treat your clothes?"

Paula continued, ignoring her attempts at distraction. "Are you going to say anything at all to explain this? Or do I need to start harassing Amber and Dad until I get some answers?"

"How do you know it was me?" Donna challenged, folding her arms across her chest.

"Because, not only is it *always* YOU, if it wasn't YOU, YOU wouldn't even be asking that question!"

Donna's brow furrowed and she said nothing.

Paula placed her hands on her hips. "Okay, so now that that's cleared up, do you have anything else to tell me about this once gorgeous silk blouse that is now ruined beyond repair, by god knows what?"

"Jelly and olive oil," Donna admitted, looking past her toward the house.

Paula blinked. "What?"

"Jelly and olive oil. I spilled jelly on it then tried to clean it with olive oil."

"What?" Paula repeated, while the breeze picked up and swiftly turned into a wind, blowing butter yellow leaves from the weeping birch tree across the lawn. "Why? Why would you do that?"

Donna fiddled with the ends of her hair. "Which part?"

"ALL of it!"

She jumped. "No need to shout."

"I disagree."

"Okay, *okay!*" She threw her hands in the air as though *she* was the one who was upset. "When I spilled the grape jelly, *by accident*, I was wearing the blouse. Then, as I said, I tried using olive oil to remove the jelly because I'd read an article that stated it would work."

"Which. Clearly. It. Did. Not," Paula said, enunciating every word.

"Exactly. And I was incensed, let me tell you. I'm thinking of finding that article and writing a strong letter to let them know they ruined your blouse."

Paula clenched her fingers into fists and breathed steadily, in and out, to rein in her frustration. Finally, she said, "Correction. THEY did not ruin it, mother. YOU did."

"Mmm," Donna murmured and shrugged her shoulders. "And now that we're talking about it, how did you find it?"

Paula peered at her. "Seriously? *That's* your response here?"

Donna gave her a wide-eyed stare in return. "I don't understand what you mean."

"I *mean*, you're not feeling you should say something like,'*sorry Paula*', or something to that effect, instead of offering a non-committal shoulder shrug and '*how did you find it*'?"

Donna pushed back the hair that had blown into her face. "Well, it's either *that* or asking the obvious question."

Paula shook her head. "What obvious question?"

Donna gave her a patient smile, as though she was slow on the uptake. "Why on Earth did you leave your delicate silk blouse out for anyone to find when you knew it could be so easily damaged? Don't you think you should keep these kind of clothes tucked away to avoid just this sort of thing happening?"

Paula's jaw went slack and she said … nothing. Nothing at all. The woman could twist anything if given half a chance. By the end of the day, it was a certainty the story would be retooled into a tale about her negligence of her things: instead of the real truth that she had left the blouse neatly folded on the dresser-top in her bedroom, the door firmly closed, assuming it would stay there and not be pilfered to have jelly and olive oil smeared across it.

Donna, oblivious to Paula's silence, cocked her head at the shirt. "I guess dry-cleaning wouldn't do the trick?"

Before Paula could think of a reply, her mother's neighbor, Dot, poked her head over the gate. "Yoohoo," she sang. "Everything okay over here? Thought I heard raised voices."

"Oh, Dot!" Donna shook out her hair and strode across the lawn to meet her at the gate. "Just a little misunderstanding, nothing life altering. You know kids, always having to be reminded about their things no matter how old they get!"

Dot chortled and Paula reached down to pick up the ruined cloth. The retooling had begun. She knew when to retreat.

"Remember to consider the dry cleaner," Donna called after her, as she turned around and marched back to the house.

Paula didn't look back. T minus fourteen days and counting: Still.

Declan drove his car along the winding curves of Mountain Pine Lane then turned right onto Mountain Pine Crescent, passing the shadowy figure of a person walking a large, yellow dog. The fog that had rolled in at the end of the afternoon was thicker here than at his work and by the time he reached Donna and Douglas' house, he felt as though he was piloting his vehicle through the clouds.

Declan's phone chirped from inside his coat pocket as he drove his car into the empty space on the driveway, so once he'd turned off the engine he retrieved it and read the message. It was from Liam and rather cryptic at that.

"Be warned, you might want to choose your words carefully when you tell Paula about the timeline extension at the house," it read. *"Sounds like there was a lot of commotion with her mom today."*

"Oh, for Christ's sake," Declan muttered, into the darkness. Clearly, his brother had been texting with Amber again.

Did he respond, or leave it?

"Leave it," he told himself, ignoring the message and opening his car door to step out into the damp night air.

He tucked the phone back into his jacket pocket then paused, taking a moment to allow the misty coolness to surround him. The street lamps were casting a subdued, orangey glow, giving the neighborhood a hushed, tip-toe sort of feeling. After a hectic day of seemingly non-stop issues, it felt good to just stand still and give his mind a rest.

The tinny sound of dog tags on a collar caught Declan's attention and he turned to watch the person he'd passed on the way into the crescent appear from within the shroud-like fog like an apparition, the dog trotting merrily at her side.

"Paula?" he said, surprised when he recognized his wife's face.

She waved and continued moving toward him.

Declan looked from her to her walking companion, trying to reconcile the two, while she stopped in front of him then leaned down to pat the large yellow canine. "Good boy."

"Who's your friend?" he asked, silently hoping she wasn't going to reveal she'd finally snapped and stolen someone's pet.

Paula gazed affectionately at the dog. "This is Mister Samson, or Sam for short."

"Mister Samson? Seriously?"

"Yup. He belongs to Helen, the neighbor three doors down."

"And you have him, why?" Declan queried, zipping up the front of his coat.

Paula stroked Sam's soft head with her mittened hand and sighed. "Because I needed a break from the house. There's been an incident and I needed a chance to cool off. Amber told me she walks him every day and that Helen would be thrilled if he got a second stroll."

"*Amber* walks him?" Declan repeated, incredulous. "Voluntarily?"

"I know, right? I had no idea but, apparently, she's been doing it for Helen ever since they adopted Sam a year ago."

"Wow."

She shrugged her shoulders. "I hear you. Apparently, my little sister has some surprises up her sleeves. Mom and Dad don't even know about it. She asked me to keep it quiet because she doesn't want any fanfare about it."

"Speaking of which," he said, "did you know that she and Liam have been talking?"

Paula shook her head. "About what?"

"I don't know. But from what I've heard, they've been texting a lot and seem to be friends, or something."

Paula pondered the information then nodded. "Yeah, I guess I can see it. They're close to the same age - how old is Liam again?"

"Thirty one."

"Right, so that's only six years older than Amber. Maybe they have stuff in common and have become friends."

Declan considered it. Maybe. Or, maybe not. Time would tell. Instead of discussing it further, he reached for her hand. "So, want me to join you while you take Mister Samson back home?"

She squeezed his fingers while they fell into step, the dog alongside, and walked down the street towards Helen's house. "Remember the blue silk blouse your Mom gave me for my birthday?"

"Uh-huh."

"Well, I'd planned to wear it tonight when we go out for dinner, but it turns out I can't because it's been completely ruined."

"What happened?"

"My *mother*," she said, simply.

They turned left and walked along the cobblestone path that led to Helen's front door, Samson pulling eagerly ahead. When they climbed the two wide steps to the landing, Paula knocked and they waited, side by side, for Helen to answer.

"I'll tell you more about it at dinner, but suffice it to say, I definitely needed the break from the house."

He nodded, then Helen opened her door: a wide smile decorating her face. "You're back. And it looks like you picked up a straggler in the fog."

Paula returned her grin. "This is my husband, Declan."

Declan held out his hand. "Nice to meet you, Ma'am."

Helen dimpled. "So nice to meet *you*, Declan. I've heard nothing but praises being sung about you from Amber, so it's nice to put a face to the words."

Declan smiled, pleased by the revelation, while Paula handed over the leash clutched in her hand. "Thanks again for letting me walk him. It's a nice break."

"How was my boy?" Helen shifted her attention to Samson as she reached down to release the clip on his collar.

He shook himself out and trotted into the house without a backward glance.

"So well mannered. A dream to walk with."

"Not surprising," she stated. "Your sister is so good with him, she's trained him up beautifully. I can never thank her enough."

"Well, thanks again. It was a treat."

"Anytime, dear, he loves a walk."

"We have to run," Paula told her. "We have dinner reservations."

"Tell your mother I said hello," Helen said, waving them off and shutting the door.

"Now why couldn't I have been born in *that* house?" Paula groused, shaking her head as they made their way down the cobblestone path toward to the street.

Declan laughed and reached for her hand, holding on as they turned to retrace their steps along the fog-shrouded sidewalk back to Donna and Douglas' house. Perhaps he'd take Liam's advice and hold off for a bit on sharing the latest information about the new house. Maybe after dinner and a few glasses of wine to soften the blow.

Chapter 6

Erin made her way around the office of *Certain Events* with practiced movements, enjoying the stillness as she brewed a fresh pot of coffee, pulled plates from the kitchenette cabinets to set beside the pink box of muffins she'd brought in for breakfast, then opened the blinds to let in the morning light. She was early, but that was more often the case than not. She preferred to start her work day a half hour before they were officially on the clock: it made the transition from calm to hectic less jarring.

She stood at the windowsill beside her desk and noted Paula's car arriving to park in her usual spot three stories below. She watched as her boss exited the vehicle, swung the strap on her messenger bag over her shoulder, and made her way to the front door of the building. 9:00 AM, right on the dot.

Erin smiled as she walked back to the kitchenette, there was something comforting in such reliability.

"Morning," Paula said, as she strode into the office a few moments later.

"That was fast," Erin replied. "Did you sprint up the stairs?"

Paula's walked over to her desk, face quizzical, making Erin chuckle.

"I was at the window when you pulled in," she explained.

"Oh, okay," Paula said, also chuckling. "You gave me a moment there to wonder if you'd become psychic overnight."

"No, definitely not," she sighed. "If so, I'd use it to win the lottery."

Paula inhaled. "It smells fabulous in here."

"Muffins. In the box on the counter, freshly baked."

Paula dumped her bag beside her desk, shucked her coat from her shoulders and laid it across the back of her chair, then quickly made her way over to the pastry box.

"You are a star. Have I told you that, lately? An absolute star."

Erin grinned. "You're easy to please."

"Ha," she shot back, opening the lid. "Tell that to my mother."

"Trouble?"

Paula chose a blueberry muffin, set it on one of the plates Erin had put out and carried it over to her desk. "When is there not?"

"Mmm," Erin murmured, in agreement.

You know my blue blouse?"

"The silk one?"

"Yup." She sat down and turned on her computer. "Well, my mother ruined it on Friday."

"Oh, no! It was so pretty."

"I know. And it was a gift from Declan's Mom."

"Aww, that sucks." Erin choose an apple muffin from the box and placed it on the second plate. "If it makes you feel any better, the one you're wearing today is gorgeous as well. Very smart."

"Thanks." Paula smoothed the edges of the dark purple top she was wearing over her grey, herringbone pencil skirt while she added, wryly, "Hopefully she won't find this one before we move out."

Erin picked up the coffee pot. "Coffee?"

"Yes, please."

She lifted their personal mugs from the strainer next to the sink and started pouring.

"Oh, and then to add to that," Paula told her, snapping her fingers as she remembered, "the pipe that was leaking at the new house has now pushed our move-in date back by *another* week."

Erin grimaced and finished pouring the coffee. "Adding insult to injury. What happened, was it worse than they thought?"

Paula stood up from her chair and walked over to the kitchenette. "No. Apparently, we have to have a mold inspection done before they can move forward which means everything else gets moved back and so on and so on like dominos."

"Bummer." Erin handed Paula her cup before picking up her own mug and plate to carry over to her desk.

Paula followed her. "I'm starting to seriously think I'm being punished for some terrible thing I did in a past life. Karma is a bitch."

Erin smirked and sat down in her chair.

"Oh, and if all that wasn't enough, the delay also means we're going to be at my parent's on Halloween," Paula revealed, putting her cup down on the desk next to her computer then settling back into her chair.

"Oh, boy," Erin said, remembering the previous year at the Hayes' house.

Donna had created a *Candy Land* theme that had ended up feeling nut-house freaky, instead of all in good fun scary, and had frightened the crap out of the neighborhood kids … and their parents, for that matter.

"Yeah, exactly." Paula picked up her muffin, took a bite and spoke around her mouthful. "And, from what I've been overhearing at the house, this year sounds like it's going to be even more over-the-top."

"*More*? How is that even possible?"

"I know, right?" Paula shuddered at the thought as she put down her muffin and pulled a tissue from the box on her desk to wipe her hands. "According to Amber, my Mom has my Dad working in his shop creating some sort of alien themed display for the entire front yard."

"Has she wrangled you guys into being characters for this mysterious alien themed extravaganza?" Erin's eyes danced with amusement at the idea as she started eating her muffin.

"Not us, but Amber."

"No? Seriously? I was just being a smart ass."

Paula snickered. "Well, you were on point. And believe you me, as soon as I heard she'd been pulled into it, I told my parent's we're going to be out for the evening. No room for discussion."

Erin pulled a frowny face. "Poor Amber."

"Hey, she could have said no just like us," Paula stated, picking up her coffee cup. "And besides, *I* think she secretly likes it. Let her be a kid again for an evening."

"Speaking of which," Erin segued, "the Carmichael's approved the ideas for their son's party."

Paula seamlessly switched gears with her. "Excellent. *Someone* should get what they want as promised and not have to wait on the mold guy to get it."

Erin laughed. "I'll get it firmed up in the calendar."

Declan exited his car and walked swiftly along the path leading to Donna and Douglas' front porch. He was having a crazy-busy morning and it didn't help he'd forgotten his cellphone when he'd left for the day; something he so rarely did, it irked him he'd done so. Clearly, the added distraction of the renovations going on at the new house were taking their toll.

He took the porch steps two at a time, strode across the wooden landing and stuck his key into the front door lock, all the while making a mental list of the things he needed to do when he got back to the office.

Once inside, he paused to recall where he'd left the phone. It couldn't have been in the bedroom, otherwise he would have taken it with him along with his wallet and keys when he'd gathered them up earlier that morning on his way out.

He slipped off his shoes and walked down the hallway, wracking his brain, when he had a sudden flash of memory: the sunporch! He was sure he'd had it with him when he and Paula had taken refuge there after dinner the night before.

"Excellent," he celebrated, under his breath, traveling into the dining room then skirting the large rectangular table and eight matching chairs sitting smack-dab in the middle of the floor.

The quicker he retrieved it, the sooner he could get back to work.

Declan strode across the tan carpet to the sliding glass door that opened to the sunporch, holding the hope no one had come across the phone overnight and moved it, then pushed the door to the right. If he remembered correctly, he'd put it down on….

That was as far as he got.

All further thoughts were smacked out of his brain by the image before him: Donna and Douglas, au naturel and wrapped around one another, clearly in the *heat of the moment*.

"Holy shit!" Declan blurted, back-pedaling so fast he nearly tripped over his own feet in his haste to exit the room.

"Oh!" Donna gasped.

"What's that?" Douglas asked, his voice holding a hint of a moan.

"Fucking hell!" Declan exclaimed, mortification wrapping around him like a straightjacket and making him clumsy and addle-brained as he turned and bolted past the dining room table and out into the hallway.

He had to get out of there, NOW. Forget his phone, he'd get a new one! He just wanted to get the hell out of the house and, hopefully, still be able to drive with that *image* burned into his retinas. He took a deep breath to clear his head then galloped down the hallway toward the front door.

"Declan!" Donna yelled, arriving a second behind him in the dining room doorway.

Declan didn't look back: didn't want to see just how much clothing she'd managed to pull on before she'd left Douglas in favor of chasing him.

"Wait! Stop!" she called out, scurrying behind him. "Please!"

Declan slowed his steps as he got to the front door, already loathing the fact his decency wouldn't allow him to continue after she'd said please. It was as much his curse as his blessing and clearly, in that moment, curse was the operative word.

"Whew," Donna breathed, taking the last few steps to bring her up beside him in the front entry. "You've got some speed on you. Must be that Irish blood."

Declan avoided looking directly at her, but even so, in his peripheral vision could tell her blousy white shirt was on inside-out and her checker-patterned skirt uneven: one side hiked further up than the other.

"First, things first," she said, one hand on her hip as she continued to catch her breath. "We didn't know you were here, we thought the house was empty."

"Stop." Declan held a hand up, traffic cop style. "You don't have to explain. At all. In fact, the less we speak of it the better."

Donna cocked her head at him. "Well, that's a bit extreme, don't you think?"

"No," he insisted, swiftly, leaning down to pull on his shoes. "No, I don't."

"Well, Declan," she soothed, "we're all adults here. Granted, this was a bit of a surprise for all of us, but…."

"Listen," he cut her off, straightening back up. "I have a whole list of things waiting for my attention back at work, so I really should go."

She nodded. "Sure, sure. Just one question though, before you go?"

Declan gritted his teeth and forced himself to make eye contact.

"What brought you home in the first place?"

"My cellphone," he said, mouth barely moving. "I forgot it."

"Oh!" Her eyes lit up. "I found it on the sofa! I put it on the kitchen counter by the house phone before Douglas and I started … well, *you know*."

Declan coughed and repressed the desire to shudder.

"Hang on." She turned around and walked back down the hallway, talking over her shoulder, "I'll get it for you."

Declan opened his mouth to tell her not to bother then shut it again when she disappeared around the corner into the kitchen. He really did need it and, at that point, what further harm could be done if he waited another minute to leave?

"Here it is," she announced, reappearing just as Douglas rounded the doorway from the dining room behind her.

It was clear, from the nakedness of his legs - thank god Donna was blocking the rest of him from Declan's sightline - he hadn't bothered to put his trousers back on.

"Whoops! Didn't realize you were still here," he chuckled, as he ducked out of view into the kitchen.

Donna laughed merrily while she closed the gap between she and Declan and handed over his phone.

"Thanks," he managed to utter, before he spun around, opened the front door and made his escape from the house.

Donna stepped out onto the porch, waved and called out, "See you later, tonight," just before he got back into his car and sped off.

Paula, driving home at the end of the workday, waited for the truck in front of her to turn right. She had Jaimie on speakerphone and had just shared Declan's story of his interaction with their parents earlier that afternoon. Needless to say, her sister's laughter was echoing through the car and Paula was giggling along with her. The picture Declan had painted when he'd called her at work all in a lather was so hysterical there was no way she stood a chance of keeping it together then, or now.

The truck made its turn and Paula drove on while Jaime's laughter continued to echo through the speakers. Finally, she took a breath and said, "God, almighty, he's going to need therapy after that."

Paula snickered and made a right turn at the next traffic light. "I know. He sounded so rattled and I was no help, whatsoever."

"This beats the time I walked in on them," Jaimie commented.

"Remind me?" Paula requested, her own experience still the most prominent in her memory.

"The laundry room. Washing machine, spin cycle...."

"Oh, right! And you were how old, again?"

"Twenty-two. You were smart to move out as soon as you could."

"Not that it saved me from my own *in-the-act* experience," Paula stated, dryly, taking a left onto Mountain Pine Lane.

"In the backseat of the car, right?" Jaimie clarified. "How old were you, again? Seventeen?"

Paula shuddered and steered the car along the winding curves of the road. "Yup. Nothing but Dad's naked ass and Mom's legs in the air, god help me."

"Augg, not so graphic! I prefer to focus on Declan's funny encounter, thank you very much."

Paula laughed and turned onto Mountain Pine Crescent.

"So, can I tell Trent?"

"Would it really matter if I said no?" Paula teased, cruising slowly down the street, her headlights illuminating the road in front of her vehicle. "You can't sit on this one and you know it. The moment he walks in the door from work you're going to start telling him."

"True," she acknowledged. "Not to mention, even if I tried to keep it to myself, my giggling would eventually have to be explained."

Paula pulled up alongside the curb in front of their parent's house and put the car into park. "Listen, I'm at the house, so I'd better go."

"Give Declan my sympathies. That's if you can ever get him back inside the house."

Paula chuckled. "I will. Give Hazel a kiss from her favorite Auntie."

"Will do, talk soon," Jaimie said, before hanging up.

Paula gingerly climbed the staircase to the second story of her parent's house, expertly avoiding the creaks in the same way she'd done when she was a teenager. Apparently, some memories were forever, she thought, as she reached the landing and paused to release the breath she'd been holding.

She padded on stocking covered feet down the hallway to her bedroom and stopped in front of the closed door.

"Hello?" she called, quietly, knocking lightly on the wood as she twisted the doorknob and pushed it open. "You alive in here?"

Declan, lying face down on his side of the bed, muttered, "Unfortunately, yes."

Paula bit her lip to keep from giggling and gently closed the door. "Wanna talk?"

"Depends," he said, speaking into his pillow. "Have you brought a melon baller to scoop out the part of my brain that holds the memory of your parents in the sunporch?"

That was too much and Paula slapped a hand across her mouth to keep from laughing out loud.

Declan rolled over, his expression a mixture of revulsion and humor. He looked like he wanted to laugh and be sick at the same time.

Paula smoothed her pencil skirt and sat down on the empty side of the bed. "It will be okay," she assured, barely able to keep her mirth in check while she reached out to pat his shoulder. "Honest, it will pass."

At that, Declan grinned. Her face was a picture.

He pointed a finger and accused, "Sure, it's funny to *you* because this is old hat for you. But can you imagine if the shoe was on the other foot and it was *you* who'd walked in on *my* parents?"

Paula's expression turned grave and she stopped patting. The idea of walking in on Bonnie and Craig in a compromising situation was … *ugg*.

"Okay, okay," she conceded, lifting her hands in surrender. "Let's agree it's all the stuff of nightmares. But what's your plan? Spend the next three weeks at work, or holed up in here?"

Declan looked around the bedroom then finally settled his gaze on the posters on the ceiling. "I don't know, I'd have the guys for company."

Paula wrinkled her nose at him and lightly slapped his arm. "Ha, ha."

He sighed then pulled himself upright. "Fine. I know I can't lock myself away. But I'm going to need a bit of space between … *what happened* and being able to pretend it never happened."

"Absolutely. No argument here. How about, for starters, we go out tonight for dinner? No across-the-table awkwardness."

"Deal."

"Okay," she said, thinking some more. "And then when we get back, we'll sneak in and go right to bed, then we'll leave early for work in the morning and that will mean you'll get another day before you have to face them head on."

Declan grinned and leaned over to kiss her. "You're my savior."

She kissed him back then admitted, "Only because this plan has been used before when I was seventeen."

"Jeez." He grimaced. "We may both need that melon baller. Drinks are on me."

Paula stuck out her hand for him to shake. "Deal."

Paula locked eyes with Declan standing directly behind her on the back steps of her parent's house and pressed a finger to her lips to remind him of their need for quiet. He nodded. They were returning from their evening out and silence was essential if they were going to get inside without detection. Knowing her parents habits, Paula figured it was late enough that her Dad had gone to bed and her night-owl mother had settled herself either in the family room or - even better - upstairs in the bedroom to read. All they had to do was follow the plan she'd laid out and they'd be good to go.

"Ready?" Paula whispered, while smoothly slipping her key into the lock on the back door.

"You're sure she's not in there, baking or something?" Declan hissed back.

"The lights are off," she stated, turning the key to the right. "My mother might be a bit batty, but I've never know her to work in the dark."

Declan snickered. "*A bit batty*, that's hysterical."

Paula chuckled, not at her own comment, but the fact that it sounded like the one-drink-too-many he'd consumed at dinner was finally hitting him.

"A bit batty, a bit batty," Declan repeated, still snickering.

Paula turned around and tapped his shoulder. "Are you done?"

He took a breath then whispered, "Okay, yes. Let's do this."

She turned back to face the door and pushed it open a crack to peer inside. It was quiet. Nothing to see but the glow of the moon shining through the window over the sink. Perfect. Exactly what she'd predicted. Paula indicated with a small jerk of her head to Declan to follow then led the way inside, tip-toeing with exaggerated movements so as to remind him of the need for stealth.

"What are you guys doing?" Amber asked, having arrived soundlessly behind Declan.

Paula nearly jumped out of her skin at the unexpected sound of her sister's voice in the darkness and screamed, "Ahhhhh!" while Declan whirled around, his eyes wide like saucers.

"Eeee!" Amber squealed back, startled by Paula's sudden yell and Declan's jarring about-face.

"Everyone, stop screaming!" he bellowed, his heart racing in reaction to both his wife's and his sister-in-law's screeches in his ears.

"Who's there?" Douglas' loud voice came booming from further inside the house. "What's going on?"

"Oh, hell," Paula sighed.

So much for being covert now. She resumed her normal gait and moved further into the kitchen.

"Who is it, Douglas?" Donna could be heard calling while he thumped down the staircase then rounded the doorway into the kitchen, his salt and pepper hair disheveled and a baseball bat clutched in his hands.

"Oh, for goodness sake, Dad," Paula chided, while Declan and Amber filed in behind her. "No one is breaking in. It's just us. Put the bat down."

"It's just the kids," Douglas yelled, over his shoulder, before resting the bat up against the door jam.

Amber kicked off her acid green, suede pumps with sharp flicks of her feet then brushed past Paula and Declan.

"S'cuse me," she murmured. "Need a drink, I'm parched."

Declan busied himself with removing his shoes and coat, anything to avoid direct eye contact with Douglas.

Paula followed his lead, handing him her jacket to hang beside his and shucking her black ankle boots to rest beside Amber's shoes.

"You didn't drive yourself home, did you?" Douglas asked Amber, after watching her unsteady trajectory across the kitchen from the doorway to the refrigerator.

She pulled open the fridge door and found a jug of orange juice.

"Course not," she replied, shaking her head then grabbing the edge of the island for support.

"Who drove home from where?" Donna appeared in the doorway to stand beside Douglas.

Paula shared a surprised look with Declan, he hadn't heard her mother descend the staircase either. She must have avoided the squeaky steps.

"No one," Douglas told her, yawning and clumsily readjusting his tartan patterned robe.

Declan kept his gaze averted and Paula winced, hoping her father was wearing *something* beneath his dressing gown. It was bad enough her mother was wearing a purple polyester kaftan which, in the right light, left far too little to the imagination: they didn't need a double feature.

"So, were you kids all out together?" Donna asked, while walking over to Amber and removing the juice jug from her hands before she spilled it all over herself and the linoleum floor.

"Hey," she complained, pouting. "I was going to drink that."

Donna nodded. "Yes, I know. Go sit down and I'll pour you a glass."

Paula noted the distraction her sister was providing and latched onto it.

"Let's move," she hissed to Declan, under her breath.

He nodded and shadowed her as she began shuffling toward the doorway that would lead them out of the kitchen.

"No, we were not out together," Amber declared, pointing at Paula and Declan while she tottered haphazardly across the floor toward the table. "I don't know where *they* were."

Paula kept moving, Declan right behind.

"But, hey, Declan!" she babbled, starting to giggle as she unwound the oversized, beige knit scarf still around her neck. "Wasn't it *you* who saw Mom and Dad going at it this afternoon?"

It was as though someone had torn the needle from the record, everything went silent and still. Except for Amber. She kept right on giggling while she finally finished unwrapping the scarf and dropped it onto the tabletop then began tugging on the sleeves of her royal blue, knitted coat, completely oblivious to everyone else's reaction.

"I'd say it's getting late," Douglas commented, attempting to start things moving again.

Paula nudged Declan from the statue position he'd assumed when Amber had blurted his name. "Yup. Agreed. We're off to bed."

"What about sleeping on the sunporch?" Amber suggested, then began laughing so hard she nearly fell over.

A flush crawled up Declan's neck to match the color of his dress shirt and Paula shot daggers at her sister - not that she noticed.

"Oh for goodness sake," Donna huffed, carrying the glass of juice she'd poured for Amber to the table then pulling her daughter's coat from her body in the same way she'd done when she was a child. "Drink your juice and pipe down."

"Jeez, pushy," Amber muttered, doing as she was told and sitting down while Donna hung her jacket across the back of the chair.

"Night," Paula said, resuming their escape.

"Wait!" Amber blurted, stopping them in their tracks.

Paula clenched her teeth. "What?"

Instead of answering right away, she held up a hand and said, "hang on," before lifting the glass of juice to her lips and downing half of it in one go.

"I'm sure, whatever it is, can wait until morning," Douglas stated, freeing them.

"No, no!" Amber insisted, putting the glass back down on the table and wiping her mouth with the back of her hand. "I just wanted to tell you, Dec, that you're not alone. I've also had the horrific misfortune of seeing these two *exhibitionists* in the act. I feel your pain."

"Oh, *now*." Donna folded her arms tightly across her chest.

Amber wagged a finger at her. "Don't you '*oh now*' me. Whether you like it or not, it's seriously scarring to see your parents going at it like rabbits. Makes you want to wash out your brain."

"Oh, believe me," Paula piped up, backing her sister. "I totally understand."

Douglas coughed then cleared his throat.

Donna rolled her eyes.

Declan gazed longingly at the doorway that would allow him to vacate the kitchen. So close and yet so far.

"You, too?" Amber went wide-eyed at Paula's revelation.

She nodded and took a couple of steps toward the table.

Declan turned to look at her, his face perplexed. "You're going the wrong way."

"How come I didn't know this?" Amber demanded, grabbing back Paula's focus.

"Because it was a long time ago," she explained, "and it's not exactly something you want to bring up at dinner parties."

"Alright, now it's time for you to listen." Donna held her hands out wide to get everyone's attention. "Yes, admittedly, we had a bit of an unfortunate *encounter* this afternoon with Declan. But no harm done."

"Wrong," Paula argued, catching her Dad's eye before he quickly looked down at the bat.

"What?" Donna put her hands on her hips then turned to face Declan.

He shot Paula a '*thanks a lot*' look and she began talking rapidly to keep her mother's inquiry centered on her, instead of him.

"I said you're wrong. There *was* harm done. And not just today, either, but also when *I* saw you, *Jaimie* saw you and," she pointed at Amber, "*she* saw you. We've all been harmed, mother."

"What are you two telling me?" Donna asked, incredulous, her head swiveling back and forth between her daughters as she spoke. "That all of my children and, apparently now, their spouses are lying in wait to watch me and their father fornicate? Who's going to try next, Trent?"

"Uggg, gross." Amber grimaced and picked up her glass to finish off the last of the orange juice.

"What? No!" Paula shot back. "Of course not!"

"Well, if not my other son-in-law then who?" Donna pressed, waving her hands in the air. "Have *you* got a boyfriend up your sleeve, Amber, that we don't know about yet?"

"This dress doesn't have sleeves," she stated, lifting her bare arm for evidence.

"That's not what I meant, mother," Paula said, between clenched teeth, trying to stop the bait and switch that was happening. "None of us have ever been '*lying in wait*', as you put it, and you know it. And no attempt to twist things around is going to change the fact we've all been traumatized by you and Dad not giving a damn who might turn up when you start *fornicating* every-damned-where."

"Ewww," Amber groaned. "Still gross."

"Traumatized?" Donna repeated, turning to Douglas. "Are you hearing this, Douglas? We've been *traumatizing* our children, all because we have a healthy sex life in our own home!"

Douglas sighed and looked at Declan.

This time he didn't try to avoid his father-in-law's eye; instead, he shrugged. Regardless of what had happened earlier that afternoon, both men were of the same thought: get me outta here

"This isn't about your ... *sex life*," Paula asserted, hands on hips, trying to dampen the drama her mother was introducing to the conversation. "No one is saying anything about that and you know it."

"Definitely not," Amber interjected, scrunching her nose in distaste.

"So, what then?" Donna insisted, her chin lifted and her tone haughty.

"Oh, for goodness sake," Paula exhaled, regretting she'd let herself get tangled up in the conversation. "It's simply about having some consideration for the fact that other people live here and there are ways to avoid this sort of encounter. Like using the bedroom, for example."

"So, you're saying what happened today is *our* fault?" Donna clarified, flicking the sides of her caftan back like a cape.

"No, not exactly your *fault* as such," Paula attempted to explain. "But—"

"Yes," Amber interrupted.

Paula shot her a look, to which she shrugged her shoulders and said, "What? *I* think it was their fault. So shoot me."

"Well, whatever you think," Donna cut in, "in case you weren't informed of the full facts, there was no one else in the house before Declan showed up. *He* walked in on *us*."

Paula sighed and looked at her sister. Amber shook her head. There was no use arguing. Their mother was never going to admit she and their father could have taken a moment to consider the idea it was possible someone might come home while they were … *you know* and; thus, chosen to go behind closed doors to avoid the chance of exactly what happened with Declan. Nope, their mother was never in the wrong and that was that.

Paula took a breath then walked over to Declan. "It's late, we should get to bed."

He looked so relieved it was almost comical.

"And we all understand and agree now?" Donna asked.

Amber rolled her eyes and got up from her seat to carry her glass to the sink.

Paula patted Douglas on the shoulder as she walked by him out of the room. "'Night, Dad."

"Goodnight, dear," he replied, yawning.

Donna pointed at the bat. "Remember to bring that back upstairs, Douglas."

"I still say it's gross," Amber stated, matter-of-fact.

"Of course you do, dear," Donna placated. "Dad and I are going back to bed. Turn off the lights before you come up."

Chapter 7

Declan clicked '*save*' on the document he was staring at on his computer screen then yawned and stretched his arms above his head. It was finally Friday and he was looking forward to the weekend. It had been a stressful week, not just with work, but at the in-laws as well. After *the incident* with Donna and Douglas and the sunporch, the past four days had continued with an awkward vibe; especially as Donna had taken to loudly announcing both where she was in the house and what she was doing, driving Paula batty.

His cellphone, resting on the desk beside his computer, pinged and Declan leaned over to read the text message. It was from his mom.

"What the hell?" he muttered, reading her question. How in the world did she know about what had happened with Douglas and Donna?

He picked up the phone and rapidly typed a reply: *"Everything is fine now. It was a bit of a blunder, but we all talked it out. Who told you about it?"*

Bonnie's response was almost immediate: *"Liam. He was here this morning to help your Dad plan out a new garden bed in the back and he told me what happened. You poor dear. Do you want to come over to talk?"*

Declan took a deep breath then exhaled, keeping his cool. Bloody Liam. How the hell did he know anything about it?

He quickly typed a reply to his mom's offer. *"No. As I said, it's fine now. Gotta run. Love you."*

"Remember Angus' birthday party tomorrow," was her response, along with a heart emoji.

Declan sent back a thumbs-up emoji then immediately switched to texting Liam. He was getting to the bottom of things. Now.

He wrote: *"How is it that you, of all people, know about what happened with me walking in on Paula's parents? And, that being said, why the hell would you share it with Mom?"* then hit send with as much gusto as one can on a cellphone and put it back on his desk.

"Hey, Tammy?" he called, closing his laptop.

"Yeah?" she replied, from reception.

"We're shutting it down early, today. Do me a favor and tell the rest of the gang."

The sound of her chair scraping across the tiles met Declan's ears, followed by the quick steps of her boots hitting the floor and then her smiling face appeared around the doorway.

"Excellent! Thanks, boss!"

He grinned as she whirled around and charged off to announce the good news to the rest of his team then picked up his phone when it pinged to announce a new text message. It was a response from Liam.

"Amber told me. Didn't know it was a secret."

Declan wrote back: *"I didn't say it was a secret, I just wondered how you knew and how it came up in conversation with*

Mom. And, besides all that, what the hell are you pulling with Amber?"

There, he'd said it.

Liam replied: *"I'm not pulling anything with Amber. What the hell are YOU implying?"*

"Oh, please," Declan muttered, then typed: *"Give me a break. You know exactly what I'm implying."*

He barely had a moment to feel righteous smug about calling his brother out because his phone started ringing in his hand, making him startle. It was Liam.

Declan connected the call.

"Okay, listen," Liam started in, before Declan even had a chance to say 'hello'. "I was out with Trina and some other friends and we ran into Amber and her friends and she told me about what happened with you and her parents. That's it."

"And Trina *was* there?" Declan verified.

"YES," Liam huffed down the line. "So stop thinking whatever shit you're thinking and give me a break, okay?"

"Okay," Declan agreed. "It's just that you've mentioned a few times lately that you've been talking to her and—"

"And, nothing," Liam cut him off.

"Got it."

"Okay, good. I have a client waiting."

"Later." Declan hung up just as another text message came through. It was from his contractor, Vince.

"Hey, Declan. Have you got a moment to swing by the house this afternoon?"

Declan replied: *"Can be there in 20 minutes."*

Vince sent back a thumbs-up emoji and Declan tucked the phone into his pocket, picked up his computer and stuffed it into his bag, all the while thinking: what now?

Declan pulled his car alongside the curb in front of the new house just in time to see the black and white cat sitting on the front porch, as natural as you please. When it spotted him emerging from the vehicle it stood up, stretched and yawned, then scampered down the steps to disappear around the side of the house.

Declan lifted his hand in a small wave and said, "See ya, Sly," then made his way along the flagstone path toward the front door. What waited for him inside was anyone's guess.

"So, you understand we have no choice but to go after it, right?" Vince was explaining, while he and Declan stood in the kitchen looking up at a dark patch on the ceiling.

Declan stared at the large blotch, sighed and nodded.

"Don't look so downtrodden," he cajoled, giving Declan's shoulder a firm pat. "Think of what might have happened if I hadn't been here keeping an eye on things."

"And none of this was evident when the mold guy was here for the inspection on Wednesday?"

Vince shook his head. "Nope."

"So, that's a good thing then, right? It means it probably just started in the last couple of days."

Vince folded his arms across his chest. "I assure you my guys were not the cause it, if that's what you're wondering."

"No, no," Declan quickly clarified. "I'm just saying, if it only started being noticeable now, maybe it's relatively new, instead of being old and more problematic?"

Vince shrugged his shoulders. "Yeah, I see what you're saying and that's possible, or not. We won't know anything for sure until we go after it."

Declan's stomach clenched. He really didn't want to ask what other possibilities there might be.

"Anyway, what matters is, we'll take care of it." Vince unfolded his arms and patted Declan a second time on the shoulder. "I already have a couple of my guys on the way over as we speak. We'll get it handled."

At a price, Declan thought, rubbing his fingers across the stubble on his chin.

"I'll put together the paperwork to show the work being added and email you the details. If you have any questions about any of it, let me know."

Declan shifted his gaze from the ceiling to the freshly patched drywall where the first pipe leak had occurred. "So, what kind of timeline are we talking here?"

"For the paperwork? Not long. I can probably get it to you by the end of the day."

"No, the timeline to get *this* dealt with," Declan verified, pointing at the blotch.

"Oh, right. Not sure exactly, but I don't imagine it'll be that long."

Declan waited. He'd learned that he and Vince had different definitions of '*not long*'.

Vince cocked his head and stared at the water mark. "First, we'll open it up and find out where it's coming from so we can stop it in its tracks. Once that's done, I'll call Marty—"

"Wait." Declan held up his hand. "Marty, the *mold* guy?"

Vince nodded. "Absolutely."

Declan looked back at the ceiling. "So, you think there could be mold in such a short time?"

"Anytime we have a water issue, there's a chance of mold," Vince stated. "Gotta bring Marty in to give us the all-clear. I've never had a lawsuit for negligence and I'm not about to start with you!"

"Right." Declan tucked his hands into his coat pockets. "Of course."

"But, no worries, it's just a minor setback. All part of the process."

"And the flooring? Is that still on schedule?"

Vince scratched his forehead. "See, that's the thing, it should be fine."

"I hear a '*but*' coming."

Vince gave him a wry smile. "Here's the thing, at first glance the water seems to be coming from the upstairs bathroom. *But* there is a chance it might be something bigger than it looks."

"And that means what, exactly?" Declan braced himself.

"It means, if it is something bigger, we could be tearing out both the ceiling here and the flooring upstairs to get at it."

Declan lifted a hand to massage the back of his neck. He could feel the beginning of a tension headache.

Vince looked up at the dark blotch again. "And that's not the real issue, of course. The real issue is the timing. Can we get the guys we need in a timely manner to do the repairs?"

Declan said nothing. He didn't know.

"Anyway, that's not for you to worry about," Vince stated, squaring his shoulders, all business. "That's why you hired me. I'll deal with it and you go home to your wife."

Declan nodded. "Do me a favor and let me know as soon as you have an idea of how much time it's going to add to the project. We're still staying at the in-laws and were really hoping to be moving outta their place and in here THIS weekend."

Vince, already tapping on the cellphone he'd pulled from his pocket, said, "You bet", then put the phone to his ear.

Home owner dismissed.

Paula hung up the phone in her office, jumped up from her chair and fist pumped the air while cheering, "Yes!"

Erin, coming out of the bathroom, started laughing at her boss's enthusiasm and asked, "Good news?"

"Great news!" she hooted, breaking into a happy dance. "The Bazzanos have decided to go with us! We won the contract!"

The Bazanno family were not just rich, they were *wealthy*. They had more money than they'd ever use, property all over the world, and their one and only daughter was turning sixteen and they intended to throw her a party fit for ... the daughter of absurdly wealthy people. The fact that they believed *Certain Events* was the planner to put that party together successfully was a huge feather in their proverbial cap.

Paula had had to interview for the contract, something she'd never before done. People came to her, not the other way around. However, when Lanzo Bazanno came a-callin' and stated he wanted to interview her for the chance to be their party planner, she'd made an exception. And now that exception had paid off.

Erin's eyes widened as she digested the information. "Ohmygod, this is seriously big," she said, finally, as it sunk in. "I mean REALLY BIG. Like, put us on the event planning map sort-of big!"

Paula stopped dancing, took a breath and nodded. "I know!"

"I can't believe it was settled while I was in the bathroom," Erin remarked, making Paula laugh.

"Don't worry, we can change the story. Put you at your desk, instead."

Erin chortled. "Perfect."

"We are going to have such a wild ride on this one," Paula enthused, not able to contain her exuberance. "The sky's the limit for these people and we're the ones who are going to have to deliver it."

Erin nodded, mechanically, and sat down at her desk. This was a whole new league for them.

Paula cocked her head. "What? What's wrong?"

She stopped nodding and said, "Nothing. I think I'm just feeling a bit … well, *intimidated* by this."

"Intimidated?" Paula repeated, sitting down on her desk chair. "Why?"

"I don't know." She shrugged her shoulders. "I guess because we've never done something this over-the-top before. The responsibility feels like a lot of pressure."

Paula leaned forward and rested her elbows on her desk. "Listen, there's no way I would have pitched for this if I didn't think we were up to it. But the fact is, we are MORE than up to it, trust me. It's like, finally, the job to really prove how good we are has arrived. We just have to take a deep breath, jump in and then rise to the occasion we've been waiting for."

Erin grinned. Paula was one of the best motivational speakers she knew and, go figure, it was working.

"See?" she said, pointing a finger at her. "You know it, too. You just needed me to remind you of how bloody good we are."

Erin's grin turned into a full-blow smile. "And we have the best contacts to back us up with whatever we need. You're right, we can do this!"

Paula jumped up from her chair and squealed, "Yes, we can!" before breaking into a terrible version of a cheerleader dance.

Erin started laughing and would have joined her, had Paula's cellphone not started to ring.

She stopped dancing and checked the display. "It's Declan," she puffed, then connected the call.

"Hey there, you."

"Hey, yourself," he replied, "you sound out of breath. Everything okay?"

"More than okay," she confirmed, sitting down and grinning across her desk at Erin. "We just got a huge contract that's going to seriously elevate our status."

"Wow, that's great! Congratulations. We'll celebrate tomorrow night."

"Absolutely. So, what's up?"

He cleared his throat. "Okay, so listen...."

"Oh, hell," Paula said, hearing the level tone in his voice. "What now?"

"It's not that bad."

"Are you sure? Because, when you start a sentence with '*listen*', it's pretty much never good."

"Okay, so I'm just going to jump right in and say it then. Agreed?"

"Agreed. Just rip the Band-Aid off."

"Vince called me over to the house this afternoon; he found another leak."

"Oh, gawwwd," she groaned, her shoulder's slumping. "I was having such a good day. Forget what I said, put the Band-Aid back on."

Erin looked up from her computer screen, her face concerned. "Problem?"

"Another leak has been found at the house," Paula told her, before saying to Declan, "Well, you've started now, may as well finish."

He took a breath and revealed the rest in one long statement. "Apparently, after I left, his guys came in to inspect it and it's coming from the upstairs bathroom. That means they have to tear open the ceiling in the kitchen to get to it and then, once they have it fixed, they have to bring back the mold guy—"

"What? Are you kidding me? Wasn't he just there?"

"I know," Declan agreed. "But this is a new leak and it's standard procedure whenever they're dealing with water damage."

"Okay, fine, so then what?"

"Once that's done, they'll probably have to get a guy in to deal with repairing the ceiling; unless one of Vince's guys can do it—"

"How long?" Paula interrupted, cutting to the chase.

"According to Vince, probably around an extra ten days."

Paula refrained from airing the expletives racing around her brain and, instead, asked, "Is that ten working days, or does that number include weekends?"

"Umm," he said, "I didn't ask. I'd assume that's working days."

Paula quickly checked her calendar and groaned again.

Erin raised an inquiring eyebrow.

"So, we're looking at ten more working days in addition to the current two and a half weeks, give or take a few," Paula stated, between clenched teeth. "Which will bring us to a grand total of four weeks, more or less, until we can get the hell out of my parent's house."

"It has to be fixed," he said, feeling as though he was in a play reenacting the part of Vince, the general contractor.

"I know," she agreed, taking deep breaths and forcing herself to rally. "And we're absolutely sure we can't move in and live around them?"

"Seriously? They'll have to turn off the water, not to mention the kitchen still isn't done...."

"Okay, okay, yes, I know," she acquiesced, rubbing the bridge of her nose. "You're right, of course. It would be a nightmare trying to live amidst all that. So, that means we'll just have to suck it up and find out what we're made of. We'll be fine. We've gone this far and survived, we can make it a few more weeks."

"I love you, Darlin'," Declan said, knowing full well how hard she was working to stay positive.

Paula softened. It really wasn't the end of the world. So they had to endure another few weeks at her parent's; there were worse things to go through, she was being childish.

"I love you, too," she said, smiling.

Erin said, "aww," before returning her focus to her computer.

"So, I'll see you in a bit?"

Paula looked at the time on the computer screen. "Yeah, I was thinking we'll take off a bit early today. We've earned it. What time are you done?"

"Now. I gave everyone a half day before I went over to the house and now I'm going to grab a coffee. Want to meet me? I'm going over to *Cuppa Caffeine*."

"Give me twenty minutes."

"Alright, see you in a bit."

"Bye." She hung up then addressed Erin. "Pack it up. We're clocking out early."

"What a great evening," Paula sighed, as she and Declan entered her parent's house through the front door.

Their coffee date had turned into a dinner date and she was feeling relaxed and much more optimistic than she had earlier that day.

Declan closed the door behind them and Paula's face lit up when she heard the sound of laughter and Jaimie's voice filtering down the hallway from the kitchen.

"I thought that was Trent's car parked out front," she said, turning toward Declan.

He shucked his jacket from his shoulders. "You didn't know they were coming over?"

"No."

She quickly slipped out of her shoes and dumped her bag and jacket on the floor beside them before speed walking away toward the kitchen.

Declan's eyebrows lifted, it was a rare occasion when his wife just dropped her things without a care. He picked up her coat and hung it next to his in the closet then stepped over her shoes and made his way along the hallway to join her and the rest of the family in the kitchen.

"So, what do you think? Will you keep him over at the new house until you move in, or keep him here with you?" Amber asked. "Personally, I vote for here. It would be nice to have a warm, furry body in the house."

Paula and Declan stood side-by-side, speechless, as they processed her questions. The last thing either of one of them had expected was to walk into the kitchen and be presented with the black and white cat that had been, until then, hanging around their new house: never mind being asked how they were going to make it a permanent part of their lives. They turned to look at one another for any sort of cue as to how they were going to proceed, but all they discovered was they were wearing matching expressions of disbelief.

"Okay, so do us a favor and clue us in: *how* exactly did it end up here?" Declan finally said, while staring pointedly at his brother, Liam, sitting next to Amber at the table.

Liam had the good grace to look sheepish under the unwavering glare, but was saved from having to speak up when Amber offered a reply.

"Oh, it's all my fault," she claimed, snuggling the cat in her arms.

"Really?" Declan's voice was laced with disbelief as he narrowed his eyes at Liam. "Just you, all by yourself?"

Amber stroked the cat's soft fur and nodded. "Uh-huh. When Liam told me about him, and we checked, it *is* a 'him', I insisted we go and see if he was still around."

"Ah," Declan said, his tone becoming icy as the other shoe dropped. "So, was this your *client* today, Li?"

Liam stayed silent to elude self-incrimination and shifted in his seat to avoid further eye contact.

Amber, oblivious to everything but the cat, continued, "Poor little thing, all alone out there in the cold. We had to rescue him."

"Oh, look at Hazel." Jaimie smiled adoringly at her baby daughter sitting in her lap, her cherubic face lit up with delight as the cat gently touched her reaching fingers with its small pink nose. "She loves it."

"Him," Amber corrected. "And his name is Sylvester."

Declan exhaled sharply and glared again at his brother.

Liam kept his gaze averted while Jaimie cooed, "Aww, great name."

"It sure seems to love *you*, Amber," Paula piped up, finally adding her voice to the conversation.

"He," she reminded.

"Right," Paula agreed. "*He* seems to adore you. Maybe *you* should keep him."

Amber shrugged her shoulders. "I don't think Mom and Dad would be on board."

"Speaking of which…." Paula looked around. "Where are they, anyway? And where's Trent? He's here, too, right?"

"They're all out in the garage," Jaimie offered, bouncing Hazel on her knee. "Dad had something he wanted to show Trent. As for Mom … well, I don't know what she's doing out there."

"So, does that mean she doesn't actually know the cat is here?" Paula clarified, while Declan walked over to the table and sat down in the empty chair next to Liam.

Amber shook her head. "Not yet."

Declan started whispering intensely at Liam, so Paula kept the conversation going.

"Do you have a backup plan if they say they don't want it here?"

Both Amber and Jaimie looked at her with surprised expressions.

"What?" she said, feeling put on the spot.

"Well, *you'll* adopt it then, obviously!" Amber stated, as though Paula was crazy for even asking. "That's what we we've been talking about all along, right?"

"Wait," Paula said, holding up her hand.

But that was as far as she got.

The backdoor opened and Trent and her parents strode into the room and the conversation sharply shifted gears.

"No!" Donna asserted, as soon as she saw the cat reclining on Amber's lap.

"Oh, for goodness sake!" she retorted, making the cat startle.

"You can say whatever you want," Donna volleyed back, folding her arms tightly across her chest. "But the answer is still going to be NO."

Amber stroked a hand down the cat's back, calming it. "You don't even know the whole story and you've already throw out a verdict. You always do this, every time I bring an animal home."

"Yup," Donna agreed, while Trent and Douglas slipped by her, doing their best to stay out of the line of fire.

"Well, that's not fair," Amber complained. "Right, Jaimie?"

Jaimie's eyes grew wide. She did not want to get in the middle. Thankfully, Hazel took that exact moment to start fussing.

"Oh, sounds like someone's wet," she announced. "Gotta change her diaper."

Trent immediately picked up the diaper bag next to her chair and said, "I'll help," before the two of them dashed from the room with Hazel in tow.

"Smart," Paula whispered to Declan, taking the seat across the table from him.

It put her back to her mother, a perfect way to avoid eye contact and stay off the radar.

"So, that's that," Donna announced, making a show of dusting off her hands. "You'd best take that animal back to wherever you found it."

Douglas walked over to the island and found his latest crossword puzzle, half finished. He picked up the paper and the pencil beside it and carried them back to the table.

"Dad," Amber whined, as he sat down.

"No," Donna interrupted. "Your father has nothing to say in this matter."

Liam and Declan exchanged a sidelong glance when Douglas didn't so much as hint at shifting his focus from the crossword puzzle. He looked as though he'd turned to stone.

Declan leaned toward Paula and asked, his voice hushed, "I get the feeling this sort of thing has happened before. Am I right?"

She nodded and pressed a finger to her lips while whispering, "I'll tell you later."

"But, why?" Amber cajoled, lifting the cat so his front paws dangled in an adorable way. "He won't be any trouble, look at him."

"Amber Jade," Donna said, her voice firm and holding a note of warning. "That's enough."

The tone brought back flashbacks for Paula of the many times during their childhood that Amber had shown up with a cat or dog, someone's pet that had managed to get out of their yard, and the arguments that had ensued before the pet had finally been returned to its rightful home.

Amber exhaled noisily. "Fine. So, it will be Paula and Declan's cat just like we agreed in the first place."

"Wonderful," Donna stated. "Problem solved."

"Wait, what?" Declan looked wide-eyed at Paula. "What did I miss?"

Paula held her hands out like a traffic cop. "Okay, hang on a sec—"

"You said you'd adopt him," Amber cut her off, then turned to look at Liam. "Right? You heard her? She agreed with Jaimie and me a few minutes ago."

"Umm," he said. "I was talking with Declan, so…."

"No, that's not what happened," Paula argued. "What happened was, y*ou* said if you couldn't keep it—"

"Where is Jaimie, anyway?" Amber cut her off a second time. "She was here, too, when Paula said it."

"Will it be staying at your new place in the meantime?" Donna asked. "Or living here until you move in?"

"Him," Paula corrected, then grimaced at the reflex while Amber nodded her approval.

Declan groaned and his shoulders slumped. They'd gone full circle and were exactly where they'd started when they'd first arrived.

"Well, look at that," Liam said, grinning at the irony. "Guess the guys working on your house were right and you do have a cat after all."

"Seriously?" Declan posed, glaring at him all over again. "*That's* how you're going to play this?"

Liam shrugged his shoulders then coughed to cover his laughter.

"And, remember, I'm free to babysit anytime you need," Amber gushed, happily snuggling the cat to her chest.

Paula sighed, giving in. "Great. Welcome to the family, cat."

"Sylvester," Amber reminded her, then smiled at Liam and said, "Right?"

He avoided Declan's stare and nodded. "Right."

Paula smoothed the skirt on her knee-length, black shift dress then stepped away from the dressing table mirror in her bedroom. Done. She was ready for Angus' surprise birthday party. His surprise *thirty-ninth* birthday party, it needed to be reiterated. She grinned, amused all over again that Linda had decided to deviate from the norm and throw the party for a non-marker year. From what Paula knew of her, and what she'd been told by Declan and his family, her sister-in-law was very much a by-the-book woman: the party was a big leap for her.

There was a knock on the bedroom door and before Paula could say, "come in", Amber pushed open the door and strode into the room.

"Are you ready?" she asked, Sylvester draped limply in her arms like a rag-doll.

Paula shook her head at the cat. "Can't accuse him of being uptight."

Amber gave him a gentle kiss on his forehead. "He's one cool dude."

Paula picked up her small, red leather handbag from the bed and checked inside it to make sure she'd transferred all of her necessities from her bulky, work satchel.

"That's cute," Amber complimented, "love the color."

"Thanks." Paula snapped the bag shut. "Did you confirm that Mom's okay with taking care of our little prince?"

Amber nodded. "Although, truth be told, I think he'll end up hanging out with Dad, not her. He seems to have already taken a shine to him."

"Really, 'cause it looks like Dad's just as smitten."

Amber giggled. "Yeah, I think that's about right."

Paula chuckled. "Okay, I'm set, are you ready? Declan's waiting downstairs."

"Uh-huh." She held out the cat.

Paula backed up. "Whoa. Don't give him to me, he'll get hair all over my dress."

Amber looked at her own clothes — a figure-hugging, black and white, off-the-shoulder lace cocktail dress — and shrugged. "Mine seems fine."

"That's because you two match," Paula quipped, turning on her heel to exit the room. "I'll brush you down with the lint roller before we leave, just to be safe."

Amber resumed cradling Sylvester while she followed in Paula's footsteps, down the stairs to meet Declan.

Declan, Paula and Amber walked three in a row, much like Dorothy and her pals in *The Wizard of Oz*, as they traveled the long length of sidewalk that lead to Angus and Linda's house. They'd been instructed to park at least a block away, so that Angus wouldn't catch sight of the car and question its presence; thus, possibly spoiling the surprise waiting for him at home.

"Yeesh, I'm glad you forced me to wear my heavy coat," Amber commented, while she reflexively moved closer to Paula - sandwiching her between her and Declan - when a brisk wind began to churn around them.

"You should have let me drop you girls off first," Declan insisted, stuffing his hands further into the pockets of his black wool coat. "No need for all of us to freeze because we need to keep the car out of sight."

Paula shivered when a line of frigid air managed to bypass her red scarf and dart down the back of her neck.

"Seriously, do you really think Angus would even notice your car in the dark?" Amber remarked, skeptically.

"Yeah, I don't know," Declan admitted. "Maybe he would, if it was right out front. But either way, the fact still remains Linda would never let me hear the end of it if it was my car that tipped him off, so I'm not taking the chance."

"Mmm," Amber agreed. "Fair enough."

"We're almost there," Paula announced, as they finally neared the house. "What time is it?"

Declan pulled his left hand from his pocket to check his wrist.

Amber did the same, except she checked her cellphone.

"Seven forty five," they said, in unison.

Paula chortled at their dual reporting and turned left to lead them along the path to the front of the house. "Okay, good. We're fifteen minutes early, just as we were told."

The front door opened as the three of them ascended the wide, concrete steps and Liam smiled warmly from the other side.

"Hey, guys. Right on time."

"Oh, thank god, heat," Amber enthused, pushing past her sister to get inside first.

"Hey, *rude*," Paula chastised, entering the house behind her.

"I'm freezing," Amber shot back.

"And we aren't?"

Liam chuckled and said, "Move it along, then," while he stepped to the right to let Declan pass as well then closed the door behind them.

"Fine," Amber huffed, at Paula, while she slipped her coat from her shoulders. "*Sorry.*"

"You don't sound it," Paula retorted, "but, fine, thank you."

Declan looked over at his brother to share an amused smile at the two sister's bickering, but Liam's focus was solely on Amber. More accurately, Amber in her skin-tight, shoulder baring, leave nothing to the imagination cocktail dress. He'd gone statue-still and it wasn't until Amber turned to face him did the animation come back into his body and he snapped to attention.

"Let me take that for you," he offered, reaching out for her coat.

She dimpled then crinkled her nose at him while she handed it over. "Thanks, Li."

"Great dress," he complimented, inspiring her to place a hand on his shoulder and give it an affectionate squeeze before she walked away toward the kitchen, her rear view as impressive as her front.

"Is Trina here?" Declan demanded, while he took Paula's coat.

Liam pulled his eyes away from Amber's retreating form, the expression on his face like that of a man who'd just come out of a trance. "Sorry, say again?"

Declan reached past him for two hangers, one for Paula's coat and the other for his own. "*Trina.* Is she here tonight?"

Liam frowned at the aggression in his tone while he busied himself with finding a hanger in the large foyer closet for Amber's jacket. "Yeah. I think she's with the kids. Why?"

"Nothing," he said, while Paula touched his arm and reminded him, "We should go into the kitchen. Linda was adamant that's where we stay so we're out of sight."

"Yeah," Liam agreed, "they'll be here any minute. You guys are the last to arrive. We should get in there with everyone else."

Declan offered no further comment and followed Paula down the hallway to the kitchen. The sooner the party was done, the sooner they could depart and he wouldn't have to keep on pretending he wasn't noticing his brother mooning after Paula's sister. While he knew it wasn't any of his business, something about staying at Doug and Donna's had made him as protective of her as he was of Paula. Regardless of the fact that Liam was his brother, he didn't want *any* guy - *including his own brother* - screwing her around.

"Hey, Dec," Emmet called out, when they walked into the kitchen. "Beer?"

Declan nodded. Time to put on his party face.

Chapter 8

Paula sighed appreciatively when contentment washed over her as she lounged in bed, enjoying the languid Sunday morning vibe. She and Declan had returned late to her parent's house the previous evening from Angus' party - a bona fide success, he'd had no idea and had been thrilled to bits by the surprise - and now the sunshine behind the window curtains was bathing the room in a warm glow and the peacefulness of the moment was inspiring her to feel at one with the world.

At the end of the bed, stretched out and looking boneless, was the cat. He'd settled into their lives like he'd always been there. Paula shook her head at the sight of him then couldn't help but chuckle at the way things had turned out: he was a cat who'd landed on his feet.

Sylvester's ears flickered and he opened his startling yellow eyes to gaze at her.

"Don't get too comfy here," she remarked, then snorted at the irony; she was more or less repeating the same thing she had said to him the very first time she'd encountered him sitting on the front steps at the new house.

He yawned widely, much as he had when she'd first said it, only this time he followed the yawn with a steady purr.

"I mean it," she insisted. "It may seem all easygoing around here, but trust me, this is a momentary calm patch. We're only going to be here as long as necessary."

Declan's cellphone buzzed on the bedside table and Paula reached to pick it up.

"It's the man who changed your destiny," she announced, to Sylvester, seeing Liam's name on the display. She swiped a finger across the screen then typed in Declan's password and held the phone to her ear. "Morning, Liam."

"Paula?" came his reply.

"The one and only," she quipped. "How are you? Calling to give us another cat, perhaps?"

He chuckled. "No, not this time."

"That's a relief," she teased, then asked, "Where are you? Are you calling from your car?"

"Yeah, good ears."

Paula glanced at the clock on the dresser, 8:30 AM. Declan had gotten up to go for a run, but she was pretty sure Liam wasn't an early riser like his brother.

"So, listen," he went on, "is Declan around?"

"He should be," she said, pulling back the covers. "He's been out for a run. Hang on, I'll get him."

"Thanks."

"Watch this for me," Paula directed, placing the phone on the bed next to Sylvester.

He sniffed it delicately with his pink-tipped nose while she retrieved her yellow, terrycloth robe from where she'd draped it over the back of her dressing table chair and slipped it around her shoulders.

"Still there?" she asked, picking the phone up again.

"Yup."

She opened the bedroom door and Sylvester jumped down from the bed to follow.

"So, whatchya up to today? Pretty early for you to be up and around after last night's party, isn't it?"

"Yeah, I suppose so," he agreed.

Paula made her way down the staircase, cat at her heels, listening for more. Liam, however, went silent instead of offering anything further. *Okay*, she thought, hitting the landing then striding down the hallway and turning into the kitchen.

Declan, seated at the table with Douglas, smiled when Paula and the cat entered the room. "Morning, sunshine and sunshine's shadow."

"Okay, found him," Paula said, into the phone.

"Thanks," she heard Liam reply as she handed the phone to Declan.

"It's for you. Your brother."

He took the phone. "Which one?"

"Liam," she said, then walked over to kiss Douglas on the cheek. "Morning, Dad."

He patted her arm affectionately and gestured to the island. "Fresh crabapple muffins. Your mother made loads."

Declan sat back in his chair. "Hey, Li, what's up? More cats?"

Paula giggled that he used the same joke as she had, then asked her Dad, "Is there food for the cat around here somewhere?"

He nodded and pointed at the fridge. "Inside. Amber got it all sorted."

Paula lifted her eyebrows, surprised. She hadn't expected her sister would take care of things. She walked over to the fridge and opened the door, impressed when she saw the container of fresh food marked 'Sylvester'.

"How much does he get?" she further questioned, while she retrieved the container.

Douglas pointed again, this time to the wall beside the fridge. "Amber left a note with all the details."

Paula turned to look and, sure enough, there was a note of instructions taped to the wall above a set of dishes - white ceramic embossed with black paw prints - on the floor next to the fridge. The note stated exactly how much food to give the cat and how often, so Paula grabbed a spoon from the cutlery drawer, peeled back the lid on the container in her hand and served a portion into one of the dishes while Sylvester purred and weaved himself around and through her legs.

"You're a lucky cat," Paula told him, feeling simultaneously surprised and pleased by the fact her sister had so responsibly attended to every last detail. Apparently, she wasn't the impulsive little girl she'd once been and had grown up without Paula noticing.

"What? Are you kidding me?" Declan straightened up in his seat, his face shifting from relaxed to intense.

Paula stepped back while the cat tucked in. "What? What's happened?"

He held up a finger while he continued listening to Liam.

She looked at her Dad, he shrugged his shoulders, so she put the rest of the cat's food back into the fridge and the spoon into the dishwasher.

"Okay, got it. Give me about ten minutes to get dressed and I'll meet you there," Declan stated, standing up.

Paula grabbed a muffin from the bowl on the island and the moment he hung up the phone, said, "What's happened? Who are you meeting and where?"

He cleared his throat and she narrowed her eyes. She knew he was stalling.

"Spill it," she demanded, then took a bite of the muffin.

"It's your sisters. Apparently, they've had a bit of an ... *incident.*"

Paula frowned and swallowed her mouthful. "Incident? What kind of incident?"

"Umm," he muttered, trying to choose his words while he took a couple of steps toward the kitchen doorway.

Before he could find them, Paula cocked her head and added, "Wait? Did you say *sisters?* Plural? As in BOTH Jaimie and Amber?"

He nodded.

She frowned. "Okay, now I'm really not following."

Declan stopped inching toward the exit, took a breath and tried to explain. "Amber called Jaimie last night before she left the party, remember?"

"Yes. She said she was going to see if Jaimie could meet up with her. So?"

"So, according to Liam, they've had a bit of an *incident* since then and—"

"Whoa, whoa, whoa," Paula interrupted, putting the remainder of the muffin down on the countertop. "Are you saying they haven't come home since last night?"

"Has there been an accident?" Douglas asked, the blood draining from his face.

"No, no." Declan held up his hands as though calming a chaotic crowd.

"So, what then?" Paula insisted, her tone sharp. "Why is *Liam*, of all people, calling to tell you about something to do with Jaimie and Amber? Why didn't they call themselves? What aren't you saying?"

Declan ran his fingers through his hair. "I'm *trying* to tell you, if you'd let me get a word in."

Paula took a breath and released it. "Sorry. Go ahead."

He gave her a small smile. "Okay, so yes, it *was* more of an accident than incident, BUT," he quickly clarified, "it was just with a golf cart and no one was hurt."

Paula's face clouded with confusion. "A golf cart?"

"Yup," Declan agreed.

She shook her head, trying to understand. "What the hell were they doing with a golf cart?"

He shrugged. "No idea."

"A golf cart," Douglas echoed, the baffled expression on his face matching Paula's. "Can you even play golf at night? Or, for that matter, at this time of year?"

Declan resumed his trajectory toward the kitchen doorway. "Okay, listen, I told Liam I'd meet them right away, so I should take off. I'm sure we'll have all of our questions answered once they're home."

Paula swiftly skirted the island to follow in his footsteps when he disappeared around the corner. "Hold on," she instructed, catching him at the bottom of the staircase. "I am sooo coming with you."

"I know," he agreed.

"Hang on," she said, then quickly returned to the kitchen. "Dad, can you do me a favor and watch the cat?"

Douglas gestured to his lap. Sylvester, finished with his breakfast, had settled in as though he'd already slept there a hundred times before.

Paula grinned and said, "Thanks," then turned around to sprint up the staircase behind Declan. Apparently, the calm patch she'd spoken of earlier was over.

Declan made a right hand turn and drove his vehicle in the direction of Boxwood Hills' art district. Paula, beside him in the passenger seat, had remained silent until that point, but now she spoke up.

"Okay, so clearly, despite being informed back at the house that my sisters were driving a golf cart, we're not headed toward any golf courses. Care to fill me in further?"

"All I know so far is what Liam told me," Declan said, coming to a stop at a red light.

"Right." She fidgeted with the green scarf she'd wrapped around her neck before they'd left the house. "And he said that Jaimie and Amber called him when they had some golf cart trouble, whatever *that* means, and he figured he should contact you since they're my sisters."

"Exactly." He accelerated when the light turned green.

"What aren't you telling me?" she accused, turning her head to stare directly at him. "You talked to him for long enough to know more than you're saying, so you may as well prepare me before we get there."

Declan made another right turn then cleared his throat. "We're here."

Paula shifted in her seat to look out the vehicle's front window and gasped. The scene before her as Declan pulled up to the curb to park the car was jaw-dropping.

Jaime and Amber, standing next to Liam on the sidewalk in front of a shop called *The Potter's Kiln*, looked as though they'd been in an explosion. Their hair, faces and clothes were covered in white powder and there were chunks of, what looked like, colored clay all over the ground. The golf cart Paula had heard about was sporting an impressive dent, not to mention gashes that had completely marred the paint job: clearly, whatever it had impacted had been done at speed.

Liam lifted a hand in greeting at Declan while Paula scrambled to get out of the car. She slammed the passenger door closed behind her then marched across the road toward him and her sisters.

"Hey, Paula," Liam said, as he brushed at the front of his clothes where he, too, was smattered in the same white dust.

"Hey, Li," she replied, stepping up onto the sidewalk. "Thanks for calling us."

"You should look both ways before you cross the street," Jaimie commented, shaking her head.

"Oh, I think I'll be fine, thank you very much, seeing as nothing is yet open," Paula shot back, folding her arms across her chest. "Which, of course, begs the question: what in the HELL are the pair of you doing on a street with no shops open, looking like you've been through an explosion in a flour factory, and driving a freaking golf cart no less!"

Amber snickered then quickly pressed her lips together when Paula's eyebrows shot up at the sound.

"Excuse me?" she demanded, unfolding her arms and taking a step forward, closer to them. "Is something funny here?"

Amber darted her eyes away from her sister's penetrating stare. "No. I guess not."

Declan strode across the street and Liam nodded at him when he arrived to join their odd party.

"Hey, Bro," he said, shaking the last of the dust from his jacket before reaching out to give him a quick hug.

Declan hugged him back then shook his head at the sidewalk around them. "Wow, this is even more impressive than I'd imagined."

Liam grinned in appreciation of the comment while Paula turned on him and accused, "I *knew* you weren't telling me everything."

Declan looked at her levelly then gestured to the mess. "Be honest, now that you see this for yourself, would it really have made any difference at all if I had tried to explain it ahead of time? Heck, I didn't even realize the extent of things until right now."

Paula lifted a shoulder up and down in a half shrug. "I suppose. Point taken."

"So," Liam said, rubbing his hands together like a man ready to get things moving. "Now that you're here, we should probably get a move on before anyone else starts showing up. Any suggestions on how we deal with this?"

Paula looked at Jaime, then at Amber. They stood side by side, silent, like bedraggled statues, so she said, "I don't even know what the hell *this* is! I mean, granted, taking into account the severely dented golf cart and the remains of…." She paused to glance up and down the street at the over-sized, lavishly painted ceramic marmots positioned at regular intervals, then continued with, "what I'm assuming *was* a marmot like the other ones down the street, I can only surmise you had a collision with an unsuspecting ceramic rodent that resulted in this … this … absurd situation we're all currently dealing with." She turned to Liam and asked, "How'd I do?"

He grinned. "Spot on, I'd say."

Amber gently fingered the material on the black and white dress she was still wearing from the previous evening. "Do you think the dry cleaner can get this out?"

"Probably," Paula told her. "And aren't you freezing? Where's your coat?"

"Umm, *in the cart*," she replied, as though Paula was slow on the uptake.

Paula took a breath, ignored her sarcasm, and wagged a finger at the pair of them. "Okay, so I still haven't heard how this all came to pass in the first place?"

"Short version, or long version?" Jaimie asked, then burped delicately.

Paula wrinkled her nose when the distinct smell of stale beer permeated the air. She shared a look with Declan that he quickly interpreted as her call for backup.

"Short will do," he stated.

Amber cleared her throat and they all shifted their focus to give her their attention. She raised her eyebrows in surprise at the sudden scrutiny. "What?"

"You cleared your throat," Jaimie told her.

"So?"

"*So*," she said, while Paula's eyes rolled so hard it was a wonder they didn't fall out of her head. "It sounded like you were going to say something."

"Oh." Amber shook her head, then reached out to grab hold of Liam's forearm to steady herself when the pavement seemed to tilt from the motion. "No."

"Oh, for god's sake, forget it," Paula barked. "You can tell us later. For now, we have to go back to Liam's question: how are we going to deal with this?"

Liam and Declan exchanged a look then nodded.

"What?" Paula insisted, watching them.

Declan turned to her. "The boys. With their help, we'll get this handled and no one will be the wiser."

Paula, despite being annoyed at her sisters, couldn't help but smirk at his statement. The way he said it made it sound like he and his brothers were a bunch of good fellas.

Declan saw the smirk and asked, "So, that's a yes, then?"

She nodded then cut her eyes at her sisters. "Do what you have to do to make this *incident* disappear without a fuss. Can you imagine the field day the newspaper would have with this if they found out? Our family would be a laughingstock."

Jaime and Amber dropped their gazes to the pavement, smartly realizing when to stay silent and be contrite.

"No worries, Paula," Liam assured her, lifting his phone to his ear. "I'm calling Emmet right now. Once I explain why he's needed, he'll come through."

She nodded, her shoulders stiff from tension.

"And," Declan added, while rapidly texting Cian, "Cian just confirmed he's on-board and he's bringing Michael as well."

Jaimie's eyes widened. "Michael? Are we sure about that?"

Michael was known to offer the warning: '*what's spoken of at the salon, doesn't always stay at the salon*', as a reminder to his clients to watch what they share at their appointments.

"Absolutely," Liam confirmed, without hesitation, while he waited for Emmet to answer his phone. "He's a listener not a talker, so while he might hear a lot of stuff, he doesn't spread it. In fact, he could end up being our ace in the hole if any of this gets further than this street. He can retool the story, if needed." He lifted a finger to interrupt himself then turned away to talk into the phone and say, "Emmet! Need your help ASAP."

Amber walked over to the golf cart and climbed clumsily into the driver's seat. "Okay, well, until they arrive, I'm taking a nap. Wake me when it's time to start."

"Done," Liam announced, turning back around. "Emmet will be here shortly and he's going to call Angus and pick him up on the way over."

Paula felt the tension loosen in her shoulders. Angus could always be relied upon for his quick thinking in moments of crisis. She looked around them at the shattered ceramic mess and thought, if there ever was a crisis that needed quick thinking this was it.

"I hope, after last night, he's not too pissed off to be dragged out," she remarked.

Liam shrugged. "I doubt it. The kids will already be up, they don't ever sleep in."

"Fair enough," Paula agreed, then noticed Jaimie staring wistfully at the passenger side seat in the golf cart and allowed herself a moment to pity her sisters.

She took off her scarf and held it out. "Here. You go sit down, too, Jaim. You look wrecked. And put this around Amber's neck to keep her warm."

Jaimie took the scarf and shot her a grateful smile before shuffling over to the golf cart. She eased herself into the seat next to Amber, wrapped the scarf around her shoulders as instructed, then leaned up against her with a sigh and closed her eyes.

Paula shook her head at them while she whispered to Declan and Liam, "Thanks for helping deal with this."

"Hey, we're family," Liam said, matter-of-fact. "It's what we do."

Paula smiled gratefully. "Truthfully, I'd expect this sort of thing from Amber, but Jaimie? She's a mother, for goodness sake."

"Maybe that's the exact reason she's involved," Declan speculated, unwrapping the grey scarf he wore around his neck and gently wrapping it around Paula's shoulders to replace the one she'd given to Jaimie. "Maybe she needed a bit of non-Mom time."

"Possibly," Paula acknowledged, rising up on tip-toe to kiss him on the cheek for his kindness. "But, whatever the reason, I don't envy her trying to explain things to Trent when she gets home."

Declan lifted his eyebrows, surprised. Trent always came across as a pretty even tempered guy. "You don't think he'll be cool about it?"

"Oh, I'm sure he will," she snickered. "And I also think he'll laugh his ass off and she'll have to live with the story being trotted out again and again at family gatherings."

Liam and Declan both grinned. She had a point.

"Speaking of which," she said, before calling out to Jaimie, "Hey, Jaim? Does Trent know where you are?"

She opened her eyes and gave a half-nod. "Sort of. When I left with Amber last night, he agreed it was fine if I crashed at Mom and Dad's and went home in the morning."

"What about Hazel?"

"She's good. She sleeps through the night."

"So, he thinks you're at Mom and Dad's right now?"

"Probably." She bit her lip then reached into her pocket for her phone. "Do you think I should call him?"

"No!" Paula blurted, simultaneously with both Declan and Liam. They all shared a look, then Paula added, "Just leave it for now while we get this handled."

"Ok," she agreed, then leaned her head back on Amber's shoulder.

Declan pointed toward the top of the street. "Looks like the cavalry is arriving."

The last bit of stress she'd been holding lifted from Paula's shoulders as she watched the Dempsey men park their vehicles in a row along the street behind Declan's car. She knew from the stories they told they'd all had their share of sibling fights and such growing up, but she also knew when it was crunch time the five of them came together and were a force with which to be reckoned.

She smiled. Today was a day for the reckoning force and they were just the damage control needed to get things done.

Douglas, seated at his workbench in the garage, paused in his hammering to pick up his cellphone when a text from Paula activated the insistent chirping alert.

"Everything taken care of. Amber and Jaimie safe, on our way back now."

Douglas put down the hammer to a reply: *"Good news. See you soon."*

He then typed a second message to Donna, in the house: *"Kids on their way home."*

She wrote back, rapid-fire: *"Did you tell them they are all welcome to come?"*

He replied: *"Yes"*, then put the phone back on his bench. "Looks like a full house," he commented, to Sylvester tucked cozily on an upper shelf between a stack of newspapers and a large, orange watering can.

The cat blinked, the only evidence he wasn't an actual statue, and Douglas chuckled.

"Right, copy that," he said, then picked up his hammer and resumed working.

Donna stood at the kitchen stovetop, yawning while she languidly stirred the soup she'd just finished preparing. It was a big deal that she was out of bed before noon, but the moment Douglas had walked into their bedroom to inform her of Amber and Jaimie being involved in a mishap - one that he was pretty certain involved alcohol and bad judgement - she'd dragged herself out of bed and set to work cooking for their return.

The pungent aromas of pickles, garlic and cilantro permeated the air and Donna inhaled appreciatively. Perfect. Her daughters, and the Dempsey men for that matter, were in for a treat. After all, just because the soup was technically for hangover didn't mean a thing. Everyone could eat it and enjoy its benefits.

"And there they are now," Donna said, to herself, as she put her ladle down and wiped her hands on the floral apron tied around her waist when she heard the sound of car doors slamming outside. The gang had arrived.

"Hey," Paula called out, as she entered the house via the back porch. "We're back."

Donna bustled out from behind the kitchen island and swiftly crossed the floor to meet them as they began filing into the house.

"Welcome! Come in! Come in! Make yourselves at home!" she sang, beaming while they removed their shoes and jackets, chattered back and forth and infusing the house with youthful energy. And then, when she asked, "Where are my naughty girls?" she made them all laugh: well, everyone except Jaimie and Amber.

"They're over here," Declan announced, his arms around the shoulders of each of his sisters-in-law, keeping them steady on their feet.

Donna gasped and laid a hand on her chest when she got a look at them.

"Believe me," Paula said, ignoring the dramatic reaction that was her mother's signature move, "they look a heck of a lot better now than they did when we got to them. We considered running them through a carwash to get the ceramic dust off. Good thing Michael had towels in his car."

He shook his head and waved away the praise. "A curse of the trade."

"Well, this time it was a blessing," she told him, making him dimple.

"Aww, Amber, your lovely dress," Donna lamented, while Declan gave both her and Jaimie a gentle push forward toward their mother then slipped off his jacket and added his shoes to the pile created by his brothers.

"Paula thinks the dry cleaner can fix it," Amber said, then added, under her breath, "not olive oil."

Jaimie snorted at the reference while, thankfully, Donna was so focused upon herself that she missed it.

Paula fanned the air in front of her face. "Wow, Mom, what on Earth is that smell?"

"Salvation," Donna stated, grabbing Jaimie and Amber by their forearms to drag them across the kitchen toward the stove.

Amber wrinkled her nose when she saw the large pot on the front burner. "Did you make hangover soup?"

Donna released her grip on them to pick up her soup ladle. She dipped it into the pot and began stirring. "Yes. And I made enough for everyone."

Liam pulled out a chair at the table and sent a questioning look to Declan. He shrugged his shoulders in return. This was new territory for him, too.

"I'd rather have eggs," Amber reported, earning herself a glare for the comment.

"Eggs would be nice," Jaimie agreed, inspiring Donna to include her in the scowl before she shifted her focus back to the pot on the stove.

"You're both wrong," she admonished. "You need hangover soup and that's that."

Emmet sat down in the vacant seat next to Liam and asked, "Did you say hangover soup?"

"Yes, she did," Douglas confirmed, rounding the kitchen doorway, Sylvester draped in his arms.

All heads turned at the sound of his voice.

"Ooh, kitty," Amber cooed, while Emmet grinned and said, "Good to see you, Doug. Where you been hiding yourself?"

He handed over the cat when Amber darted toward him, arms outstretched. "Working on a project in the garage."

Angus, meanwhile, rose from his seat at the end of the table and indicated for Douglas to take it. He waved away the gesture. "No, no. You sit. I'll get a few extra chairs from the dining room."

"Let me help," Declan offered, following him out of the kitchen.

"You have a cat?" Michael asked. "Since when?"

"Long story," Paula said, leaning up against the island.

"His name is Sylvester, but he's not mine. He belongs to Paula and Declan," Amber explained, while she walked over to the table and sat down next to Liam.

Cian's eyes went wide at the information and he turned to fix Paula with a stare of disbelief. "What now? Did she just say *my* little brother has a cat? How did *that* happen?"

"Believe me, we're still asking the same thing," she quipped.

"Moving on," Emmet interrupted and got up from his chair to join Donna and Jaimie beside the stove. "Tell us about this hangover soup. Does it really work? 'Cause it smells pretty powerful and if it works as well as it smells, I definitely want the recipe."

Paula snorted and shared a look of amusement with Liam. Emmet, thirty five going on twenty five, was the party boy of the family and no stranger to a hangover.

"You could make a tidy sum selling it to our clients, Donna," Cian piped up, smirking.

He and Emmet were massage therapists and business partners at their studio, *Muscle Through, Massage Therapy*. They saw many clients at their worst 'the morning after'.

Michael snickered and threw in, "And at the salon as well. You'd be amazed at how many of our clients come in hungover. Vanity takes precedence over almost anything, including alcohol poisoning."

"Sounds like you'll need to check into acquiring a street vendor license, Hon," Douglas teased, returning from the dining room with Declan and more chairs.

Donna laughed and began ladling soup into the large, eggshell blue bowls she'd piled on the counter beside the stovetop for their arrival.

"Be a dear, won't you Emmet," she requested, handing the first bowl to him, "and carry this to the table for Amber? She's been through so much today, she's probably still a bit unsteady on her feet."

"Of course," he said, taking the bowl.

"Oh, for goodness sake, Mom. I'm perfectly capable of doing it myself," Amber griped, while Emmet delivered the soup to the table.

Donna raised an eyebrow at her, said, "Put the cat down," then returned to ladling.

She glared back, but stopped arguing and put the cat down on the floor. The truth was, there were too many examples that highlighted her propensity for stumbling and dropping something - more often than not an item of food on herself or, even worse, on someone else - when she'd been drinking. Her history was her downfall.

Donna handed the next bowl to Jaimie with a cheery, "bon appetit!", then began working on the rest. "Alright, everyone line up," she instructed. "I know you all don't have hangovers like my wayward daughters, but there's more than enough for everyone and you shouldn't miss out. This is my best batch of oyster mushroom and pickle soup yet!"

Five pairs of Dempsey eyes - which included Michael, a Dempsey by marriage - turned to stare at Declan.

He chuckled at their skeptical expressions. "Come on lads, we're Irish. Since when do we back down from a challenge?"

"Here, here," Liam laughed and stood up to lead the charge.

Paula walked into the bedroom, closed the door behind her and sighed.

Declan, reclining in bed and reading on his iPad, grinned when he heard her heavy exhale. "Quite the day," he offered, putting the tablet down beside him on the comforter.

"That's a kind way of putting it," she acknowledged, padding across the carpet in bare feet.

"Where's the cat?"

"In with Amber. Did you fill my Dad in on everything that happened?"

He nodded. "Uh-huh."

Paula picked up her lip balm from her dresser, opened it and swiped it across her lips. "I still can't believe the two of them," she said, putting the cap back on the lip balm and tossing it back on the dresser. "I mean, seriously, what would they have done if your brothers hadn't been available to literally pick up the pieces and manage the situation?"

"Figure out something else, I guess."

She snorted. "Doubtful. They would have gotten caught out and then Jaimie would have had to call Trent and tell him that, instead of simply going for a drink and to play some pool with Amber, things had escalated into a pissing match with a couple of guys they met in the pub."

He laughed. "It would have been funny to see those guy's faces when they realized, too late, how skilled your sisters are."

"I am, too." She couldn't help but remind him as she joined him on the bed.

"I know," he agreed. "Your Dad taught the three of you very, very well. Remember how shocked Emmet was when you basically ran the table the first time we all played?"

Paula chuckled while she fluffed her pillow. It *had* been funny. His surprise had been so great, he'd been without words. And that was saying something, indeed. Emmet was a man of many words; most of them used for the art of seduction, but still.

"I guarantee those guys that Jaimie and Amber played were just as blown away."

"Yeah, but at least with us, we didn't all get stinking drunk and start throwing out asinine bets."

The story they'd been told was: Jaimie and Amber had met up at *The Tipsy Pigeon* and were minding their own business, having some fun playing pool, when a couple of guys who worked at *Marmot Hills Golf Club* challenged them to a game. Of course, they hadn't known how skilled the sisters were when they challenged them and, as often happens when there is a mixture of too much alcohol and bad judgement, pretty soon one thing led to another and the guys laid down a bet that involved a golf cart from the club.

When pressed as to why they hadn't stayed at the golf course and, instead, had driven into the art district, Jaimie and Amber had given the drunken explanation: '*because of the marmots, of course*'. Apparently, one of them - they were unsure as to who - got the brilliant idea to park the golf carts with the clay marmots and take a photo of them together because, '*the golf course is NAMED after marmots and the clay sculptures ARE marmots, sooo....*'

Paula had listened to their drunken logic and had had to resist knocking their heads together to sober them up while bellowing, "And how did that work out for you?"

"That marmot seriously exploded," Declan said, still marveling at the obliteration of the clay sculpture while he reached for his iPad and moved it over to the bedside table.

Paula pulled back the bedcovers and crawled in beside him. "God, can you imagine what could have happened if Amber had kept on driving? Thank god she hit the brakes after she hit it. Granted, it would have been even better had she not accidentally been in reverse in the first place, but we can't change the past."

Declan snorted at the idea of his sisters-in-law slamming the golf cart into the sculpture, probably screaming blue murder when they realized they were moving backward instead of forward.

Paula smirked, she knew what he was picturing in his head because she was, too. "Shhh. We don't want Amber to hear us. She'll know we're laughing at her and Jaimie."

He took a breath, calming his laughter. "Anyway, the important thing is that *The Potter's Kiln* stays closed on Sundays and we got it all handled before anyone else showed up."

"Mmm," she murmured.

"What?"

"What about those guys from the golf course? Where did they go? Were they even there when it happened? 'Cause neither of my sisters seems to remember if they were actually there when they drove into the sculpture, or if they booked it after it happened. What if they were there and decide to spill the beans?"

Declan shook his head. "I don't think that'll be a problem. Whether they were there or not, there's no way they'll admit being connected to a missing golf cart. They've probably washed their hands of all of it and, even if they did see it happen, will claim they know nothing if questioned by their boss."

"Yeah, you're probably right. They won't want to be implicated." She turned her head to look directly at him. "But how about this, what sort of reaction is there going to be when that shop owner turns up tomorrow and that marmot is gone. Disappeared. Not a trace left. Will he, or she, start a manhunt to get to the bottom of things? Because, while I can totally see Amber being indifferent to any of it, Jaimie is another story. She had a chronically honest heart, I don't know if she'll be able to keep quiet."

Declan nodded. It was true. "You don't think this situation will be different? Considering that, if they're caught, they take the entire family down with them?"

"Yeah, that's true," she agreed. "The one thing that will keep Jaimie from coming clean is loyalty. We had a few times, growing up, where she totally kept some stuff we did quiet."

"There you go. No need to worry."

Paula smiled. "Thanks. That reminder makes me feel better."

He reached out to turn off the bedside table light, the room going dark around them, and snuggled next to her under the covers.

"Good. I'm glad you feel better and I'm sure none of this will amount to anything. Worst case scenario, someone will think it's an early Halloween prank by some bored kids."

"Damned kids," Paula said, giggling into the comforter to muffle the sound.

Declan chuckled. "Trouble makers."

Chapter 9

"Happy Hump Day!" Erin sang, striding into the *Certain Events* office, a pink box filled with pastries held in her grasp.

Paula sat back in her seat and shot her a wry smile. "For *some*, I suppose."

"Yikes, cryptic," she replied, carrying the box over to the kitchenette and putting it down on the countertop. "What's *that* all about?"

Paula shrugged and turned back to her computer screen. "Nothing."

"*Oh, please*," she snorted, walking over to her desk.

"What?"

"Who do you think you're talking to?" she insisted, draping her jacket across the back of her chair and dropping the overstuffed bag hanging from her shoulder onto the floor. "That so-called *nothing* is clearly full of a lot of something. You may as well spill. Trouble in paradise?"

Paula smirked at the word *paradise*. It wasn't one she'd choose to describe her current state of affairs.

Erin cocked her head. "Am I missing something?"

Paula lifted her hand and waved away the inquiry. "No. Never mind."

Erin's brow furrowed. "Oh, come *on*, already."

Paula stopped pretending to work and leaned back in her chair. "Okay, fine. Let's just say that, since we moved into my parent's house, there hasn't been any … *happy hump day*."

"Oh." Erin nodded, putting two and two together.

Paula stood up and stalked over to the pink pastry box on the countertop. She needed sugar.

"Wait, so nothing at *all*?" Erin dared to query.

Paula chose an apple fritter then shot her a grave look. "Nope."

"Seriously?"

"Seriously." She grabbed a napkin from a pile next to the box and carried her confection with her back to her desk.

"Wow," Erin said, mentally doing the math. "That's been what now? Two and a half weeks?"

"Yup." Paula took a large bite of her fritter.

Erin went back over to the kitchenette to choose a pastry for herself, her face a picture of incredulity.

Paula swallowed her mouthful. "Oh, for goodness sake, no need to look so gob smacked. Yes, it's been a while, but just a couple of weeks, not *years*. And, go figure, under the circumstances can you blame us?"

"No," she admitted, lifting a cherry fritter from the box. "But it's not like the only place you *could* is at their house."

Paula's lips curved into a small, devilish smile. "What are you saying? That Declan and I should come here? Get ourselves sorted on the sofa?"

Erin's face twisted into a mortified expression as she glanced at the couch in their reception area making Paula release a bark of laughter.

"Exactly," she said, chuckling. "Not the most appetizing thought. And before you say anything about *his* office, he has staff that come and go at odd hours, so that's a no-go as well. And never mind the new house either. With all the coming and going there as well, it would be just our luck to have our contractor show up unannounced. God, that'd be beyond embarrassing."

Erin wrapped a napkin around her fritter. "And a hotel?"

"Yeah, no. Our schedules are all over the place and with all of the surprise fixes at the new house, we need to keep our extra cash on hand."

"Alright," Erin acknowledged, walking back to her desk, pastry in hand. "Point made."

"Good. So, let's just keep the sugar and caffeine coming until Declan and I can finally move the heck out of there and no one will get hurt."

Erin laughed. "Agreed."

"Good. Because with the Bazzano party getting more and more outlandish and—"

"Speaking of outlandish," she interrupted, putting her fritter on the desktop and sitting down in her chair. "Did you see the latest on the mystery disappearance of the marmot in front of *The Potter's Kiln* in the *PT Post*?"

Paula stiffened. It had been three days since *the incident*, how on Earth was it still making news? Didn't Boxwood Hills' local newspaper, *Pine Tree Post* aka: *PT Post*, have something else newsworthy to report? A kitten caught in a tree, perhaps? A pumpkin patch raid?

"Hang on, I'll read it to you."

Paula finished eating her pastry while Erin tapped at her keyboard.

"Okay, here it is," she said, before starting to read. "New intel has been delivered, via an anonymous source, regarding the mystery disappearance of *The Potter's Kiln* marmot."

"Intel?" Paula repeated. "Seriously? They actually used the word '*intel*'?"

Erin grinned and nodded. "Uh-huh, right here in black and white."

"Oh, for goodness sake. What's next, are they going to insinuate it may have been an attempted hit gone wrong on the pottery store?"

Erin laughed and continued reading. "A photo has been given to the *Pine Tree Post*, revealing that the missing marmot—"

"Wait," Paula cut in, her heart rate increasing. "They actually have a photo?"

Erin gave her a funny look when her voice squeaked then pointed at the screen. "Yup, come take a look."

Paula scrambled from her chair and darted around her desk to Erin's, directly opposite, to peer over her shoulder. The *Post's* article displayed a very grainy, blurred black and white photo and Paula took a steadying breath while her heartbeat returned to normal.

Erin, mistaking her relief for an expression of distain, nodded in agreement. "I know, right? It's pathetic. It almost looks like a still shot from a security camera. A pretty crappy security camera at that." She began clicking on the photo, making it larger. "Even if you make it bigger, it still shows basically nothing. There's what, two people there? Maybe more? And they aren't even facing the camera, what good is that?"

Paula returned to her desk, her knees shaky from the sudden rush of adrenaline.

"Heck, it could be a total coincidence of some people just passing by at around the supposed time the *alleged* marmot-napping occurred."

Paula forced herself to chuckle at the comment. "Seriously, ridiculous. All of it. Oh, hey, did I tell you we now have a cat?"

"No, you didn't!" Erin exclaimed, closing the tab on her browser and giving Paula her full attention. "When? How? Do you have a photo?"

Paula let her shoulders relax. Diversion achieved.

"Liam on line one," Tammy called out, to Declan, from reception.

"Did you say *Liam*?" he replied.

"Yes, I did."

"Okay, thanks," he said, frowning when a shiver of trepidation ran up his spine.

Liam wasn't given to phoning and, as fate would have it, the last time he'd done so had been on Sunday, about *the incident*.

"Line one. He's waiting."

"Got it." Declan leaned back in his chair and picked up the phone. "Hey, Bro. Is your cell dead or something?"

"No. But you weren't picking up on yours, so here we are."

"Wait, you called?" Declan ran his gaze over his desktop, his cellphone was nowhere in sight. Damn it, where had he left it? If it was back at Donna and Douglas' house again, he was definitely calling first.

"Yeah. Have you seen the *PT Post* today?"

"No." Declan tucked the phone receiver between his shoulder and chin then started rummaging through his messenger bag with both hands. "Why?"

"Pull it up on your computer. I'll wait."

"Just tell me what's there," Declan insisted, reaching into a side pocket on the bag.

"No, you have to see it for yourself."

"Found it. Found my phone. It was stuck down the side pocket of my bag and still on vibrate."

"Don't give a shit. Google the *PT Post.*"

Declan put the cellphone down on his desk and said, "Fine, hang on," while he opened the browser on his computer. As he was doing so the cellphone vibrated, alerting him to a new text message.

"Got it yet?"

"No," he said, reaching for the cellphone. "Did you just text me?"

"What? No, of course not. I'm on my cell right now."

Declan opened the message, it was from Paula.

"Check out the PT Post when you have a moment. We may have to do damage control."

Declan quickly sent back, "*OK*".

"Hello?" Liam said. "Are you still there?"

"Yeah. Paula just texted me, telling me to check out the *Post* as well. Why is she saying we might have to do damage control?"

"Just bring up the god-damned page on your computer, already!" Liam bellowed.

Declan put down the cellphone and did as instructed then said, "oh, hell", when he saw the headline about the missing marmot.

"Three bloody days later and it's still making news? Isn't there some sort of parade or something going on that should be taking precedent?"

"And they have a photo," Liam stated. "A shitty one, but a photo nonetheless."

Declan clicked on the photo. It was crap, no doubt about it, but it begged him to ask the question: "How the hell, or should I say, *who* the hell took this photo? There was no one around while we were there."

"Exactly what I thought when I first saw it," Liam agreed. "But then my second thought was that it could have come from a surveillance camera from one of the shops across the street."

"That would explain why it's in black and white."

"And so grainy."

"So wait, if we're right, does that mean there could be more than just this one?" Declan asked, exhaling slowly at the implications of the question. "Or even actual video footage?"

"Possibly."

"Jeezus."

"Language," Liam reprimanded, doing a spot-on imitation of their mother.

Despite the gravity of their conversation, Declan couldn't help but laugh.

Liam chuckled along with him.

"Okay, seriously though. What the hell are we going to do about this?"

"Don't worry, I've already got Angus on it."

Declan leaned his elbows on his desk. "Angus? Are you for real? Our pillar of the community, GP brother is going to directly link himself to this in order to smooth the unexpected wrinkle in this situation? I mean, I know he was fine when we were cleaning up *the incident*, but this?"

"Yup. He's totally onboard. Turns out a couple of the shop owners across from *The Potter's Kiln* are his patients. He's going to find out exactly what sort of footage, video or photo, was taken of *the incident* and make it disappear."

Declan rubbed a hand across the stubble on his chin while he digested the information. When they were kids, there was no questioning that Angus was the brother to keep calm and make a plan to get things straightened out when any of them got into hot water. Declan didn't know if it was because he was the oldest and saw it as his responsibility to take care of his brothers, or it was just a natural instinct to protect. Whatever the case, with four younger brothers *and* his own mishaps with which to contend, Angus had become very adept at it. It stood to reason he'd still have that skill set in his arsenal, except for one small - very poignant - possible roadblock: Linda.

"Don't worry," Liam insisted. "Angus will come through. He always did when we were kids and he will now."

"Linda," Declan said, bluntly.

"Taken care of," he replied.

"What the hell is *that* supposed to mean?" Declan demanded, alarmed at the implications.

Liam laughed. "Not like *that*, idiot. I meant she knows the lay of the land and said she'll cover for him."

Declan added his own laughter to the conversation, albeit laced with a strong dash of incredulity, and said, "Are you shitting me? *Our* sister-in-law, the one and only saint Linda, is going to cover for Angus while he does the shady work of making photographic evidence of *the incident* disappear?"

"Yup."

"Well, blimey O'Reilly," he remarked, shaking his head. "Who'd a-thought we'd see the day."

Liam chuckled at his usage of their Dad's expression. "She already knows everything about *the incident* and is keeping quiet about it. Of course Angus is going to tell her about this, too. She's his wife."

"Yeah, alright. You've got a point there. There's no way I could keep something like this from Paula."

"Exactly. And, besides, Linda's a lot cooler than you'd expect once you take the time to get past the prickly exterior."

"I'll take your word for it," Declan said, closing the browser on his computer.

"Especially when there are a lot of drinks involved," Liam added. "Get a few drinks into her and she's a much cooler woman. Didn't you get a chance to talk to her at Angus' party? She was alright."

Declan released a bark of laughter, inspiring Tammy to poke her head inside the office.

"What's all the commotion in here?" she demanded, her eyes bright with curiosity. "And how come I wasn't invited?"

"Nothing," he replied, still grinning, then said to his brother, "Hey, Li, I gotta go. Thanks for the heads up, I'll pass along the info to Paula. Keep me updated."

"You bet. Later."

Tammy waggled her eyebrows while Declan hung up the phone. "Oooh, sounds mighty intriguing. Care to share?"

"No." He smiled to soften the bluntness of his words. "And it's not intriguing. Just run of the mill stuff."

She shrugged her shoulders. "Well, if it changes, call me in to share. I could use a distraction from this whole work thing."

Declan picked up his cellphone to text Paula the news that Angus was doing cleanup on *the incident.*

"Did you hear me?" Tammy pressed. "I *said*—"

"I heard," he cut in, grinning at her teasing tone. "Want donuts and coffee? They're on me."

"Yay!" she cheered, then announced loudly for the rest of the office to hear, "People, I'm going for a donut run! Give me your requests! Ten minutes and I'm outta here!"

Declan hit 'send' on his phone and got up to join the rest of his team in the reception area. When all else failed, sugar and caffeine were a good distraction from so many things.

Amber's cellphone alert sounded loudly for the fourth time and Douglas marched into her bedroom, his face agitated.

"Amber," he started, then stopped when he saw the room was empty.

"Well, that's a surprise," he commented, to the vacant space.

His daughter's phone was basically an additional appendage; to hear it without seeing her attached to it was an anomaly. The phone went off yet again and Douglas tracked it to her dresser top. It was charging.

"Ahh," he said, the mystery as to why it wasn't with her was solved.

"Hey!" Amber blurted, the cat lounging bonelessly in her arms as she rounded the corner of the doorway to her bedroom and laid eyes on her father. "What are YOU doing in here?"

Douglas held his hands up, as though readying himself to be frisked. "I didn't touch anything, I swear! It was your phone. It kept making noise and I came in to see what was going on and you weren't here and—"

"Okay, okay," she cut him off, before he started declaring he wanted legal counsel. "I believe you."

"Who *is* that, anyway?" Douglas asked, dropping his hands back down to his sides. "And could you at least do us all a favor and turn down the volume?"

She put the cat down on the bed then picked up the phone to check the screen. Her face stiffened and she said, "Oh, shit."

Douglas' eyebrows lifted. "Problem?"

"I'll say." She sat down next to Sylvester on the daisy patterned comforter. "It's Jaimie and she says that *the incident* is still making news in the *PT Post*. Apparently, they have a photo."

"A photo?" Douglas repeated, his eyebrows dropping down into a furrow. "Of what, exactly?"

"I don't know," she began, before the loud alert sounded yet again - making Sylvester's pupils dilate - and she read the message. "Oh, wait, here we go. Jaimie says the photo is really grainy, so it makes it hard to tell who it is."

"We'd better get ahold of the paper and check it out ourselves," Douglas declared, striding out of the bedroom. "I'll get my wallet."

"We don't need an actual physical copy, Dad," she called after him. "We can look it up online."

Douglas, heading for his bedroom, changed directions and turned left to walk down the hallway toward the home office and his computer.

Amber got up from her bed and trailed behind him.

Sylvester yawned and stretched, then jumped down from the bed to follow in her path.

"I wonder if Paula knows about this," she speculated, flopping into the overstuffed, brown corduroy armchair tucked into one of the corners of the office.

Douglas turned on his computer then sat in his antique regency swivel desk chair, the cherry red leather glowing in the overhead light. The cat leaped effortlessly onto his lap and curled into a black and white ball.

"Knowing your sister, I'd say there's a very high probability she does."

"Yeah," she agreed, grimacing. "That's what I thought, too."

"Calm down," Paula insisted, into her cellphone, while adjusting the pillows on her bed behind her head. "It's all getting taken care of, there's no need to go off the deep end."

It was Jaimie on the other end of the line and she was having a slight panic attack over the idea that the facts of *the incident* could be revealed in the local newspaper. She'd just claimed that, if that happened, she and Trent would have no choice but to pack up baby Hazel and all of their worldly possessions and move away from Boxwood Hills.

"You're sure about that?" Jaimie demanded.

Paula shifted her position on her bed, sliding further into the softness of the comforter. It had been a busy day and she was taking a moment to decompress before diving into the evening. Her sister was making that impossible.

"Yes, I'm sure. You're being way too dramatic about this."

"Or you're being way too blasé," Jaimie countered.

Paula laughed.

"Oh, sure, it's funny now," she continued. "But, when—"

"Stop!" Paula blurted. "You're spiraling. Declan said Angus is going to take care of it and I believe him. As soon as I know more, I'll let you know, okay?"

Jaimie took a deep breath then released it. "Okay."

"Good. Now relax, go and make dinner for you and your husband and play with your daughter, and I'll talk to you in a bit."

"I'll be waiting."

"I know."

"The package has been obtained," Declan announced, striding into Paula's bedroom.

She startled awake at the sound of his voice then yawned widely: what time was it? How long had she been asleep?

Declan crossed the room to the window, completely oblivious to the fact he'd woken her up.

Paula sat up and cleared her throat. "What's *package* code for, exactly?"

Declan turned away from the window, it was already too dark to see much of anything outside besides what the street lamps illuminated.

"Angus got all of the footage from the day of *the incident*."

"So there was actual full-on video footage? Is that where the photo came from?"

"Yup."

"Good god," she said, shaking her head. "One blurry photo was bad enough, actual full-on video footage would be a nightmare."

"AND, even better, he even got the neighboring businesses to give up whatever they had so there's no worries of any leaks of any kind."

Paula goggled. She'd never have thought in a million years that Angus could be so … conniving. "Wow, gotta be honest, I'd love to see footage of *that* going down. I can't imagine mister straight-laced doctor wheedling them to give up the goods."

Declan laughed and walked over to sit beside her on the bed. "You'd be surprised, seriously. He honed the talent when we were kids."

Paula shook her head. "Your poor mother."

Declan laughed, again.

"So, can I share the good news with Amber and Jaimie?"

"Absolutely," he said, then added, "and there's a bonus to all of this, too. Angus is going to show us whatever is on those tapes!"

Paula squealed and clapped her hands. "Ohmygod! When?"

"He invited us over on Halloween."

"Perfect! I've already told Mom we won't be here, so now there's no way she can try and convince us to stay and get trapped in Halloween hell."

Declan laid back on the bed and stared up at the ceiling. "Really? Do you think it will be that bad, especially after last year's debacle? Don't you think they'll be more careful and pull back this year?"

"Please. Learning from their mistakes is not something they do. Have you not heard the pounding going on in the garage? Whatever Dad's working on in there for this year's theme needs a *hammer* and god knows what else. I'm pretty sure pulling back isn't a part of the game plan."

"So, I should tell Angus and Linda we're in?"

"Immediately."

There was a knock on the bedroom door and Paula called out, "Come in."

The door opened and Douglas poked his head inside. "Have you kids seen the cat?"

Paula shook her head. "No. Why? Isn't it in with Amber?"

Douglas stepped further into the bedroom. "I checked, he's not there either. He came into the garage with me, he seems to like to watch me work, and then he disappeared. I haven't seen him since and was getting a bit concerned."

Paula looked at him fondly. He was such a tender heart, her Dad.

"He can't have gone far," Declan said, standing up. "Let's have another look around, I'm sure he'll turn up."

The doorbell sounded below and Douglas raised an eyebrow. "Wonder who that is, this late in the evening."

They all listened as Donna opened the front door, then Douglas said, "I'd better join her," and left the room.

Declan walked over to the bedroom window and peered out between the curtains.

"See anything?" Paula asked.

"No," he said, just before raised voices began to echo through the house vents.

"Paula!" Donna hollered, from the bottom of the staircase. "Come down here, please!"

"Ok!" she yelled back, then got up off the bed.

Declan led the way out of the room, while tossing over his shoulder the statement: "Never a dull moment."

"Here she is," Donna announced, pointing at Paula as she and Declan walked into the front hall.

"What's going on?" Paula asked, then smiled when she noticed Sylvester tucked into her Dad's embrace. "Oh, hey, you found him."

Douglas nodded then gestured toward the open front door and their neighbor's daughter-in-law, Kimberly, standing on the porch. "Yes and we can thank Kimberly for that. She's visiting Ginny and spotted Sylvester in the yard."

A gust of wind blew through the foyer and Donna said, "For goodness sake, you can come inside. We don't bite."

Kimberly pursed her lips as though she'd been sucking a sour lemon. "Thank you, but as I said, I don't plan to stay."

"Okey-dokey," Donna agreed, stepping forward to reach for the door.

"*However*," Kimberly added, taking a small step forward to stop Donna closing the door in her face. "Before I go, I'd like to share that *thanking me* for bringing over the cat is a bit much, mister Hayes, considering I'd actually like to issue a formal complaint about that animal."

Declan, standing behind Paula, lifted his eyebrows at the statement.

"Formal complaint?" Paula echoed, folding her arms across her chest. "To who? And for what, exactly?"

"Apparently, your cat was bothering their cat," Donna stated, a smirk on her face.

"More like tormenting," Kimberly elaborated, cutting her eyes at Sylvester.

He blinked in return, giving nothing away.

"Seriously?" Paula questioned. "*This* cat? Are you sure?"

"Quite," she replied, tightly.

"Here's the thing," Donna remarked, cocking her head. "Could we *really* call it tormenting when your cat was inside and behind glass while theirs was outside? Or, was it more like your cat—"

"Ginny's cat, actually," Kimberly corrected.

"Right," Donna agreed. "Or was it more like your *mother-in-law's* cat happened to be in a pissy mood at the same time you spotted Sylvester, so you just laid blame where it didn't belong?"

"Martini does not have *pissy* moods," Kimberly stated, wrinkling her nose when she had to say pissy.

"Did you say, Martini?" Declan clarified. "As in the drink? That's the cat's name?"

"Yes," Donna answered, for Kimberly, before rolling her eyes and adding, "And I'm sure he *does* get pissy and then some. He's a cat, for god's sake. It's part of the job description."

"Okay," Paula jumped in, cutting the conversation off before it went from *pissy* to all-out war. "Let's take a breath."

Douglas immediately backed her up. "Agreed. Who did what, or felt what, or whatever, doesn't matter. What does matter is that you, Kimberly, brought Sylvester home and for that we're grateful. When I noticed him missing from my workshop I was worried sick about him."

Kimberly narrowed her eyes and looked first at the cat then at Paula and Declan. "And it's actually *your* cat?"

"That's right," Declan confirmed.

"*He's* our cat," Paula said, unable to help herself when Kimberly called Sylvester *it*.

"So, that means it will go home with you," Kimberly pressed. "Instead of living here?"

Donna nodded. "Yes. Thank goodness."

"*He* will, yes," Paula interjected, again.

Kimberly's face brightened at the information and her blue eyes suddenly looked soft, instead of steely, her long hair like spun gold instead of yellow straw. It was quite the transformation. "And while it's here, it's an indoor cat?"

Paula took a steadying breath and spoke between clenched teeth. "Absolutely. *He* is an indoor cat."

Kimberly nodded, her features relaxing further to reveal just how pretty she actually was when she didn't look as though she'd been sucking a lemon.

"Alright, well, hopefully it will stay put now until you take it home."

Paula shot a wide-eyed look a Declan, afraid if she had to correct the woman one more time she might smack her as well.

"Oh, *he* will," he said, stepping in and reaching out to pet Sylvester still tucked in Douglas' arms. "*He's* a good cat. *He* must have been pretty interested in whatever *he* saw outside to sneak out. But don't you worry, we'll keep an eye on *him* for the rest of our stay."

Donna's eyebrows furrowed at all of the over-emphasizing and she stared at Declan. "Are you feeling okay?"

"Fine." He winked at Paula, making her giggle.

Douglas stepped forward to see Kimberly off.

"Thanks again," he said, waving as she descended the porch stairs and walked back to Ginny's house next door.

"Well, thank goodness *that's* over with," Donna grumbled, making a show of smacking her hands together to free them of imaginary dust before she strode away toward the kitchen. "*I'm* going to order pizza."

Paula smirked. Apparently, Declan's over emphasizing was contagious.

"Like I said," he stated, chuckling. "*Never* a dull moment."

Chapter 10

"Perfect, wonderful," Paula enthused, grinning so hard her face was starting to hurt.

The person on the receiving end of her perma-grin was none other than Lanzo Bazzano, the so-wealthy-it-would-be-rude-to-mention-it client who had hired *Certain Events* to create a celebration worthy of royalty for his daughter's sixteenth birthday. So far, things were going swimmingly and he was loving the ideas and plans they'd shared: with, of course, the added notes and suggestions coming from his wife that Paula was expected to follow to the letter.

Keep grinning.

"Okay, so we'll chat again at the top of next week and see where we're at, at that time," Paula stated, playing with the slim gold necklace around her neck. "Sound good?"

Lanzo, his dark eyes warm and his smile equally engaging, nodded on her screen. He had a magnetic personality, no question about it, and Paula was starting to understand why he had gained the confidences of many powerful and wealthy people; thus, securing his place and fortune among them.

"That sounds perfectly agreeable, Ms. Dempsey," Lanzo replied, his voice smooth like melted chocolate.

Paula had to work to suppress a giggle, before saying, "Please, we agreed, it's Paula."

"Right, right. Excuse me, *Paula*." He nodded and flashed another disarming grin, his teeth so white against his olive skin they were nearly as mesmerizing as his eyes. "I look forward to our next meeting."

Paula gave a little wave and said, "Talk soon," then disconnected the call and let out an agonized groan.

Erin, listening in from her desk, began to laugh.

"You're only human," she chuckled, tucking a lock of hair behind her ear. "And that man is a serious charmer."

"I know," Paula agreed, slumping back in her chair. She's been unconsciously holding herself taut like a pageant contestant. "But I'm supposed to be a professional - not to mention a married woman - and instead of acting like either of those, there I am playing with my jewelry and giving out little waves and chipper 'talk soon' sound bites! All that was left was for me to state I want world peace, for goodness sake."

Erin laughed again, then offered the assurance, "I'm sure he doesn't even notice. He's probably so used to woman going mushy around him, he thinks it's normal."

"Okay, if *that's* supposed to be comforting, I'm here to tell you it's not."

Erin shrugged. "It's the best I've got on short notice."

Paula straightened herself back up in her seat. "Well, you need better material."

"Speaking of which," Erin said, picking up a piece of note paper and leaning across her desk to hand it over. "Your mother called while you were talking to the *alluring Lanzo*."

Paula shot her a grimace then took the note. "God, don't call him that. I'll never be able to keep a straight face the next time we talk with him."

"The next time y*ou* talk with him, you mean."

"What? Are you feeling left out? You want in on the next call? You've got it, sister. Pull up a chair, please, and join me."

Erin smirked and waved her hand dismissively. "Nope. Someone has to keep the place running while you're shmoozing. Sorry, boss, you're on your own."

Paula read the note about her mother's phone call and her grimace returned. "So what did my mother say, exactly?"

"That she had something urgent to talk to you about and that she knew you'd be thrilled to be a part of it."

"Oh, god," Paula groused. "What now?"

Erin narrowed her eyes, thinking. She snapped her fingers when an idea came to mind.

"You know, it's almost the end of the day. You could tell her I gave you the message late and use that as an excuse not to call her back. Maybe you'll be lucky and by the time you get home, whatever was so urgent will be forgotten and it won't even come up at all."

Paula nodded. It was a good idea, except for one detail.

"But you realize, if she does remember I didn't call back, that puts the blame on you and throws you under the bus."

Erin shrugged. "No worries."

"You're sure?"

"Positive."

"Okay, deal. That's what I'm going to do. And don't pick up pastries tomorrow morning, I'll get them as my thank you for saving me the grief."

Erin smiled. "Agreed."

Amber sat outside on the front porch swing of her parent's house and pushed her foot against the wooden floorboards, making the seat swing backward and forward in a soothing manner. She was grateful *something* was soothing at the moment, considering the next world war seemed to be threatening to erupt inside the house. Her mother and Paula were at each other's throats, *again*, and as soon as it started she'd taken cover outside while her Dad had grabbed Sylvester and split for the garage and the project he was working on for Halloween.

Declan's car pulled into the driveway and Amber felt relief begin to course through her veins. *He* could do something, she was sure of it.

"Hey," he called, exiting the car and giving a small wave as he began walking along the path toward the house. "What are you doing out here in the dark?"

"Better than being in there in the war zone," Amber replied, pushing her foot against the porch floor again to keep the swing moving.

Declan climbed the stairs then paused at the top step to listen. Sure enough, the sound of raised voices could be heard through the closed windows.

"They've been going back and forth for the past half hour," Amber told him, as he walked over to join her on the swing.

"About?"

"This one is on Mom," she stated, shifting herself to the left to make room for him. "Which, let's be honest, is pretty much the norm. She's got it in her head she wants to host Thanksgiving."

Declan shook his head, he didn't follow.

"Mom's a shitty host, party planner, organizer, whatever you want to choose that involves being able to stick to a timeline, she's crap at it. Period. But she NEVER acknowledges it, which means she signs up for stuff then ends up dropping the ball and heaping whatever half-assed crap she's come up with on the rest of us, expecting us to run with it and make it look like she's the one who did it all."

Declan nodded. He'd heard much the same from Paula. "Okay, so *this* time what happened?"

"This time she was actually pretty straight forward - well, straight forward for *her* - and told Paula she wants to host Thanksgiving for the entire family and that she wants her *help* because, and I quote: *'you do this sort of thing for a living, don't you?'*."

Declan frowned. He wasn't sure which part was the issue.

Amber saw the confusion on his face and raised an eyebrow. "Seriously? You're not getting it?"

"Indulge me."

She sighed. "Fine, but I shouldn't have to."

"Sorry, it's been a long day."

"Right," she said, not believing him. "As you know, my sister, *your* wife, does a hell of a lot more at work than plan little family Thanksgiving house parties. And for Mom to act as though that's all she does is fucking insulting. Even *I* know that and I'm as bloody self-centered as they come."

Declan chuckled at her self-awareness.

"So, now that you know, mister *it's been a long day*, how are you going to fix it?"

He stopped chuckling and stared into her wide, unblinking eyes. "Time to play mediator?"

"Good for you. Got it in one this time. I'll stay here until you get things in hand."

She tilted her head against the back of the swing and closed her eyes.

"It's kinda cold out here," he offered, hoping to sway her to come inside with him.

She snorted. "Not as cold as in there. Off you go."

Declan stared at her. She was clearly done talking. He shifted his focus to the front door and thought: Once more into the breach.

Paula pulled on a grey t-shirt then reached for her lip balm on the dresser. Declan, already in bed, watched her and waited. He knew she was still decompressing from the argument with her mother and didn't want to interrupt her process.

"Thank you," she said, softly, her back to him.

"Pardon?" he asked. "Did you say something, sweetie?"

She turned around and nodded. "I said thank you. Things would have just kept on spiraling with my mother if you hadn't broken things up and sent us to our respective corners."

"I wish you could have actually resolved things, instead of just agreeing to disagree, but it didn't seem like that was going to happen."

She walked over to the bed and he pulled back the covers to let her slip in beside him. "Yeah, the reality of it is she's never understood what I do for a living, or even tried to understand for that matter. It's pretty straight forward, what I do, but—"

"BUT, it also isn't," he said, matter-of-fact. "You're an organizing ninja and clearly, from what I heard tonight, she has no idea of all that you do to make things run smoothly for so many complicated projects at once."

She smiled and leaned over to give him a kiss. "Thank you."

"It's true."

She smiled at him again. "Anyway, I'm tired of trying to get through to her, so thank you again for bravely stepping into the fray and helping shut things down."

He grinned. "Just doing my duty, ma'am."

Paula chuckled and slid closer to him beneath the sheets. "Speaking of which, what do you say to the idea of us daring to doing another *duty*, albeit silently and in total darkness like furtive teenagers?"

Declan's eyebrows lifted. "Seriously?"

She met his eye. "I'm game, if you are."

"Challenge accepted," he replied, reaching to turn out the bedside light.

Chapter 11

Paula sat at the dressing table in her bedroom, humming to herself as she finished applying the last touches to her makeup. It was finally the weekend and time to celebrate not just Halloween, but the fact she'd managed to get through the entire last week of dealing with one outlandish request after another from Lanzo Bazzano; as well as avoiding having any sort of altercation with her mother. Two for two, she was on a roll.

Paula smiled at her reflection while she adjusted the long brunette wig she was wearing adorned with a single yellow bow. Declan walked through the doorway at the same moment and his eyes widened in surprise when he saw her.

"Wow," he said, stopping in his tracks.

Paula's grin widened. "Convincing?"

He moved closer and nodded. "It's amazing. You look exactly like Belle."

She patted the wig and stood up, her long golden gown falling smoothly over her hips. "Well, if there's one perk to what I do for a living, it's the connections.

Wait until you get your outfit on, you'll look just like Beast: non-animal version, of course."

"I'm sure I'm going to pale by comparison, costume or no costume." Declan said, walking over to the bedroom window.

"Ah, but that won't change the fact you're my prince for real. You worked a miracle."

"I did?"

"Absolutely. Instead of just agreeing to disagree about Thanksgiving like we thought, my mother has changed her tone completely."

"Really? Since when?" He reached over to pull back the window curtain and look outside.

"About an hour ago. She stopped me before I came upstairs, said she's been thinking about our conversation and has decided she's going to do all of the work for the gathering herself."

"Holy crap." Declan shook his head.

"I know, right? I'm not sure if it means she actually understood what I was saying about my work, but—"

"No, not that," he interrupted, indicating with a jerk of his chin toward the window. "Out there. Have you looked out there in the past hour?"

The 'out there' to which he was referring was just beyond Donna and Douglas' front porch: namely, their front yard. The entire space had being transformed from a suburban garden into an alien landing site, complete with an adjacent dinner party zone, for a group of green and purple aliens.

A huge wooden table, illuminated by the glow of six black candelabras, displayed twelve place settings and the spoils of a questionable feast. Five of the lifelike aliens sat around the table, another three were scattered around the yard, and the remaining four were huddled around the wreckage of the front end of a spacecraft.

Declan shook his head again. "Seriously, if you haven't looked, you should. Your Dad's work is amazing, he could be a set designer. Talk about taking things to a whole new level."

"Just like they do every year," Paula stated. "Did you get a look at Amber yet?"

He shook his head.

"Well, when you do, you'll feel you know my sister better than you ever wanted to. She's been kitted out with a costume that basically leaves her naked and that was my mother's doing, not hers."

Declan couldn't help but laugh at her description. "You can't accuse them of lack of enthusiasm."

Paula chuckled. That was certainly true. Ever since she could remember, her parents had loved all things Halloween. They reveled in the fact there was a day designated for candy, silliness and fantasy, and embraced it wholeheartedly. Growing up, she and her sisters were always dressed in the best costumes on the block, something they'd taken for granted until it occurred to them how many hours their mother had put into making them.

"Sure you don't want to stay here for a bit and head over to Angus and Linda's later?" Declan asked, closing the curtain then pulling his grey t-shirt over his head and tossing it into the laundry basket next to the dresser.

Paula smoothed her hands down the skirt on her gown, enjoying the feeling of the silky material. "God, no. We can hear the highlights later. I don't want to be here when something goes awry."

"You sound pretty sure about that," he remarked, reaching for the white dress shirt laid out for him on the bed and slipping into it.

"Because I am." She tucked her feet into a pair of black pumps. "Every year, without fail, something happens. Hopefully, this year's incident will be tame."

He made a sharp, wolf-whistle sound while he buttoned the shirt. "Wow, I gotta say it again, you look gorgeous, missus Dempsey."

Paula shot him a grateful smile and did a small twirl to show off the fullness of her skirt.

Declan reached out and pulled her close then spoke softly into her ear. "Maybe, as you're so appealing, we should be staying in. I am Beast, after all. I'll show you my fangs."

Paula leaned into his warmth and wrapped her arms around his waist. "Not a chance. We'll get no privacy and no reprieve from the alien adventure set to begin outside."

A loud bang shook the house and Declan raised an eyebrow.

"That's our cue," she announced, untangling herself from his embrace. "We gotta get out of here while we still can. Grab the vest for your costume, you can put it on in the car."

"Do you think we should make sure everything is okay?" he asked, picking up the gold vest from the bed.

She reached for his hand and pulled him along behind her out of the bedroom. "Nope. Just follow my lead. Duck and cover and run like hell."

Declan and Paula stood side by side on Angus and Linda's front step, the porch light illuminating them in their costumes.

"Ready?" he asked.

She nodded and then together they called out, "Trick or treat!" before falling all over themselves laughing.

A moment later, the door swung open to reveal Linda; a large grin on her face.

"Ooh, *Beauty and the Beast*!" she gushed. "Love it!"

Paula gave a small curtsey and offered a return compliment to her sister-in-law's outfit. "And you make an absolutely adorable cat."

"Paula's right, but come on Linda, that's my wife you're calling a beast," Declan quipped, earning himself a slap across his shoulder from Paula and an eye roll from Linda.

She stepped aside to welcome them into the house and retorted, "Better watch it there, Dec, or you might find yourself sleeping in the yard tonight."

Before he could think of anything witty to say, the cries of: "Uncle Declan and Auntie Paula are here!" rang out from further inside the house.

"Brace yourself," Paula laughed, when the pounding of fast moving feet vibrated the floor.

In the next instant, Angus and Linda's sons, Ethan and Finn - ages ten and eight - came barreling from the family room into the foyer.

Finn hurled himself at Declan's legs, nearly bowling him over, while Ethan wrapped his arms around Paula's waist and grinned up at her.

"Boys!" Linda reprimanded, while closing the front door. "Be careful! You're not babies anymore, you could hurt your auntie and uncle." They started giggling and Linda threw her hands up in the air. "I don't know why I even bother. They're Dempsey's, through and through. I just have to hang on by my fingernails to survive until they're grown."

"And drink a lot of wine," Paula advised, kissing the top of Ethan's head then tickling him to make him giggle more.

"You look pretty, Auntie Paula," he said, leaning his cheek against her soft skirt. "I like your dress."

Paula gave him a gentle squeeze. "Thanks, sweetie."

"Whoa!" Emmet whooped, laying eyes on Declan and Paula as he walked down the hallway from the kitchen. "Get a load of you two! Love the boots, Dec. Who are you supposed to be, ye old town barman and his way-out-of-his-league wife?"

Declan lifted Finn into his arms and shot back, "At least I have a way-out-of-my-league wife."

"Wow, hurtful," Emmet replied, feigning indignation.

Declan smirked. "Whatever. What are *you* doing here, anyway?"

Emmet shifted from fake indignation to mock defensiveness. "What's *that* supposed to mean?"

"It means," Declan began, before Paula cut in.

"It's Halloween," she finished, while Ethan unwound himself from around her then took off without a backward glance, disappearing around the corner.

"Exactly," Declan agreed.

"So?" Emmet challenged.

"Please," Declan retorted, setting Finn back down on the tile floor. "Since when are you not out on Halloween, taking advantage of the…."

He paused and looked at Finn, listening to the conversation.

"What?" Emmet pressed.

"Finn," Linda said, stepping in. "Don't you want to go with Ethan and finish getting ready for trick-or-treating?"

That was all the encouragement he needed. He took off at speed in the same manner Ethan had.

"And you two, behave," she ordered, once her son was out of hearing range, pointing a finger at both her brothers-in-law.

Declan lifted his hands up, quickly defending himself. "Hey, don't look at me. I was just standing here, he—"

"*Please*," Paula interjected, sounding like an echo of him from moments ago. "You're both as bad as the other."

Linda laughed and led the way into the house. "Everyone out of the hallway, already. Angus will be ready to take the kids out right away and once they're done we'll watch the video."

"I'm going with them, right?" Declan confirmed, while he followed her and Paula into the kitchen and Emmet went into the family room.

"Yes, you are," Liam answered, sitting at the kitchen table with a beer in hand.

"Li," Declan said, pleasure lighting his features as he crossed the room to join him at the table. "No costume?"

He shrugged. "Figured I could go without."

"But you were wrong," Linda sang.

Liam stood up to give Paula a hug. "Love the costume, Belle."

She squeezed him back. "Thanks."

Declan pulled out a chair and sat down. "Why was Liam wrong?"

Linda's grinned, her eyes dancing with amusement. "'Cause Finn has a Darth Vader mask that he insists Uncle Liam must wear when you guys go out."

They all laughed while Liam chuckled along good-naturedly.

"Wine, Paula?" Linda lifted a bottle of red from the island.

Paula pulled out a chair at the table, next to Declan. "Yes, please, but do you have white? I don't want to risk the dress."

"Of course." She put the bottle back on the countertop. "How about you *Beast*? Wine or beer?"

He laughed. "Beer, thanks, but don't worry about it, I can get it myself."

"Absolutely," Paula agreed with Declan. "We can serve ourselves, you go and check on the kids."

"Yeah, you're probably right. Angus may be in over his head." She wiped her hands on a dish towel. "Both the white and the beer are in the fridge."

"Go." Declan waved her away. "We're fine."

She nodded and sped out of the kitchen.

"So, where's Trina?" Paula asked Liam.

He leaned back in his chair. "At her Mom's, helping out with candy duty."

"What about at your place, no kids there?"

He shook his head. "Barely any, not worth worrying about, whereas Trina's parents get a huge turnout in their neighborhood, easily over two hundred."

"Sounds like Doug and Donna's neighborhood," Declan commented.

"Hey, speaking of your parent's," Liam said, taking a swig from his bottle of beer then placing it on the tabletop. "Are they going all out with decorating tonight?"

Paula exchanged a look with Declan. "I think your brother can answer that question for you," she said, then got up to retrieve the white wine from the fridge.

Declan leaned in toward Liam. "Holy Moses, you should see it over there. Doug went above and beyond."

Paula chuckled as he began expounding on the decorations her parents had created, unaware that Emmet had sidled up beside her.

"Where's your sister, tonight?"

She jerked at the sound of his voice in her ear. "Jeez, Em, what's with the stealth maneuver? You nearly gave me a heart attack."

"Sorry. Thought you heard me."

"Seriously," she couldn't resist teasing, while she opened the bottle of wine. "I think you've had too much practice moving around silently, making your getaway the morning after without being noticed."

He shot her a downcast look. "Oh, come on. Is that really what you guys think of me? Some playboy, slipping in and out like a snake?"

She smirked and nudged his shoulder with her own, turning his anguished expression into a shit-eating grin.

"Yeah, that's what I thought," she said, shaking her head while he laughed. "And why aren't you wearing a costume?"

He affected a shocked look and gestured to his brown suit. "You mean you can't tell *whooo* I am?"

She lifted an eyebrow and poured the wine into the glass Linda had left for her. "Is there supposed to be a hint in there, somewhere?"

He shook his head at her. "I'm disappointed, lovely *Belle*. Maybe this will help."

Paula cocked her head when he put his bottle of beer on the island then pulled a white flashlight from his pocket and pointed it toward her like he was going to zap her with it.

"Oh, come *on*," he insisted, when she frowned, instead of getting it. "It's a *sonic screwdriver*."

"He's *Doctor Who*," Declan announced, before resuming his conversation with Liam.

Emmet pointed the screwdriver at Declan. "Ah-ha! See? Even the barman gets it."

Paula released a bark of laughter and placed the bottle of wine on the countertop. "Alright, forgive me for being slow on the uptake. *Now*, I get it."

"About time. Now, about your sister—"

"Stop." Paula held her hand up like a traffic cop.

Emmet shrugged his shoulders. "Can't blame a guy for trying."

Paula lifted her glass and took a sip of wine, then said, "No, you cannot. Is that why you're here, tonight? Did you think she'd be coming with us?"

He reached for his beer as an excuse to avoid her direct stare then tipped it to his lips to further avoid answering.

Instead of pressing him further, Paula put down her wine then reached into the fridge for a bottle of beer.

"Here," she said, handing the bottle to him. "Go bring this to your barman brother, *Doctor*."

He took it then leaned over and kissed her cheek. "Dec got the last good catch, I'm telling you," he stated, before walking over to join the conversation at the table.

"Unless my sister is available, apparently," she shot back, flashing a cheeky smile then beating a hasty retreat out of the kitchen before he could offer a retort.

Linda strode into the family room and announced, "Okay, we're all set. The boys are occupied with their candy and a movie, so now we can watch ours."

Paula settled herself between Declan and Liam on the oversized, cushy L-shaped sofa and sighed. The night had been unfolding easily, she was reveling in it. She and Linda had stayed at the house to hand out candy while Angus, Declan and Liam took the boys out for their treats - Emmet had made his escape not long after he'd been made aware Amber would not be joining them at any point - and now Trina had arrived and they were all ready to view the surveillance footage Angus had liberated from his patient's shop across the street from site of *the incident.*

Declan smiled when he heard her sigh and reached out to take her hand. "Having a nice night?"

"More than I can say," she replied, grinning back at him. "It's been a perfect Halloween."

"Glad to be out of that wig?"

"God, yes." She ran her fingers through her hair. "It was starting to make my scalp itch."

"I think Belle suits short and red better anyway," he said, nodding his approval. "Makes her more edgy, like she can keep up with the Beast."

Paula laughed. "Don't you mean the barman?"

Declan chortled. "That would be a whole different movie."

"Everyone have drinks?" Angus asked, standing up from where he'd been kneeling in front of the DVD player. "Trina?"

"Yup, all good," she confirmed, gesturing to a glass of wine on the side table.

"We're all good, too," Declan chimed in. "Go ahead and start it up."

Linda tucked herself into the far corner of the couch, leaving room for Angus. Paula couldn't help but grin, all of them in a row like kids at a movie.

"Okay, here we go." Angus pressed 'play' on the remote control then sat down next to Linda.

They all watched as the black and white footage of the street outside *The Potter's Kiln* appeared on the TV screen.

"So, who gave this to you again?" Trina asked.

"Claire, one of my patients," Angus replied, then added, "Well, to be accurate, her twins are my patients."

"She owns the shop across the street, *Pipe Dream Glassworks*," Linda explained.

"I love that shop," Paula commented. "She does gorgeous work."

"Oh, oh," Trina piped up, pointing at the TV. "Here we go."

They all went silent, not that they actually needed to as there was no sound on the footage, when a golf cart carrying two guys came speeding into view from around the corner.

"That's not them," Trina said.

"Must be the guys they met at the pub," Liam offered.

"You said they were gone by the time you got there, right?" she confirmed.

He nodded.

"There's Amber and Jaimie!" Linda squealed, caught up in the moment, when Paula's sister's came into view driving a second golf.

Angus jerked at her sudden outburst then started laughing. "You're cut off," he teased, making them all chuckle along with him.

"Man, they're seriously all over the place," Trina remarked, wide-eyed, watching the screen.

"That's 'cause they were seriously hammered," Liam stated. "I'm still amazed they were able to drive at all."

They all went silent again as the 'story' unfolded on the TV. Amber, sitting in the driver's seat of one of the carts with Jaimie by her side, was laughing and pointing at the two guys in the other. They were showing off and zipping around at speed; narrowly missing slamming into both the ceramic marmot in front of *The Potter's Kiln* and Amber and Jaimie's golf cart.

"Jeez," Angus offered, flinching as he watched. "It's like a Three Stooges movie, except that there's four of them."

Liam released a sharp bark of laughter while the rest of them chortled at the observation.

"Oh, they're leaving," Trina observed, then turned to Angus. "Are you sure this is the footage of the hit?"

"Absolutely," he said, keeping his eyes on the screen and watching the two carts and their occupants disappear. "They must come back, that's the only logical explanation."

"You didn't watch it first?" Paula asked.

He shook his head. "I wanted to wait until we were all together."

Declan shifted in his seat to look at his brother. "Can you fast forward?"

Angus pointed the remote at the DVD player and moved the footage forward. They all waited a beat until Amber and Jaimie, still in the golf cart, reappeared.

There they are!" Linda blurted, sitting on the edge of her seat.

Angus stopped fast-forwarding, put down the remote and let it run.

"Okay, so they've clearly ditched those guys, we must be getting closer to what happened," Trina said, stating the obvious, while on-screen Amber brought the cart to a stop a few feet in front of the marmot.

Paula sat forward and watched her sisters lurch out of the vehicle, barely maintaining their balance, then pull out their phones to take multiple photos of each other in silly poses with the marmot.

"Do either of you know if those photos still exist?" she asked, looking first at Declan, then at Liam.

Liam shook his head. "No idea."

"Me, neither," Declan confirmed while, on-screen Jaimie and Amber stumbled back to the cart and climbed back into the seats.

Paula returned to watching the footage. "Well, let's hope they had the good sense to delete them once they sobered up."

"It looks like they're getting ready to leave again," Linda remarked, when on-screen Amber looked over her shoulder as she prepared to reverse the cart. "Maybe the incident is further along."

"I can check," Angus offered, reaching for the remote again, but then stopping dead when the footage on the screen showed the golf cart shooting forward at speed with Amber clutching the steering wheel and Jaimie slamming back into her seat.

"Ohmygod!" Linda blurted, when the forward moving cart plow straight into the ceramic marmot, blowing it open and creating an explosion of white dust.

"Holy crap," Trina exhaled, while on-screen Amber managed to bring the golf cart to a stop without sending them ass over tit. "That was a serious hit."

"Didn't they say they reversed into it?" Declan asked.

Paula lifted an eyebrow. "Does it really surprise you they remembered it wrong?"

He thought back to how drunk they'd been and smirked. "Fair enough."

Angus pointed at the screen where Jaimie was turning her head to look at Amber and they exchanged words before slowly easing themselves out of the golf cart.

"Oh, man, look at their faces. They're in shock. I was so intent on helping get things sorted, I didn't stop to think how they were."

"You're kind, Angus, and a good doctor," Paula soothed. "However, no need to feel badly as I'm pretty sure what we're seeing here isn't shock, but the fact that they're so drunk they're having a hard time processing what happened."

His face was skeptical as he watched the TV and he said, "I don't know," just as Amber and Jaimie suddenly doubled over, clearly laughing their asses off.

"And there it is. Processing complete." Paula shook her head at her sisters, even though they were only a screen image.

Angus lifted his hands in mock surrender. "Conceded."

"So, that's that," Liam said, standing up. "I'd guess the rest of this footage will just be them calling me and then hanging around until everyone arrived to clean up, that sort of thing. No need to watch that, we lived it. Boring."

Declan narrowed his eyes at his brother. He recognized the speeding-things-along tone. Something was up.

"We can still watch it," he stated, observing Liam closely to see his reaction.

"Why?" he retorted, sharply, leaning forward to try and snatch the remote off the couch.

Angus moved sharply to his left and grabbed it, immediately picking up the thread. "Or, more to the point, why *not*?"

"Okay, what's going on?" Linda piped up, while Angus pressed the remote to start moving the recording forward. "What's happening?"

"Oh, for Christ sake," Liam barked, lunging at Angus.

He laughed and darted out of the way while Declan stood up and started running interference.

"Ohmygod, you guys!" Paula shouted, scooting to her right on the sofa, trying to stay out of the crossfire.

"Liam!" Trina demanded, as he attempted to shove Declan aside to get to Angus. "What the hell are you doing?"

"Oh, there!" Paula jabbed a finger at the TV. "Look, look! There's Liam!"

Angus stopped the recording moving forward and they all went still and watched the screen. Liam strode onto the scene, took one look at the situation and burst out laughing.

"*This* is what you didn't want us to see? You laughing?" Declan challenged, while they watched Amber and Jaimie, now seated in the golf cart, scramble out to join him at the curb, their faces twisted in mirth.

"Oh, fucking hell," Liam muttered, under his breath.

Paula's eyebrows shot up and she shared a look of surprise with Declan, while Trina asked, "What's the big deal?"

Before Liam could answer her; however, she got to see for herself why he'd cursed. There, in black and white, on the sidewalk outside *The Potter's Kiln*, Amber threw her arms around him and pressed herself fully up against the length of his torso to lay a kiss on him that would make anyone's mouth drop open.

And it did.

On the screen, Jaimie's face was a picture as she stared slack-jawed at the heat-filled snog unfolding in front of her and, in Angus and Linda's living room, the five of them held expressions that were much the same.

Liam slowly exhaled, waiting for the next reaction. He didn't have to wait long.

"What the FUCK?" Trina bellowed, before pointing at Angus and saying, "Pause that, NOW!"

"Language!" Linda blurted, then took a step backward at the intensity on Trina's face.

"Never mind," Angus quickly interjected, doing as he'd been told then pulling his wife out of the line of fire. "If the boys overheard, they've probably heard worse at school."

Paula, her cumbersome ball gown making her awkward, scrambled off the couch to join Declan. He'd taken a step back as well, leaving Liam as a lone man in the middle of the family room.

"Trina, honey, listen," he began, before she cut him off.

"I don't bloody think so!" she retorted, her shoulders rounding like a bull preparing to charge.

"It didn't mean anything!" Liam insisted. "She was drunk, she'd just survived a crash and I was in the right place at the right time. It wasn't about *me*, she would have done that to any guy who'd shown up to help them out."

"Oh, I'm well aware of *that*," she said, her face flushed as she started swaying back and forth like a prize fighter.

Paula frowned at Declan. After all, it was *her* sister they were speaking about with such disrespect.

"I don't think we want to get involved in this," he hissed, between almost-closed lips, answering her frown.

Reluctantly, she nodded. He was right.

"Okay, then," Liam wheedled. "So, you agree that there's no need to—"

"BUT, *that's* not the issue here," she cut him off, again. "No, the *issue* is YOUR reaction, you fucker."

Liam lifted his hands like a blackjack player showing he had nothing hidden. "What reaction?"

Trina turned her laser-like stare on Angus, making him flinch, and demanded, "Replay that last part."

He looked at Linda and she nodded. The faster things got resolved, the better. He pressed the remote, rewound the part with the kiss, then looked at Trina for further instruction.

"Play it," she barked.

They all turned their gaze to the screen as, yet again, video Amber pressed herself up against video Liam and kissed him as though their lives depended upon it.

"And THERE is it," Trina stated, as on-screen Liam did not pull back from the kiss, but instead wrapped one arm around Amber's waist and drew her in even tighter; if that was possible. "You fucking fucker."

Angus stopped the footage while Liam ran his fingers through his hair and said, "Okay, admittedly, *that* doesn't look so good."

"*That's* why you were covered in dust," Paula chimed in, snapping her fingers. "I was wondering and now it makes sense, because—"

Trina whipped around to stare at her and she stopped short.

"Oh, right, not helping," she said, grateful that the cellphone in her purse began ringing loudly. "I'll just get that."

Declan took the opportunity offered to follow closely on her heels out of the family room and into the adjacent dining room, making sure to keep his eyes down to avoid the desperate 'take me with you' expression on Angus' face.

"What?" Paula asked, into her phone, her face pinched. "Well, I guess so. We're pretty much done here, anyway."

Declan had no idea who it was, but nodded in agreement with her statement. Whatever, or whomever, it was on the other side of the conversation seemed to be offering a legitimate way out of the house and he was on-board.

"Okay, we'll be there shortly, bye."

"What?" Declan asked, hopeful. "Do we need to leave right now?"

Paula glanced at the ugly scene still unfolding in the family room and nodded. "Uh-huh. Right now."

"Good," he exhaled, relieved. "You sneak in and tell Linda, I'll get our coats and start the car."

"Deal."

Declan drove to Donna and Douglas' house, his vehicle smoothly parting the low-lying mist illuminated by the fog lamps. Beside him, in the passenger seat, Paula was silent. They'd covered the conversation of: 'What the hell was that between Liam and Amber?', and had finally arrived at the agreement they would keep their noses out of it; even though it riled Declan and made him want to shake his brother. Now they were just enjoying the calm before, what Paula was certain was, the storm.

"I can't believe we're delivering barbecue lighters, of all things," she commented, staring out the side window. "Why barbecue lighters specifically? Are they having a cookout? Which would be a totally weird thing to do on Halloween, but yet, right up their alley."

Declan steered the car onto Mountain Pine Crescent where the mist turned into a fog. "Yeah, well, whatever they need them for, I'm just glad your sister called and got us the hell out of that house."

"Got that right," she acknowledged. "I hope Angus managed to convince Liam and Trina to take their issue elsewhere. You'll have to text him later and find out how things turned out."

Declan slowed the car to a crawl as multitudes of adults and children - most dressed in costumes - started to become visible through the thick haze on the street.

"My god, look at that," Paula said, pointing a finger in the direction of her parent's house at the top of the crescent: there was an eerie green glow lighting up the throng. "I knew things were going to get nutty around here, but that crowd is seriously large."

And "crowd" was not an exaggeration.

There were so many people in the cul-de-sac that Declan was forced to stop a few houses short of Donna and Douglas' and park at the curb in front of a neighbor's property.

"Holy crap," he muttered. "Can you see anything at all?"

Paula shook her head. "No. And I'm surprised one of the neighbor's hasn't called the cops yet. Maybe we should just stay here until the crowd thins."

Declan checked his rearview mirror and saw a car pulling up behind them. He recognized it and sighed. "Yeah, I don't think we're going to have that luxury. Look behind us."

Paula turned in her seat then sucked in her breath when the driver side door on the car behind them swung open and Liam stepped out. "Jeez, what the hell is he doing here?"

"Only one way to find out," Declan said, opening his door.

Paula grabbed the bag of barbecue lighters on the floor next to her feet and exited the car as well.

"What the hell are *you* doing here?" Declan demanded of his brother, meeting him on the sidewalk.

Liam shrugged his shoulders. "Anywhere was better than at Angus and Linda's house. I figured this would be the last place Trina might look for me."

"You're an idiot, you know that right?" Declan stated.

Before Liam could offer any sort of defense, Paula joined them and shook her head at her brother-in-law.

"Seriously?" she insisted. "You're here? You don't think Trina might guess that you'd come looking for Amber and that *here*," she made a wide, arcing gesture toward her parent's house at the top of the street, "would be a good place to start searching for you?"

"Yeah, I guess, but…." he began, but was cut off by a violently loud bang that shook the pavement beneath their feet.

"OH!" Paula exclaimed, grabbing ahold of Declan's arm.

The crowd around Donna and Douglas' house all seemed to take a uniformed step back - opening a gap that allowed a view of the front yard - when smoke and sparks began emanating from something on the lawn.

"Okay, I don't know what that is making all those sparks, but that at least it explains why the fog is so much thicker here than at the top of the street," Paula offered, coughing and trying to get a better look.

"Holy shit," Liam breathed, taking in the scene.

Muliti-colored strobe lights had been set up beneath the hulking weeping birch trees, making their streaming branches look like tentacles waiting for their next victim. The glowing green alien scene of dinner feast and crash landing zone - that had seemed a bit cheesy to Paula in the daylight - had been transformed by nightfall and the low-lying fog, making the entire yard look as though it belonged on another planet.

"Is that your *sister*?" Liam's eyes were out on stalks when Amber came into view, her body paint and few patches of fabric covering exactly what Paula had said … nothing.

"In the flesh," she confirmed, snickering at her own joke.

"*Jeezus*," he muttered, finally blinking.

Paula exchanged a look with Declan then said, "*Anywaaay*, we may as well get in there while there's a break in the crowd."

Needing no further words of encouragement, Liam strode full-steam toward the house.

"Oh, for Christ's sake," Declan remarked, watching him go. "Idiot."

"Yup," Paula agreed, handing over the bag of lighters then grabbing handfuls of her voluminous skirt and lifting the hem above her ankles. "No good is going to come of that."

He tucked the bag into the inside pocket of his coat. "So, what do you think—"

That was as far as he got.

An even larger bang than the last rang out and shook the street, followed by serious set of flames shooting skyward from the lawn, making the crowd cry out.

"Oh, shit!" Paula yelped, hiking her skirt even higher and dashing behind Declan as he started running toward the house.

He pulled out his phone while he weaved through the retreating crowd and tapped in nine-one-one when he realized the flames weren't getting any smaller. The closer he got to the yard, the thinner the throng and he could see Amber through a rapidly widening gap. She was frantically fumbling with the garden hose while, a few feet away, Douglas was hauling a shovelful of dirt from the flower bed toward the flames.

"Did you make the call?" Paula yelled, across the throng of people bumping into them.

It felt like they were moving against a very loud and clumsy current.

"Done!" he confirmed, then focused on getting to Douglas. "I'm going to help your Dad!"

Liam appeared from within the crush and bellowed, over the din, "I'm with Declan!"

"Good! Go!" Paula hollered back.

He nodded and took off in the same direction as his brother, shouldering aside anyone in his way, while Paula scrambled around the other remaining rubberneckers to get to Amber.

It was definitely the wrong day to be wearing a princess gown.

An eerie sort of calm settled itself over Donna and Douglas' front yard, despite the obvious presence of both the police and fire department. The crowd that had gathered in front of the house earlier than evening had disappeared, the only people left were the family and, of course, the authorities.

Paula, seated on the front porch stairs with her cellphone pressed against her ear, hunched further into her coat while listening to Jaimie going, "ohmygod," on the other end of the line. She'd sent her photos of the yard once the chaos had abated and she was still reeling from what she'd seen.

"I cannot believe that happened," Jaimie marveled.

"*You* can't," Paula replied, looking dejectedly at the state of her once pristine golden gown. "*I* lived it and I'm having a hard time believing it. Not to mention, I don't think I'm getting my deposit back on our costumes. My dress is trashed."

"When Amber called me yelling about a fire I felt like I might have a heart attack." Jaimie sucked in her breath and released it slowly, trying to calm herself down.

"Again," Paula reminded her, "*from my end*, it wasn't exactly a picnic."

"How are Mom and Dad doing?"

Paula snorted sharply. What a question.

"Have you *met* our mother?" she threw back, looking around the yard until she laid eyes on Donna. "Even now, after all that's happened, she's acting like the god-damned bell-of-the-ball, instead of what she should be; humiliated."

And she was.

Donna had managed to corner one of the police officers on the scene and, judging from her over-the-top, flailing arm gestures, was clearly regaling her tale. He was nodding and looking at, what used to be, the pretend wreckage from the alien space craft scene: now a blackened, unrecognizable mess. Nearly every bit of Douglas' workmanship had been disintegrated by the fire, all that was left was a smoking pile of papier-mâché, some hubcaps and charred wood. As for the aliens who had been on the scene attending to the grounded space craft, they'd been reduced to nothing more than an ashy memory.

"Arm gestures and everything?" Jaimie confirmed, referring to Donna's storytelling.

"Yup, full on," Paula agreed, then coughed when the lingering smoky haze irritated her throat.

Declan, seated a few feet away on the wooden porch chairs with her father, heard her and asked, "You okay, hon?"

"Fine."

"Who's on the phone?"

"Jaimie."

"Tell her, we're all okay," Douglas instructed. "Nothing a bit of elbow grease and grass seed won't fix."

"Did he seriously just say grass seed will fix it?" Jaimie asked.

Paula snickered at the incredulousness in her tone.

"'Cause judging by the pictures you sent me, those burn marks on the lawn look like bloody crop circles and they're going to need a helluva lot more than grass seed to make them disappear."

Paula looked at the burn marks that had been scorched into the ground beneath one of the two weeping birch trees - miraculously unaffected by the fire - and sighed. It was true, the new landscape of charred circles was definitely not going to disappear without some serious intervention.

"So, what now?" Jaimie inquired.

Paula glanced over to where Amber was standing with Liam, their heads close together and said, "Clean up, I suppose. But, never mind that, why the hell didn't you say anything about Amber and Liam?"

"What about them?"

"Umm, well, to start, their kiss comes to mind."

"WHAT?" Jaimie's voice rang shrilly from the phone and Paula winced as she pulled it back from her ear. "They kissed? Seriously? When?"

"What do you mean *when*?" Paula insisted, her voice irate. "When you guys had *the incident*, that's when. Why didn't you say anything?"

"Wait, what?" Jaimie said, confused.

"I saw it tonight on the tape at Angus and Linda's," Paula told her. "You were right there when it happened."

"I was?" Jaimie paused, wracking her brain.

"Good god," Paula lamented. "How bloody drunk *were* you two?"

"Ohmygod, wait! I DO remember! That was *Liam*? I thought it was one of the guys from the pub."

"Seriously? You didn't notice that it was Liam, who is a part of the family and who showed up after YOU called him, that she was kissing?"

"So sue me. I was a little over my limit."

Paula couldn't help herself and snorted with amusement. "Uh, yeah you were. And then some."

"Oh, be quiet, you brat," she shot back, chuckling. "Like you've never had one too many."

"Well...," Paula began, before Jaimie cut her off.

"*Anyway*, back to the Amber, Liam thing. Do you realized how big this is? The shit is going to hit the fan if Trina ever finds out about it."

Paula reached down and brushed at some mud clinging to the hem of her skirt. It didn't budge. "She *has* found out about it and the shit had definitely hit the fan."

"Ohmygod, really? When? How come I haven't been told about any of this?"

"Because all of it just happened earlier tonight when we watched the tape." Paula shook her head at the memory. "Believe me, while Mom and Dad's display turned into a shit-show, the one good thing it did was give Declan and me a legitimate way to get out of that house when Trina saw the kiss on the video footage."

"Holy hell. Is she out for Amber's blood?"

Paula frowned, remembering the way Trina slagged off Amber's behavior. "I don't know. But I'm pretty sure she's out for Liam's."

"Really? You'd think she'd be pissed at Amber, too."

"Yeah," Paula acknowledged, "but she was more focused on him because of the way he reacted to the kiss."

"What do you mean?"

"You were *there*, remember?"

"Oh, cut me some slack already," Jaimie groused.

Paula chuckled. "Fine. After Amber laid her kiss on him, which was seriously something by the way, instead of stopping it he actually pulled her in closer. It was movie grade stuff."

"Clearly, I gotta see that footage," Jaimie stated.

"Yeah, probably a good idea so you know what actually happened, not just what you think you might remember," Paula teased.

"Ha, ha."

"Oh, wait, hold on. We have a new development in the yard. It looks like Mom is going to invite the cop she's been harassing on a tour of the alien dinner party. Apparently, since it somehow managed to survive everything, it's become an opportunity to showcase her ingenuity."

Jaimie laughed at the sarcasm in her voice.

"And you should see her, by the way," Paula expanded. "She's painted in the same green body paint as Amber and has some sort of patchwork costume on that makes her look like she recently emerged from Oscar's trash can."

Jaimie laughed a second time at the *Sesame Street* reference. "Get a picture."

"I will, hang on a sec."

Paula pointed her phone toward the yard to capture a shot of their mother gesturing wildly while the cop wore the expression of a person in way over his head.

She snapped the photo and forwarded it to Jaimie's phone.

"K, sent it."

"Yup, heard it. Hang on while I look."

Paula yawned while she waited, then started to giggle when she heard her sister laughing.

"Ahahaha! The cop's face is hysterical. And I love how everything looks now, as though the aliens around the table are sitting vigil for their fallen comrades."

Paula chortled. She was right, it did look like that. Instead of a party scene, it looked like a creepy wake.

"So, do you think Mom and Dad will leave it there?" Jaimie joked, snickering. "As a sort of memorial to the Halloween blaze?"

Paula giggled harder, until her giggles got caught in her throat by what happened next: A white van turned speedily into the crescent, tore down the street and came to a sharp halt next to one of the police cars.

"Oh, shit," she grumbled, her stomach dropping when she saw who it was.

"What? What's wrong?"

"A *Channel Five* van just pulled up in front of the house."

"Oh, shit," Jaimie echoed. "Just when you think it can't get worse."

"It does," Paula finished. "I'd better go, I'll phone you back."

"Yup. Bye."

Paula hung up and looked over at Declan and her father, just in time to see them share a look of camaraderie, and thought at least one good thing seemed to have come out of a disastrous experience. Her Dad was finally getting the son he'd always hoped to have.

Declan positioned himself in front of Douglas, shielding him from the reporter and cameraman from *Channel Five.* Standing tall and still dressed in his Beast costume, he looked like a nobleman brought forward from the past to protect the innocent and downtrodden.

"We don't have anything to say on the matter," he declared, lifting his chin and staring down calmly at the reporter. "Things got a little out of hand and we took care of it. It's no longer news."

The reporter kept her perma-grin in place and nodded encouragingly. She'd dealt with this sort of non-starter response before and was quickly realizing, if she wanted a story, she'd have to get the brunt of it from the neighbors.

Paula stayed back and watched from the shadow of the birch tree, the last thing she needed was to be seen on camera in her soot and dirt smeared Belle costume. An image like that, especially when the Beast had already been recorded standing guard, had the potential to inflict serious damage to her credibility with her clients.

"Oh! Paula!" Donna exclaimed, when she rounded the tree trunk and found her there. "Where did you come from? I was just going to greet the press, you should join me."

Paula stared at her mother, unsure of which statement to address first. They were equally maddening. Not only did her mother not even notice that she, Declan and Liam had been crucial to the fire not getting out of hand before the fire department arrived, but she also had no idea that going on camera would cement her being a joke to all of Boxwood Hills and beyond when it hit the internet.

"What? Why are you staring at me?" Donna insisted. "Is my hair mussed?"

Paula cleared her throat, keeping her thoughts to herself, and said, "No, it's fine."

Donna nodded and attempted to smooth the hair she'd backcombed into a large, shaggy helmet and generously coated with hairspray earlier that evening. It didn't work. Her hair stayed firmly in place, doing a great impression of a crazy clown wig.

"And, in regards to the press, I think you should stay out of it and leave it alone. Declan's got it covered," Paula told her, hoping it would stall her mother further.

She cocked her head. "You think so? Nothing I need to add? I mean, he looks a little out of place in that outfit doesn't he? How will anyone take him seriously?"

Paula gritted her teeth, refusing to address the comment. It was bad enough Declan was going to have to live down the repercussions of being documented on video in his costume, there was no way she was going to debate the merits of its seriousness versus her mother's scrapheap outfit.

Paula pointed at her husband, still shielding her father from the camera's scrutinizing eye, and said, "Just stop talking for a minute and listen."

"While we appreciate your interest in the situation, human curiosity never lets up, we hope you'll respect our wishes and leave us in peace," Declan stated, his tone clear and firm. "There really isn't a story here, sorry you've wasted your time."

Douglas began taking steps backward, putting distance between him and the reporter and the glaring camera light. Paula didn't blame him one bit for keeping as low a profile as possible. In his costume, some sort of troll-like alien, he looked more than a little deranged. And, while *Hayes Happy Zone* could always benefit from advertising, there was no need to showcase its owner/operator as a man who might not know how to keep from burning the place down.

"That was a little abrupt," Donna huffed, while the reporter kept her camera-ready grin still fixed firmly to her face.

"And necessary," Paula clarified, watching Declan wave the woman off then turning around to follow Douglas. "Trust me, mother, the last thing you want to do is give those people an opportunity to twist a story for increased ratings."

"Well, that's not always...." Donna began, then snapped her mouth shut when Paula darted out of the shadow of the tree and bolted away, leaving her talking to no one but herself.

Paula didn't look back, just kept on walking as fast as her gown would allow; her goal to get the hell way from her mother's almost assuredly half-baked logic.

"THAT was abrupt, too," Donna called after her.

Declan's brow furrowed as he looked over his shoulder at the sound of Donna's voice, then noticed Paula falling into step beside him. "Problem?"

"Ignore her," she instructed, taking hold of his arm and pulling him aside, away from the prying eyes of, well, everyone. "Listen, we need to talk."

"Agreed," he said, then pointed to the house next door. "But first, is that that Kimberly woman over there? The one who found Sylvester. She looks seriously pissed off."

Paula followed his gaze. "Yup, that's her. She's tried a few times to convince Ginny to move out of the crescent. I would imagine this little fiasco will inspire her to start nagging again and, truthfully, I can't really say I blame her."

Declan watched the TV reporter and her cameraman approached Kimberly. He had no idea how much she has witnessed and hoped, fingers crossed, it was nowhere near enough to turn the night's events into a viable story.

Paula sat down on the porch steps and patted the space beside her, inviting him to join her.

He sat, then looked further off into the yard. "Did Liam leave?"

"Yup. As soon as the TV van showed up, he beat a hasty retreat."

Declan smirked. "Didn't want to accidentally get caught on camera is my bet. I don't know what he's playing at, but he better be careful. Trina's already out for blood, so god forbid she sees him here on the local news."

"Yeah, pretty much my thoughts as well. And that's all I want to know about any of it. Did you see the two of them?"

He nodded.

She shook her head. "Playing with fire, no pun intended."

Declan ran his hand across the stubble on his chin and sighed. "Yeah, just like we said before in the car, even though I'd like to smack him one and tell him to he'd better not string Amber along, I'm going to do my best to stay the hell out of it. I don't want any crossfire."

"And, just like *I* said, while it's lovely that you're protective of her, Amber can take care of herself. Trust me." Paula leaned her shoulder up against him. "So what were you and Dad talking about, anyway? Did he tell you exactly what happened here tonight?"

"It was an accident."

"Clearly. But what went wrong?"

"Basically, it was an effect that backfired."

Paula looked at the charred lawn. "What on Earth was it *supposed* to do?"

"Give the impression of crop circles without actually touching the lawn. That's why there was the film between the grass and the butane canisters."

"Butane!" Paula gaped at him, horrified.

"I know, I know," he said, placatingly.

"I want to see the house."

Declan looked at her, confused. "It's fine. The fire didn't move past what's here."

"No, *our* house. I want to go there tomorrow."

"Are you sure? I thought you said you didn't want to see things until they were finished. The whole big reveal thing."

Paula hunkered down into her jacket and gazed across the yard, watching her Dad carrying a coat out to Amber.

"I've changed my mind. I need to see it to remind myself it's actually there and all of *this* isn't going to be our reality forever."

Declan wrapped his arms around her, tucking her comfortingly into his side. "We'll go tomorrow morning."

Chapter 12

Declan held the door for Paula as they exited *Cuppa Caffeine*, each of them grasping a large takeaway cup. They were ready to visit the new house.

Paula turned to meet Declan's eye and say, "Thank you", just as a well-dressed blonde man came speed-walking toward the doorway and nearly smacked right into her in his rush to enter the shop.

"Oh, my!" he yelped, stopping just shy of jostling Paula's full-to-the-brim cup from her hand to land directly onto himself.

She tightened her hold on it and squeaked, "Oh!" while Declan steadied her from behind.

"I'm sooo sorry," the man began, before Paula interrupted him to say, "Oh my gosh, Travis! Hey, how are you?"

"Nearly covered in coffee!" he bantered, laughing at his own joke.

Travis Walker was a part of the real estate team, *G&T Real Estate*, that had worked with Paula and Declan to purchase their new house. He was as over-the-top enthusiastic as he was gorgeous, and as gorgeous as he was generous of spirit, which was to say VERY on all counts.

"It is sooo good to see you guys!" he went on, his exuberance giving a sparkle to his green eyes, despite the overcast day. "How's the new house? Are you just loving it?"

Paula exchanged a look with Declan then stepped clear of the doorway to let other people pass.

Travis saw the look and his smile dropped. "Uh-oh," he said, pointing an index finger at Paula. "I saw that look? What was that about?"

"Umm," she said, unsure where to begin.

Thankfully, Gerry Carrion, the "G" in *G&T Real Estate* and; thus, Travis' partner in both business and life, came striding along the sidewalk toward them, buying her extra time to ponder.

He and Travis were polar opposites in their looks: Travis fair with a lean, swimmers build, while Gerry sported hair the color of dark chocolate and stood broad as a barn door. Together, they looked like something out of a fashion advert and turned heads wherever they went.

"For goodness sake, Travis," Gerry chastised. "I turned around and you were gone!"

"Sorry," he apologized, shrugging his shoulders beneath his tan, wool overcoat. "I was on a coffee mission. But never mind that, look who it is!"

Gerry's face lit up when Travis stepped aside and Paula and Declan both smiled in greeting. "Well, look at you two!" he enthused, extending a hand toward Declan to shake. "It's so good to see you both! I'd hug you, but I don't want to spill your coffee. How are things? Are you loving the new house?"

Travis made a frowny face. "I just asked the same question, Gerr-Bear, and they gave each other a *look.*"

"Oh, dear." His dark eyebrows furrowed.

"It's fine," Paula assured.

"Nothing a bit of reno isn't fixing," Declan added.

"Still?" Travis asked, his eyes wide with surprise. "It was the kitchen, if I remember correctly, right?"

Declan and Paula both nodded.

"But that was just a remodel," Gerry said. "Surely, it's not still going on?"

Paula looked at Declan. "You wanna take this?"

He nodded. "Basically, in a nutshell, there were some glitches."

"Glitches?" Gerry echoed. "What kind of *glitches*?"

"Oh, where to start," Paula quipped, then took a drink of her coffee.

"No!" Travis exclaimed, reaching out to clutch Paula's shoulder.

"They haven't even told us anything yet." Gerry snickered, grinning at Travis' over-the-top reply.

He released Paula's shoulder and sniffed. "I *know* that. But clearly, from what's been said, my response is called for."

Gerry caught the twinkle of amusement in Travis' eye at being called out and shook his head.

Paula grinned at the pair of them, remembering why she'd so enjoyed the house hunting experience. They were a delight.

"Okay, so there's been *glitches*," Gerry reiterated. "But are they fixable?"

"And what *are* they?" Travis pressed, ever nosey.

That made Paula laugh out loud.

Declan chuckled as well. "Okay, bullet points. There was a kitchen pipe leak that ended up having to have a whole section of pipe replaced, drywall torn out, the works."

"And *that* glitch pushed into the timeline of when the flooring guys were supposed to come in," Paula further expounded, "so they had to leave for another job and then come back to ours when they were done." She met Travis' eye and nodded. "*Now* you can say it."

"No!" He immediately effused, making them all laugh.

"But, seriously, that's terrible," Gerry sympathized, patting Declan's shoulder. "I'm so sorry you're going through this."

"I wonder if the Turners knew about any of this, but didn't divulge," Travis mused, referring to the former owners while he stroked his immaculate beard, sculpted to accent perfectly his sharp cheekbones.

Gerry shook his head. "I doubt it. They didn't come across as shady, just a retired couple looking to downsize."

"And that's not all of it, either," Paula offered, drinking more of her coffee.

"Get out!" Travis demanded, making a few people exiting *Cup of Caffeine* turn their heads.

Declan drank from his cup then nodded. "It's true. But we don't want to keep you guys."

"He's right," Paula agreed. "And we're heading over there right now to see how things are coming along."

Travis lifted his hands up like a traffic cop. "Wait. Are you telling me you haven't even *moved in* yet?"

"Our *stuff* is there," Paula said.

"Are you kidding me? It's so bad you can't even live there yet? Where on Earth are you staying then?" Travis pressed.

Paula and Declan exchanged another look, which inspired Gerry and Travis to do the same.

"At my parents," Paula revealed, bracing herself.

If they'd seen the Halloween debacle on the late news, this would be the thing to trigger their memory.

"Ohmygod," Gerry exhaled, placing a hand across his heart.

"You poor things," Travis added, his face despondent.

"It's not as bad as it sounds," Declan quickly assured them. "Honestly."

Paula released the breath she was holding. Nothing. No references to the news. They were in the clear.

"We just feel so badly," Gerry explained, seeing that Travis was - for once - at a loss for words. "If we'd known about any of it—"

"There's no way you could have," Paula interjected. "No one could have, not even the Turners. We had the inspection done, as you know, but it was inside the wall. Barring tearing them all out, how could we have known?"

Declan patted Gerry's shoulder. "She's right. These things happen. And what's most important is that it's getting fixed. Once it's done, the house will be even more gorgeous that we'd all imagined it would be when we signed the papers."

"Okay, I guess…." Travis said, still clearly upset.

"You guys are fabulous," Paula assured him, smiling. "The best in the business. We feel lucky we had you as our agents. The house is sound, other than a few hiccups, but that's home ownership, right?"

Travis reluctantly nodded. She was right, but he just wished they'd managed to get moved in at least before any *hiccups* had shown up.

"So, please, don't worry about it," Declan instructed, meeting Gerry's eye. "There are far worse things in life than a few house renos."

Gerry grinned. "Okay, okay. You guys are really something else. We only wish more of our clients were like you."

Travis dimpled at that statement. "God, isn't that the truth!"

Paula leaned over and gave him a peck on the cheek. "How are the dogs doing?"

Both men sparkled at the question. They were avid long-haired dachshund owners and their fur-babies were their pride and joy.

"They are so good!" Travis enthused. "You two should seriously think about getting a dog now that you have the house."

"Would a cat suffice?" Paula posed.

Gerry's eyebrows shot up. "You're cat people?"

Declan laughed at the way he said it, as though he couldn't believe what he was hearing.

"In a forced manner, I suppose," Paula admitted. "Long story short, a cat has claimed us."

Travis nodded in a knowing manner. "Um-hmm, they do that, cats do."

"But that doesn't mean we're anti-dog," Declan assured them. "We accept all pets equally."

"Lots of dogs are great with cats," Gerry said, matter-of-fact, to Travis.

"That's true!" he agreed, then added excitedly, "In fact, our friend, Pat - she owns the bookstore *Possibilities* on Main Street - her cat, Whiskey, is great with our dogs."

"That's true," Gerry reiterated. "And I've even heard that dachshunds are exceptionally good with cats."

Paula and Declan exchanged a look. Time to stop this train in its tracks.

"Hey, listen," Declan said, smiling warmly. "We'd love to chat more, but we really do have to run."

"Of course!" Travis waved a hand at Gerry. "You're keeping them too long."

Paula bit her lip to keep from giggling at the pair of them. Such fun and kind people.

"It was so great seeing you both," she said, meaning every word. "We'll invite you to the housewarming once we're settled in."

"Looking forward to it," Travis gushed, while Gerry offered his hand once more to Declan and said, "Next time, coffee is on us."

"Deal. Talk soon." He gave a small wave then put an arm around Paula's shoulders.

"Whew, dodged that dog-laced bullet," Paula said, chuckling good-naturedly once Travis and Gerry had gone inside the shop. "I was preparing myself for one of them to suddenly whip open their coat and produce a puppy for us to take home."

Declan laughed. "I think a cat is quite enough for the moment, not to mention we need to get *us* into the house before we start adding even more creatures into the mix."

"Amen to that. And, that being said, shall we?"

"Absolutely. To the new house," he declared and they set off down the street to where they'd parked the car.

Declan unlocked the front door to the new house then stepped aside to allow Paula first entry.

She crossed the threshold, the same excited feeling beating in her chest that she'd had the first day they'd looked at it. Home, she thought, letting it wash over her.

"So, as I told you," he reminded, leading the way into the living room, "it looks worse than it is."

"I know, I know," she assured him, walking over to run a loving hand across the wood mantle on the fireplace. "Yikes, dusty."

"Everything is."

"To be expected, but I don't care. Just being here makes me think I should have come much sooner. It feels like forever since I've seen the place."

He nodded, understanding, then pulled his cellphone from his pocket when it trilled.

"Who's that?" she asked, rubbing her hands together to rid them of the dust from the mantle.

He read the screen. "It's my Mom."

"What's up?"

He quickly typed a reply, then said, "Okay, that should do it. She was just wondering how we're getting on and wanted to know if we want to go there for dinner later."

"Did you tell her yes?"

"Of course."

"Excellent. All breaks from the house of Hayes are welcome."

He laughed, knowing she'd be glad of the opportunity for some space from her mother. It wasn't his first rodeo.

"So, anyway, I can't wait to get everything set up properly," she went on, then stopped short.

"What?" He looked around, trying to figure out what she'd seen to halt her in her tracks.

Paula walked over to the couch. "So, it's true," she said, chuckling as she picked up black and white cat hairs from the cushions. "Sylvester *was* making himself at home here already."

Declan grinned. "Yup."

"Do you wonder if he belongs to someone in the neighborhood and we … well, not *we* exactly, but *Amber* cat-napped him?"

He nodded. "I thought about that, too, but then I considered the factors - the main one being that the workmen all confirmed he hung out here most of the day and the other one being that no one seems to be looking for him in any way when I asked the neighbors."

"Are you kidding me?" she insisted, hands on her hips. "You actually did that? You asked around the neighborhood?"

He shrugged. "It was the decent thing to do. I didn't want to find out we'd ended up stealing some poor kid's beloved pet."

"You mean find out *Amber* stole some kid's pet," Paula corrected.

"Either way, we can rest easy knowing he was a stray who hit the jackpot."

Paula reached out for him and wrapped her arms around him. "You are a good man."

"Yes," he said, hugging her back, his voice teasing. "Yes, I am."

She laughed and pulled back to smile at him. "And modest, can't forget that."

"Of course," he agreed, then nodded toward the hallway. "Are you ready to see the kitchen?"

"Lead on."

"Okay, now seriously, remember what I said," he warned, as they left the living room and walked down the hall then rounded the corner into the kitchen. "It looks worse—"

Paula's loud gasp interrupted his attempts to soften the blow and she stood, slack-jawed, in the face of what was before them. Even though the original space had desperately needed renovation, it had at least *looked* like a kitchen. *This*, well, this looked more like a construction site.

"I told you, it isn't pretty. Not now. But as soon as the guys get moving on it again, it will be gorgeous; just as we imagined."

Paula looked at the wall where the pipe had leaked and been fixed. The new expanse of drywall stood out in stark relief next to the original, giving the impression the area had gone through some sort of graft: which, for all intents and purposes, it had.

"Ignore the walls," Declan instructed, as though reading her mind. "They'll get painted and disappear behind the new cabinetry."

Paula shifted her focus to the tiles beneath their feet. "Well, at least the floor is in and it's gorgeous. No more yucky, yellowing linoleum."

Declan let his gaze drop to the floor as well, thrilled to see something completed. While he'd never admitted it out loud, he had been starting to feel a bit discouraged by the ratio of things that still needed attention compared to what was actually done. Seeing the stone-look porcelain tiles solidly beneath their feet gave him hope it would all get done.

"It looks even better than I'd hoped."

Paula nodded then looked up at the open ceiling where the second leak had been discovered. "How about that leak? Has Vince updated you on how that's going?"

"Yup, all good. The leak from the bathroom is fixed, there's no mold and they just have to bring in their ceiling guy to close it up."

"How about the bathroom, upstairs?"

"They were able to access it from down here."

"That's a relief," Paula breathed. "One less thing to deal with."

Declan reached for a light switch on the wall and flicked it upward. Nothing. He frowned and looked up at the light that was supposed to be on, then turned the switch off and on again. Still nothing.

Paula cleared her throat. "Umm, so what's happening there? I assume the light was supposed to turn on?"

Declan flicked the switch off. "Yup."

"Right, so…?"

"Maybe they disconnected it while they were dealing with the bathroom leak."

She took a deep breath and released it. "Maybe."

The defeat lacing her words was almost palpable and Declan slapped on a grin. Damage control was in order.

"Forget that. It's nothing. Did I tell you that the cabinetry will be arriving this week? That means the deadline for move-in could actually be on track this time."

Paula let him placate her and reached for his hand. "Listen," she said, looking into his eyes.

"Uh-oh," he responded.

She grinned. "No, this is a good 'listen'."

"Is that possible?" he teased.

"Yes," she insisted, dropping his hand and moving closer to wrap her arms around his waist.

"Okay, shoot."

"First, I want to apologize for being such a crab."

He squeezed her and shook his head. "No need. It's been stressful. It happens."

"Still," she argued, "I shouldn't have been taking it out on you. We're a team and my negativity isn't helping the situation."

He regarded her. "Don't worry about it, I get it. I know how hard it is for you at the best of times, dealing with your family. Living with them, like we have—"

"Yeah, but," she interrupted, loosening her grip around his waist and taking a step back, "that's the thing. I want to let that go. It's time. I need to get a handle on the fact that, when I'm back in that house, I haven't stepped back in time. Regardless of how it was when I was a kid, picking up Mom's slack and basically being the only one who seemed to be able to act like an adult, it's not that way anymore. I don't have to be a part of that anymore."

"You had a lot on your plate as a kid," he acknowledged, sympathetically.

She nodded her head. "Yes, but to use the old cliché, that was then and this is now. And I want to be able to laugh it off like you do, instead of feeling like I'm morphing into the person I was before I got out of there." She sighed and added, "I didn't like that version of me then and I definitely don't like it now."

"Okay," he said, rallying. "So, what's the plan? Do we create some sort of code word for the next week that I can say when things get nutty - and you know they will - to help you pull back from feeling you have to take care of everything?"

She laughed. It was a funny idea, but also a good one. "Like what?"

"I don't know." He scanned the room while he began to pace the floor. "How about ... kitchen sink?"

Paula giggled some more. "Kitchen sink?"

"Sure, why not?" He stopped pacing and faced her, then noticed she was looking past him to the dog door, or *cat* door as the workmen had renamed it.

"How about, instead of kitchen sink, we use *new cat*?" Paula offered, an amused grin on her face.

Declan chuckled and rubbed a hand across the dark stubble on his chin. "Sounds perfect."

Chapter 13

Jaimie bounced baby Hazel on her knee, pulling silly faces to make her daughter smile.

Amber, seated across from her at the kitchen table, moved her thumbs rapid-fire on the screen of her cellphone.

"Who are you texting? And why are they so much more important than your niece?" Jaimie demanded, indignant.

Amber looked up from the screen. "It's Tara."

"And what is so important that *Tara* cannot be put off?"

"Halloween."

Donna came into the kitchen in time to watch Jaimie throw her head back, laughing.

"What's so funny? Did Hazel do something? Did I miss it?" She charged across the floor to scoop the baby out of Jaimie's grasp and began cooing at her granddaughter. "Are you a funny bunny? Hmmm? Funny bunny? Or are you the prettiest little baby in the world?"

Hazel gave her a gummy grin and said, "buh-buh-buh."

"Very good!" Donna praised, smiling. "Bunny, bunny, bunny."

"Amber was just commenting on the Halloween debacle."

Donna flicked her gaze at Jaimie then returned her attention to Hazel.

Jaimie smirked. Her mother was the queen of avoidance when need be. "I told you about Trent, right?" she went on, referring to her husband. "He laughed so loudly when he saw you guys on the news, I thought for sure Hazel was going to wake up."

"It wasn't *that* funny and it was barely even a story," Donna said, rocking Hazel and walking her around the kitchen to point things out and say their names. "Toaster. That's a toaster for making toast."

"Oh, but it *was*," Jaimie countered, snickering while she pulled her brown hair into a ponytail then secured it with an elastic she slipped from around her wrist. "Another folly to add to the list."

Donna paused in pointing out coffee maker to Hazel and shifted her focus to Amber. "Amber, will you say something for goodness sake? Back me up. Tell your sister it was barely a story; most people missed it altogether."

Amber, still texting, looked up from her phone again. "What?"

"Forget it," Jaimie said, picking up her cup of tea from the table.

Amber dropped her eyes back to the screen.

"You know, if you'd watched," Jaimie continued, "you'd have noticed that it was Paula who really stood out."

"No one watched," Donna stated.

"Yeah, but those who might have would have noticed Paula for sure."

Donna cocked her head, her face puzzled. "You're not making any sense. What did Paula do? She was barely even there."

Jaimie sipped her tea then cupped the mug in her hands. "She was definitely there, Mom. *You* may not have noticed, but she was. They caught her on camera when she was striding across the yard, if you need proof. Her dress was eye catching."

"Oh, that gown," Donna groused, carrying Hazel back to the table. "Why was she wearing something so attention getting in the first place?"

Jaimie lifted an eyebrow, but held her tongue. She'd seen what Amber had been wearing, or *not* wearing, Paula's costume had been tame by comparison.

"All I'm saying is, between that dress and the shots they got of her face when she was sitting with Declan told the real story. I haven't talked with her about it since, I hope no one has recognized her in the past few days. Not great for her work."

Donna sat down and began gently bouncing Hazel on her knee. She frowned, contemplating the information.

"Does she need changing?" Jaimie asked.

She lifted her eyebrows. "Hmmm?"

"The baby. Does she need changing?"

Donna looked at Hazel then back at her daughter. "I don't know. Why, has it been awhile?"

"Well, you're frowning like you've smelled something unpleasant, so I just figured."

"Oh," she said, smoothing her features. "I wasn't frowning about that. I was thinking about what you said about Paula."

Jaimie put down her mug and reached for the baby. "I'll check her anyway."

Donna handed Hazel over. "Anyway, it wasn't as bad as all that. And, even though you think otherwise, Paula was barely even there. I'm sure whatever you think you saw was just her being overly-sensitive, or worried about the yard. The burnt lawn will grow back in the Spring after we add some seed and water, you'll never know anything happened. Just a silly Halloween adventure."

Jaimie picked up the diaper bag beside her chair and said nothing. Her mother had no clue she'd been on the phone with Paula that night and there was no way she was going to enlighten her. As usual, history would be rewritten and the Halloween debacle would eventually become a lively tale where no one had been in any real danger and no one had been ignored.

"Amber," she said. "Stop texting and come with me while I change the baby."

"Why?" Amber asked, not looking up from her phone.

"Because I want company."

Amber exhaled noisily, tucked her phone into her pocket and said, "Fine,", as she got up from her seat to follow her out of the kitchen.

Jaimie placed Hazel on the changing mat she'd laid on the floor of Amber's bedroom then reached into the side pocket of the diaper bag for a soft, blue monkey shaped rattle to keep her occupied.

Amber flopped down on the bed. "So I'm here, why?"

"I said, to keep me company." Jaimie handed the toy to Hazel then set to work. "And to tell me about Liam. What's the deal there? Was it just a bit of nothing, or something else?"

Amber watched her efficiently finish up and offered, "You could enter a baby changing competition and win. You're fast."

"Avoiding," Jaimie stated, by way of reply, while Hazel waved her chubby legs in the air then stuffed the rattle into her mouth.

"Okay, fine," Amber acknowledged. "The *deal*, as you called it, is we've been hanging out."

Jaimie picked Hazel up off the mat and extended her toward Amber to hold. "Define, *hanging out*," she pressed, clearing away the last of the changing paraphernalia then joining them on the bed.

Amber sat Hazel between them and offered her one of her stuffed bears that she kept on her bed. Her niece's face lit up as she pulled it into her embrace and squeezed it with abandon. Amber giggled at the pure joy on her little face.

"I don't know," she finally answered. "I guess it means we've been spending time together—"

"How much time?" Jaimie interrupted.

"God," Amber huffed. "Let me finish."

"Sorry. Go ahead."

"A lot of time," she expounded. "If you must know."

"Before or after *the incident?*"

"After. Before *the incident* we talked once in a while if we crossed paths, and we texted a fair bit as well, but then … well, you know the rest."

Jaimie put her hands out on either side of Hazel to catch her if she started to topple from her sitting position. "And what about Trina? What's happening there?"

"You're not going to let up are you?"

"Not until I get the information I want," she agreed, moving her left hand gently against Hazel's shoulder to help steady her back to center.

Amber sighed and nodded. "Okay, here it is. But," she pointed a finger, "you can't tell Mom."

Jaimie gently applied her right hand to her daughter's other shoulder when she began to tilt in that direction. "Understood."

"Ever since *the incident*, we've been meeting up for coffee and stuff."

Jaimie lifted her focus from Hazel to meet Amber's eye at *and stuff*.

Amber frowned. "No, not that! At least, not at first."

Jaimie's eyebrows shot up. "Meaning?"

"Well, once Trina saw that video of us it was pretty much out in the open, right?"

She got up from the bed and began pacing the floor.

Jaimie said nothing, letting her continue.

"Then, after the Halloween debacle here at the house, Liam said he was going to have an honest discussion with Trina and…."

"And what?" Jaimie scooped Hazel and the bear into her arms so she could focus completely on what Amber was saying.

"They broke up."

"And she's okay with that?"

Amber shrugged her shoulders. "I think so. He hasn't said much else except that he explained things to her and that was that."

"So, what does that mean for you two? Does that mean you're, *you know*."

Amber flushed.

"Ohmygod," Jaimie gushed, seeing the color in her sister's face. "It's more than a fling then."

Amber, her cheeks still pink, tried to repress a grin. She failed and it took over her face.

"Wow." Jaimie smiled with her. "And you're happy? He's happy?"

"Yes," she admitted. "It's still new, but I'm kinda shocked at how well we fit together." She saw Jaimie raise an eyebrow and quickly clarified, "And not like *that*, you perv. Although, if we're mentioning it, I gotta say...."

"Stop," Jaimie insisted, while she bounced Hazel in her lap. "Your face says more than enough, thank you."

Amber giggled.

"So, have you told Paula and Declan how things have turned out?"

"No, but I probably should, right?"

"I think so. And the sooner the better. They've had so much stuff lately with the house and living back here with the 'rents, they don't need to have this sprung on them."

Amber frowned. "You think they'd be against it?"

"No." She shook her head. "And they probably won't even be all that surprised after seeing the video, But, that being said, I still think it would bug them to hear it as gossip."

Amber nodded. "Yeah, makes sense. Okay, I'll mention it later tonight."

"Good." Jaimie stood up and shifted Hazel onto her hip.

"She can keep the bear," Amber offered. "She loves it."

Jaimie smiled and picked the diaper bag up from the floor. "Thanks. You're a good Auntie. Now let's go back downstairs and tease Mom some more about Halloween."

Amber laughed and followed her out of the room.

Douglas yawned and stretched his arms above his head. He'd been working and lost track of time, the daylight once streaming brightly through the garage window had grown dim. He looked at his work and nodded in satisfaction. A six foot by six foot, carved-wood Horn of Plenty: it was a sight to behold. He'd really outdone himself, his attention to detail was inspiring, and he knew it was going to be brilliant once painted. Donna would be delighted.

He grinned. There was nothing better for him, no greater joy, than the girlish pleasure on his wife's face when he surprised her with the end product of his work. Sure, he made his living running *Hayes Happy Zone,* and it was a good living and he enjoyed his days there, but this sort of work with his hands and taping into his creativity was the most satisfying of all.

"Looking good?" Douglas asked, directing the question at Sylvester.

The cat, tucked up on a shelf above the workbench, twitched his nose while he gazed at the carved wood.

"I'll take that as a yes," he chuckled.

His phone buzzed, a text message from Donna, and he picked it up from his workbench to read the screen.

"Kids are home."

"That's our cue," he announced, giving the Horn of Plenty a gentle pat. "Time for us to call it a night."

Sylvester, as though understanding, flexed his paws then stood up to jump effortlessly from shelf to workbench to floor.

"Good lad," Douglas praised, and got up to follow the cat toward the door.

Trent rapped his knuckles sharply against Donna and Douglas' front door before opening it, then flinched when the raised voices of Paula and Donna nearly bowled him over. If it hadn't been for the fact his wife and baby daughter were inside, he might have turned on his heel and retreated back outside. But, as is the case when it comes to family, he stayed put to weather the storm with the rest of them.

Amber gave a small wave to her brother-in-law and he furrowed his brow questioningly in return as he stepped across the threshold into the house and closed the door. She waved him over as there was no way to communicate over the verbal battle.

"What the hell's going on?" he asked, after darting around Paula and Donna to arrive at Jaimie's side.

She shifted to her left on the love-seat to make room for him to sit down. "Mom just won't let up, *as usual*, and now there's a bloody war, *as usual*."

Amber, sitting on the couch, rolled her eyes by way of agreement.

"War about what?" he pressed, taking off his jacket and laying it across the back of the love-seat before settling in beside Jaimie.

Amber sat forward. "Thanksgiving."

Trent frowned. "What about it? I thought it was all settled."

Amber laughed and sat back in her seat.

Jaimie patted his knee, affectionately. "Oh, if it were only that simple. No, Mom made the statement that she was going to host without anyone's help, but, as usual, she had no bloody idea what she's doing and, *as usual*, she's trying to heap it on Paula."

Trent nodded, finally understanding. He'd heard the stories about their childhood. He knew the lay of the land.

"I am neck-deep right now at work!" Paula bellowed, staring at her mother. "Do you even understand what that means?"

Donna huffed and tossed her arms around, trying to make eye contact with one of them in the room. They all averted their gaze, refusing to be dragged into the middle of things.

"Because," Paula continued, pointing her finger, "I don't think you have any clue."

"So, enlighten me," Donna snapped back, her mouth set as she folded her arms across her chest.

"It means, I have clients - stinking rich and influential clients - who are paying me to get events organized for them at deadline. If I don't, it will mean I don't get paid, my assistant doesn't get paid, the rent doesn't get paid and our reputation is destroyed."

"*Reputation,*" Donna exhaled, scornfully.

Paula's mouth dropped open.

"Uh-oh," Amber said, her eyes wide as she exchanged looks with Jaimie and Trent.

"Should we try to get out of here?" Jaimie whispered.

"Where's Hazel?" Trent asked, noting the absence of his daughter.

"Upstairs. Asleep."

He nodded. Hazel was a sound sleeper. Once she was out, nothing short of a siren would wake her. He dared to peek at his mother-in-law and sister-in-law and thought they might offer something fairly close.

"Hey, all, I'm back!"

Paula, about to unleash a verbal assault on her mother for her rude remark, was jarred from her stance by the sound of Declan's voice from the kitchen.

"Where is everyone, anyway?" he called. "I've got the donuts as requested."

"In here," Jaimie squeaked, hiding slightly behind Trent's shoulder in case her reply caused her mother or sister to shift their focus to where they and Amber were sitting.

Declan strode into the living room then paused, his face confused by the tableau before him. He'd been gone less than thirty minutes and now his wife and mother-in-law were squared off in the middle of the floor like they were in a boxing match, while the rest of the family were cowering into the furniture as though they were afraid they'd get caught in the cross-fire.

"What's going on in here?" he demanded, before noticed his father-in-law's absence. "And where's Doug?"

"What's going on is," Paula informed him, "*new cat.*"

Declan's eyebrows shot up at her reference to their conversation at the new house. They'd been kidding around, or so he'd thought, but apparently things had gotten serious while he was out.

Amber shook her head. "What does that mean? What does the cat have to do with anything?"

"It means," Paula told her, "Declan and I are outta here."

"*Paula*," Jaimie pleaded.

"No!" She held her hand up. "We've been here long enough and *clearly* we've outstayed our welcome."

"Seriously," Declan insisted, moving further into the room. "What the hell happened?"

"Go ahead," Paula prompted her mother. "Tell him. Apparently, you're the only one who deserves any respect around here, so you may as well fill him in."

"*I'll* fill him in," Amber offered, standing up.

Declan turned and gave her his attention.

"In a nutshell, Mom has totally dropped the ball for Thanksgiving."

"No, no." Donna shook her head.

"Yes, yes," Amber countered, then spoke directly to Declan again. "And now she's being totally rude to Paula and insisting she has plenty of time to organize everything for Thanksgiving even though it's only two weeks away!"

Donna threw her hands in the air. "Slander! That's what this is! By my own daughter!"

"Oh, *please*." Jaimie got up to stand beside Amber. "She's saying exactly what's happened and you know it. You've gone ahead and invited at least twenty people and you've done exactly nothing to prepare for it. Not even one bloody list!"

"Okay," Declan soothed, wrapping his head around the information. He dealt with this sort of thing every day at work, just with tech related issues instead of turkey related. "We can get this handled if we all pull together."

Paula's mouth set in a hard line. She shook her head, so pissed off she couldn't find the words.

Declan reached out and gently took her by the arm, while asking, "Can we go into the kitchen and talk about this? Try and deal with this *new cat?*"

"Fine," she agreed, and let him lead her from the room.

"Okay, before you say it," Declan assured, once they were seated at the kitchen table, "I know exactly how overwhelmingly frustrating this is for you."

Paula scrubbed her scalp with her fingers, trying to release some of the tension that had built up over the past hour.

"It's just one more time that your mother basically gets bailed out by everyone else," he expanded. "And you are at your limit and don't want any part of it."

She dropped her hands limply into her lap. "Then why are you suggesting we do it?"

"Because, I care about everyone who's been promised a Thanksgiving dinner here at this house. I don't want to see them suddenly left high and dry."

Paula pursed her lips. "Well, obviously, I don't want that either. But—"

"*Aaand* if we don't all pull together," he offered, gently. "You know damned well it's going to be a bust."

Paula leaned forward to lay her forehead on the tabletop. "I knooooow, but I'm so busy at work right now you can't imagine. The very idea of trying to organize and pull everything together in two weeks is…."

"You're not going to do a thing."

She lifted her head and looked at him, confused.

"I'm serious," he said, firmly. "I'm going to go back in there and organize everything. I'll get in touch with my brothers and my Mom and Dad, and Thanksgiving is going to happen without you being involved at all."

"I can't let you do that. They'll all think I'm terrible for not helping."

Declan shook his head. "Your family certainly won't. As you heard, they know exactly what's going on. As for my family, I'll keep it simple and explain that work is swamped, *not* that your Mom is dropping the ball. Seriously, I'll handle it and no one will end up looking bad. Trust me."

Paula's face relaxed as she let his words sink in.

"Okay?"

She smiled softly and nodded. "Okay."

His cellphone trilled from inside his pants pocket and he pulled it out to read the text. "Speak of the devil, it's my Mom."

Paula chuckled.

"And she's asking if she can bring anything for Thanksgiving."

"She must be psychic."

He grinned and stood up. "Okay, I'm going back in there to organize the troops. You stay here, out of the fray."

"Can I say one last thing?"

He tucked his phone back into his pocket. "Of course."

"While I appreciate all that you're doing, maybe we *should* consider just biting the bullet and leaving here to go and stay at your parents." She held up a hand when he frowned. "Before you start offering a counter argument, we can, or *you all* can, still help get Thanksgiving arranged, but maybe we should leave here in the meantime. My Mom and I aren't going to stop locking horns and it's not like she's obligated to have me here, maybe it's for the best that we bail out."

"I guess. I mean, if that's what you want," Declan began, before Amber charged through the door and interrupted him.

"No way," she barked, shaking her head.

"It *is* their house," Paula started.

"Oh, blah, blah, blah," she finished. "That's just Mom-speak for *everyone do what I say, no matter how many times I change my opinion.* If I had a dollar for every time she pulled that bullshit out, I'd be rich. You go ahead and try and tell her that and, sure as shit, she'll turn it around on you and act as though your leaving is somehow a betrayal, instead of respect for the fact it's their house. She lives for conflict, you know that. You can't win."

Paula exchanged a look with Declan and snickered. She had a point.

"Okay, so we'll shelve that idea and agree my plan stands?" Declan confirmed.

"I didn't hear it," Amber told him. "I only heard the part where Paula was trying to bail out."

He smirked, but kept his focus. "In a nutshell, I'll get everything organized for Thanksgiving, you guys and my family all help out, and it isn't heaped on Paula to save the day as usual."

"Deal." Amber held out her hand.

Declan shook it then looked at Paula. "Got that?"

She smiled. "Got it. And thanks. You guys are the best."

"We know," Amber agreed, before telling Declan, "You want to go out to Dad's shop and tell him it's safe to come inside now?"

He chuckled. "Decided to duck out, huh?"

"He's had lots of practice," she stated, wryly. "Oh, and the *new cat* is out there as well," she added, then walked out of the kitchen to return to the family room.

Paula and Declan shared a look. If only she had any idea of what that meant to them when they used it.

"Wanna come with me?" he offered, rising from his chair.

Paula looked first toward the door to the family room, then to the one leading outside to her Dad's workshop. It was a no-brainer.

She nodded and stood up. "Lead the way."

Chapter 14

"Hey, Mom?" Declan called out, as he pushed open the front door of his parent's house. "You here?"

"Upstairs," came Bonnie's reply. "Be right there."

Declan closed the door and slipped off his shoes and coat, draping his jacket across the pine bench in the foyer.

"Hey, honey," his mother said, all smiles as she descended the staircase. "Cold out there today."

Declan returned the grin and anyone watching would have observed his smile matched hers exactly. In fact, he and his brothers had all inherited Bonnie's wide, welcoming grin.

"How come you always look so great?" he complimented, opening his arms to her for a hug.

They were an affectionate family, the Dempsey's, and hugging was as normal to them as a handshake.

"Oh, you're a kind boy," she praised, squeezing him back.

He let her go and shook his head. "Nope, just honest."

"What do you want?" she teased, making him laugh.

"Hey, can't a guy give a compliment without an ulterior motive?"

She patted his shoulder and led the way to the kitchen. "Not around this house."

Declan chuckled some more. She wasn't exactly exaggerating. Raising five sons, plus having a husband, had taught her to be wary of compliments.

"Well, in this case, there's no ulterior motive," he insisted. "Just noticing you look great."

"Alright, fine, I'll believe you." A small pleased smile curved her lips as she smoothed the front of her blue checked blouse over her black slacks. "Thank you, dear."

"So, where's the cat?" Declan asked, looking around the kitchen.

More often than not, his mother's white cat could be found tucked up on the shelf that held her cookbooks. Today, however, the shelf was lacking a furry accessory.

"Outside, I'd gather," she said, walking over to the stainless steel carafe on the countertop. "Why, doesn't your cat go outside?"

"Not anymore. It's funny, even though he was outside when we found him, he shows no inclination whatsoever to go out now that he's with us. He went out once, but that was by accident, and seemed relieved to be back with us when the neighbor found him."

Bonnie lifted the carafe and poured coffee into her mug on the countertop. "I'm not surprised. Why would he want to be anywhere that you aren't?"

Declan walked across the kitchen and fetched a glass from the cupboard. "Yeah, I'm guessing he's just smart and knows where his bread and butter are coming from and wants to make sure he doesn't lose it."

She chuckled and held the carafe toward him. "Coffee?"

He shook his head then filled the glass with water from the tap. "No, thanks. Is Dad around?"

"Out for a bike ride with Angus."

"They're still doing that?"

"Yup." She put the carafe down on the counter. "Three times a week, rain, shine or cold."

"Good for Dad," he praised, knowing fully well his father was more or less being told by both his wife and son he had no choice in the matter.

When his doctor had informed him his blood pressure was a tad high, that had been that. Angus had taken it upon himself to make sure Craig was consistent with his exercise and diet.

"I think he's hoping it will snow sooner than later, truth be told," Bonnie revealed, giggling.

"Yeah, but I'll bet Angus has something up his sleeve to replace the cycling."

She nodded. "Yup. He's already said they're going to get cross-country skis."

Declan released a bark of laughter then took a drink of water from his glass. The idea of his Dad with skis strapped to his feet was comical.

"I know." Bonnie giggled some more while she carried her cup over to the table and sat down. "It's a hysterical thought."

"Make sure you take pictures."

"Absolutely," she agreed. "So, you still haven't told me what brings you by. Everything okay with Paula?"

"Of course."

"Mmm, that's good," she said, before asking, "Then is it because of all of the alien activity around the house as of late?"

Declan smirked then drank the rest of the water from his glass.

"Sorry, honey, I just couldn't resist," she apologized, grinned cheekily while resting her elbows on the tabletop. "It looked like it was quite the show, though, I'm sorry we missed it."

She and Craig had been out of town over Halloween and had just arrived back a few days ago; thus, they'd missed the debacle.

Declan placed the empty glass in the sink then joined her at the table. "Who told you?"

"Cian," she said, tucking one side of her brown, bobbed hair behind an ear. "Or, rather, Michael heard about it at the salon and then told Cian, who Googled it and sent the link to us."

Declan shook his head. "God, nothing that goes on in Boxwood Hills seems to get by Mike. He should have considered a job in reporting."

Bonnie snickered and picked up her coffee cup. Her son-in-law was not just the family hairstylist, but their foremost authority when it came to gossip.

"Anyway," Declan said, moving things along. "The reason I came over was to talk to you about Thanksgiving."

Bonnie lifted her eyebrows. "Something wrong?"

"No, not exactly. It's still going to be at Donna and Doug's, but there's been a bit of a glitch."

She took a sip from her cup, letting him continue.

"It seems Donna's bitten off more than she can chew," he revealed, then warned, "which, by the way, you did not hear from me and we won't be telling anyone else."

She nodded. "Understood."

"So, I was hoping I could count on you and Dad and the rest of the family to pitch in. Paula's got a ridiculously overflowing work schedule right now and just can't pick up the slack on this one, so I told her I'd rally the troops and she wouldn't have to worry about it."

Bonnie put her cup down and cocked her head. "So, just to be clear, what you're saying is *you're* basically hosting Thanksgiving at *their* house, right?"

Declan shrugged. "I like to think of it as helping to make Thanksgiving a success for everyone."

Bonnie smiled at her son. His kindness and willingness to help were just some of the traits that made him so endearing. If she ever questioned her value on the planet, all she had to do was look at him and her other four sons to know she'd contributed well.

"So, can we count you and Dad in?"

"Of course, dear. We'll do whatever you need."

Declan grinned. He knew he could count on his parents to join in and help everything go smoothly. He'd told Paula he'd get it handled and he would.

"That's a huge relief," he said, standing up. "And now, I'm sorry to cut things short, but I need to take off and get back to work. I'm going to make a list of what needs to be done and I'll text you."

"Sounds good. And you're sure you two are doing okay living there all this time?"

He paused and rubbed a hand across the stubble on his chin. "It's been challenging for Paula living back at home—"

"What about you?"

"It's easier for me, of course," he admitted. "I didn't grow up there."

"And you're trying to make the best of a difficult situation."

"Exactly."

She stood up as well and reached out to give him a hug. "You're a good person."

"And my wife is even better," he replied, squeezing her back. "She deserves to have someone in her corner on this."

Bonnie released him and smiled. "Well, she has all of us now. Let's make this a happy Thanksgiving."

Paula stepped from the cold street into the warm, sweet smelling shop of *The Bakery*. The door closed behind her and the shift in temperature inspired a shiver to run up her spine. She pulled her green, knitted hat from her head and ruffled the short layers of her hair as she scanned the interior of the cafe for her sister.

Amber, seated across the room, waved from her table near the window.

"Paula," she called out. "Over here."

Paula tucked her hat into her coat pocket, and weaved her way between the wooden tables toward her. "Hey," she said, pulling out the chair across from her sister and sitting down. "It's getting seriously cold out there, feels like snow."

Amber nodded. "I know. Dad's had to turn the heater on in the garage so that the paint on his Horn of Plenty will dry before he puts it outside."

"God, did you see the size of that thing?" Paula asked, while shucking the coat from her shoulders and hanging it and her bag across the back of her chair.

"It's really good, though," Amber acknowledged.

"Beautiful," she agreed. "But he's going to need all of our help to carry it into the yard."

"He'll figure it out," Amber said, then leaned forward in her chair. "So, listen, thanks for coming. I know it's short notice and you're super busy at work and all, but—"

"No, no." Paula held up a hand to stop her. "Your text said it was urgent and that matters more than anything. Erin can hold down the fort, work isn't going anywhere."

Amber's face softened. Her big sister. Always there when she needed her.

"So, what's going on?"

"Should we get some coffee, first?" she asked, looking over at the board above the bakery cases that displayed the numerous selections available to them.

"You bet, it's on me. What do you want?"

Amber clutched the mug of mocha peppermint latte she'd ordered; her face tense with expectation. She'd never felt so nervous before about revealing she was dating someone; however, to be fair, the person she was dating wasn't just any old someone, it was Liam.

"So?" she prompted, while Paula sipped her macadamia nut flavored coffee.

Paula placed her cup down on the tabletop. "So, you're saying that you and Liam have been nearly inseparable since *the incident*."

She nodded

"And it's serious?"

A flush warmed Amber's cheeks in the same way it had when she'd first started talking about she and Liam and she hide her face behind her mug.

Paula looked into her eyes and started to grin. The grin turned into a full-on smile and she started to giggle. Her little sister and Declan's brother, who'd a-thought?

Amber put down her cup and stared at her, not sure what to think.

"Well, I can't tell you I'm surprised," she admitted.

Amber's eyebrows lifted. "What do you mean?"

"We all saw the," she lowered her voice, "*video footage* of you two, after all. And ever since then you've been in a fabulous mood, so…."

"So, you're not mad at me?"

It was Paula's turn to lift her eyebrows. "Mad? Why would I be mad?"

"I don't know, maybe because you know my track record and you might be worried if something happens and we break up it will cause problems in the family."

Paula leaned forward and placed her elbows on the table. "Do *you* think that's going to happen?"

The pink in Amber's cheeks deepened to match her sweater and she shook her head.

"I didn't think so," Paula stated. "In fact, if I'm to be completely honest, I don't ever think I've seen you like this with any guy."

Amber giggled and leaned in as well. "I know! It's nuts, but I've never been this much … *me*, with anyone."

Paula reached across the table to squeeze her hand. "And that's all that matters."

Amber's eyes sparkled in the cafe's overhead lights and she took a steadying breath. "I'm a little scared, too, how quickly we seem so together."

Paula nodded. She understood. She and Declan had been much the same. "Just enjoy it," she counselled, leaning back in her seat. "Let it unfold and relax."

"That's exactly what I'm trying to do," Amber agreed.

"And besides," Paula added, picking up her coffee cup and raising it in a toast. "At least you know that the only crazy people between the two of you belong to us!"

Amber laughed and clinked her mug against the cup. "Cheers to that."

Declan's phone chimed once, then again, indicating he had two text messages waiting. He hit *save* on the document he was working on his laptop then reached across his desk to pick up the phone.

The first text was from Vince: *"Declan, issue with cabinets. We were sent the wrong color. Contact me as soon as you can."*

"Oh, hell," he grumbled, while checking the second text.

It was from Amber: *"Hey, Dec! Serious shit going down here at the house. And by shit, I mean turkey shit. Mom went and bought a live turkey and it's in the backyard! No lies! I haven't told Paula, this is just the sort of thing that will send her over the edge, so you gotta get home before her to help keep things from blowing up."*

"Oh, for fuck's sake, are you kidding me?" Declan complained, loudly, to his office walls.

Tammy walked through the doorway, her face concerned. "What's wrong?"

He looked up from his phone and took a deep breath to regain his calm before he spoke. "The contractor just informed me that the wrong color cabinets were sent to the house and if that's not enough, apparently, my mother-in-law has brought home a god-damned live turkey for Thanksgiving. Business as usual."

Tammy's face twisted in shock. "Are you serious?"

"About which part?" he asked, putting his phone back down on the desk before shutting down his computer.

"The turkey, of course!"

"That's what my sister-in-law tells me," he said, matter-of-fact. "And that means I have to get the rest of this work done later, so that I can get out of here and get home before Paula to make sure she doesn't murder her mother when she finds out about this latest stunt."

"Does Paula have something against turkeys?"

Declan shot her a wry grin then slid his computer into his messenger bag. "No. She has something against having to bail her mother out of a situation the moment it goes south: which this clearly is going to do at any moment."

Tammy cocked her head. "What about her Dad? He runs *Hayes Happy Zone*, doesn't he? Surely, he can deal with it?"

"Yeah, no. Doug's not the kind of guy that deals with things, more the kind of guy who has staff to deal with things."

Tammy raised an eyebrow.

"Don't get me wrong," he clarified. "I love him, he's a great guy and a fantastic father-in-law. It's just that when it comes to handling stuff, Doug's the sort of guy who knows his limits and makes sure he hires people to do the stuff he can't. He's a people person, which is why *Hayes* has been so successful. Not only is he great at dealing with the public, but he has an eye for talent. Case in point, the woman who basically runs *Hayes*, Nicole, is super talented and totally on her game. She reminds me of you."

Tammy grinned at the flattery. "Aww, whether you mean it or not, I'll take it. Thanks."

He laughed. "I do mean it."

"So, I'm guessing that means Paula is the mess cleaner-upper around that house then?"

Declan nodded. "You got it."

"Sounds like there's never a dull moment around there."

"Doesn't seem like it. And, believe me, I've gained a much greater understanding of why my lovely wife moved out when she was nineteen."

Tammy pulled a sympathetic face. "You go and get things handled. I'm on top of everything here, no worries."

He smiled at her gratefully. "Thanks. I owe you some gladiolas to show my appreciation."

She laughed and waved his words away while she exited the office. "Get going, already! Time waits for no turkey!"

Declan chuckled at the sound of her giggles as she walked back to reception. At least someone was deriving some entertainment out of, what seemed to be, the Hayes' household circus.

He picked up his phone from his desk, typed and sent a reply to Amber that said: *On my way*, then tucked it into one of the pockets on his messenger bag. First stop the new house, second stop the in-law's house. It was a tie as to which one he was dreading more.

"Lanzo Bazzano called, while you were out," Erin announced, as Paula opened the door and entered the office.

She set her bag on the floor then pulled off her hat and scarf. "Man, it is seriously cold out there."

"I think he was a bit disappointed he had to talk with me, instead of *you,*" Erin revealed, grinning.

Paula laughed and hung the hat and scarf on the wooden coat rack adjacent to the door.

"It's true," she insisted, leaning back in her desk chair. "He was very polite, but nowhere near as chatty as he is with you. You're *special.*"

"Were you on the phone or Skype?" Paula asked, shucking her jacket next and hanging it with the accessories.

"The phone."

Paula picked up her bag and carried it over to her desk. "Ahh, okay, well that explains it."

Erin pushed her hair back from her shoulders. "Explains what?"

"If Lanzo could have actually *seen* you, I guarantee he would have been a whole lot more friendly." She tucked her bag away on the other side of her desk and sat down.

"Oh, please."

"Hey, when you've got it, you've got it," Paula stated, turning on her computer. "And speaking of someone who's *got it….*"

Erin leaned forward, all ears.

"It's official, my sister is dating Liam. She told me when we met for coffee."

"Wow, well good for her." Erin nodded her approval. "Another Hayes woman with a Dempsey man. How…."

"Odd?"

Erin laughed. "I was going to say *unexpected*, but yours works too."

"Yeah and they seem to be pretty serious already."

"So, did she say how it all happened that they got together? What was the catalyst that started things?"

Taken off guard by the question, Paula coughed and cleared her throat, buying time. She wasn't about to mention *the incident*, so what else would she say? Thankfully, she was saved from having to come up with something when her cellphone beeped.

"Hang on," she said, reaching into her bag.

Erin turned her attention back to her computer while she checked her text.

She read the message and frowned at the screen.

"What's wrong?" Erin asked, when she looked up and saw Paula's face.

"It's Declan, asking if I'm still at work. Where else would I be?"

"Out with your lover?"

"That's what I should write back," she said, giggling while she sent a fast '*yes*' reply.

Her phone beeped again. Another text.

She read it and blurted, "Oh, crap on a cracker!"

Erin's eyes widened. "Yikes. What now?"

Paula put the phone down on her desktop and ran her fingers through her hair. "The wrong kitchen cabinets were delivered to the house."

"No. Seriously?"

"Yup," she said, pointing at the phone. "That's what he says. Our contractor called to tell him that the wrong color cabinets were sent to our house."

"How does that even happen?" Erin insisted, indignant on their behalf. "Don't they check the boxes before they send them?"

Paula slumped in her chair. "God, we were so close to moving. Just days away. I knew I shouldn't get my hopes up."

"So, what are they going to do about it?"

"Hang on." She picked up her phone yet again.

Erin waited while she rapidly typed another text.

A moment later there was another alert.

Paula read it and said, "So, he says he's going to fill me in later on the gory details, but he just wanted to keep me in the loop of what's going on."

"Do you think it's going to delay your move in date?"

Paula lifted an eyebrow while she met her eye. "Gory details? I'm going to go out on a limb and say that's a firm yes."

Erin grimaced.

"Exactly."

"Okay," she said, trying to rally. "Let's forget about that for now and, instead, you fill me in on Amber and Liam."

Paula nodded. She could alter the story as necessary to omit details of *the incident*. May as well. No amount of fretting was going to magically change the wrong cabinets into the right ones, so focusing on something else was the smart way to go.

"Okay," she said, leaning in, again. "So, apparently they'd been texting back and forth for a while, just as friends…."

Declan sat on the front porch swing at Donna and Douglas', waiting for Paula to arrive home. Sure the temperature was frigid and he was feeling the chill settling into his bones through his wool coat, but he'd already been inside the house and experienced the chaos that was going on there and figured his best bet was to head Paula off at the pass to prepare her for what her mother had done. Which, if he was honest with himself, was going to be near impossible.

How did you prepare someone to be all laissez faire about a live turkey in the backyard? They weren't in farm country, for god's sake, they were in the suburbs! The situation was absurd at the very least and bat-shit crazy at most - leaving not a lot of room for middle ground.

Declan sighed and thought, between the turkey and the kitchen cabinet mix-up, he was starting to think that Paula's idea of pitching a tent in the yard of the new house wasn't such a bad idea after all.

A set of headlights came around the corner at the top of the crescent and Declan watched a car approach. He slowed the back and forth swinging motion he'd been creating with his foot on the porch floor and took a breath to center himself. He could do this.

The vehicle pulled up next to the curb and Declan frowned. It wasn't Paula's car. In fact, it looked more like his brother's car, but that made no sense. The driver's side door opened and out stepped … Liam? What was Liam doing at Paula's parent's house, again? Declan stood up and walked across the porch and down the steps toward the driveway.

"Hey, bro!" Liam called, lifting his hand in greeting while he moved around his car.

Declan met him on the sidewalk and reached out to give him a quick hug. "Hey, yourself. What brings you by?"

"I wanted to talk to you, so—"

"Is something wrong?"

"No." Liam gave him a funny look. "Why?"

"'Cause it's not exactly like you to show up unannounced saying you need to talk to me in person. You're a texting sorta guy."

Liam shrugged a shoulder. "Fair enough. But, no, nothing's wrong."

Declan waited.

"What?" Liam asked. "You want me to talk *out here*? It's freezing, can't we go inside?"

Declan turned to look at the house. "Trust me, you'd rather be here than in there."

"Because of the turkey thing?"

"You know about the turkey?"

"Yeah."

"Amber?"

He nodded. "And it sorta connects to why I'm here."

Another pair of headlights came around the corner at the top of the crescent and they both turned to watch another car approach.

"Hold that thought, this might be Paula and I need to warn her about the turkey before she goes inside."

"Not a sentence you hear every day," Liam quipped, making Declan grin.

Paula's vehicle slowed as it neared the house and she gave a small wave before she pulled up into the empty space on the driveway. She turned off the car and opened the driver-side door, her face puzzled as she stepped out onto the pavement.

"What are you guys doing out here?" she asked, reaching back into the car for her bag, swinging the strap across her shoulder, then closing the door and locking it up. "You look cold, why aren't you inside?"

Declan exchanged a look with Liam.

He nodded and said, "I'm just going to head in."

Paula made to follow him when Declan reached out and put a hand on her arm to stop her.

"Can we talk out here for a sec, before we go inside?"

The puzzlement on her face grew deeper, but she nodded. "Okay, what's up? Is this about the cabinets? Because I've worked through what you told me and have accepted our move-in date will probably be bumped back, *again*."

"No," he said, while Liam slipped into the house, closing the front door behind him. "Do you want to go sit down on the porch?"

Paula's expression changed from puzzlement to concern. "Okay, now you're freaking me out. What's wrong?"

Declan sighed and rubbed a hand across the stubble on his chin. "Okay, I'm just going to cut to the chase and say it. Your Mom bought a turkey for Thanksgiving."

Her face cleared. "Okay. That's good, right? It sounds like a move in the right direction. Although, I'm thinking we'll need more than just the one."

Declan braced himself as he elaborated, "No, not a store-bought turkey. An *actual* turkey."

Paula's brow furrowed as she contemplated what he'd said. She shook her head as though her ears weren't working properly. "Wait. I'm not following, or at least I hope to hell I'm not. Are you telling me she bought a *live* turkey?"

Declan nodded. "Uh-huh. It's in the backyard, as we speak."

Paula's bag slipped from her shoulder and hit the ground with a thump. She blinked rapidly, processing the information.

Finally, she said, "What the hell is she planning to do with it?"

"That's the thing," he began, before she stepped around him and began speed-walking toward the house, dragging her bag behind her.

"Oh, hell," he said, following in her footsteps.

In a matter of seconds she'd rapidly ascended the porch stairs, yanked open the front door and charged into the house; all before he'd had a chance to catch up.

The shit, or turkey shit as Amber had stated, was about the hit the fan.

Declan eased the front door open, bracing himself for the assault of raised voices he was sure would meet his ears. Except, they didn't. He stepped across the threshold and paused, listening for … anything.

"Huh," he said, closing the door behind him when the only sound he could hear was the steady, low rumble of voices coming from deeper within the house.

At least he knew Paula hadn't murdered Donna: one small blessing in the sea of crazy.

He shucked his shoes from his feet and eased his coat from across his shoulders to hang in the front hall closet, reveling in the heat of the house seeping into his chilled bones. Finally, curiosity now well-piqued, he made his way down the hallway, following the rumble of voices coming from the kitchen.

"I get it," Paula was saying, standing next to the island, her arms folded across her chest. "You wanted to punish me and this was the best way you could think how to do it on short notice. It's blatantly obvious."

Donna pressed a hand over her heart, her face twisted in shock. "That's just ridiculous! I was simply attempting to do my part for Thanksgiving—"

"By getting a *live* turkey?" Amber, seated next to Liam at the kitchen table, interrupted. "Get real, Mom."

Declan, standing in the doorway, cleared his throat and Paula turned her head.

"Oh, good," she said, "you're just in time to hear my news. We're leaving and this time I mean it. New cat, new cat, new cat."

Liam caught Amber's eye and quietly mouthed, "New cat?"

She shook her head and muttered, "No idea."

Declan looked at Paula and said nothing. He was torn as to whether or not he should try and convince her, *again*, why they should stick it out until they could move into the new house. In light of recent events, he wasn't sure he'd be able to be very convincing.

"Oh, no," Donna argued, waving her arms around as she spoke. "Now you're just being foolish."

Paula turned back to her, her eyes wide. "*I'm* being foolish? Seriously?"

Amber and Liam exchanged a look, but stayed silent.

"I think the winner for foolish, nay *asinine*, behavior belongs to you, mother. You cemented your win by bringing a god-damned live turkey into the house!"

"It is not in the house," Donna countered, lifting her chin. "Your father is building it a lovely home as we speak."

"Oh, that's just *great*," Paula replied. "So, instead of a turkey for dinner, you've brought home a pet. Will you name it as well?"

Donna rolled her eyes. "Sarcasm doesn't make you witty, you know."

Paula threw her hands up in the air as she looked over at Declan. "You see what we're working with here?"

He walked further into the kitchen and looked at his mother-in-law. "Donna," he said, "can I ask a question?"

She smiled, sweetly. "Of course, dear, what is it?"

"What's the end game?"

All heads turned to stare at her, waiting. She frowned, not following.

"What do you mean, *end game*? Is that a sports metaphor for something? Because I don't watch sports games."

"Ooh, ooh!" Amber raised her hand insistently. "I know this one!"

Declan gave her an amused grin then refocused on Donna. "What I mean is, what's your end game with the turkey? *Is* it going to be a pet, *or*…?"

He left the implication hanging.

Everyone waited, again, for her reply.

"Oh, well…," she muttered, flustered, as she fluffed her hair then fidgeted with the hem of her blousy, orange cotton top. "I mean, I *did* say I got it to do my part for Thanksgiving, so…."

"So, what, exactly?" Paula pushed, refusing to let her leave her statement unfinished. "It's going to be a family mascot? Or is it destined for slaughter to grace our table for dinner?"

Donna flinched at the sharpness in her tone.

"And, that being said," Paula went on, starting to pace the kitchen floor. "Who exactly did you have in mind to slaughter it, hmm? 'Cause, I can't speak for anyone else here, but I'm sure as hell not doing it!"

Amber grimaced and went, "Ewww!" making Liam reach over and take her hand in his. She looked at him gratefully then said, "I'M not freakin' doing it either."

"Let's face it, no one is doing it," Declan declared, lifting his hands up like a traffic cop while he stared directly at his mother-in-law. "Right, Donna?"

She swallowed audibly then nodded.

"Right," Paula said, tightly. "So then the whole reason for this … *stunt*, was exactly as I said: to punish me for not taking over Thanksgiving as you'd tried to make me do."

"No," Donna began, then stopped abruptly when Paula pointed a sharp finger at her.

"YES. And, quite frankly, I am done. You and your turkey can gobble off into the sunset for all I care. I'm not cleaning up your mess. We're leaving."

"But your house isn't ready yet!" Donna insisted.

"We'll find somewhere else," Paula declared. "Bonnie keeps on insisting we can live there, maybe we'll take her up on it. Or maybe we'll just set up camp at my office if we have to."

Declan, wincing at the idea of those options, looked over at Amber with wide, desperate eyes.

"If Paula goes, so do I!" she announced, standing up and pushing her chair back with a firm hand.

Declan suppressed a groan. Okay, maybe he should have thought it through before he'd sent her his pleading look.

"Oh, for goodness sake!" Donna groused, facing her youngest. "That's ridiculous! Where would you go?"

"I don't know," Amber blathered, walking around the table to stand next to Paula. "Maybe to Jaime and Trent's. Or … Liam's!"

All focus shifted to Liam and he stared at them with wide eyes, startled by her statement. Declan felt a tremor of laughter building in his chest at the expression on his brother's face and had to cough to cover it up.

Donna stamped her foot. "Okay, okay, everyone just calm down!"

Amber grasped Paula's hand in a show of solidarity and Paula softened slightly. While her sister was being completely silly - she wasn't about to move in with Jaimie and her family, nor with Liam - she still greatly appreciated the gesture.

"No one is going anywhere," Donna insisted. "And, *perhaps*, I missed the mark with the turkey and I should find another way to do my part for our Thanksgiving gathering."

"So, what *are* you going to do with it?" Amber challenged, still holding Paula's hand like she had when they were children.

"Yeah," Paula agreed. "It can't stay here. You don't know how to take care of a turkey."

Donna waved her hands dismissively. "That's none of your concern. As you pointed out, it's *my* mess. I'll take care of it."

"Which means *Dad* will have to take care of it," Amber whispered, at Paula.

Donna gave herself a little shake, not unlike a dog, and made flicking motions around herself with her hands.

Liam gave Declan a puzzled look, and when he shrugged and said, "Clearing her aura", he clenched his jaw to keep from laughing. This family was too much.

"Okay," Donna exhaled, satisfied her aura was sufficiently cleansed. "I'm going to check on your father. There's leftovers in the fridge."

The four of them watched her flounce out of the house via the backdoor then Paula shook her head and said, "Oy."

Amber went back around the table to sit next to Liam. "Yeah. Either Dad has to re-home that bird, or we've got a new pet. And I'm guessing the neighbors won't be very happy about that. It's pretty, don't get me wrong, but still."

"Sure you don't want to leave?" Paula asked Declan. "The couch in my office is pretty comfortable and we have a kitchenette."

He smiled and reached out to pull her into a hug. "We're almost at the finish line, we can make it."

"*If* that damned line stops would just stop moving," she clarified.

"It will," he assured her, before turning to Liam and pointing a finger back and forth between him and Amber. "So, what's going on here?"

Amber blushed and nudged Liam with her shoulder. "I thought you were going to tell him."

"I was," he confirmed. "But this whole turkey thing got in the way."

"Tell me what?" Declan reached out for a chair at the table, sat down and pulled Paula with him to sit on his lap. "You two an official item now?"

Liam nodded. "Yup."

"Cool," he said.

Amber gave Paula a wide-eyed look.

Paula snickered at the incredulous expression on her sister's face. She was new to the Dempsey way of communicating; so vastly different and straight forward than what they'd grown up experiencing.

"Trust me," she said, smiling. "It seems odd now, this Dempsey communication, but soon you'll find it wonderfully refreshing. No agenda, just the straight forward goods."

Liam and Declan shared a puzzled look.

Paula chuckled and patted Declan's hand.

Amber followed her lead and did the same to Liam.

"So, whatever you two are talking about," Declan said, meeting Paula's eye, "I'm going to assume it's a compliment?"

She gave him a quick kiss. "Absolutely."

"Good by me," he stated, then turned to Liam. "You?"

He nodded, just as he'd done when Declan has asked if he and Amber were together. "Yup."

Amber grinned at her sister and patted Liam's hand again. "Straight forward goods."

Chapter 15

"Easy does it, now," Douglas coached, while he grasped one corner of the Horn of Plenty; completely finished and ready to be displayed in the yard. "On the count of three. One, two, THREE!"

Declan and Liam, each clutching a corner, hoisted the wooden work-of-art off the workshop table in Douglas' garage in unison with his count.

"Jeezus," Liam breathed, his biceps straining against the fabric of his shirt beneath his jacket. "This thing weighs a tone. What the hell is it made of, Doug?"

"Reclaimed oak," he sputtered, setting his end on the garage floor while they did the same.

Declan stretched his back then shook his head at the carving. "There's gotta be an easier way to get this thing into the yard than carrying it."

Liam glanced around the shop. "Do you have a dolly, Doug?"

"Yes!" His face lit up. "Of course, good thinking. Keep it steady while I find it."

Declan held onto the carving as instructed while Douglas began moving things around in search of the dolly.

"This is quite the piece," Liam complimented, admiring the details on the Horn of Plenty.

Declan nodded in agreement. "It looks 3-D."

What had started as a raw slab of wood, was now an intricately carved masterpiece. The horn itself was beautifully sculpted: all golden curves, the funnel ridges smooth to the touch after hours of sanding then painted with precision to create texture and shadow.

The 'food' was just as impressive. There were pumpkins; both large and small, some orange, some striped white and green, and others almost red, that looked as though they were spilling from the Horn's open end. Filling in the spaces between the pumpkins were yellow and green zucchini, and their relative the purple squash,; all meticulously hewn and painted, so lifelike it was hard to believe they were made of wood.

"Ah-ha!" Douglas exclaimed, pulling a forest green, upright dolly from behind a stack of wood.

"Seriously," Liam continued, while Douglas wheeled the dolly across the shop floor. "You could make money doing this for other people."

He chuckled and set the dolly next to the carving.

"I'm not kidding," Liam insisted. "I have clients who would pay good money to be able to add a one-of-a-kind, hand-carved piece of art like this to their landscaping."

Douglas pointed at the bottom of the Horn. "You boys each lift an end and I'll slide the dolly underneath. Then, while I wheel it out, you can watch the sides and hold it steady as we take it into the yard. Put your gloves on first, there's a bite in that air."

Liam looked at Declan for guidance. Clearly, Douglas had heard him, but the way he was acting you'd never know it.

Declan smiled and shrugged his shoulders. While his father-in-law was one of the most easygoing people he'd met, he also wouldn't be pushed into anything he didn't want to do. He didn't offer a fight, just carried on in the direction he'd set for himself. It was a trait that had served him well, if his solid business success was any sort of gauge by which to measure.

"Right," Declan said, pulling his gloves from his coat pocket and slipping them on, indirectly offering Liam a direction to follow. "You lead the way. It's your piece, you know what's best for it."

Liam got the message and nodded. "Lead on, Doug."

Jaimie placed Hazel on her change-mat and handed her a plush, butterfly shaped toy with a mirror in the center. Her daughter grinned for a moment at her reflection then stuffed one of the butterfly's wings into her mouth. Jaimie chuckled while Paula spoke into her ear via the headset she had connected to her phone: the only way to be able to talk and get anything done at the same time.

"So, we're still waiting," Paula was saying, from her desk at her office, "and Vince is trying to pull some fast strings to get the proper cabinets exchanged for the ones they dropped off."

"How long has it been since they dropped them off?" Jaimie asked, finishing up with Hazel and grabbing a sani-wipe for her hands.

"Four days."

"Are they nice?"

"What, the cabinets?"

"Yeah."

"I suppose so. Why?"

Jaimie lifted Hazel from the mat and stood up, nestling her against her hip as she exited the bedroom. "Well, if you like them, maybe you could just keep them."

Paula laughed, while the sound of her fingers tapping swiftly on her keyboard echoed behind her chortles.

"What?" Jaimie insisted, carrying Hazel into the kitchen for a snack. "At least this way they'd get installed and you could get into the house."

"That's ridiculous and you know it," Paula stated, still smirking as she opened a document on her desktop. "They belong to someone else and, besides, they're completely the wrong color and style, so they wouldn't fit anyway."

"Ah-ha, but you thought about it," Jaimie teased, while setting Hazel in her highchair and clipping the safety belt around her tiny waist.

Hazel echoed, "Ah-ha!" in a perfect imitation then picked up the baby spoon and cup on the tray and started banging them to hear the noise.

Jaimie grinned and went to retrieve the snack from the fridge.

Paula winced when the spoon and cup cacophony hammered through Jaimie's headset and into her own. "Is Hazel getting ready to audition for *Stomp*?"

Jaimie laughed. "It's snack time, so she's keeping busy while I get her applesauce."

"Snack time," Paula approved, stopping typing. "Nice. I should think about doing the same."

"Is Erin out of the office?"

"Yeah, she started getting a cold, so I told her to take the day. She's been working like a demon, getting everything arranged for our biggest client. She deserves the break, not to mention I cannot afford to catch it."

Jaimie retrieved the applesauce from the fridge. "And how are things at Mom and Dad's?"

"Tense. Mom and I are basically keeping out of each other's way and, meanwhile, I'm starting to feel like a real bitch."

"What? Why?" Jaimie pulled up a chair next to Hazel in her highchair and sat down.

Paula sighed. "It's still her house, after all. Who am I to dictate to her?"

"You did nothing but tell the truth," Jaimie insisted, offering a spoonful of applesauce to Hazel. "That's not dictating, that's pointing out much needed reason."

"I suppose, but—"

"But, nothing," Jaimie cut her off. "I'm having déjà vu. You're falling back into your old patterns because you've been there too long."

"What patterns?" Paula asked, picking up her coffee cup then rising from her chair to walk over to the kitchenette.

"You did the same thing when we were kids," Jaimie stated, continuing to feed Hazel. "You'd get roped into stuff because of Mom's ability to push your buttons, *then* you'd tell it like it is while straightening out whatever blunder she'd created, *then* you'd end up feeling guilty and think you'd overstepped when what you'd actually done was the complete opposite and saved her ass from the repercussions of her actions. Face it, Mom would have been screwed without you."

Paula picked up the carafe on the countertop and poured coffee into her cup. She was without words. She'd had no idea just how acutely aware Jaimie had been of what was going on while they were kids.

"And now, here you are doing it again," she said, feeding the last of the applesauce to Hazel.

"I know, but—"

"But nothing. Seriously, you need to stop it right now. Things have managed to get done in that house since you moved out, you don't need to pick up where you left off and get stuck back in old habits. Stick to your guns and don't be roped in. Declan is handling things, let him. We'll have a nice Thanksgiving, without a live turkey in attendance, and Mom will see that she has to stop guilting you into being her cleanup crew."

Paula sipped her coffee while her sister's words sunk in.

"Okay?" she pressed, standing up and walking over to a kitchen drawer for a clean cloth.

"Okay," Paula finally agreed.

"Good. Now, speaking of which, what's happening with the turkey?"

Paula carried her mug back to her desk and sat down. "It goes tomorrow. Dad found a family with an acreage who are thrilled to be gifted a turkey as a pet."

"Seriously?" Jaimie wet the cloth with warm water from the tap then took it back to the highchair and set to work wiping her daughter's face and hands.

"Absolutely. One of his regulars at work hooked him up with these people and everyone is happy. Apparently, they have some chickens, a goat, dogs, the works. A turkey will fit right into the mix."

"Wow, that's something," she said, tossing the cloth into the sink then releasing Hazel from her chair and hoisting her up onto her hip. "And you're sure they're not just going to slaughter it for Thanksgiving?"

Paula grimaced. Against her better judgment, over the past few days, she'd developed a protectiveness toward the bird.

"Hello? Paula, are you still there?" Jaimie asked, while she carried Hazel into the family room.

"Yes, I am, and no, they're not going to slaughter him. You should see him, for a turkey he's gorgeous. He has a huge white and black feather plume, definitely show quality, not table food. Not to mention, the people taking him are vegetarians, so they really do want Ernie as a pet."

Jaimie chuckled and set Hazel into her ExerSaucer to play. "Pardon me? Did you just say 'Ernie'? As in your named it?"

Paula winced. Damn it. Now she'd never hear the end of it.

"Fine," she admitted. "I may have started referring to him as Ernie, but it's all Amber's fault."

"Fantastic. Ernie the turkey."

Paula snickered and sipped her coffee.

"Anyway, listen, I gotta run," Jaimie said. "But make sure you remember what I said, okay? You don't need to clean up after Mom. Ever since you moved out, Dad's been taking care of it. Let him continue."

Paula nodded, even though her sister couldn't see her. "I know, you're right."

"Good, remember that as well," she teased. "Talk to you later. Love you."

"You, too, bye."

Paula disconnected the call then gazed out the window next to her desk, the skies above overcast, and drank the last of her coffee. She was going to need the caffeine kick to get her through the rest of the day, doing the work of two on her own.

"Alright, Mrs. Dempsey," she instructed herself, while placing her cup on the desk and returning to the work on her computer. "Time waits for no man, or woman."

Amber snuggled up to Liam on the sofa in the sunroom and sighed contentedly. The contrast between the darkness outside the windows and the soft, intimate light inside made her feel as though they were the only two people in the world. Bliss.

"Happy?" Liam asked, running his fingers through her dark hair.

"Very," she told him, looking into his eyes.

He nodded, understanding exactly how she felt. "You really are something else, you know that?"

She grinned and leaned in closer to give him a long, deep kiss.

When they came up for air, he said, "Good god, girl, you're going to turn me inside out," making her chuckle and ask, "And that's a good thing?"

"A very good thing," he agreed.

It was her turn to nod, while she revealed, "Then you should know I feel the same way."

Liam frowned and sat upright, not the reaction Amber was expecting.

"What?" she asked. "What's wrong?"

He sniffed the air. "Do you smell that?"

"Oh, god," she lamented. "Is this a gross guy joke?"

"What? No," he said, giving her a peculiar look. "What kind of guys have you been hanging out with?"

Amber shrugged and her cheeks flushed. It did sound like she'd been associating with less than desirable men.

"Anyway," he said, moving things along, "you seriously can't smell that?"

Amber inhaled deeply then nodded. "Okay, yeah. Smells like someone in the neighborhood is using their fire pit."

"Okay, fair enough," he began, before being cut off by Donna's shrill shriek from the other side of the house, calling, "AMBERRR!"

"Jeez!" she yelped, startled by her mother's voice. "What the hell?"

The sound of rapidly approaching footsteps thundered down the hall and Donna careened into the dining room, her eyes wide like saucers.

"Quickly! Quickly!" she insisted, bolting past the table and chairs before charging into the sunroom. "The Horn of Plenty's on fire!"

Liam and Amber leaped up from the sofa, nearly bowling Donna over as they rushed by her.

"Goodness!" she bleated, grabbing hold of the sofa to regain her balance. "You almost flattened me!"

"Sorry!" Liam called, moving at speed through the dining room toward the front of the house.

When he reached the foyer, he hauled open the front door then stopped in his tracks at the threshold.

Amber, close on his heels, nearly smacked into him from behind.

"What are you doing?" she asked, before peering around him to see why he'd remained in the doorway instead of continuing outside.

Liam just stared, speechless.

Amber, however, did not.

"Holy shit!" she exclaimed, at the sight before them.

The Horn of Plenty was engulfed in flames, the tops of them reaching at least eight feet high, creating a blaze that threatened to spread at any moment.

"What *is* it with you people and fire?" Liam remarked, stepping out onto the porch while the sound of sirens could be heard in the distance.

Douglas appeared around the corner of the garage, his cheeks marked with black soot.

"It's okay," he said, wearily. "I've told the neighbors not to worry, I'm keeping it contained and I've called the fire department. They're on their way."

"Oh, Daddy," Amber sympathized, waving him over when she saw the expression on his face. He looked so downcast, her heart clutched. "Your lovely Horn of Plenty."

Liam nodded. "I'm really sorry, Doug. It was a thing of beauty."

Douglas shrugged then squared his shoulders. "Nothing we can do about it now. At least we got some photos of it, that's a blessing."

Liam patted him on the back, impressed by his inclination to rally. It had been fun, that morning, working with him and Declan to get it all set up, then taking photos with it to commemorate the moment. Who knew those photos would end up being the only evidence it had ever existed.

Douglas looked past them at the house. "Where's your mother?"

"Inside," Amber said. "I don't think she can face it."

He nodded while the sirens grew closer and a fire truck rounded the corner at the top of the street. "Time to face the music," he said, descending the porch steps to meet the crew as they pulled their vehicle up in front of the house.

Just a few blocks from her parent's house, Paula drove her car away from the curb to resume course after pulling over to let a firetruck, sirens blaring, speed past. She hoped, wherever it was headed, everyone was okay.

She approached her turn and signaled right, only to have her jaw drop when she rounded the corner and looked further up the street. The firetruck that had shot past her was in front of her parent's house.

"You're gotta be kidding me," she said, driving further down the street until she had no choice but to pull up, *again*, in front of a neighbor's house because, *again*, it was unsafe to park in her usual spot on her parent's driveway.

She got out of the car, the last light of the flames reflecting off the firetruck, and stared: dumbstruck. It looked like they'd had a huge bonfire that had gotten out of control, which begged the question: why on Earth were they having a bonfire on the front lawn in mid-November?

"Ohmygod, Paula!" Amber called, waving her hand high in the air as she and Liam dashed down the porch steps, sidled up next to the house to keep out of the way, then jogged down the far-side of the driveway to meet her at the curb.

"What the hell happened?" Paula demanded, the moment they stood in front of her.

"Dad's Horn of Plenty caught on fire," Amber told her.

"What? Are you kidding me? Someone set it on fire?"

"No, no." Both she and Liam shook their heads in unison. "It *caught* fire."

It was Paula's turn to shake her head as she tried to understand. "How?"

Amber leaned in, as though she was sharing a shameful secret. "Dad decided to light it up, so that everyone could still see it in the evening, and…."

"Oh, god, Do *not* tell me he used faulty lights."

Liam nodded, while Amber shrugged her shoulders.

Paula groaned and hung her head.

"And," Amber added, "apparently, Dad now thinks there's also a good chance he wasn't paying close enough attention when he was attaching them and the nails damaged and frayed the cord around the wiring."

"The *already faulty* wiring," Paula clarified.

Amber nodded.

"And now here we are with the fire department trying to put out something akin to an out-of-control bonfire on the front lawn," Paula stated. "Jeezus, if their insurance company gets the full story…."

"Oh, shit," Liam said, looking past her.

Amber followed his gaze. "Crap."

Paula turned around to see the Channel Five van driving down the street directly toward them.

"Oh, bloody hell," she bitched. "This is all we need."

"What do you want to do?" Liam asked, ready to take action.

"Get both Mom and Dad into the house," Paula instructed. "And us, too, for that matter. If they want to try and make this into a story, we're not going have any part of it."

"But what about the neighbors?" Amber asked.

"I don't give a rat's ass about the neighbors," she stated, scanning for their parents in the yard. "They can say whatever the hell they want, but those vultures aren't getting anything from any of us. Maybe, if we're lucky, it will end up a puff-piece because we're not around to give it any weight."

"There's Dad!" Amber pointed toward the porch. "And Mom's with him."

"Perfect," Paula said, while the three of them scooted along the path toward the house. "Let's work as a team and haul them inside before they can argue. Mom's already noticed the news van, you can tell by her face, we need to stop her doing anything stupid."

Amber and Liam linked arms and barreled up the porch steps, Paula in behind in case there was any chance one of them got away. They grabbed both Douglas and Donna by their arms and did as Paula had instructed: frog-marched them toward the front door.

"Hey!" Douglas barked, the sudden momentum taking him off guard as he found himself moving at speed toward the house.

"What on Earth?" Donna exclaimed, when Liam practically lifted her off her feet.

"Don't fight it," Paula called out, while they all motored as a unit through the front door and into the house. "I'll explain once we're out of sight."

It had taken some serious persuasion, but Paula had finally gotten through to her mother that speaking to the press was a very bad idea. Donna had tried wheedling, but Paula had refused her so-called reasoning and both Amber and Liam had backed her up. Outnumbered, Donna had finally flounced over to the family room windows to watch the action outside from behind semi-closed blinds.

"They must be almost done getting things under control out there," Paula remarked, while she and Amber and Liam all sat at the kitchen table, the window curtains drawn, drinking hot chocolate as they waited for the all clear from Douglas.

"It looks like the Channel Five van is leaving," Donna announced, as she came into the kitchen. "I saw them talking to the fire department, but that was it."

"No neighbors?" Amber asked.

Donna shook her head.

"Well, that's good news," Paula said. "Maybe it'll barely get a mention in tonight's lineup."

"Or, even better," Liam offered, "dropped altogether."

"I *still* say I could have cleared things up quickly if you'd let me speak to them and they would have realized there wasn't any story to be told," Donna huffed, smoothing the wrinkles from her green and black paisley print blouse.

"They found that out just fine without your *help*," Paula stated, firmly.

"Mmm," Donna muttered, then cocked her head and stared at Liam. "Did *these two* make you do what you did when you all ambushed me and Douglas and dragged us into the house?"

Liam's eyes widened as he drank from his mug. He wanted nothing more than to be out of the discussion. There was no way he was offering any insight, no matter what he knew.

Paula stepped in, saving him from comment. "It doesn't matter now. What's done is done."

He gave her a grateful look just as Douglas pushed open the backdoor and strode into the kitchen.

"So?' Donna asked, her face so eager it was almost comical.

Amber called her out on it. "God, Mom. Look at you. We've only been in here for, like, a half-hour. It's not like we've been cut off from the outside world."

Paula snickered. Her sister had nailed it.

Donna frowned. "I *know* that. I was just concerned about … the turkey."

"Uh-huh," Amber said. "Sure."

"Ernie's fine," Douglas assured them, pulling his gloves from his hands and stuffing them into his jacket pocket. "He didn't even realize what was going on."

"Well, that's a relief," Donna stated, refusing to budge from her stance.

Paula had pity on her, put down her mug of hot chocolate and posed the question she knew her mother was dying to ask. "How do things look in the front yard?"

Donna's face brightened while she waited for his answer.

"Pretty much what you'd expect," he replied, taking off his jacket and hanging it on a hook on the wall. "When wood is that dry it burns fast. But it's all out now, so no fear of accidentally causing more damage. We'll deal with the cleanup in the morning."

Amber, Liam and Paula all exchanged looks, unsure of what to say. Thankfully, the front door opened and Declan called out, "Pizza delivery!"

"I didn't order pizza," Donna said, just before Declan rounded the corner, four large cardboard pizza boxes in hand.

"I heard there was some excitement around here today," he said, winking at Paula. "So, I figured pizza and beer would be a good first step toward putting it behind us."

Douglas' shoulders straightened from their slump and he grinned at his son-in-law. "You know, that sounds perfect. Just perfect."

Declan put the boxes on the island and said, "Get 'em while they're hot," then pointed at Liam and added, "Want to help me bring in the beer?"

Needing no further invitation, Liam got up to follow him out of the room.

"I've got the plates," Amber announced, standing up and striding across the kitchen to the cupboard.

"I'll get napkins and glasses," Donna stated.

"And I'll give *you* a hug, my lovely daughter," Douglas said, quietly, reaching out to embrace Paula. "Thanks for bringing in the cavalry in your old Dad's time of need."

Paula kissed him on the cheek just as Sylvester rounded the doorway, his nose twitching at the food smells. "Anytime. Now go get your pizza before the cat tries to convince Amber to give him your share."

He gave her another gentle squeeze then did as he was told.

Chapter 16

Paula cupped her coffee mug between her hands and stared out her bedroom window to the yard below. It wasn't a pretty sight. The artwork that had been the Horn of Plenty was now a heap of ugly black soot and charred wood, and the grass beneath it had taken a serious beating. At this rate, it was looking more and more like her parents were going to have to re-seed the entire lawn in the Spring.

"A small price to pay," she mumbled, considering how much worse it could have been. With the intensity that the Horn had burned - not surprising, considering it had been reclaimed wood - all it would have taken was a brisk breeze to turn it into a whole other animal.

Paula sipped her coffee and her thoughts shifted from bonfires on the lawn to the new house. They now had a new move-in date and it coincided with the sweet sixteen birthday party she'd been killing herself to arrange for Lanzo Bazzano's daughter.

Of course.

She sighed and let her shoulders relax. No use wasting energy on what she couldn't change. It would be fine, they'd bump their moving day back one more time. After two months instead of the originally planned two weeks, what did it matter?

She reached out and pressed her fingertips against the window pane, the glass cold to the touch, then lifted her gaze from the lawn to the surrounding low-lying mountains. Their tops were concealed by grey cloud and looked almost as though at any moment they could begin to….

"SNOW!" Amber bellowed, from her neighboring bedroom.

Paula watched as, sure enough, fluffy white flakes began falling in front of the glass, spiraling lazily downward toward the waiting Earth below.

The floor shook slightly as Amber charged out of her room, rapped sharply on Paula's door then flung it wide open.

"Did you see?" she demanded, breathlessly enthused, before beetling across the floor to stand beside Paula at the window. "Isn't it beautiful?"

Paula watched her press her nose against the glass in an attempt to see the ground below and had a flashback of her when she was just a little girl, doing the same thing, and it made her chuckle.

"I wonder if it's going to stick?"

"It's a bit early," Amber admitted. "It may just last today and we'll have to wait for more later."

Paula turned away from the window. "Have you checked the forecast?"

Amber whipped her phone out of the pocket of her purple robe and began tapping on the screen while Paula settled herself next to the cat on the bed's soft comforter.

"Okay, it says light snow this morning," she reported, reading from the screen. "Tapering off later this afternoon with a chance of more overnight."

"So, I guess we'll just have to wait and see." Paula tipped her mug to her mouth to drink the last of her coffee.

Amber pointed to the bed, just noticing the absence of her brother-in-law. "Where's Declan?"

"He had a callout at the crack of dawn."

"On a Saturday morning?"

Paula nodded. "It happens more than you'd think."

"That sucks." She reached out to stroke Sylvester's fur, he was snuggled deeply into the comforter where Declan would have been had he not vacated the bed.

Paula considered her statement. "I guess. I've gotten used to it."

Amber's eyes widened and she stopped petting the cat.

"What is it?" Paula cocked her head.

"Ernie. It's going to be cold."

"Oh, I'm sure Dad's already taking care of him," Paula assured her.

Amber nodded, her face relaxing. It was true, one thing they knew about their Dad, when he took on a project he left nothing to chance.

"So, what now?"

"I'm going to get a jump on things and dig out the shovels. You never know, it might turn out to be more than what's forecasted. A surprise blizzard!"

Paula watched her stride out of the room and grinned. Her sister's excitement was endearing and it was nice to have something positive going on. Maybe it was a sign they were finally turning a corner and by the time she and Declan left to the new house things would be flowing more easily.

She put her empty mug on the adjacent nightstand then began settling back into her pillow to watch the snow falling on the other side of the window. It really was pretty. And soothing. And….

"Hey!" Amber barked, poking her head around the door.

"WHAT?" Paula bellowed back, her pulse racing from the sudden intrusion.

Amber frowned. "Why are you yelling?"

"I'm not," she said, her hand pressed against her yellow flannel pajama top over her heart. "You startled me, it was a reflex."

"Oh. Well, sorry, but don't get too comfy," Amber ordered. "We may need all hands on deck if this gets any more intense."

She turned on her heel and disappeared from the doorway to pound down the staircase, calling out to anyone who could hear that the snow was falling.

Paula reached out to pet Sylvester while more childhood memories of her sister pushed to the forefront: in addition to the cute moments, snow days had often turned Amber from a happy-go-lucky little girl into a mini sergeant general.

Clearly, nothing had changed on that front.

"Remember the positive," Paula advised herself. "Remember the positive."

"Sweet Caroline, it's really coming down out there." Douglas stamped his snow-clad boots against the doormat and shook the hat he'd pulled off his head, scattering snowflakes like confetti.

Donna threw her hands up in exasperation. "Well, isn't that a fine kettle of fish. And I was planning a grocery run this morning."

Douglas removed his down-filled coat and hung it on a hook by the door. "Might want to reconsider that."

"Reconsider what?" Paula asked, walking into the kitchen.

"The grocery shopping agenda," Douglas told her. "The roads aren't looking very friendly at the moment."

"I'm starting to get things prepared, *early* you'll note, for Thanksgiving," Donna bragged, a self-congratulatory smile on her face.

Paula ignored her mother and picked up the coffee pot to pour herself another mug of the strong brew. She could almost hear Jaimie in her head, cheering her on for choosing not to be baited.

"How's Ernie holding up, Dad?"

"Good. Warm and cozy."

Paula smiled. He'd put together an amazing enclosure and roosting house made from recycled crates from his workshop - apparently, in his extensive research, he'd found out turkeys don't like feeling boxed in, so the slats in the crates alleviated that problem - and concrete blocks to set them on because turkeys feel safe if they can roost up high, and he'd been correct on all counts. The turkey was a contented bird, not a care in the world.

"I think I did it a favor, in the long run," Donna offered, lifting her chin.

Choose to ignore, Paula silently reminded herself while asking her Dad, "Are the people coming today to pick it up?"

"That's the plan, but with the weather going as it is…." he began, before the backdoor swung open with a flourish, nearly knocking him sideways. "Whoa! Watch it there!" he yelped, steadying himself.

"Wow! Can you believe it?" Amber gushed, completely oblivious to the fact she'd come close to flattening her father. "We may have to think about breaking out Big Blue, if this keeps up."

Donna gasped, "No!", then darted out of the kitchen toward the living room to get a better look at the front street.

"Oh, come on," Paula said, after taking a sip of her coffee. "It can't be Big Blue weather yet."

They were, of course, referring to the ancient snow blower than lived in the garage. It had managed to survive for decades - thanks to Douglas' steadfast upkeep - and only when the weather was truly intense was it brought out to perform snow removal magic.

Amber looked at their father. "Dad?"

Paula continued to drink her coffee, but also watched her father for his verdict. He was always the final authority when it came to Big Blue.

Douglas cleared his throat and nodded. "If it continues like this for much longer, Blue will have to make an early appearance this year. And, to finish what I was telling Paula, Ernie may be here a bit longer."

Amber clapped her hands and grinned, triumphant.

Paula chuckled at her sister's glee and left the room to check her phone for messages from Declan.

"Jeez," Declan muttered, when the wheels of his car spun yet again as he pulled away from a stop sign.

His windshield wipers were working steadily as the snow fell thickly and without hesitation, sticking wetly to his windscreen. The weather had moved in so fast, he'd been shocked to leave his client's office and step out into the near blizzard.

"Nearly there," he counselled, creeping along Mountain Pine Lane toward home. Or, rather, his in-law's house. God, it was getting harder to remember to separate the two.

His cellphone rang and Declan pressed the button on his console to connect the call. "Hello?"

"Where are you? Are you okay?" his mother's voice demanded, through the car speakers.

"Of course, I'm fine." He reached to turn up the heat.

"Then why weren't you answering your phone? I called and called and it kept going to voicemail."

"Yeah, sorry about that. I didn't realize it was turned off until I was in the car."

"You're driving?" Bonnie's voice took on a shrill note of alarm. "It's nearly a blizzard out there! Why are you driving?"

"I had a callout," Declan told her, turning on his right signal light.

"Oh, well, then please be careful," she instructed.

"I will, I'm almost back at Doug and Donna's." The phone beeped, signaling another call, and Declan said, "Listen, Mom, I have another call. Can I phone you back?"

"Of course. Let me know you made it back safely to the house."

"I will." He turned the wheel and the car drifted slowly around the corner onto Mountain Pine Crescent.

"Okay, love you," she said, signing off.

"You, too," he said, pressing the button on his steering wheel to hang up and connect the next incoming call. "Hello?"

"Oh, thank goodness." Paula's voice rang through the speakers. "Where are you?"

"Just up the street," he replied. "You got my message, right, about the sound being off on my phone?"

"Yeah, thanks," she said. "I'm just glad you're okay and not in a ditch somewhere."

Declan grinned. "No worries. I have all-wheel drive, remember. Not to mention the roads are practically deserted and I've been moving at the speed of a turtle."

"I was going to go into the office today, but now—"

"I wouldn't. It's like an ice rink out here."

Paula exhaled in frustration. She already knew it was true, but it still irked her. Darn weather. "Okay, I'll meet you out front."

Declan drove the car toward the top of the crescent. "You don't need to. It's really coming down, stay inside and—"

"Oh, believe me," she said, cutting him off. "I've been stuck in this house all morning without a break, I *need* to."

"See you in a sec."

Paula hung up, tucked her phone into her jacket pocket and watched for his car from the family room window. The moment he pulled into the driveway she darted over to the front door, whipped it open and stepped out onto the porch. She closed the door behind her and wrapped her arms around herself in her coat, smiling in welcome as he got out of the vehicle and approached the house.

"Good thing the callout wasn't later in the day or you'd never have been able to go," she commented, while he waded through the snow accumulated on the front path.

"The roads are crap," he told her, climbing the porch steps. "I'm going to put my stuff inside and start shoveling out here."

'You should get something to eat first," she urged, reaching out to give him a hug.

He wrapped his arms around her and squeezed her back. "Okay, first food, then shoveling. Oh, and I need to text my Mom to let her know I made it back safely."

"On a positive note," she offered, teasingly, "chances are good there won't be any more lawn fires for a while."

Declan laughed and released her. He looked over to where the Horn of Plenty had stood in the yard. In the past hour, the charred remains had been covered in a blanket of white. If they hadn't known what had happened, no one would have been the wiser.

"How's the turkey doing in all of this?"

Paula tucked her hands into her coat pockets. "Good. Dad's got him all taken care of."

The front door opened and Amber stepped out, her eyes alive with excitement. "Can you believe this? Looks like we're going to have a white Thanksgiving as well as Christmas."

"I'm going to get something to eat," Declan said, moving toward the house.

"After you're done, come out and grab a shovel," Amber ordered, then tromped down the steps in knee-high heavily treaded snow boots.

Declan raised an eyebrow at Paula.

She smirked. "Drill sergeant Amber takes her job seriously."

"I'm starting to understand why you wanted a break from inside the house."

"Between her barking orders and my mother lamenting about how the weather has interfered with her supposed plans to get a jump on Thanksgiving prep, I've been just trying to lay low."

Declan chuckled and took her hand. "We'll go in together and stay together. No man, or woman left behind."

Paula grinned. "Copy that. Lead on."

The loud rumble of - what sounded like - a helicopter startled Declan awake. He'd retired to the bedroom for a mid-afternoon nap to catch up on sleep he'd lost from his morning callout and now he was groggy and confused, trying to match the sound to anything familiar. He blinked and peered into the darkened bedroom, trying to get his bearings.

Next to him on the bed, Paula stirred, and he shifted toward her, hoping she could shed some light on the situation. "Paula? Do you hear that?"

"Hmm?" she murmured, still half-asleep.

"That sound," Declan clarified, as the noise got louder. "Do you hear it? What the hell is it?"

The roar from outside gentle rattled the windows and Paula finally woke up. She listened, then groaned and pulled her pillow over her head.

"What? What's going on?" Declan pressed.

"Big Blue," she said, from beneath the pillow.

Declan frowned, not following. "What? Beg Lou? What does that mean?"

Paula pushed the pillow from her face and sat up. "Big Blue. I said, Big Blue."

He looked at her, blankly. "Okay, but that really doesn't make it any more clear."

"The snow blower. Big Blue, the snow blower."

Comprehension dawned as Declan recalled the back and forth conversation from earlier that afternoon about whether or not Big Blue was going to be called into action. It had seemed to go on forever.

"Oh, okay, but why the hell is your Dad starting it up now? We already shoveled."

"Why do these people do anything when they do?" Paula countered, yawning and placing her pillow behind her head. "Go look outside. Maybe that will explain things."

He got out of the bed and crossed the room to the window then pulled open the drapes.

"Well?"

"Wow," he exhaled. "Okay, so it definitely snowed more."

"Seriously?" Paula climbed out of the bed.

"Oh, yeah," he said, nodding. "There's gotta be another foot out there."

Paula didn't bother responding further as her words would have been drowned out by the sound of Big Blue roaring out of the garage and onto the driveway below. She and Declan watched as Douglas came into view behind the monstrous machine, looking more like he was hanging onto it for dear life as opposed to guiding it.

Next came Donna, hauling a large object that seemed to be threatening to pull her over as she slipped and slid on the freshly fallen snow.

"Is that…." Declan began, when Blue was far enough away for him to be heard.

"Yup," Paula agreed, as her mother set a lifelike, six foot tall Santa Claus on the driveway.

"Are they having a yard sale in a snowstorm?"

Paula laughed at the idea and turned away from the window. "No."

"So, what then?"

"They're decorating the house," she said, returning to bed and tucking herself under the covers.

"For what?" he asked, just as Amber emerged from the garage carrying a glittery red and green Christmas tree ornament the size of a large footstool. "Christmas? Get outta here!"

Paula chuckled and snuggled further into the comforter. The incredulous tone in his voice was comical.

Declan left the window to join her back in bed, shaking his head while he shifted the cat out of his spot. "Why are they decorating so early? What about Thanksgiving? Is it because of what happened to the Horn of Plenty?"

Paula watched Sylvester reluctantly move to the bottom of the bed and curl himself into a ball. "They always decorate for the holidays at Thanksgiving. I'm sure I've mentioned it at one point, haven't I?"

Declan shook his head, again, then shrugged. "I don't know, maybe. Either way, you're telling me that every year they start decorating the house for Christmas before Thanksgiving even fully arrives? Seriously, every year?"

"Yup. Ever since I was a kid. They're probably overjoyed this year is an early snow year, makes it feel more authentic."

"Do they decorate for Thanksgiving every year, too, or is that a new thing this year?"

"Oh, no. They do that every year, too."

Declan finally laughed. "Impressive."

"Or crazy," Paula offered, before the sound of Big Blue cutting another swath through the snow drowned out further comment.

Chapter 17

Tammy used a black, dry erase marker to write *apple pie and pumpkin pie* next to Donna's name on the whiteboard set up in Declan's office.

"Okay, check," she said. "Your mother-in-law will make the pies for dessert."

"Perfect, shouldn't be too hard to get her to do that," Declan commented, a wry grin on his face.

"And," she continued, "your Mom is doing not one, not two, but three types of potatoes, 'cause Bonnie is a boss and knows how to do things right!"

Declan read the words *mashed*, *scalloped* and *sweet* next to his mother's name on the board. God, while he more than appreciated her going the extra mile, it had not been fun when Donna hadn't been able to resist a dig at Paula: reminding her about when she'd taken such offence when he'd been asked about potato suggestions. Clearly, Donna had declared, Bonnie's willingness to tackle all the potato choices made it glaring obvious *she'd* been correct in stating that the Irish knew potatoes and *Paula* had just been being overly sensitive.

Declan had watched Paula's face twist in irritation and he'd wanted to demand of his mother-in-law, "Why? Why do you need to voice every damned thought in your head?"

But, he hadn't.

Instead, he'd taken his wife out for drink and a game of pool. A place for her to channel her annoyance. It had seemed to do the trick.

"You said Cian and Michael volunteered to bring a green bean casserole and cranberry sauce, right?" Tammy asked, unaware she'd broken Declan's train of thought.

"Uh-huh," he agreed, grateful she'd interrupted his spiraling thoughts. "And a Brussels sprouts dish."

She wrote *green bean casserole, cranberry sauce* and *Brussels sprouts* in her looping script beside Cian's and Michael's names on the board.

"And we managed to get Emmet to commit to bringing dinner rolls, which is a small miracle, and he said he'd bring pumpkin pie."

Tammy frowned and pointed at Donna's name. "Your mother-in-law is pies."

Declan nodded. "I know, I told him, so he said he'd bring brownies instead."

Her eyebrows lifted while she leaned toward the board and wrote the items next to Emmet's name on the board.

"Don't be too impressed," he told her. "They'll either be store bought, or he'll manage to convince some woman to make them for him."

"Still," she said, finishing writing *brownies*, "at least he's bringing something besides beer."

Declan lifted his hands in mock surrender. "True enough."

"And the main event is being brought by Angus and Linda," she stated, referring to the turkey.

"Yup and the stuffing and gravy."

"Wow," she said, shaking her head.

"Agreed. This time you can be impressed."

She started writing the additional information next to Angus' and Linda's names. "So, tell me again, *why* the turkey is being brought in instead of being cooked at Paula's parent's house?"

Declan ran his fingers through his hair and cleared his throat. "Because Donna doesn't think she can bring herself to cook a turkey after having one as a pet."

She snickered, still writing. "But she's okay to *eat* one?"

Declan chuckled. "Apparently."

"You don't buy it?"

"Let's just say, cooking meat isn't her strong suit," he offered, magnanimously.

"So, what about the turkey? Did the people show up to adopt it?"

"Not yet. The snow interfered with their intentions to come into town, so now they've said they'll come after Thanksgiving."

"Ah, gotchya." She pointed at the names with blank spaces beside them. "So, Liam and Trina, what are they bringing?"

Declan lifted an eyebrow while she gasped, "Oh!", and slapped a hand across her mouth. He started laughing at the look on her face.

"I cannot *believe* I did that! Can you imagine if Paula's sister had heard me? I don't know her, but being a woman, I'd bet she'd be livid."

Declan, still chuckling, picked up his phone and checked his list. "Liam and *Amber* are contributing a carrot dish and three cheese, mac and cheese."

"Ooh, sounds yummy." Tammy erased Trina's name and wrote *Amber* next to Liam.

"Wow, looks like I'm just in time," a woman's voice announced, from the doorway, startling both Declan and Tammy.

Tammy whipped her head around just as Declan said, "*Trina*, hey, how are you?"

She strode into the office and gestured to the board. "Pretty good, considering I'm just in time to watch myself being *literally* wiped out of the family."

Tammy blushed and put the cap back on the marker; any excuse to not make eye contact.

Declan cleared his throat. "Aww, come on, you know it's not like that."

"Isn't it?" she demanded, starting to pace. "Because, from over here, it sure looks like it."

Tammy bit her lip, feeling horribly out of place and yet, didn't want to leave Declan alone when Trina's behavior was so erratic.

"It's just a list," Declan placated. "Nothing more."

Trina gave a harsh laugh and stopped pacing. "Right. To *you*, maybe. But, to me, it says everything. It says not only have I been shoved out of the family I *thought* I was going to marry into, but I've already been replaced without a backward glance."

Declan looked at Tammy and said, softly, "It's okay, you can go back out to your desk."

She looked hesitantly from him to Trina, unsure.

He smiled. "It's fine. Really."

She nodded and skittered out of the office, avoiding getting too close to Trina, leaving the door wide open behind her just in case.

Trina released a large exhale and met Declan's eye. "Look, I'm sorry to bring this to your door, but no one else will acknowledge me."

He nodded then gestured to the couch. "Wanna sit down? Can I get you a coffee? Water?"

She softened her stance, relaxing her shoulders. "No, I'm good, thanks."

"Okay," he said, walking around to the other side of his desk to sit down in his chair. "So, what do you want?"

She walked over to the sofa and perched on an arm. "Truthfully? For Liam and I to be back together like nothing happened."

Declan smiled kindly. "Okay, let me rephrase that, what do you realistically want?"

She had the good grace to snicker.

"Seriously, Trina," he went on, "I get that you're upset and I think it's completely normal to want to get some sort of … *closure*, on things."

She bit her lip, her brow furrowed, and nodded. "I just want to know why."

"Why what?" he dared to ask.

"Why didn't he want me," she stated, then spat, "Why *her* instead of me?"

Oh boy, Declan thought, hearing the animosity in her voice.

"So, didn't Liam speak with you about this? I could have sworn he said you two had a talk and he explained how he was feeling," he said, hoping to reestablish calm.

"Yeah, yeah, we did. But I honestly still don't get it. What's so bloody special about *her* that makes her better than me?" She stood up and started to pace again. "Is it her hair? 'Cause I can fix that with a pair of scissors, fast. Give her a pixie cut like Paula's, then we'll see how Liam feels."

"Whoa," Declan warned, standing up and coming back around his desk. "That's too far, Trina."

She stopped pacing and looked him in the eye again. "Fine, maybe it is, but whatever. All I know is, I wasted part of my life on him and for what? To be tossed to the curb when someone new comes along? All that time and he turned out to be an unworthy ass."

"Fair enough," he acknowledged.

She pushed her hair back from her face and said, "So, since he's pretty much gone off the grid and your family's done the same, you can deliver a message to him for me."

"Absolutely," Declan agreed, hoping his lack of resistance would keep her rational.

"Tell him I've thought about everything and I don't forgive him and I never will. He's a selfish fucker and he and *Amber* deserve each other!"

Declan nodded. "Got it."

She stalked over to the doorway then paused and turned her head. "And don't worry, I won't touch your precious *sister-in-law*. She's already had way too much attention as it is."

"Thank you," he said.

"Whatever." She strode through the doorway and disappeared.

Declan released the breath he'd been holding when the sound of the exit door slamming let him know she'd fully gone.

"Holy crap!" Tammy bleated, as she ran into his office, her eyes round like saucers.

"Lunch," Declan replied, leaning on the edge of his desk. "If we're going to rehash this, we need food."

"Agreed, I'll grab the takeout menus."

She ran back to her desk, leaving Declan a moment to send a text to Liam.

"We need to talk."

Liam stepped across the threshold into *The Tipsy Pigeon* then blinked a few times while his eyes adjusted to the contrast between the late afternoon light outside and the dim lighting inside. Declan's ominous text earlier that afternoon had come as a surprise, he had joked that it sounded like a warning they were breaking up. Declan hadn't been amused, which was why he was here to meet him in person to get all the information.

"Li," Declan called, lifting a hand to indicate he was sitting at a booth near the back.

Liam nodded and walked through the pub, a fairly easy task at that time; nothing compared to the crush of people that filled the place after work hours and into the night.

"Hey," he said, sliding onto the bench style seat across the table from Declan. "Little early to start drinking, don't ya think?"

Declan lifted his mug of beer, took a drink and placed it back down on the table. "It's five o'clock somewhere and, besides, you may want one as well when I tell you who visited me earlier this afternoon."

"Okay, so tell me," he said, shucking his jacket from his shoulders and letting it slip behind him on the seat.

"Trina."

That got Liam's attention.

Declan nodded when his brother's eyebrows lifted in surprise. "Yeah, exactly."

Liam leaned forward, his face a picture of confusion. "Why would she visit you?"

"Okay, first I should clarify it was more of an ambush than a visit," Declan acknowledged. "And she was seriously wired."

Liam's face twisted from confusion to shock. "She was high?"

"What? No!" Declan barked, shaking his head. "I just meant she was all hyped up. And pissed off. Seriously pissed off. At you."

Liam sat back in his seat, digesting the information.

"Anyway, what matters is, I let her vent and that seemed to help."

Liam cleared his throat then asked, "About what? We settled everything."

"Yeah, well, apparently she's still holding a grudge, *go figure*."

Liam narrowed his eyes. "What the hell does that mean?"

"It means, I'm not surprised she's still a bit bent out of shape about what happened. You guys were together for a while, of course she's going to still be pissed."

"So, you're on her side?"

"Oh, for Christ's sake," Declan growled. "There are no sides here, Li. You're my brother, of course I support you. But I'm not blind and can see why Trina would still be upset about what happened."

Liam relaxed his shoulders and nodded. "Okay, fair enough."

"Go get a drink and I'll tell you the rest of what she said," Declan instructed.

"There's more?"

"Yeah, but as I said, I think letting her vent was a good thing and she won't be back again." He leaned forward and looked Liam in the eye. "And, even more importantly, I don't think you should share any of this with Amber. I'm not telling Paula, there's no point and it would just freak her out."

Liam slid out of the booth. "Sounds like I need that drink. I'll be right back."

Declan watched him walk over to the bar then couldn't help but smirk when unexpected amusement bubbled up in his chest. What was happening? It was bad enough having Paula's nutty family to contend with, now it seemed his was getting affected by association. First with *the incident* and now there were unhinged ex-girlfriends showing up without warning: was he next to fall down the proverbial rabbit hole? And, if so, should he resist?

Raucous laughter echoed through the house venting, causing Declan to startle awake in bed. Beside him Paula continued to sleep, muttering nonsensical words softly into her pillow. He blinked into the darkness then reached for his phone to check the time.

"Whoa," he whispered, when he read the screen. Ten minutes past two - in the morning. It seemed a bit early to start baking pies, didn't it?

Another bout of laughter reverberated through the floor from downstairs and Declan gently lifted the comforter and slipped out of the bed, careful not to jostle Paula from her slumber. He was fully awake now and curiously had gotten the best of him. May as well see what all the commotion was about.

Paula rolled over in bed and reached out for Declan. Nothing.

She moved her hand back and forth across the covers and still, nothing.

Finally, she gave in and opened her eyes to peer into the dark bedroom.

"Declan?"

Silence met her query. Not even Sylvester was around to answer her call.

Paula pulled herself upright and rubbed her eyes as she attempted to get her bearings. What time was it? She turned to look at the clock on the nightstand and her jaw nearly dropped. Four AM? That couldn't be right.

She leaned over to retrieve her cellphone from beside the clock when, in the exact same moment, the sound of voices rumbled through the ducting, adding to her confusion.

"What the hell?" she muttered, picking up the phone and turning it on.

Yup, there it was on the screen as well: four o'clock in the morning. Paula stared at the display, trying to reconcile the time with the sounds traveling through the house - was that singing? And was that bacon she was smelling?

She pushed back the covers and got out of bed, sliding her feet into her orange slippers on the floor. Time to get to the bottom of things.

Declan threw his head back and roared with laughter. Beside him, Amber and Liam were so overwhelmed by mirth that *she'd* given herself a case of the hiccups while *he* was wiping tears from his eyes. Sitting around the other side of the kitchen table, Donna slapped her thighs and emitted high-pitched snorts and giggles.

The cause of their spirited merriment? Douglas.

Pour him a few drinks and he turned into a one-man show. He had material dating back decades and with every tale - and impression to fill it out - he just became funnier and funnier.

At least, that was the consensus of the crowd he was currently entertaining and they were not just family, but also three - or possible four or five - sheets to the wind.

Paula walked into the kitchen just as her mother rose from her seat and stumbled across the room to retrieve a plate of bacon from the countertop beside the stove. She wrinkled her nose when the combined smells of stale beer, grease and something else she couldn't put her finger hit her like a noxious wave.

"What on EARTH is happening in here?" she demanded, hands on hips. "Do any of you have any idea what time it is?"

The crowd around the table, and Sylvester reclining in front of Liam on the tabletop, all swiveled their heads in her direction. Their startled expressions quickly gave way to smiles and Amber raised her hand in welcome.

"Hey! You're up! Come and have some bacon, there's lots."

Donna passed by Paula and placed the plate she was carrying onto the table, a few feet away from Sylvester.

"You should, it's delicious," Douglas agreed, reaching for a slice. "This is our third plate, your mother is a bacon master."

"Hear, hear," Declan cheered, raising his bottle of beer in salute then tipping it toward his mouth to take a long swallow.

Donna dimpled as they all copied him and lifted their drinks to her name.

"Oh, give me strength," Paula muttered, taking a deep breath while trying to hold onto her patience.

It was bad enough *her* family was crazy, but now her husband and his brother, too? Was there something in the air only she was missing?

"Just be careful not to drop any on the floor," Douglas cautioned. "Don't want our vegetarian to accidentally become a meat eater."

Paula frowned, wondering how he figured the cat was a vegetarian, until she followed her father's gaze to the corner of the kitchen. Tucked in beneath the coats hanging from the hooks on the wall was a large wooden crate - door open - and inside that was the turkey, fast asleep and snuggled up with a fluffy blanket. Paula restrained herself from commenting and, instead, thought that it explained the unidentifiable smell: sleeping poultry.

"Can I get you a beer?" Liam offered, rising unsteadily from his chair.

Amber lifted her hand like she was in school, asking the teacher a question. "Or, better yet, can you get us a refill?"

Donna snorted and popped a piece of bacon into her mouth.

"No, to both things," Paula replied, through clenched teeth. "Sit down, Liam, before you fall over."

He nodded and sat.

"So, what's going on here? Are you baking pies now?"

Amber blinked, her face a picture of confusion. "Baking pies? Who's baking pies?"

Paula folded her arms across her chest. "You are."

"*We* are?" She looked at Liam in alarm. "Do we have pies in the oven?"

"I don't think so," he said.

Declan patted Amber's arm. "Liam's right. You don't."

"Not *you*, directly," Paula huffed, then fixed Donna with an accusing stare. "*Mom* is supposed to be doing it. For dessert, remember?"

Amber's face relaxed while Donna's eyes grew round, like saucers, and she exclaimed, "Oh! Is it Thanksgiving? I thought that was tomorrow, did we miss it?"

"It *was* tomorrow," Paula stated, rubbing her temples with her fingertips. "But now it's today."

Douglas' brow furrowed. "You mean an entire day has passed and we didn't notice?"

"No, I mean…." Paula said.

"So, we *didn't* miss Thanksgiving?" Donna clarified.

Paula threw her hands in the air, giving up. "Oh, for god's sake. No. You didn't miss Thanksgiving."

"Okay then," Donna declared, "so we still have time to bake pies. Good to know."

"You okay, hon?" Declan peered at Paula. "You look a little tired. Maybe some bacon would be a good idea, give you some energy."

Paula fixed him with a glare, but refrained from comment. There was no use wasting words, they were all hammered and would never remember anyway. She spun on her heel and marched out of the room, determined not to get roped into baking pies while her mother watched.

Paula sat at the kitchen table a few hours later, sipping Chamomile tea and keeping calm. Thankfully, her Dad had returned Ernie back to his house, so she was alone. After she'd left the five of them - seven, including the bird and cat - she'd returned to bed, caught another couple hours of sleep then took a shower. She also did *not* start the prep for baking pies. It was her mother's contribution to the Thanksgiving dinner and that was that.

"Oh, man," Amber groaned, shuffling into the room, Liam trailing behind. "It's way too early. My head is killing me."

"Ditto," he agreed, yawing widely.

Paula said nothing, just sipped her tea.

"Seriously," Amber went on, "it feels like someone with a tiny jackhammer is pounding away inside my skull."

"You do kinda look like shit," Paula commented, breaking her silence.

Amber glared at her, then winced when the effort of frowning caused her further discomfort.

"I do NOT recommend the couch in the sunroom for sleeping," Liam stated, referring to where he and Amber had inadvertently passed out.

"Did we even sleep?" Amber complained. "Wouldn't it be more like we took a nap?"

Paula sipped more tea, refusing to commiserate. Under other circumstances she might have offered sympathy, she knew all too well how uncomfortable that couch was, but not today. Not when it was becoming glaringly obvious she was the only one who seemed to remember they had a house-load of guests scheduled to arrive later that afternoon.

Amber walked over to the fridge, opened the door and pulled out a bottle of beer. As Paula watched, she twisted off the top and took a long swallow.

"What the hell are you doing?" she demanded.

Amber burped delicately and said, "Hair of the dog."

"Smart," Donna commented, shuffling into the kitchen. Clad in her baggy tartan robe, hair looking as though she'd had an encounter with a light socket, she was a sight.

"No, it's not!" Paula countered. "It's an old wives' tale. What about hangover soup? Wouldn't that be a better way to go?"

Liam stared at the bottle of beer in Amber's hand, unsure if he should comment or not. He chose not and sat down at the table.

"It would be a great way to go," Donna agreed. "But I can't make it in my state, so the old wives' tale will have to suffice."

Paula didn't get a chance to respond because Douglas took that moment to enter the house, pushing open the backdoor and letting a gust of cold, damp air inside.

"You won't believe it, it's raining out there!" he announced, slightly wild-eyed. "The snow's going to all melt away and Santa's going to look seriously water-logged if it keeps up."

"You doing okay, Dad?" Paula asked.

Douglas shoved the door closed and clapped his hands together. "Fit as a fiddle! Made up a batch of hangover soup and haven't looked back. I even found a solution to hide the burnt wood from the Horn of Plenty if the snow all melts away."

"*That's* what I'm smelling," Declan said, while easing himself around the corner and into the room.

Paula's eyes went wide as she took in the sight that was her husband. "Wow. You look rough."

Declan ran his fingers through his hair and grimaced at his own touch. He squinted his bloodshot eyes and peered at Douglas. "Seriously, did you say hangover soup? Is there any left?"

"Yup. In the fridge," he said, removing his black slicker. "I made enough for everyone."

"Yay," Amber cheered, putting the half-empty bottle of beer in the sink.

Donna pulled out a chair next to Liam at the table to sit down. "I thought we were out of the ingredients."

"We are now," Douglas told her. "We'll have to restock at the next grocery shop."

"Or, here's a crazy thought, just don't drink enough to need it," Paula muttered, under her breath.

"Here it is," Amber announced, lifting a large pitcher from inside the fridge and placing it on the countertop. "No more hair of the dog needed."

"Thank god," Declan said, easing himself into a chair at the table, across from Liam.

"That better work," Paula warned them, without a trace of pity. "Because we have a house-full of guests showing up in a few hours and by my calculations there's still a lot to be done."

Not one of them looked her way, instead they all sat in silence while her Dad bustled about, taking the soup from Amber and pouring it into a large pot on the stovetop to start heating.

Paula picked up her cup of tea and walked out, leaving them to it. It was the only way she was going to save herself from being dragged further into their circus.

"Hello, Hello!" Donna cheered, opening the front door to welcome more guests into the house.

She was in full-on party hostess mode and Paula, in the kitchen tackling the cleanup while two apple and two pumpkin pies finished baking, clenched her teeth.

She was feeling seriously fed up. Fed up that she'd been a fool for believing her mother would even be able to set her mind to the simplest task of baking pies, and even more fed up at herself for doing the work in her stead. The truth was, if they didn't have everyone coming to them for the holiday, she would have seriously considered bailing out completely, pouring a drink and ordering in Chinese food.

Paula gave a final swipe to the stovetop and sighed: between cleaning the house - which somehow had been forgotten on the list of things to be done for the party - *and* preparing the dining room for the buffet of food everyone was bringing over, *and* baking the pies her mother had not, she was already feeling overheated and exhausted and the gathering hadn't even gotten started yet.

She dropped the cloth into the sink and walked over to open the windows beside the kitchen door to allow some of the cool, damp air into the room while, at the same moment, Bonnie breezed into the kitchen all smiles.

"Happy Thanksgiving, Paula!" she sang, Craig behind her with a cooler in tow.

Paula pasted a smile on her face, hoping it looked welcoming instead of menacing, and greeted her in-laws. "Right back at ya," was all she could manage to utter without swearing.

"We have the potatoes." Bonnie gestured to the cooler in Craig's grasp.

Paula looked around the kitchen, every available space occupied. "Will they be okay to stay in your cooler until we're ready to reheat them?"

"Of course," she agreed. "The cooler will probably keep them warm, anyway, we didn't put ice in it."

"Okay, so it should be fine on the back porch. Just put a brick on the lid, so there's no chance of anything getting inside."

Craig's eyes widened, but he kept quiet and shuffled the cooler around the table toward the backdoor as instructed.

"Is there a brick handy?" Bonnie asked, as though it was the most normal thing in the world to say.

"Yup," Paula told her, then turned to her father-in-law and laughed when she saw his face. "Don't look so alarmed. It's just a precaution I take when I put anything food related out on the porch. We've never actually had anything happen, I just like to over-engineer things. A reflex from the business I'm in."

Craig smiled, looking relieved. "It's a smart idea. But then you're one smart cookie, sweetheart."

Paula felt her shoulders soften. Kind words were exactly what she needed to hear right at that moment. "Thanks and, hey, you're looking good. Still working out with Angus?"

He flushed, pleased at the compliment, and nodded. "Whether I like it or not, he's keeping me on task."

"Soon, he'll be ready to start modelling swimsuits," Bonnie teased.

Craig laughed and shook his head at his wife. "Cheeky," he retorted, before carrying the cooler out to the back porch.

Paula giggled at the pair of them. So cute and still so obviously adoring of each other.

"So, what can I do to help?" Bonnie insisted, rolling up the sleeves on her blue blouse. "It seems like a real party has already started in there and you look like you could use some extra muscle in here."

Paula felt such a wave of gratitude for her mother-in-law she could have wept. She wiped her hands on her apron then untied the back of it and pulled it over her head. "The pies are pretty much ready to be taken out of the oven...."

"Say no more." Bonnie held out her hand to take the apron. "I'm on it."

Craig came back inside and smiled at the two women. "Can I get you ladies a drink?"

Paula looked at Bonnie who immediately took the wheel.

"Two glasses of red wine, good sir," she said, playfully. "And leave the bottle."

Paula laughed. Maybe Thanksgiving was going to be alright after all.

"You look pretty rough there, bro," Emmet said, sidling up beside Declan at the dining room table. "What's up?"

Declan continued to fork dark meat from one of the three platters of turkey on the table, refusing to be baited by the smirking tone in his brother's voice. He was already embarrassed as hell by his behavior the night before, he didn't want to open a discussion about it.

Emmet turned away from Declan and called out, "Hey, Angus, come here and have a look at Dec. He might not be feeling well."

"I'm *fine*," Declan hissed. "Shut up."

Angus watched them for a moment then returned to his conversation with Douglas. He'd been around *that* block too many times with his brothers to take the bait that easily.

Emmet chuckled and turned back to face Declan. "Okay, so are you going to share *why* you look like shit, and Liam too, or do I have to ask Paula?"

"You are such a nosey prick," Declan grumbled, making Emmet crow with laughter.

"So that's a *no* then to asking Paula?"

Declan heaved a healthy portion of garlic mashed potatoes onto his plate and kept moving down the line.

"Okay, so we have protein and starch on your plate," Emmet observed, assessing Declan's choices. "Hungover it is."

Declan paused, the gravy boat poised above his potatoes. "*Please*, you know nothing. It's Thanksgiving. It's all starch and protein."

Emmet shot him a shit-eating grin. "Uh-huh. *Riiight*."

Declan sighed, giving in. "You're not going to let up, are you?"

"No. Obviously."

"Okay, fine." Declan put down the gravy boat and rested his plate on the table. "You're right, I do feel like shit because I had some drinks with Paula's family last night - well, more like early this morning - and ended up drinking to *excess* and now she's pissed at me for being a useless, hungover lump. Happy now?"

"Uncle Declan?" A young voice interrupted, before Emmet could respond.

Declan turned away from Emmet to look down into the face of his eight year old nephew. "Hey, Finn. What's up?"

"What always comes at the end of Thanksgiving?"

Declan cocked his head and pretended to think. "Hmm.... A big nap?"

"The letter G!" Finn bellowed, then doubled over with laughter.

Emmet laughed along with him while Declan chuckled and shook his head.

"Who taught you that one?" Declan asked.

"Until Liam," he said, grinning. "He gave me a whole book of jokes."

Declan shared a knowing look with Emmet. Liam got a kick out of stirring the pot and there was no question he'd given the joke book to Finn not just for their nephew's entertainment, but knowing full well it would make Linda bananas.

"Finn," Angus called.

He turned around to look at his father. "Yeah?"

"Your dinner's getting cold."

"Okay." He shrugged at his uncles. "Gotta go eat."

Emmet ruffled his hair. "Come back after you're done and tell us another one, buddy."

"But, not until you're really finished," Declan added. "Or your mom will have our heads."

Finn giggled and ran back to the kid's table to join Ethan, already sitting down and eating his dinner.

"So, you tied one on with the in-laws," Emmet said, immediately resuming their conversation once Finn was out of earshot. "And Liam too, I'm assuming, from the way he looks. What happened to the hangover soup Donna cooked up the last time we were here?"

Declan picked up his plate and stepped to the side of the buffet table. "Oh, we had it this morning, thank god. Otherwise, I doubt I'd even be standing upright."

"Wow. You impress me, bro."

Declan rolled his eyes. The last thing he wanted was for his behavior to earn the respect of his party-animal brother.

"Think Paula will get over it?" he asked, grabbing a roll from the basket on the table. "I brought these, by the way."

"I hope so." Declan shoveled some of the potatoes on his plate into his mouth. "She hasn't made eye contact with me yet today. *And* when she took a walk when the weather let up for a bit this afternoon, she went with Sam and did not invite me along."

"Whoa, back up." Emmet's face was grave. "Are you serious right now? Who's this Sam? Do we need to make a visit and have a *talk* with this guy?"

Declan grinned and Emmet lifted his hands imploringly.

"This isn't a time for laughs, man. If this Sam character is a serious concern—"

Declan laughed and cut him off. "Relax, doofus. Sam is the neighbor's dog."

"Oh." He nodded, processing, then lifted his fist to give a sharp knuckle-jab to Declan's shoulder.

"Hey!" Declan blurted, flinching at the sudden hit. "What the hell?"

Bonnie, entering the dining room from the kitchen, heard Declan's lament and fixed a laser-stare on both him and Emmet: just as she'd done when they were kids.

Emmet's eyes widened at their mother's glare and he lowered his voice. "You asked for it, *doofus*. Stop me sooner next time and I won't have to hit you."

Declan also caught Bonnie's frown and followed his brother's lead by slapping an easy smile on his face to give the impression they were just pleasantly chatting.

"I don't know, Em, you do a really convincing good fella impression. Just needs a bit more menace and you've nailed it."

Emmet grabbed a turkey leg from a plate laden with meat and stalked away, leaving Declan to laugh at his indignation just like when they were children.

Paula, overhearing the laughter, caught Declan's eye from across the room: he quickly clammed up when he gazed into the depths of her stony scowl. It rivalled his mother's.

Perhaps, he thought, while forking up more food from his plate, he might be wise to make a call on Sam and see if he had any spare room available in his doghouse.

Angus and Douglas were in the backyard for some fresh air after the heavy Thanksgiving meal and, more importantly, for Angus to see Ernie. He'd heard all about the turkey and when the opportunity had presented itself, he'd taken Douglas aside and asked to meet the bird before he left for his new home.

"This is seriously impressive, Doug," Angus praised, hunching into his coat against the wet weather that had decided to stick around.

They'd arrived at the back of the garden and were standing in front of the turkey house Douglas had created. The solidly built crate structure was six feet high and four feet wide with a perch set into it at the back where the turkey was tucked up and looking like the king of all he surveyed.

"It was easier to make than you'd think," Douglas offered, magnanimously, tugging the rim of his grey, Greek fisherman-style cap to keep it from being blown from his head.

Angus flipped up the collar on his wool coat. "For you, perhaps. But not us common mortals."

Douglas chuckled.

"And I had no idea he had such nice plumage," he went on, referring to the turkey's abundance of snow white and metallic black feathers. "I was expecting a regular old, grey looking turkey, not one that looks like he belongs on a parade float. Donna must have paid a fair price for him."

Doug smiled fondly at the bird. "Ernie is a Royal Palm turkey, bred for domestication."

"Ernie?" Angus repeated.

"The girls named him."

As though aware he was the topic of conversation, Ernie stood up on his perch and fluffed out his feathers.

"Wow," Angus breathed, taking in the splendor of the bird's fanning white tail. It displayed a perfect arc of inky black feathers across the top, giving the impression they'd been carefully painted there for contrast.

Douglas' small smile turned into a full-blown grin and encompassed his face. "He is something and, to tell you the truth, I'm going to miss him."

"So why don't you keep him?" Angus asked, then braced himself when a gust of cold wind whipped across their faces.

Ernie lifted his wings and let the wind plump up his feathers, then settled himself back on his perch. If it was possible for a turkey to look content, he did.

Douglas shook his head. "No, we can't. He deserves the room of an acreage so he can eventually have a few hens of his own."

Angus cast a sidelong glance at his brother's father-in-law: he was a good, kind man. "Maybe Declan and Paula can set him up at their new place, then you'd be able to visit?"

Douglas threw his head back, laughing, then had to grab at his cap before the wind took it.

Angus chuckled along with him. It was a hilarious idea, the two of them with not just the cat, but Ernie in tow. "Or maybe," he added, "Paula could bring him to work as her new mascot."

Douglas chortled some more while he resettled his cap on his head. "I think it's safe to say that Ernie will be off to his new home in a few days with no resistance from either your brother or Paula."

"Can I bring the boys out to have a look at him?"

"Of course," Douglas agreed, turning around into the wind and leading the way back to the house. "But don't blame me if they want one once they see him and Linda ends up sending you to live in the turkey house."

Angus bent his head against the rain that had begun spitting down on them.

"Noted," he said, patting Douglas on the shoulder as they headed inside.

Paula shlepped yet another load of used dishes from the dining room to the kitchen, willing to do pretty much anything that would keep her from being in the living room where her mother was holding court by regaling their guests with stories from their family archives. Stories that, more often than not, contained some sort of humiliation that Donna twisted like a balloon animal until it appeared humorous, instead of cringe-making.

"Can I help?" Linda offered, walking into the kitchen.

"Oh, it's okay," Paula told her, waving her hand.

"I don't mind, honest," she said, while laughter drifted into the kitchen from the living room. "You shouldn't be missing your own Thanksgiving."

Paula picked up one of the many dirty forks on the countertop to use as a scraper for the leftovers stuck to the plates.

"Believe me," she said, pulling out the trash can under the sink and setting to work, "I've *lived* the stories my Mom is telling, I don't need to visit them again."

Linda shot her a sympathetic smile. She'd had the thought that the stories were not exactly flattering, but didn't want to say anything to cause further discomfort.

"Did she tell the one yet about how I got caught out in my underwear with my teenage boyfriend, Josh Dunbar?"

Linda shrugged and held out her hand for the first cleared plate. "I think that was the one she was starting to tell when I left to follow you in here."

Paula gave her the plate then picked up another and started working on it. "You should go back. The way she tells it, it sounds hysterical."

Linda opened the dishwasher, rolled out the lower rack and slotted the dirty dish into it. "But it wasn't?"

"I was seventeen, so, no, it definitely wasn't."

"You must be looking forward to getting into your house," she stated.

Paula paused, fork held aloft. "You have no idea."

"Paula! Linda!" Donna's voice rang out. "Where have you two gone? We're making a toast!"

They exchanged looks and Paula sighed.

"We may as well go in there," she said, putting the plate and fork down on the counter then wiping her hands on a dish towel. "Otherwise, she'll send out a search party."

Linda shot her a second look of sympathy and led the way.

"And, finally," Donna announced, her voice thick with emotion as she gazed into the faces of the guests in her living room. "I want to thank Declan. Without him, none of this would have been possible."

The family all raised their glasses, ready to drink, but Donna wasn't quite finished.

"Because," she went on, "our Paula was just not ready to step in this year. So Declan, the amazing man that he is, stepped up in her place and willingly put himself out."

Amber exchanged a wide-eyed look with Liam. Was her mother really saying this out loud?

"Well, now," Douglas began, awkwardly clearing his throat. "That's not—"

"*He* had work to do!" Donna spoke louder, not giving him a chance to finish his thought. "But did he put that before his family? Before all of us? No, *he* didn't." She pressed a palm to her chest, over her heart. "Instead, he rallied and picked up the slack and got everyone on board and we should all raise our glasses to him in thanks for being willing to show us how much he values us."

Bonnie shot an incredulous look at Craig, shocked to the core that Donna was saying such things in front of everyone. Granted, the woman was almost falling down drunk, but still, it was mortifying she was speaking in such a manner about her daughter.

"Okay, then," Amber interjected, loudly, attempting to help her father in his effort to shut her mother down.

"To Declan!" Donna declared, jabbing her glass of wine into the air with such gusto that some of it sloshed over the rim and down her hand.

Everyone rapidly offered muttered agreement, the general vibe of the room being one of such discomfort they all wanted to put an end to the toast as swiftly as possible.

"Speech!" Donna screeched. "Declan! Speech!"

Declan ignored her and, instead, scanned the room for his wife. She wasn't there.

Douglas, with some help from Liam, began taking Donna in hand; strong-arming her out of the family room and into the kitchen while Amber did her best to offer apologies for her mother's unexpected outburst.

Declan didn't care about any of it. All he cared about was where Paula had gone. He slipped away from the group and headed upstairs to start his search.

Thanksgiving was officially over.

Chapter 18

"Snow!" Amber bellowed, her voice so loud it carried through the house venting.

"Oy," Paula groaned, jarred awake from her deep sleep. "I'm having déjà vu, how about you?"

No one replied.

She turned over and the empty space beside her in the bed reminded her that Declan had camped out on the pullout couch in her Dad's office down the hall. After the day they'd had yesterday, topped off with her mother's toast, she'd just wanted to be left alone. Now, in the light of day, she wondered how he'd slept: then had a brief, mean-spirited hope it was poorly.

There was a gentle tap at the door and she thought, speak of the devil, when the door eased opened and Declan poked his head around the edge.

"You awake?"

"Of course. No one gets to keep sleeping when the snowfall alarm starts ringing."

He stepped into the room. "Can we please talk now?"

Paula nodded. Truth was, she was tired of being angry and wanted to make up.

Declan walked over and sat down on the edge of the bed. "I'm so sorry. Really, I am. I can't say it enough. I let you down and I promise it won't happen again."

"It's fine," she said, pulling back the covers as an invitation for him to get into the bed.

"No," he argued, while accept the invitation and climbing in beside her. "It's not."

"Okay, fine. Then I forgive you. They are a persuasive group, my family, and I'm well aware of the fact that - unless you're a seasoned pro - they can drag a person down the crazy path pretty fast."

Declan sunk into the bedclothes, his face still troubled. "Well, thanks for understanding, even though I don't think I deserve it."

Paula snuggled up next to him and sighed, glad they were back on speaking terms.

"And about your Mom…."

"Forget that, too." Paula's voice was steely. "She was drunk."

Declan wrapped am arm around her. "I know, but still…."

"We have just over a week now until we get into the house," she stated. "And I'm going to be crazy busy at work getting the last minute stuff done for the Bazzano sixteenth birthday party. I can't afford to put any more energy into her and her antics."

"Ok," he agreed.

She snuggled closer, pressing herself against the length of him in invitation of a different manner.

He grinned and got the message.

Jaimie sat in her car outside her parent's house, the engine running, waiting for her mother to join her. She adjusted the heat vents then turned up the sound on the radio to hear what was playing.

Nothing good. Just news.

She turned it back down.

"Come on," she muttered, tapping the steering wheel impatiently.

She'd told her mother she'd be there at eleven, what was the hold up?

Finally, just as she was debating giving a solid blast of the horn, Donna appeared around the side of the house.

"Yay," Jaimie said, before reaching for the door handle to exit the vehicle to help her mother navigate the slushy pavement.

Donna waved and shook her head, making Jaimie pause, then increased her speed to get to the vehicle faster.

"Hey, there!" she enthused, pulling open the passenger side door and slipping into the seat.

"I was going to get out and help you," Jaimie told her, while she waited for her to buckle up.

Instead of doing so, Donna waved a dismissive hand. "No need. I have my traction shoes on. I'd probably have been holding you up."

Jaimie continued to wait while her mother lifted her oversized purse and swung it into the backseat.

"Okay, that's better," she said, then laid her hands in her lap and gave Jaimie a quizzical look. "Are we going, or what?"

"Once you have your seatbelt on, we will," Jaimie replied, tightly.

"Oh, for goodness sake," she groused, reaching for the belt and giving it a hard tug: which, of course, caused it to tighten up instead of release.

"Don't pull on it like that," Jaimie tried to explain, before her mother cut her off.

"What's wrong with this thing? Is it broken? It probably is, so you can just drive and no one will worry about it."

"No, it is *not* broken," Jaimie said, between clenched teeth. "You just need to be less aggressive with it and it will work fine."

Donna made an exaggerated show of gently pulling the belt out then finally clipping it across her lap. "Goodness, so sensitive. Must be a car made in this generation."

Jaimie refused to be baited, instead she took a deep breath and shifted her focus to driving.

Jaimie carried a cup of coffee in each hand while making her way to the table she and Donna had secured near the windows at *The Bakery*. She'd originally considered the idea of driving the two of them to her house to talk, but then her mother would have been completely distracted by Hazel and Trent; thus, destroying any opportunity for real communication. And they definitely needed real communication. Fast. Otherwise, Jaimie feared her mother might destroy her relationship with Paula beyond repair. And now that she was also a mother, she couldn't imagine something more devastating than her own daughter wanting nothing to do with her. She hoped by expressing her thoughts it might stop things from unravelling past the point of no return.

"Thank you," Donna said, when Jaimie set one of the cups of coffee on the table in front of her.

She pulled out the chair on the other side of the small, square table and sat down. "My pleasure."

"So, are you finally going to tell me to what I owe the pleasure of this last-minute coffee date the day after Thanksgiving, or do I have to start guessing?" Donna glanced around the shop and added, "I'm actually rather surprised this place is open at all, truth be told."

Jaimie took a large gulp of her coffee then cringed when it burned her tongue.

Donna raised her eyebrows. "Is that face about me, or the coffee?"

"The coffee," she croaked. "Hot."

Donna leaned back in her chair. "Well, that's a relief."

Jaimie set her cup back down on the table. "Maybe. Unless what I need to say doesn't sit well with you and then you could be making the same face for another reason."

If possible, Donna's eyebrows lifted even higher.

"It's about Paula, Mom," Jaimie began, jumping right in.

Donna held up a hand to stop her. "Say no more. I know what this is about."

"You do?"

She nodded. "Of course. I was out of line, yesterday."

Jaimie brightened. Maybe this was going to go more smoothly than she'd thought.

"I could have put more thought into baking the pies," she stated, looking contrite and pushing her riot of ginger hair from her face. "But, instead, I let the excitement of the day get in the way and I didn't do my part."

Jaimie stared at her. *That* she wasn't expecting. While she knew her mother was self-absorbed, it was unsettling to have such blatant evidence of just how deeply it ran.

"Oh, don't look at me like that," Donna complained. "In the end it was just pies and Paula will get over it."

Jaimie shook her head. "But it wasn't just pies, Mom. In fact, it wasn't the pies at all."

Donna frowned. "How do you know? You weren't even there."

Jaimie leaned forward in her chair. "Yeah, but I still know what happened."

"Third person."

Jaimie took a steadying breath and rested her elbows on the table. "Still, I did hear about all of it, so will you do me the courtesy of letting me talk and not interrupting?"

"Goodness, so serious."

"Do. We. Have. A. Deal?"

"Fine, fine." Donna picked up her coffee cup. "Say whatever is it you feel you need to say. I'll just drink my coffee."

"Thank you," Jaimie said, then jumped back in. "To put it bluntly, you are seriously screwing up with Paula."

Donna swallowed her coffee and opened her mouth to speak, but Jaimie pointed a finger at her.

"No. You agreed you'd let me talk."

"Alright." Donna lifted her free hand in surrender. "Go ahead."

Jaimie nodded. "So, anyway, not only are you screwing up with Paula, but you're screwing up to the point of no return."

"What does *that* mean?" Donna demanded, then quickly verified, "And that's technically a question, not an interruption."

'Where do I start?"

"On come *on*," Donna shot back, then mimed zipping her lips when Jaimie narrowed her eyes.

"As I was saying, where do I start? I could go so far back into our family past it's seriously not funny, but I'll just say that for too long now you've taken her for granted and it's finally taken its toll on her." Jaimie sighed and sat back in her seat. "I could site example after example, but I think if you really look back on things from the time we were kids—"

"From the time you were kids!" Donna echoed, aghast.

"Yes, Mom," Jaimie confirmed. "That's how far back your utter disregard and expectations and general taking-for-granted of Paula has been. She's always been super reliable and you've taken advantage of that. Surely, you can see it can't you?"

Donna's face hardened and she drank more of her coffee.

Jaimie sighed and picked up her cup. She hadn't expected the conversation to go smoothly and her mother was proving her right.

Donna put down her mug with a solid thump on the tabletop. "Does this mean I'm *allowed* to comment now?"

Jaimie raised an eyebrow as the belligerence in her tone and nodded.

"Well, all I can say is, it sounds like you have your opinion set, so I don't imagine I can offer anything to change your mind. So, I had a little too much to drink and my toast was a little more over the top than it should have been. So sue me."

Jaimie set her cup down as well and leaned forward. "What are you talking about?"

"Yesterday. Thanksgiving," Donna stated. "Amber and your father said my toast was too personal and, clearly, you've been told the same thing."

"Oh, for the love of god," Jaimie exhaled, mentally regrouping. "Have you not been listening to a word I've said? I am not talking about your bloody toast, although I did hear about it and it sounded mean, I'm talking about the way you treat Paula in general; not just via one shitty toast. You take her for granted. Period."

"Sez who?" Donna demanded.

"Pretty much all of us who've watched how things have happened over the years. From the time she was able to start doing it, Paula has always been the reliable one to clean up your messes and you just act like it's normal."

"Messes," Donna grumbled. "Please."

Jaimie narrowed her eyes. "I'm sorry, what would you call the more-than-we-can-count instances where things have gone sideways and Paula has stepped in to put things right?"

Donna flapped her hands. "Well, sure, we all know there have been some *adventures* that took some unexpected turns, but…."

"No, Mom," Jaimie stated. "Not *adventures*. Not at all. No one thinks that, but you. But you won't believe it because you have an almost pathological need to never be wrong. Instead of facing the facts, you passive-aggressive the shit out of everything and the moment you get called out on it you turn it around and act as though you're the victim."

"That's not true."

"Case in point," Jaimie declared, folding her arms across her chest.

"Oh, for goodness sake," Donna huffed. "So, is this why you asked me to join you for coffee? To ambush me into feeling guilty about the past?"

Jaimie stretched her neck back and forth. Clearly, she had more talking to do and that was definitely going to require more coffee.

Chapter 19

"Oh, shit," Amber cursed, when she walked into the kitchen and saw snow falling on the other side of the window above the sink.

It had been amusing for the first bit, announcing when the flakes started flying, but three snow-laden days later and she was already bored of both reporting and of snow. It had been a lot more fun when she was a child, go figure, and didn't have to actually deal with the weather other than to play in it.

Her cellphone chimed and Amber retrieved it from her pocket. It was Declan, asking if her Mom was home.

"Of course," she wrote back.

"Good. Keep her there. I'm on my way over," he replied.

Amber lifted an eyebrow, almost hearing the insistence in his tone. She rapidly typed back, *"Will do"* and sent a thumbs-up emoji.

She tucked her phone back into her pocket and thought *cryptic*, then wondered if she should stick around for whatever was clearly going to go down once he arrived. Maybe she'd hang out in her room with the door open, out of sight but still able to overhear whatever transpired. She grinned. Win-win.

Declan pulled his car into Donna and Doug's driveway and turned off the ignition. He took a deep, steadying breath, then got out of the vehicle and headed toward the house. He was on a mission, self-imposed, but one he knew would benefit the greater good.

Upstairs, hidden behind the blinds on her bedroom window, Amber peeked through the slats and watched him ascend the porch steps then disappear from sight as he crossed the landing and entered the house.

He looked serious.

Show time.

Declan sat at the kitchen table while Donna bustled about offering coffee, tea, a sandwich, whatever came to mind.

He shook his head and said, "I'm fine," while gesturing for her to sit down across the table from him.

"Well, you have to eat, it's lunch time," she insisted. "How will you make it through the rest of the work day?"

"*Donna*," he snapped. "Please *sit*."

"Goodness," she replied, plunking herself down in the chair across from him. "So serious. Am I in trouble?"

"Truthfully? Yes," he told her, making the teasing grin drop from her face.

She lifted her chin and folded her hands across her lap. "I'm not sure I appreciate your tone."

"Well, then you'd better brace yourself because you're probably not going to like what I'm about to say next, either."

Donna's face hardened, but she stayed silent.

Declan took that as his cue to jump in. "First, I want to state that Paula has no idea I'm here. I want that made clear right off the top."

Donna's brow furrowed. "Why?"

"Because I'm here to talk about *her.*"

"What about her?" Donna demanded. "Has something happened? Did she lose her job?"

Declan stared at her. Was she serious?

"Why are you looking at me like that?" she asked, frowning.

"Because I can't believe you'd even ask me that question," he exhaled, running his fingers through his hair. "*Of course* she hasn't lost her job. She IS the job. She's the bloody owner. Jeez, Donna, you should at least remember that."

"Well, of course I do," she countered, fluffing her hair. "It's just that I've had a lot going on and I can't remember every little detail—"

Declan smacked a hand down on the table, loud enough to stop her stream of chatter. "Okay, stop talking and listen."

Donna's eyes widened at his vehemence.

He leaned in. "Okay, here it is, in a nutshell: you are going to lose your daughter if you keep on treating her the way you have been … *her entire life.*"

"Lose her?" she repeated. "What do you mean, *lose her?*"

"I mean, the way you acted at Thanksgiving was the final straw. Your so-called toast was reprehensible. Just downright mean. You treated your daughter, *my wife*, with such disrespect it's embarrassing. And I'm warning you, if you don't get a grip on yourself, you're going to lose her for good. As in, she's going to cut you out of her life."

She cocked her head. "Have you been talking to Jaimie?"

Declan frowned. "No. Why?"

"So this is all coming from you? Your own thoughts and observation?"

"Yes, of course," he agreed, sitting back in his chair. "Why?"

Donna shook her head, saying nothing more. What could she say? Clearly, Jaimie had been telling the truth about how everyone perceived the relationship between her and Paula. She hadn't wanted to believe it, but now….

Declan waited. He'd said his piece. It was time for her to decide if it mattered.

Tears formed in Donna's eyes and she blinked to keep them at bay. She looked at Declan, but he averted his eyes, unwilling to be pulled in. She took a deep breath, let it go, then nodded.

"You're right."

Amber, having snuck from her bedroom to the top of the staircase to eavesdrop, had to grab the railing to keep from tumbling forward when her knees went weak from the shock of hearing her mother's reply. Had she heard correctly? Had her mother actually acknowledged that her behavior had affected someone negatively?

Amber's first impulse was to call Jaimie and tell her what was happening, but if she did so she'd miss whatever came next. And it was too gripping. She had to know what came next.

Sylvester poked his head from around Paula's bedroom door, saw Amber crouched on the landing and padded over to join her.

"Shh," she whispered, settling herself cross-legged on the hardwood floor and pulling him into her lap.

The cat went boneless in her embrace and began to purr contentedly while she leaned forward to keep listening to the conversation in the kitchen.

"Pardon me?" Declan said.

Donna sighed. "I said, you're right."

"Really. Just like that, I'm right." He stared at her, skeptical.

She didn't blame him.

"And you came to this conclusion when, exactly?"

"The day after Thanksgiving."

"Okay, so are you planning to do anything about it?" Declan demanded, still refusing to be sucked into any possible emotional manipulation.

Donna watched his face, knowing full well by his expression he'd drawn the line. On one side was he and Paula and the other her. She had to convince him she was sincere.

"I have been wracked with guilt over that toast … and so many other things," she revealed, standing up to pace the floor. "And I've been going over it and over it since Jaimie and I talked —"

"Wait." He held up a hand. "You and Jaimie talked about this? Is that why you asked if I'd been talking to her?"

She stopped pacing. "Yes. We went for coffee the day after Thanksgiving and she expressed very clearly her thoughts about Paula … and some other things … and said pretty much the same things as you have. It's been haunting me ever since."

Declan was still skeptical. "Really? So, are you telling me if I hadn't come to talk to you, you would have tried to make amends regardless because of your conversation with Jaimie?"

"Yes. Exactly," she further revealed, her face earnest. "And I've been trying to come up with some way to let Paula know I'm sorry. Not just for the toast, but for a lot of other stuff as well."

Declan rubbed the stubble on his chin. He wanted to believe her, but her track record was so damned dicey.

"I know, I know, it seems sudden and even hard to believe, but trust me, Jaimie talked to me for a *long* time and I mean what I'm saying." She sat down again and rested her elbows on the tabletop. "I was actually planning to come to you about it, once I'd figured out how I could show her my remorse."

"I have a crazy idea," he offered, sardonically. "What about expressing this to *her*?"

Donna fixed him with a grave stare. "You and I both know words would be pointless. Anything I say will go in one ear and out the other."

"Do you blame her?"

"No, she's fully justified in that," she quickly clarified. "And that's why I need to *show* her."

"Okay," he reluctantly agreed, "fair point, so—"

"And I came up with something," she interrupted, hoping to move things in a positive direction.

Declan lifted an eyebrow. He wasn't expecting that.

She leaned in. "I want to throw her a surprise holiday party at your new house. The whole shebang, the house all decorated, lots of food and drink and all of her family and friends. Basically a housewarming party with a festive theme."

Declan rolled his eyes. He'd just witnessed her party throwing skills, or lack thereof, in action.

"I know, I know," she said, waving her hands. "Thanksgiving was a debacle, you'll get no argument from me on that. But this will be different, I promise."

Declan finally looked directly at her. Her expression was open, completely lacking in … bullshit, to put it not so politely.

"Okay," he said, sitting up in his seat. "For sake of argument, if you really were going to try to do this, how would you manage it? We're supposed to be moving in next weekend, so surprising her might be a bit of a challenge."

"We could pretend there's another issue to stall your moving in!" Amber yelled, from the staircase as she came charging down the steps.

"Oh!" Donna exclaimed, her hand flying to her throat when Amber rounded the corner into the kitchen, Sylvester clutched in her arms. "You scared the hell out of me! Where were you and why were you eavesdropping?"

"Sorry," she apologized, putting the wild-eyed cat down on the floor and pulling out a chair to join them at the table.

"What sort of issue are you thinking of?" Declan queried, watching Sylvester dart across the room and settle himself next to his food dishes.

Amber grinned. "We could say they're having another water pipe problem because of the cold weather."

"Setting the date back again," he finished, nodding.

"Exactly," she agreed. "And instead of you guys moving in on this coming Sunday, you could tell her it's going to be one more week. That would give us almost two weeks to get everything done for the party, which is totally doable."

Donna reached out to touch Amber's forearm. "Did you say *we*? Does that mean you'll help?"

"Of course I'll help," she said, slightly exasperated at the question. "But only as long as you stick to your promise and arrange everything. If that's the case, I'm happy to be a part of your crew. I'll even make Liam help."

Declan snickered. His poor brother didn't know what he was in for.

"I will," Donna affirmed. "I'll do my part."

"And I'm sure if you ask her," he added, "my Mom would be happy to pitch in. And me, too, of course."

Amber snapped her fingers. "And we can get Jaimie to tell Paula *she's* hosting the party, which would mean we could do the planning in plain sight. If we get caught with anything, we can just say it's for Jaimie."

Donna clapped her hands and beamed at the two of them. "Oh, this is going to be wonderful. I have some fabulous ideas and we'll make it a housewarming party to remember."

She got up from her chair and rushed over to rummage in a drawer for a notebook and pen. They had less than two weeks, time to make some lists.

Amber shared a look with Declan, they both smiled. Seemed they were about to witness a holiday miracle, or something resembling it. And, just maybe, it would be a start toward mending fences.

"God bless us, everyone," Amber chanted, smirking.

Declan chuckled then asked, under his breath so Donna wouldn't overhear, "Do you really think this is going to go smoothly and without a hitch?"

Amber shook her head. "No. Not a chance."

He sat back in his chair and laughed.

Donna and Amber did their best to keep their facial expressions neutral as Declan paced the living room floor and repeatedly said, "uh-huh" into his cellphone.

They'd just finished up with dinner and had settled themselves on the sofa, Paula on the adjacent armchair, when Declan's phone had rung and, now, were readying themselves to play their part in his story: the story he was about to make up to Paula about there being another issue at the new house. As for Douglas, they'd agreed it was best to keep him in the dark during this part of the plan, fearing he wouldn't be able to act convincingly and give them all away. He was out in his workshop, none the wiser.

Declan finally hung up the phone and heaved a heavy sigh.

"What?" Paula asked, shifting in her seat. "What's going on?"

"That was Vince," he began explaining, even though it hadn't been and, instead, had been Jaimie pretending to be Vince.

Donna gasped, too loudly if truth be told, and Amber nudged her. Thankfully, Paula was focused on Declan, so didn't give any attention to her mother's dramatics.

"*And*," he continued, cutting his eyes at Donna. "There may be another pipe issue at the house."

Donna kept quiet this time.

Paula stood up and walked over to him. "Another one? What did he say?"

"Umm, well, it sounds like it might be from the weather this time and he thinks I should go and see for myself."

She nodded. "Good idea, let's go."

"No," he said, putting his hand up.

She frowned. "Why not?"

He shot a look at Amber.

She immediately spoke up. "BECAUSE you said you were going to show me the plans from work for the big party you're creating next weekend, remember?"

Paula turned to look at her. "No, I didn't."

"*Yes, you diiid*," she insisted, throwing a slight whine into her voice. "You *saaaid* it was going to be a huge extravaganza and that you'd show me what you're *doooing*."

Declan, behind Paula, gave her a thumbs-up.

"She's right, I remember," Donna confirmed. "We were in the kitchen when you said it."

Declan grinned.

"Did I?" Paula asked, starting to second guess herself.

"I'm sure it's just because you've been so busy that it slipped your mind," Donna offered. "Why don't we go into the kitchen and get some wine and you can tell Amber all about it while Declan deals with the contractor thingy."

"Sounds like a good idea to me," Amber said, getting up from the couch to lead the way into the kitchen.

Paula turned back to Declan. "Is that okay? Do you need me to come with you?"

He smiled and shook his head. "No, it's fine. You go chat with your sister and I'll be back before you know it."

"See you in a bit," Donna sang, waving as she followed Amber's path into the kitchen.

He planted a kiss on Paula's lips and said, "Save some wine for when I get back," then quickly slipped away to put on his shoes, grab his coat and exit the house.

Paula stood for a moment, feeling a little off-kilter. Things had happened too fast and she felt like she was trying to get up to speed.

"Come *ooooon*," Amber called, while the sound of Declan's car starting outside met Paula's ears.

He was gone.

She shrugged and set off for the kitchen.

"So, the good news is that it can be remedied," Donna confirmed, picking up the bottle of red wine on the kitchen table.

"Yup," Declan agreed, watching her pour a generous serving into his glass.

He'd returned from his, supposed, investigation of the pipe at the new house; when in fact he'd driven around for forty-five minutes, enjoying the Christmas decorations in the neighborhood.

"*And*?" Donna prompted, smiling encouragingly.

Declan cleared his throat and picked up his glass. Unlike her and Amber, he was not comfortable lying to Paula: even if it was for the greater good of the surprise party.

"Thankfully, Vince caught it early before it burst," he said, stiffly, feeling like a fraud. "Otherwise we would have had a whole helluva lot worse water damage."

"More good news," Donna stated, placing the bottle on the table.

Paula picked up her glass and took a long swallow of the dusky colored merlot. She was afraid to pose the next, obvious, question.

Amber, however, was not.

"So, does this all mean another delay for moving in?" she asked, over her shoulder as she rummaged through a cupboard for crackers.

"Yup." Declan avoided eye contact with Donna across the table and took a healthy slug of his wine.

Amber pulled out a box of crackers and shook it. Jackpot.

Paula put her glass back on the table and forced herself to say, "So how long are we talking?"

Declan said nothing and took another drink.

Amber turned around and exchanged a look with Donna, who then prompted, "Declan? Did you hear

Paula? Do you have an idea of how long it will be to get it fixed?"

He tried not to look guilty as hell. "I think we can safely say there's a chance we'll be here for Christmas."

Amber cheered, "Yay!" then pressed her lips together when she saw the grave expression on her sister's face.

"Awww, honey," Donna soothed, chuckling and reaching out to pat Paula's arm. "Don't look so downcast. There are worse things than some pipe issues and having to spend the holidays with your family."

Amber shook the crackers into a bowl and brought them to the table. "She's right. I know you're disappointed about the delay, but maybe it's the fates aligning."

Paula lifted an eyebrow. "The fates?"

Amber nodded and pulled out a chair to sit down. "Uh-huh. Maybe."

Declan said nothing. He already felt guilty enough fibbing to his wife, he wasn't about to add anything more to the conversation unless directly addressed.

"And the time will fly by," Donna assured. "The holidays are always a whirlwind."

Paula took a cracker from the bowl. "Do we have more wine in the house?"

Amber grinned and Donna nodded.

"Good. I think we're going to need it."

Chapter 20

Bonnie sat at Donna's kitchen table while she bustled about the room, piling cookies on a plate, setting a fresh pot of coffee brewing, gathering cups and spoons and cream and sugar. When Declan had called the previous evening from his car to inform her of his mother-in-law's party plans, as well as to warn her he had taken the liberty of declaring she would probably be agreeable to help, what could she do? Her son needed her and she was going to be there for him, end of story.

"Sure I can't help with anything?" she offered.

"No, no," Donna assured her, pouring two steaming cups of coffee from the pot and carrying them over to the table. "You relax. I've got things covered."

Bonnie felt a twinge of pity for her; it seemed she was trying to make up for what had happened at their last encounter at Thanksgiving by demonstrating her competence in that moment.

"Well, thanks," she said, kindly. "The cookies look delicious."

Donna pulled out a seat opposite her and sat down. "Don't thank me, I should be thanking you for being willing to help out. I can't tell you how much I appreciate it, every bit helps with such a short timeline."

Bonnie shook her head. "Oh, it's nothing, really. I'm happy to do it."

Donna chose a peanut butter cookie from the white plate between them on the tabletop and silently wondered just how much Declan had revealed to his mother.

"As a matter of fact," Bonnie went on, reading her mind, "when Declan called me to tell me of your plans, I thought it was a wonderfully kind and fun idea."

Donna dunked her cookie into her coffee cup then took a large bite and chewed methodically.

"I'm sure Paula is going to be so surprised and thrilled," Bonnie further expounded, adding creamer to her coffee while she continued to fill the silence that had fallen.

A surprising silence, it must be noted, as she had no memory of witnessing Donna without words.

Donna placed the remainder of her cookie on a blue plate next to her mug. "I really hope so," she finally said, reaching for a paper napkin from a pile on the table. "We've had a pretty rocky relationship and since the kids have moved back in, it's become downright tumultuous."

Bonnie picked up the spoon Donna had provided and stirred her coffee, nodding. "It's the nature of kids and parents. Trust me, after raising five boys, I've learned no matter what the age, there are moments of upheaval. Don't beat yourself up."

Donna appreciated her kindness, but had to clarify, "Thank you for saying that, but I'm afraid I've been the cause of a lot of it. That's why I really want to try and put things right and make a fresh start. I'm hoping this surprise housewarming will be the first step."

"I'm sure it will be," Bonnie affirmed, placing the spoon on her plate. "How could it not?"

Donna picked up her cup. "Cheers to that."

Bonnie lifted her own mug from the table and gently clinked it against Donna's. They both took a swallow of their coffee, went "ahhh", then set their cups back down.

"Okay," she said, leaning forward and taking a peanut butter cookie for herself. "So, what sort of ideas do you have so far and what can I do to help? I'm all yours."

Donna smiled. No wonder Declan and his siblings were such good people. With a mother like Bonnie, it would seem they couldn't be anything but. She was inspired just being around her and hoped, fingers crossed, this party would be the start of foraging a new relationship with her middle child.

"I'll get my list," she said, eager to get the ball rolling.

Liam read Amber's text then typed a reply: *"Yup, texted Emmet and he says he can hook us up with a guy for the cutouts."*

She sent back a smiley face and a thumbs-up emoji.

"And you want them by tomorrow, at your parent's house, for your Mom to decide if they're what she wants, right?"

She wrote back: *"Yes. Is that possible?"*

A cheeky grin spread across Liam's face as he texted: *"Please, do you need to ask? We're Dempsey's, remember? We get things handled."*

She sent back an emoji winking and sticking out its tongue, knowing full well to what he was referring: *the incident.*

"Why are they being delivered to your parent's house before they go to Dec's and Paula's? Why not just have them delivered to the new house and decide there?"

"Because that's how my mother is," Amber wrote back. *"She's got it in her head she needs to see them before they go to the new house and there's no use arguing it."*

"No worries, was just curious. It'll get done," Liam replied. *"I'll text once I have confirmation of everything. Gotta run, client waiting."*

Amber replied with another emoji; this one blowing a kiss.

Liam felt a flutter in his stomach. God, she made him weak in the knees. It was the last thing he'd ever expected - Paula's sister - and yet it felt like the best thing he'd ever experienced. It made him think of Trina and how he'd never felt this way about her, which led to the feeling of gratitude for Declan handling things when she'd showed up at his office. He'd dodged a bullet there and he hoped she'd eventually be okay and find someone who adored her the way he did Amber.

He grinned while he returned Amber's reply with an emoji of a smiling face, its eyes in the shape of red hearts, then tucked his phone into his pocket. Time to get to work.

Donna's phone pinged on the coffee table in the family room and she put down her knitting to check the message. She was working on personalized Christmas stockings, in secret, to hang over the mantle at Paula and Declan's new house to add an extra loving touch to the surprise housewarming party.

She leaned forward from her seat on the couch and picked up her phone. The text was from Jaimie and read: *"Did my part in setting the stage, told Paula I'm having a Christmas party."*

Donna grinned and typed back: *"Wonderful! Thank you, sweetie! I had a great visit with Bonnie and she's all excited about helping. Going to be a great surprise."*

"Perfect," Jaimie replied.

"Do you want to come over for dinner tonight?" Donna asked, her fingers tapping away at her screen.

Jaimie responded: *"Sounds good, thanks. Trent is doing rounds at the hospital, so it will just be Hazel and me."*

"Okay, see you girls later." Donna sent back.

Jaimie sent a waving girl emoji and Donna giggled. She put her phone back down on the coffee table, sat back in her seat and reached for her knitting. She was already halfway through Declan's stocking: the foot in a shade of forest green with white snowflakes, then a wide red band stitched with white poinsettias. Next she planned to knit a wide white band stitched with green trees, then she was going to add another layer with snowmen and candy canes, then his name, then a solid green band to complete it.

Perfect.

Everything was falling into place.

Declan drove his vehicle onto Mountain Pine Crescent, easily maneuvering the car through the freshly falling snow. He smiled to himself, appreciating the hush that had enveloped the streets. Not a creature was stirring, he noted, taking pleasure in the quiet. After the past few days he'd had - it felt as though any and every tech issue that could have happened, happened - he was looking forward to spending some uninterrupted time with Paula. He knew she'd been burning the candle at both ends as well, maybe they'd treat themselves and go out for dinner or a movie, or both.

He approached Doug and Donna's house - still slightly staggered by the plethora of seasonal decorations they'd scattered across the lawn - and just as he was about to pull up to the curb was nearly blinded by a sudden blast of light that lit up not just their house, but their neighbor's homes as well.

"Holy crap," Declan blurted, slamming on the brakes and sending the car skidding to the edge of the sidewalk with a thump.

A moment later, while he threw the gearstick into park, the garage door started opening and Amber ducked underneath it to step out onto the snow covered driveway.

"That might be a bit much, Dad!" she yelled, while Declan squinted and lifted a hand to shield his eyes from the light.

"You think," he muttered, shutting off the car.

Amber turned away from the house and caught sight of him behind the wheel. She waved broadly while calling out, "Dad! Declan's home! He can help, too!"

"Oh, boy," Declan said, then sighed in relief when Douglas cut the lights.

Amber grinned when she saw his face through the windscreen.

"A bit much, yeah?" she said, as he stepped out of the car and closed the door.

"Just a tad," he agreed, wryly, rubbing his eyes. "I'm still seeing spots."

She laughed and pulled the faux-fur lined hood on her army green parka more securely around her face. "I *told* Dad it was too much. We'll get complaints from the neighbors like last year."

"You had complaints?" He glanced at the houses on the crescent.

"Big time. They said they couldn't sleep because of the light."

Declan chuckled. Based on what he'd just seen, he believed it.

Douglas ambled out of the garage to join them, lifting his hand in greeting. He was dressed in a white puffa jacket and knitted red and white stripped scarf with a matching slouch cap. He looked like a happy-go-lucky snowman.

"Hey, Doug," Declan said, while gesturing toward the house. "Adding more lights, huh? I thought you guys were done decorating."

"Me, too, but Donna thinks we should have more now that we're having the surprise housewarming party. She thinks it will help throw Paula off the scent."

Declan lifted an eyebrow. "How so?"

"No idea," he replied, cheerfully. "But she asks and I deliver. I just gotta find a happy medium between giving her what she wants and not inspiring the neighbors into a riot."

"I think if we go with more colored lights, instead of white, that will help keep the peace," Amber offered, lifting her chin skyward to catch the falling snowflakes with her tongue.

Douglas nodded. "Right. Like we tried to do last time, before we were shut down."

"Shut down?" Declan parroted. "I thought you just had complaints."

"It started out that way and then we offered up the colored lights suggestion," Douglas explained.

"No go?"

He shook his head. "No, at first it seemed a good compromise, but…."

"Then Kimberly weighed in," Amber finished, cryptically, pointing at the neighbor's yellow bungalow.

Declan followed the direction of her pointed finger.

"And the stupidest part is she doesn't even live on the crescent," Amber huffed, shaking her head. "It's Ginny who actually lives here."

Douglas tapped his cap. "This year, we won't give her a chance to complain. We'll get it right the first time."

Declan looked toward the house. "Do you mind if I change first, before I help?"

"Of course," Douglas affirmed, clapping him on the back. "Do what you have to do."

Declan left them standing in the steadily falling snow, talking quietly about their next move. He chuckled to himself as he made his way to the front porch. Never a dull moment at the Hayes' house.

Paula drove her car along the same path Declan had earlier that afternoon and the closer she got to her parent's property, the slower she traveled.

Holy Moses, she thought. *The Griswold's* had nothing on them.

The snow covered lawn sported a life-sized Santa exiting a wooden outhouse, the structure surrounded by numerous oversized tree ornaments and garishly wrapped presents, countless wooden signs inked with swirly, time-worn sentiments of holiday merriment, and two clusters of plywood snowmen engaged in - what looked like - a game of winter lawn bowling.

And now, clearly added into the plethora of holiday jumble since she'd left earlier that day, there were lights. So many lights. Rudolph's nose wouldn't have stood a chance next to the glow.

A movement at the side of the driveway caught Paula's eye as she pulled up next to the curb behind Declan's vehicle. She turned off the car and peered through the passenger door window, then smirked at what she saw. Her husband, sporting one of her father's brightly colored toques - this one florescent orange - was laughing merrily as he coiled a string of lights around a wooden stake driven into the flowerbed at the edge of the house.

"Done!" She heard him yell, just before a spark flashed visibly from the freshly woven strings of lights and he hollered, "Whoa! Stop! Turn it off!"

"Oh, no, not again," Paula muttered, throwing open her door and dashing from the vehicle.

"Hey, Hon," Declan called, while she shuffled toward him, trying to keep her balance despite the slipperiness of the pavement. "Didn't even see you there. Was kinda busy."

"Yeah, I saw," she retorted, stopping in front of him, hands on her hips. "Busy almost getting electrocuted."

Declan laughed. "It's fine."

"Sure didn't look like it from where I was sitting."

"No worries," he assured her, before shifting his gaze to her vehicle. "Looks like you left your door open."

"Because I was so worried about getting to you," she stated, while Amber walked around the side of the garage.

"Hey, Paula!" she said, striding over to join them. "What do you think? Pretty nice job this year, huh?"

Paula folded her arms across her chest as she stared at her sister. "I guess. Unless we have to be worried the whole thing is going to light the house on fire."

Douglas appeared from around the corner, following in Amber's snowy tracks. "Hey, sweetheart! You're just in time to witness what a valuable helper your husband has been this year!"

Paula groaned, she should have known her father was masterminding all of it.

"You should congratulate him on his creativity," he went on. "He really brought this year's display to life while simultaneously sparing us the neighbor's wrath."

Paula cut her eyes at Declan.

"It wasn't as bad as it looked," he insisted, trying to temper the effects of what she'd seen. "It was just one bulb."

"What?" Douglas looked back and forth between them. "What's going on? What did I miss?"

"A bulb barely sparked and Paula's worried we've created a fire hazard."

"*Again*," she couldn't keep herself from adding. "And it wasn't *barely* a spark, either. I could see it all the way from the curb."

Douglas laughed and waved his hands in the air. "No worries, darling! Every year we get sparking bulbs.

It's the nature of the game. They just need to be replaced and everything is fine."

She gave him a skeptical look, to which he replied, "What? Do you *see* a house burned down? No, you don't. The proof is in the pudding."

"Mmmm, pudding," Amber said, clapping her mittened hands together. "I could go for some pudding. Anyone else wanna join me?"

"We'll just replace the bulb that sparked then be right in," Douglas said, then turned to Declan. "Which one was it?"

"Here." He pointed to one of the green bulbs on the string.

"Have you never heard of LED lights?" Paula remarked. "No sparks. No worries."

"Follow me," Douglas instructed, as though she hadn't even spoken.

"You should close your car door, Hon," Declan reminded her, before trailing her Dad back to the garage for a replacement bulb.

"Seriously, though," Paula began, turning toward Amber, then stopping when she saw her sister had already begun shuffling through the half foot of fluffy snow on the path toward the house - pudding in mind.

"Well, this is a fine turn of events," she breathed, a vapor cloud forming in front of her face in the crisp evening air.

No one was left to respond, so she made her way carefully back to her car to retrieve her things and close her door.

Donna chopped zucchini at the kitchen island while Paula shucked corn at the table. Jaimie, seated across from her, sighed contentedly and lifted her feet to rest on the vacant chair next to hers.

"This is nice," she said, smiling at Paula and their mother. "So calming and relaxing."

"Too bad Trent is working," Paula replied.

Jaimie nodded. "Yeah, but I told him I'd bring him leftovers, so he's happy."

"You know, it occurs to me," Donna offered, pausing with the knife in her hand held aloft. "You've probably gotten pretty good with party planning."

Paula exchanged a look with Jaimie. They'd grown up hearing many conversations started in just that manner and, in their experience, they'd never turned out well.

"I mean," Donna went on, putting down the knife to replace it with a glass of red wine, "you do *do* that sort of thing, right?"

Paula kept her mouth shut.

Jaimie, unsure as to what her mother was trying to achieve, finally filled the silence. "Who are you talking to, Mom?"

Donna took a sip of wine then put the glass back down on the counter. "Paula, of course."

"Why, *of course*?" Jaimie asked, trying to sound indignant while barely repressing a smirk. "Are you saying you don't think I can plan a party?"

Donna picked up the knife and resumed chopping the zucchini. "Of course you can!"

"I don't know," she said, peeling the label from her bottle of beer. "Didn't sound like you thought so."

Well, it's not so much you can't," Donna admitted, waving the knife in the air. "Just that I was thinking, since Paula apparently gets paid for such things, it would make sense to include her in your party plans."

Paula snorted when her mother used the word 'include'. Please. She was being *recruited*, not included.

Jaimie looked at her mother, wide-eyed. What the hell was she doing? Trying to get Paula to unwittingly plan her own party? Donna gave her a covert wink, which explained nothing except for the fact that, apparently, what she was saying was calculated.

Paula placed the final ear of corn in the green bowl on the tabletop. "Yes, Mom," she said, finally joining the conversation. "To quote you, I have *gotten pretty good with party planning*. What's your point?"

Donna abandoned her chopping and dropped the knife back onto the counter "Good question," she praised, while wiping her hands on the blue apron tied around her waist.

Jaimie and Paula waited, assuming she'd continue.

They were correct.

She picked up her wine glass and navigated around the island. "Since this sort of thing is in *your* wheel house—"

"Nope," Paula declared, swiftly cutting her off. "Jaimie and I already discussed it. Not happening."

Donna winked at Jaimie a second time then shrugged and said, "Oh, I didn't know that. Well, perhaps *I'll* just have to help her out then."

Ahh, Jaimie thought. So this was her way of letting Paula know she was going to be involved with the party and; thus, freeing herself from having to hide what she was doing. A little advanced warning of her plan would have been nice.

"There's Momma," Declan announced, all smiles as he walked into the kitchen with Hazel in his arms.

Jaimie grinned at her daughter. "Everything okay?"

"Perfect," he assured her. "She's a sweetheart. Must take after her Momma."

Jaimie chuckled. "And you're a charmer. And, as I've met your father, I'm guessing you get that lovely trait from him?"

Declan threw his head back, laughing. Hazel blinked her large brown eyes a number of times, revealing her surprise at the suddenness of the sound, then giggled at her uncle's merriment.

"So, how're things going in here?" he asked, handing Hazel over to Jaimie. "Need any help?"

"Funny you should ask," Paula stated, flatly, picking up the bowl of corn then rising from her chair to carry it to the island. "Because Mom apparently thinks Jaimie needs help planning her Christmas party."

Declan stiffened then said, "Christmas party?" while inwardly wincing at the woodenness of his delivery.

Paula didn't notice. She was too focused on her annoyance to register anything else.

"Oh, now," Donna placated, sipping her wine and settling herself on a chair at the table. "It's not so much *her* party as it is the family's. That's why I thought—"

"But," Paula interrupted, "you thought wrong."

Jaimie lifted her eyebrows at Declan then swiftly moved her beer bottle out of Hazel's reach.

Donna tipped her glass to her mouth and took a cheek-bulging swig of wine.

"Can I get anyone a refill?" Declan offered, trying to fill the silence.

Paula shook her head, wiped her hands on a dish towel, then turned on the burner under a pot of water on the stove for the corn.

"I'm good," Jaimie said, standing up. "I should change Hazel."

Declan shot her a desperate look as she quickly exited the kitchen. He snuck a look in Donna's direction - she was staring off into the distance while drumming her fingers on the wooden tabletop - and wished he was anywhere else. Subterfuge was not one of his strong points.

"Hey, all, what's the good word?" Douglas inquired, all smiles as he opened the back door and walked into the kitchen carrying the cat.

"Oh, thank god," Declan muttered, before slapping on a grin. "Hey, Doug! How was it out there? Need some more help with anything? *Anything* at all?"

Douglas stole a glance at his wife, still silently strumming her fingers, and raised an eyebrow at Declan.

Declan widened his eyes by way of reply, hoping he'd get the message.

"Absolutely!" he agreed, catching the cue. "And you're just the man I was looking for. Grab your coat and let's head back out!"

Like a dog being surprised with a ride in the car, Declan practically sprinted toward the backdoor. He snatched his jacket from a hook and eagerly followed Douglas out of the house.

"Be back in a jif!" Douglas called out, before they firmly shut the door and made a beeline for the safety of the garage.

Jaimie stood outside Paula's closed bedroom door, readying herself for the task at hand: making sure her sister was okay after the conversation that had transpired in the kitchen. After Paula had left the room, Donna had insisted Jaimie go up and commiserate to keep things seemingly normal. Which would have been fine, if they were. But they weren't.

No, *this* time she knew the conversation downstairs had been put into play on purpose, which was the opposite of normal, and being privy to that information was making her feel terribly self-conscious. She was sure she'd come across just as wooden as Declan had earlier and Paula would suspect something was up.

She took a breath, released it slowly, and silently assured herself everything would be fine. Then she knocked: three firm raps.

Nothing.

She tried again.

"Enter," Paula said, her voice muffled by the door between them.

Jaimie twisted the knob and pushed the door open then poked her head around the edge. "Are you sure it's safe?"

"Sorry," Paula apologized, slumping back into her pillow on the bed. "Didn't mean to be so sharp. I thought you might be Mom."

Jaimie walked into the room and closed the door behind her.

"Where's Hazel?"

"With Amber." Jaimie gestured to the bed. "Can I?"

Paula nodded and shifted herself to the right to make room.

Jaimie climbed onto the bed and laid back with a satisfied, "Ahhhh", making Paula chuckle at her obvious enjoyment.

"Sounds like you need a nap."

"Since the day Hazel was born," she quipped, closing her eyes.

Paula pulled herself up onto her elbow. "So, what's up?"

Jaimie opened one eye briefly, looked at her, then closed it again. "Do you want to talk about it?"

"About what?"

"You know."

"What, Mom? What's to say? Same old, same old."

Jaimie opened her eyes again. "Yeah, but you got up-in-arms pretty darn fast down there."

Paula sat up then got off the bed to begin pacing the floor. "You would, too, if you'd been living here for the past couple of months."

"No argument there, but…."

Paula stopped pacing and put her hands on her hips. "But, what? You remember what it was like, growing up. Well, since we moved in here, it's like she's gone right back to being that person again."

Jaimie sat up on the bed and nodded. "Okay, I get that. And while there's no question it's really shitty, aren't you tired of the conflict?"

"Obviously." Paula folded her arms across her chest. "But what do you suggest? I should just let her do her usual thing without saying a word so as to avoid conflict?"

"No. But—"

"Because I've seriously started having flashbacks to our childhood and all the times she had some *great idea* and we got suckered in *every damned time*, only to have it go wrong because she had no follow through and we had to scramble to pick up the pieces of her great idea and slap them together into something worthwhile."

Jaimie watched as she gestured wildly throughout her rapid-fire speech and nodded along. She remembered.

Paula paused to catch her breath then further elaborated, "Like that time, I think I was around eight, and she got the idea into her head to have an Easter egg hunt for us and our friends."

Jaimie winced.

"*Exactly*. And there we were, hours before the hunt, and that's when she suddenly remembered she had to actually boil and color all the eggs before she hid them. One hundred fifty freakin' eggs!"

Jaimie couldn't help herself and smirked at the memory.

"Oh, sure," Paula said, pointing a finger at her. "It's sort-of funny *now*, twenty years later, but it sure as hell wasn't at the time. At the time, we were in panic mode for hours and hours and ended up so exhausted from having to get all of the work done in time that we didn't even enjoy the party. At least I didn't, anyway."

Jaimie's smirk shifted into an expression of sympathy.

"Let's be honest, that's just one of many, many examples." Paula sighed and shook her head. "God, any good therapist would probably say that's why I went into the business I'm in. I felt so out of control as a kid, I'm making up for it in adulthood."

Jaimie said nothing. It was something she'd thought before, too, but she wasn't about to add that speculation to the conversation.

Instead, she tried to soften it and said, "Yeah, but you love your work right?"

"I do," Paula acknowledged, sitting down on the edge of the bed. "So as least there was one good thing that came out of all of the instability, I found the path that makes me happy."

"Silver lining," Jaimie commented.

Paula nodded. "Agreed. So anyway, that aside, I hope you understand the reason I was so swift to shut down Mom's comments about me getting involved in your holiday party. If I would have told her I'd help, you know damned well she'd just assume she could dump whatever she'd volunteered to do, on me."

"I know," Jaimie said, her voice soothing. "I get it. I really do. But as I was going to say, regardless of Mom and her *ways*, don't you think it's time you threw in the towel and stop pushing against it?"

"And do her bidding, you mean?"

She shook her head. "No. I mean, just let it go. Accept her as she is and free yourself from the conflict of it all."

Paula stared at her.

"What? Do I have something on my face?"

"Are you telling me that's what you've done? Is that why you're so bloody calm around her now? Because you've thrown in the so-called towel?"

"Pretty much," she admitted. "I just came to the decision life is too short to keep on battling against the wackiness that is our mother, especially when it gets me nowhere anyway."

"So, what you're telling me is, you've basically come to the conclusion that nothing you do to get through to her registers on her radar no matter how hard you try. It's like trying to reason with a crazy person."

Jaimie snickered. "Yeah, something like that."

"So, it's not so much giving up," Paula said, digesting the idea. "As it is *getting out*."

Jaimie got up from the bed and stretched her arms over her head. "However you need to approach it is fine, as long as you feel better."

Paula smiled. "I do."

Jaimie dropped her arms back down to her sides and matched her grin. "Excellent."

A sharp rap at the door and Amber calling out, "Jaimie? Are you guys in there?" put a halt to the conversation.

Jaimie walked over to the door and opened it.

"There she is!" Amber cheered.

Hazel, tucked into her auntie's embrace, gave Jaimie a gummy grin.

She reached out to take her daughter. "Is she starting to get whiny?"

"A bit." Amber handed her niece over then pushed her long, dark hair back from her shoulders. "I figured she needed some Mommy time."

Hazel yawned widely.

"And a nap," Jaimie added, snuggling the baby against her. "Which is our cue to get going."

"Thanks for the talk," Paula said, as her sister and niece exited the room.

"Anytime," Jaimie replied, making her way down the stairs, Amber following behind.

"Hey, Amber?" Paula called, before she was out of hearing range. "Have you seen Declan?"

"I think he's still out with Dad in the garage," she called back.

"K, thanks."

Paula walked over to the bedroom window and looked out, hoping to catch sight of her husband. Nothing. He and her Dad were clearly using the garage as a hide-out of sorts, laying low until the storm passed.

Well, she'd just have to go out and tell them they could re-enter the house without fear. She was going to take Jaimie's advice and throw in the towel. Heck, she was going to throw it in so solidly, it would be a challenge to ever find it again.

Chapter 21

Paula raced through the house, searching for her messenger bag. She was sure she'd put it in the bedroom, but then she *had* been doing some work in the sunroom the previous evening, so it was just as likely - given all of the things she was trying to remember - she'd left it there.

She strode down the hallway and turned into the dining room, then came to a dead stop. "What the hell?" she said, taking in the sight before her.

The ten-seater, heavy oak table and matching chairs had been moved aside and in their place were faceless, life-sized, stand-in cutouts of Santa and missus Claus, two elves and, wait … here came Liam, via the sunroom, directing two men carrying three reindeer cutouts to add to the holiday menagerie.

"Yup, right in here with the others," he was saying, arms waving like a ground marshal. "Right there next to the elves, line 'em up."

Paula readied herself to get his attention once he was finished, but her mother took that moment to step out of Santa's shadow.

"Oh, Paula!" she gasped, when she noticed her daughter standing as motionless as the stand-ins.

Donna had been hoping she would have already left for work when the cutouts arrived, but was also feeling a bit self-congratulatory they'd had the forward thinking to create the fib about helping with the party at Jaimie's house; no worries about being caught out and having to explain.

Paula attempted, and failed, to sidle past the figures. "Can I move that so I can get by?" she asked, pointing to the first of the two faceless elves blocking her path.

"Perfect timing!" Donna enthused, taking the proverbial bull by the horns. "I'm thinking of renting these stand-in cutouts for Jaimie's party. Wouldn't it be fun to let everyone take photos of themselves?"

Paula gave up on waiting for a reply to her question and started shuffling the plywood elf aside so she could pass.

Amber came speeding in from the sunroom, her dark eyes glittering in her excitement. The two men who'd been carrying the reindeer grinned and exchanged a look, inspiring Liam to scowl at them and growl, "Alright, move it along. She's spoken for."

Not needing to be told twice the duo did as they were told, stepping around Amber and returning to the truck outside. While they didn't know much about Liam, they knew his brother Emmet: and playboy or not, he had a reputation of being willing to back up his words if pushed. They had no inclination to find out if it was a family trait.

Donna eased her way around the second elf then reached out to grab Paula's arm. "Come on," she encouraged, tugging at her. "Let's try them out and see what we think."

"Ooh, good idea!" Amber rushed over and began shoving the elf Paula had just moved, back into line with its twin. "Let's be elves!"

Before she could argue, Paula found herself being dragged along and her head pushed forward so she was gazing out of a hole where an Elf's face should have been.

Donna sprinted around in front of the cutouts and held up her phone. "Smile!" she cheered.

"Wait," Paula said, but it was too late. The flash went off and the photo was taken.

Donna giggled and held up the phone for them to see. While Amber darted over to gush at the photo, Paula sighed and stepped back from the cutout. "Listen," she began, before her mother cut her off.

"See! It's cute, right? Our guests would love it!"

"Oh-em-gee, I love the face you're making!" Amber declared. "Next time, I'm going to do that."

"I wasn't *making a face*," Paula tried to explain, before being interrupted by Liam.

"That's hysterical," he laughed, looking over Donna's shoulder. "You should share it with Declan."

"Oooh!" Amber clapped her hands, her face lit up. "Let's get one of me and Liam as missus Claus and Santa and we can send that, too!"

"I have to get my bag," Paula stated, slipping by them and the faceless reindeer to continue her quest.

"Oh, come *on*," Donna insisted, trailing her to the sunroom. "It's a good party activity, right? You can at least tell me that much. And we'll hire someone to take photos. A wonderful memento of their holiday fun."

"Sure. Fun," Paula agreed, relieved when she saw her bag on the floor beside the couch. "But I really have to go."

"Of course." Donna stepped aside to let her pass.

Paula stopped and stared.

Donna stared back. "What?"

"That's it?"

Donna frowned. What was she getting at? Then it hit her. In her old ways, she would have pushed for more input, not just moved aside. No wonder Paula was looking at her as though she was an alien. She had to deflect.

"No, it's not," she said, haughtily, hands on hips. "You didn't let me finish. I was *going* to say, *of course* I know you don't want to help out with anything party related because you already made your thoughts loud and clear about *that*. But there's no reason you can't think of someone else for a moment and take just one or two more photos before you leave."

Paula rolled her eyes and Donna repressed a smirk while she reached out and began tugging on her arm again. Clearly, she'd hit the right note.

"I don't have time," Paula told her, trying to shake her off.

"Sure you do," Donna argued, cheerfully playing her part. "Just a couple more!"

Amber nudged Liam and he piped up, "Let's try the reindeer this time, there's three of them."

Paula managed to throw her mother off her arm then stalked out of the room, calling back over her shoulder, "I don't have time!"

"Maybe later, then!" Donna yelled back, joyfully. "And we have eggnog to add to coffee, if you want!"

The sound of Paula's feet pounding up the staircase shook the house and Donna's smirk turned into a full-blown smile. "Mission accomplished, I'd say?" she whispered.

"And then some," Liam agreed.

Amber nodded. "Absolutely. She totally thinks you were just trying to get her involved. No way she suspected anything else."

"Perfect," Donna said, before gesturing to the stand-ins. "So, now that we've tried them out, I think we can all agree these are a great idea. Let's take that photo of you two as Santa and missus Claus before we get those guys back in here to move them over to the new house."

Amber grabbed Liam's hand and they scrambled around the backside of the cutouts.

Erin hummed quietly while she walked along the third floor hallway to the office. She'd stopped at their mailbox at the building's front entrance on her way in and was now flipping through the pile in her hands; mostly flyers for fast food outlets and a couple of bills. She stopped humming as she got closer to *Certain Events,* surprised to hear, what sounded like, someone seriously yelling.

"Well, I don't care WHAT the reason is! GET. IT. DONE. RIGHT!"

Erin's eyes widened and she pushed opened the office door. Wow. She stared at Paula's back and watched her slam the phone down onto her desk then snap, "For fuck's sake!"

"Paula?" she ventured, slowly easing her way inside.

Paula whirled around in her chair. "Oh, sorry! I thought I was alone."

"Problem?"

Paula leaned back in her chair and exhaled sharply. "Nothing that can't be fixed."

Erin pressed her lips together. It certainly hadn't sounded like *nothing*, but she didn't think her pointing that out would be appreciated at that moment. She crossed the room and dropped the mail onto the kitchenette countertop.

"And, speaking of which, if you want coffee you'll have to go out to buy one."

Erin's eyebrows lifted while she unwound her purple scarf from her neck and walked over to the coat rack to hang it on an empty rung. "Because…?"

Paula's face grew sheepish. "Because the coffee pot's broken."

"Okay." She nodded, digesting the information while she slipped out of her heavy coat and settled it on the same rung as her scarf. "So, I should get another one then, yes?"

Paula rubbed her temples. "Yes. Sorry. Apparently, the combined pressure of the Bazzano party and my mother have finally gotten to me."

"What now?"

"It's the party Jaimie's having. Mom is *helping out*," she said, making air quotes with her fingers. "Which would be fine if she wasn't doing her damnedest to get me involved in the process."

Erin grimaced and walked over to her desk and sat down.

"My feelings exactly. You should have seen what was going on before I left the house. She had a menagerie of those life-sized stand-in thingies. You know the type with the faces cut out?"

Erin nodded.

"Right. Well, she seems to think they'd be a welcomed addition to Jaimie's party and had them set up all over the dining room when I left."

"Wow." Erin tried to picture what that would look like: a room full of faceless stand-ins. "So, what did they look like?"

"All Christmas themed. Santa and his wife, a group of elves, some reindeer, and who knows what else was added after I left."

Erin grinned at the new mental image in her head while she logged into her computer. "Sounds festive."

Paula's phone pinged and she reached into her bag beside her desk to retrieve it. "Speak of the devil," she remarked, turning her phone around and holding it across her desktop for Erin to see.

Erin couldn't help but giggle at the photo displayed on the screen. It was the one Donna had snapped of Paula and Amber behind the elf stand-ins. Amber was grinning merrily while Paula's face was twisted, as though she'd been talking as the photo was being taken: which she had been.

The phone pinged again and Paula turned it back around to check the next message.

"And here's another one."

Erin tried to keep her composure and not snicker a second time when Paula whipped the phone back around to reveal the photo of Amber and Liam as mister and missus Claus. Her efforts; however, failed and she exhaled an amused snort.

Paula shot her a wry grin. It *was* amusing, no question, but unfortunately her mother's attempts to drag her into the mayhem had soured the humor of it all.

"Looks like it's going to be an interesting party," Erin offered, returning her focus to her computer screen.

Paula took a steadying breath. "As long as I can survive to see the Bazzano job done without having a mental breakdown, I'll be happy."

"No worries." Erin waved her hand dismissively. "We're at crunch time. T minus twenty-eight hours. We can do it."

Paula smiled at her, grateful for her easy-going demeanor. "Agreed. By tomorrow night, this will all be a memory."

"Speaking of which, don't you need to be heading over to the venue?"

Paula's eyebrows shot up. "What time is it?"

"Twenty past eight."

"Aack!" she yelped, working quickly to shut down her computer. "You'll be okay here?"

"Absolutely."

Paula asked the same thing every time they had a big event. It was like a script the two of them followed that reassured her everything would turn out okay.

"Okay, then," she said, tucking the last things she needed into her bag. "My cell is at the ready, so call for whatever you need."

"Got it," Erin agreed, watching her beetle across the room to grab her black, wool car coat. "Drive safe, the roads are kinda ugly."

Paula slipped on her coat and fastened the buttons down the front. "Will do," she said, striding back over to her desk to pick up her messenger bag. "I'll give you an update on how everything is going along at the venue once I'm there."

Erin clipped her headset on and gave a small salute. "Roger that."

Paula chuckled and waved as she exited the office.

Bonnie stood at the living room window in Declan and Paula's house, watching for both Liam's vehicle and the large white van carrying the Christmas stand-ins.

She'd been at the house for the past couple of hours with Linda, the two of them cleaning. Linda had had to leave to go to her son's elementary school to help out with the lunch program leaving Bonnie on her own to wait for the others to turn up; thus the reason she'd resorted to staring out the window like a child waiting for a parent to return home. Or for the mailman to arrive. Or a friend coming over to visit. The list could go on and on.

"There they are," she sang, when Liam's SUV pulled up into the driveway beside her car and the white van eased in behind both vehicles.

She moved away from the window and went to the front door to welcome them all into the house.

Donna was the first to step out of Liam's vehicle and she began waving excitedly when she saw Bonnie in the open doorway.

"Hello! Hello!"

Bonnie waved back. "Glad you made it safely."

Amber stepped out next and she and Donna made their way to the house while Liam went to join the two moving guys at the back of their van.

"The roads were gross," Amber stated, reaching out to hug Bonnie. "But Liam drives like a boss, so all good."

Donna stepped in for a hug when Amber was done and Bonnie said, "I'm just glad you're all here safely," while she squeezed her back. "Come inside and see how well Linda and I did getting things cleaned up. In addition to her many other talents, my daughter-in-law cleans like a pro."

Donna scanned the foyer while she slipped her boots from her feet and set them next to Amber's on the floor mat. The last time she'd been to the house had been just after Paula and Declan had decided to put a bid on it and had invited her and Douglas to have a look. Everything looked the same as she remembered, so she followed behind Bonnie as she led them further into the house and down the hallway toward the kitchen.

"Is Linda still here?" Amber asked.

Bonnie stopped a few feet shy of the doorway that led into the kitchen. "No. She had to get to the boy's school to help with the lunch program. She's an amazing woman. My son is a lucky man."

Donna blinked, impressed that she would offer such lovely compliments about her daughter-in-law, even though Linda wasn't there to hear it. She studied her for a moment and thought she could do well to hang out with her more and let her good vibes rub off a bit. It might be just the thing to help with her relationship with Paula.

"Okay," Bonnie said, excitement lacing her words. "Are you two ready for this? Because you're not going to believe your eyes when you see it."

"Yes, show us!" Amber enthused.

She stepped aside to let them walk past her into the kitchen. "Tadaaa!"

"Ohmygod!" Amber exclaimed, her eyes wide like saucers.

Donna's jaw went slack. Declan had said it was beautiful, but this was more than she'd expected.

Amber dashed further into the room, darting around the newly built, curved island to stand in front of the pecan colored, alder wood cabinets gracing the walls.

"Aren't they just beautiful?" Bonnie enthused.

"Gorgeous," Amber gushed, running her hands along the doors then pulling on the brushed nickel handles to open them and peek inside.

"And a far cry from those chipping, yellowing pine things that were here before," Bonnie stated. "I know they were popular once-upon-a-time, but it was time for them to retire. No amount of cleaning or polishing was going to save them."

"Wow, you sure have a great memory," Donna remarked, surprised by the comment.

Bonnie smiled. "What do you mean?"

"And these countertops and backsplash," Amber raved, turning away from the cabinets to trace her index finger across the smooth, glossy, cool surface of the sand-toned, gold and brown flecked island top. "Did Paula say they were made of quartz?"

Bonnie nodded.

"I'm just saying," Donna explained, by-passing Amber's narrative, "it's been months since the kids bought the house and yet you remember the old cabinets perfectly. Impressive."

Bonnie's brow furrowed and she shook her head. "I'm not following."

"Well…," Donna began, but her words ground to a halt when things clicked into place in her head.

Oh. Of course.

Bonnie, unlike she and Douglas, had been invited back to the house since Paula and Declan had first put a bid down on it. And, judging by her familiarity of the place, it sounded likely she'd been there quite a bit. *That's* why she wasn't understanding what was being said about her memory.

"Everything okay?" Bonnie asked, noticing the mixture of emotions on Donna's face.

"Fine," she stated. "It's nothing I haven't done to myself."

Before Bonnie could ask anything further, Amber interrupted the awkward conversation by announcing, "This floor is totally stunning."

They all looked down at their feet.

"But the best thing, I think," she went on, pointing her index finger toward the opposite side of the space, "is how they opened up the two rooms into one. You'd never know there used to be a wall there. It's amazing."

Donna followed her daughter's pointed finger to where the wall that had once separated the kitchen from the dining room used to be. She was right, no trace of it existed. Instead, it was now one large entertainment space and Declan and Paula's brand new twelve-seater table was easily accessible for whatever sort of gathering they desired.

"Getting some ideas, Mom?" Amber asked, walking back around the island to stand next to Donna. "Thinking of making some changes at your house?"

"Oh, well," Donna said, shrugging.

"Oooh, think of how great it would be if you updated the kitchen! You said you like white cabinets, right? You could do that!"

Donna laughed and said, "Maybe," before quickly adding, "but let's worry about that at another time. Today is about getting things done here."

Bonnie grinned at Amber, enjoying her child-like enthusiasm. She could understand why Liam was so charmed by her and hoped the relationship blossomed into something lasting.

"Fine," Amber agreed, knowing full well her mother was placating her.

She shucked her jacket from her shoulders and plunked it onto the island top then reached into one of the pockets to retrieve her cellphone.

"Hey!" Liam called out, pulling all of their attention back to the task at hand. "Where are these going?"

Amber looked at Donna and they shared a grin. Amber tucked her phone into her jeans pocket and walked over to Bonnie, grabbing her arm. "Come on. You have to see the stand-ins, they're hilarious!"

Bonnie let herself be led from the kitchen by, finger's crossed, the next woman to eventually take the Dempsey name. Not that she'd ever say that to Liam, of course, but if the transformation that had happened in the kitchen was any indication to go by, wishes *could* turn into dreams.

Donna, seated cross-legged on the living room carpet, frowned as she looked at recipe after recipe in the worn cookbook on her lap. She peered at the pages, flipped them back and forth and, finally, pulled her reading glasses from her face and dropped them onto the coffee table with an audible clatter.

Douglas, seated in his armchair reading the newspaper, looked up from the pages. "Trouble?"

"I can't make a decision and it's making me crazy," she grumbled, shoving the cookbook aside and laying backward onto the carpet.

Declan glanced at his mother-in-law sprawled across the floor then snuck a look at his wife seated beside him on the sofa. She wasn't biting. Instead, Paula continued to focus on her laptop, reviewing the notes she'd made for the Bazzano party.

"Can I help?" Douglas offered. "Do you want me to come there and have a look?"

Declan, playing a word scramble game on his tablet, covertly watched the back and forth exchange between his in-laws. Something was up, he was sure of it.

"No," Donna sighed, sitting upright again. "I just think it would help greatly if *someone* who dealt with this sort of thing in a professional capacity could offer their opinion."

Douglas exchanged a look with Declan.

"Paula?" Donna finally pressed. "Could *you* offer an opinion in this matter?"

Paula looked up from her computer, smiled sweetly and said, "No, thank you."

Donna's eyebrows lifted. "Pardon?"

"I said, *no thank you*," she repeated.

"Well, that's a fine how-do-you-do," Donna huffed. "I ask for some help and this is the response I get?"

Paula closed her laptop and got up from the sofa. "Excuse me," she said, brushing by Declan to leave the room.

Donna waited a beat until she was sure she was out of sight, then giggled.

"So, I'm assuming that was all on purpose?" Declan asked.

She nodded. "Of course. I have to keep up the pretense, otherwise she's sure to become suspicious."

He raised an eyebrow skeptically.

"She *would*," she insisted. "Think about it. I agree to help Jaimie with her holiday party then never make any more obvious effort to get her involved? Doesn't that seem a bit odd? A bit out of character for me? Or, rather, the former me?"

He thought about it. She was right.

"Uh-huh." She pointed a finger at his face. "It would."

Declan returned to his tablet.

"Douglas?" Donna said, turning to her husband.

"Yes, my dear?"

"I would actually welcome your input."

He sat forward in his recliner. "Let's have a look."

Declan eased open the door to the bedroom and tentatively crossed the threshold. He was nervous. After what had transpired downstairs, he wasn't sure what he would be facing when he entered the room. Donna may have been being purposeful in her actions, but Paula didn't know that and, as a result, he had to weather the possible backlash.

Paula was snuggled into the bedclothes and looked up from her book, a smile decorating her face.

"Hey," he said, shutting the door behind him.

"Hey, yourself," she replied.

He sat on the edge of the bed. "You okay?"

She closed her book and set it beside her on the bed. "Yeah. Why?"

He looked at her levelly. "Seriously?"

"Okay, *fine*," she said, smirking. "Yes, it's bothersome that my mother won't stop trying to rope me into helping with the Christmas party, but that's who she is, so it's to be expected, right?"

"Right," he agreed, thinking Donna clearly did know what she was talking about. Paula saw her mother's actions as business as usual.

"So, since that's the case, I chose to avoid a scene and take Jaimie's advice."

"Which is?"

Paula shifted herself into a sitting position. "She advised I basically throw in the towel."

"Throw in the towel," he repeated. "I'm not following."

"She suggested I just accept Mom for who she is and that she's never going to change and stop trying to fight it."

"Good advice."

"I know. And that's why I'm just stepping away like I did downstairs and not letting her engage me anymore. Avoids a whole lot of unnecessary upheaval."

"And you're sure you can stay unengaged and not react, even if she's being … *her*?"

"Yup," she said, settling back into the pillows on the bed. "Like water off a duck's back."

"Okay."

"What? Why do you sound so skeptical?"

"Because I know your mother, that's why."

"Bah." Paula waved his words away with a flick of her hand and picked up her book. "She's no match for me."

He said nothing further. He'd done as Donna had instructed: kept things normal by performing his part as the concerned husband. Paula seemed fine, time to let it drop.

Chapter 22

Paula tip-toed around the bedroom, using her cellphone as a makeshift flashlight so as to not wake Declan still asleep in bed. It was early, five AM early, and she wanted to get a jumpstart on what was certain to be a crazy day. There was so much riding on the Bazzano party, she needed everything to go as smoothly as glass. A whole new level of party planning was standing on the doorstep of *Certain Events* and today's event would be the push needed to send it across the threshold.

"Oh!" Paula yelped, bumping her knee against the dressing table. Damn, that hurt.

Declan rolled over, squinting in the dim light, his cheek creased from sleep. Beside him, tucked into the comforter folds, Sylvester yawned and flexed his pink toes.

"Go back to sleep," she said, reaching down to rub her knee. "Both of you."

Declan yawned as widely as the cat had just done. "What are you doing up? It's still dark out."

Paula repressed a frustrated exhale. She'd told him more than once that today was the Bazzano event. Hell, she's told them all.

"Is the venue for the party even open this early?" he asked, rubbing his eyes.

"Not usually," she said, feeling a stab of guilt for her knee-jerk annoyance. Clearly he did remember. "I asked them to make a special concession for me, so I'm heading in early to make sure everything starts smoothly. Go back to sleep."

"Can I make you a coffee or some food before you go?" he offered, while she slipped on her gold hoop earrings and grabbed a long, peacock blue silk scarf from the back of the dressing table chair.

She looped the scarf loosely around her neck. "No, no. You sleep, I'll grab a coffee on the way out."

"I look forward to hearing your stories later."

Paula walked over to the bed to give him a quick kiss.

He reached out and ran a hand down her side. "You look great, by the way. Gorgeous."

Paula grinned. She'd chosen the red shift dress because it not only fit like a perfectly tailored glove, but the power of the color made her feel she could tackle any challenge she might face.

"Thanks, get some more sleep."

"I love you, sweetie," he said. "Knock 'em dead."

Paula picked up her leather satchel, tucked her cellphone into the side pocket and crossed the shag carpet to ease open the bedroom door.

"I love you, too," she whispered, then stepped out into the hallway and closed the door behind her.

"What are you doing up so early?" Donna demanded, her face a picture of surprise when Paula strode into the kitchen.

Paula put her satchel on the floor next to her feet and chose a plain white cup from the mug-tree on the countertop next to the sink. "I could say the same to you. You've never been an early riser."

Donna shrugged. "I haven't exactly gone fully to bed yet. I had things on my mind, so I've been sort of napping through the evening."

"Well, it's morning now," Paula said, pouring herself a half-cup of coffee from the carafe next to the mug-tree. "You might want to catch some sleep before the day gets into full swing."

Donna's leaned forward in her chair to rest her elbows on the table. "So, what on earth are you doing that's so important to be up so early?"

"Work."

"A party?"

Paula nodded and Donna's face lit up while she said, "Speaking of which, guess who *I* have coming here this afternoon?"

Paula shrugged her shoulders and drank her coffee.

"Oh, come on, guess," Donna prompted. "I'll even give you a hint: some people call him *the king*."

"You have a dead person coming over?"

Donna threw her head back and laughed. "No, no," she said, catching her breath. "The men coming here are very much alive."

"Men?"

She pushed back her chair and stood up, too excited to sit still. "Yes! Ten Elvis impersonators are coming here this afternoon to audition for the holiday party!"

Paula's face went blank. She had no response to that information.

"Oh, I wish you were going to be here!" Donna enthused, coming around the table to grin into her daughter's face. "In that dress, you'd add such great flare to the Christmas energy. Is there any way you could get off early to pop round and see the auditions?"

"No." Paula swallowed the last of her coffee.

"Oh, come *on*," she wheedled. "I'm sure that your girl, Emma? Emily?"

"Erin," Paula corrected, teeth clenched.

"Right. Her. I'm sure she can handle your little party so that you can get back."

Paula took a deep breath then let it out. Throw in the towel, she silently coached herself.

"Well, anyway," Donna gushed, flicking her hair back from her face. "It's going to be a hoot!"

Paula put her empty mug in the sink, picked up her bag then crossed the room to the back door.

"Off so soon?"

"Yup. Lots to do." She slipped on her black coat while simultaneously tucking her feet into her driving boots.

"Okay," Donna said, waving her off. "But remember, if you're bored with your thingy, pop home for the auditions."

Mustering all of her willpower, Paula closed the door with a firm hand instead of slamming it soundly behind her.

Donna snickered. Clearly, she was doing a good job channeling the side of herself that set Paula off. In fact, when she'd offered up the '*if you're bored with your thingy*' comment, she'd felt slightly concerned as to what Paula would do with it; her face had gone positively rigid with annoyance.

Donna grinned, pleased with the way everything was coming together for the housewarming party. She was so looking forward to finally coming clean and being able to tell her daughter she'd been soul searching - courtesy of a no-holds-barred intervention from Jaimie - and realized how much time she'd wasted not appreciating her.

"Only one more week," she said, to the empty kitchen.

Declan scanned the busy shopping mall hallway, looking for an empty bench seat. His feet were killing him, ironic as he spent so much of his day on them, but he attributed their fatigue to his mental state and the fact he was trying - and failing - to find a Christmas gift for Amber: his designated person in the family name draw. Finally spotting a vacant seat on a bench in front of a shoe store, he quickly strode over and claimed the space; his sigh as heavy as the resignation he felt weighing on his shoulders as he sat down.

What did one get for a twenty five year old woman who still lived at home, took part-time classes at the local community college, worked in a flower shop and was dating his brother? Sure, there were lots of generic options: bath products, specialty candy, gift cards and so on, but he wanted to find something that showed he'd actually thought of her when he'd chosen her gift. She was his sister-in-law, not to mention his friend, and he always felt that if it was worth the time to give a gift, it was also worth the time to be thoughtful about the gift being given.

His cellphone chirped and Declan pulled it from his jacket pocket, hoping it was divine intervention calling with the perfect suggestion. Instead, he saw Paula's assistant's number. That was a surprise.

He swiped his finger across the screen and said, "Hello?"

"Hey, Declan, it's Erin."

"Hey," he replied. "How are you?"

"Good, thanks," she said. "You?"

"Good, thanks," he echoed, then waited a beat for her to say something else. When she didn't, he said, "So, this is an unexpected thing receiving a phone call from you. Is everything okay?"

She sighed. "Listen, first of all, I don't want Paula to know I'm contacting you, okay? She's out of the office right now dealing with the Bazzano party stuff, so I figured it would be a good time to call you without her knowing."

Declan sat back on the bench seat. "Sure, no problem."

"Okay, good," she said, sounding relieved.

Declan's intrigue shifted to concern. "Is there something wrong?"

"Yeah, sort of," she said, before quickly clarifying, "nothing life threatening or anything like that. It's just that … well, for the past week or so, Paula's been acting really off."

"Off?"

"Yes."

Declan blinked, unsure of how to take the statement. "What do you mean, exactly?"

"Well, I know she's not truly been herself since you guys moved into her parent's place."

"Right," he agreed. That was stating the obvious.

"And I know she's been doing her best to let it slide and all that," she continued, "but I think the effort of trying to *not* let things bother her, combined with so much work stuff, is starting to take its toll."

Declan rubbed his free hand across the stubble on his chin. "Okay, but you gotta give me more. Taking its toll *how*, exactly?"

Erin cleared her throat. "She's developed a really short fuse. Like, REALLY short. Normally she had unlimited patience, but lately she's started to unnerve me a bit with her intensity. It's like she's been repressing stuff and it's coming out in unexpected ways."

"Like how?"

"Okay, well, off the top of my head, she's usually really great with our suppliers; that's why we have such a positive working relationship with them and they always come through for us. But lately she's been the opposite of patient with them: almost shrew-like. It's at the point where I've been having to apologize for her behavior behind her back."

Declan ran his fingers through his hair. "Anything else?"

"Nothing but the coffee pots."

"What?"

"She didn't tell you about the coffee pots?" she asked, hearing the confusion in his voice.

"No."

"Well, she managed to destroy - or as she put it, 'accidentally broke' - not just one, but two of them. It's making me a bit worried about what's next."

"Yeah, I get it," Declan agreed, taking a breath and assimilating the new information. "And I gotta be honest, I'm not all that surprised."

"She's been breaking stuff at home, too?"

"No. *That part* is definitely a surprise. I just meant she's been claiming she's learned from her sister how to let things go with their mother, but I didn't fully buy it. Clearly, from what you're telling me, I was right."

"I didn't know who else to talk to."

"No, no," he quickly reassured her. "I'm glad you told me. Thank you. And I'm going to do my best to deal with things."

"Okay, good," she said, relieved. "But please don't let it slip that I put you up to it, okay? I don't want her thinking I'm tattling behind her back. It's just that, as I said, I'm worried about her."

"Absolutely," he confirmed, grateful his wife had such a good friend. "I won't reveal a thing."

"Okay, great. Thanks for listening, talk soon."

"Bye."

Declan tucked the phone back into his coat pocket and resisted the urge to groan out loud at the new information. While he'd had a pretty strong hunch that Paula was putting on a calm facade, it was seriously disconcerting to think of her getting so angry she was taking it out on things like coffee pots. The image did not reconcile in any way with the woman he knew.

He stood up from the bench and squared his shoulders. It was time to find a Christmas gift for Amber then speak to his mother-in-law. Clearly her plan to keep Paula off the scent of the party by acting like her old self was working *too* well and the repercussions were causing real damage. If it was bad enough for Erin to notice and be concerned, who knew how much more destructive his wife might become be in another week's time? Yikes.

Declan slotted his key into the front door lock to the new house and twisted it to the left, only to discover it already open. He frowned and reached down to turn the knob then push the door forward to step inside, a gust of cold air following on his heels.

"Hello?" he called out, closing the door behind him. "Vince? You around?"

Nothing but silence met his greeting and Declan raised an eyebrow. He was award that his Mom, brother, Donna and Amber had been there earlier that day working on party stuff, but he was sure they would have locked up. He reached into his pocket for his cellphone then paused when he thought he heard a murmur. It was coming from upstairs.

"Hello?" he called out, again, kicking off his shoes and following the noise to the bottom of the staircase.

Now it sounded like banging.

Declan climbed the staircase, curiosity making his steps swift. If it was Vince, he wouldn't hear anything over that clamor, but the real mystery was: what was he doing upstairs when the work that had been done was in the kitchen?

Declan got to the landing, the noise even louder than it had been on the first floor, and followed it down the hallway toward the master bedroom. He shoved open the door and....

"AHHHHH!" Paula screamed, pounding her fists into the mattress on the king sized bed.

Declan jumped at the volume of her screech ringing above the heavy metal music blaring from her cellphone, not to mention she was doing it clad only in her underwear, what the hell?

"PAULA!" he yelled, hoping she would hear him over the racket.

She whipped around, her startled face pink from exertion, then quickly grabbed her phone and turned off the music.

"What the hell?" he demanded, repeating the thoughts in his head out loud.

She took a breath and cleared her throat. "Hey, what are you doing here?"

"*Seriously*?" he asked, striding further into the room. "*That's* what you have to say right now?"

She had the good grace to look contrite.

"What the hell were you doing?" he went on, pacing the room. "And why are you almost naked doing it?"

Paula sighed and flopped backward onto the bed. "My mother is making me crazy."

Declan stopped pacing.

"And not the usual crazy," she said, sitting up. "This is a whole new level. She's so obsessed with wanting me to be a part of that fucking party, she's started calling and emailing me at work!"

Declan sat down on the bed. Oh, boy. He *really* had to talk to Donna, and fast.

"She won't let up. I was so exhausted from the morning prep work that I decided to take a late lunch break before the Bazzano party gets into full swing and the real chaos begins, and do you think I got a moment's peace? Nope. My phone kept pinging and pinging, it was maddening. She even sent me videos of the guys auditioning to be the Elvis impersonator for the party."

"She's having Elvis impersonators?"

"Oh, yeah," she confirmed. "Wanna see the videos?"

He shook his head. "I'm good."

"Smart choice," she said, rolling her eyes. "Anyway, since I'm doing my damnedest to take Jaimie's advice and not react, I had to find some way to release my frustrations before I make myself a pariah with all my work contacts."

Declan nodded, putting two and two together. "Right. So, beating up the bed—"

"Is the best solution I could find in a hurry."

"And your dress?"

"I didn't want to ruin it." She pointed to where she'd draped it over the back of a chair under the window.

"Awww, Hon," he said, reaching out to gather her into his arms.

She leaned into him and sighed contentedly at the feel of his jacket against her cheek. Home.

Declan kissed the top of her head. "Okay, listen, I know we talked about this sort of thing before, but I'm going to up my game now and instead of just helping to pull you back from reacting, I'm going to do some serious deflection."

Paula shook her head against his chest. "It's okay, you don't have to do that. We'll be past it all soon and moved out of their house. It's fine."

He released her so he could look into her face. "No way. We're a team and you shouldn't have to weather this on your own. I know I dropped the ball at Thanksgiving, but I'm serious this time. I'm your man."

Paula smiled at him gratefully.

He grinned. "Your mom is going to be in for a big surprise when I start getting involved every time she mentions wanting help planning the party."

Paula snickered.

"Seriously, if she emails you, throw it my way. *I'll* reply back with *my* suggestions."

Paula laid back down on the bed, feeling decidedly more relaxed.

"Do we have a deal?"

"Deal."

"Excellent," he said, laying down beside her.

"Hey, speaking of which, we only have a week to go now. I didn't even look at the kitchen when I came in, I was so intent on getting up here. Wanna go peek on our way out?"

Declan stiffened. Oh, crap. What if there was surprise party stuff in there?

"I have a better idea," he offered, turning over and pulling her toward him. "We have an empty house and you're basically naked anyway, why don't we make use of it before you have to head back to the Bazzano party? Guaranteed stress reliever."

Paula laughed and moved in closer.

Declan leaned forward to give Paula one more kiss through her open car window before she drove off. She'd parked across the street, instead of in the driveway, hence the reason he hadn't noticed her vehicle when he'd arrived at the house.

"Drive safe," he said, before pulling himself back upright.

"I don't know what time I'll be home."

He shook his head. "No worries. Do what you have to do and I'm sure the party is going to be a huge success."

She grinned. "I'll text once I have a better idea."

"Sounds good," he agreed, searching through his coat pocket for his car key. "Remember to have fun."

"Always do," she said, closing her window then giving a small wave before she pulled away from the curb.

Declan lifted a hand to wave her off then walked across the street to the driveway where he'd parked his car. He still had one thing to do before he returned to work: call Donna. He opened the vehicle's door and slipped inside, then turned on the car and dialed the house number from the stereo panel on the dashboard. While it rang, he fiddled with the heat controls.

"Hello?"

"Hey, Donna," he said, settling back into his seat.

"Declan?" she asked, her voice coming from the speakers and filling the interior of the car. "What's wrong?"

"Nothing," he immediately replied. "Well, not nothing exactly, but nothing that's an emergency."

"*Okaaay*," she said, confused.

"Listen," he went on, "I'm just leaving the house—"

"*Your* house?"

"Yeah. And Paula was here—"

"WHAT!"

Her voice was so loud, Declan winced and reached to turn down the volume.

"It's okay," he quickly clarified, rubbing one of his ears to stop the ringing. "She didn't see anything."

"Oh, thank god," she breathed, before calling out, "it's okay, everything is fine. Just Declan with some news, but nothing bad."

Declan waited. Clearly, she was talking to Douglas.

"Sorry," she apologized, into the phone. "Douglas heard me holler and wanted to know what was the matter."

"Right, so about Paula…."

"My god," she interrupted. "What was she doing there? Are you absolutely sure she didn't see anything?"

"I'm sure," he re-confirmed. "She was in the bedroom and told me she'd gone right upstairs after she went into the house."

"Didn't she find that suspicious, that you were asking where she'd been in the house?"

"No," he said, running his palm across the stubble on his chin. "She'd only been there for a few moments before I arrived and she volunteered the information. *And*," he added, before she could offer further questions, "further proof is that she suggested we take a peek at the kitchen before we left because she hadn't looked when she came in."

"Ohmygod! You didn't, did you?"

Declan rolled his eyes, but kept his voice even. "Of course not."

"Then how did you managed to keep her from—"

"The details don't matter," he said, swiftly cutting her off. "What *does* matter is that I got her out of there without any incident."

"Why was she there, anyway?" Donna pressed.

"Because, apparently, she needed some time alone. Because you're driving her nuts."

She went silent in the face of his bluntness.

"Your plan to throw her off the scent is working *too* well, Donna. Not only does she definitely believe you're involved in arranging the holiday party at Jaimie's, she's also starting to feel the strain of trying to keep from being dragged into it."

"Perfect!" she enthused.

"No, not perfect. While we want her convinced, we don't want her having a total meltdown. That would probably defeat all of the effort you're putting in, don't you think? I think you need to pull back a bit."

"Oh," she said, less enthused. "So what do you suggest? I stop talking to her about it? Won't that seem a bit suspicious, all of a sudden?"

Declan sat forward, as though he was talking to her across a table instead of through his car's speakers. "No, you don't have to do that. I came up with a plan. I told her I would run interference and anything *you* asked of her, *I'll* do. That way she'll get a buffer from things and, at the same time, I can help out without us having to find ways to hide the fact that I'm doing so."

"Ooh, that's a good plan," Donna complimented.

"I thought so," he admitted, a little proud of himself.

"Is she going to be home for dinner?"

He pulled his seatbelt across his torso and secured the buckle. "Not sure. Depends on how things go with the client party and whether or not thinks she needs to stay to the end to see it all finished and cleaned up."

"Okay, so, if she is home tonight, I'll say something about Jaimie's party and you intervene and she'll see your plan in action. And if she isn't home early enough tonight, I'll do it tomorrow after dinner."

"Sounds perfect."

"Oh, speaking of tomorrow, Ernie's new guardians are coming out to pick him up in the morning. He'll be off to the good life with his new family."

Declan smiled. Despite the whole absurdity of them having a live turkey in the first place, he was glad Douglas had managed to get things sorted for the bird.

"Glad it all worked out," he said. "Gotta run."

"See you later at home," she sang, then hung up.

Declan ended the call on his end and shook his head. Here he was at his new house and, yet, she was calling her house home. The irony? It didn't feel all that off the mark.

Paula nodded her approval as two muscle-bound young men lifted the rhinestone laden *Happy Sweet Sixteen* banner into position above the head table in the ballroom being decked out for 'Baby Girl Bazzano' - as she and Erin had been referring to Lanzo Bazzano's daughter. He never referred to her by an actual name, just the pet name of 'Baby Girl', so she and Erin went along with it.

"Careful there," Paula cautioned, as one of the men came dangerously close to bumping the equally jewel-encrusted, five foot by three foot, purple and gold masquerade mask positioned just above the banner.

Once the banner was in place and secured, she breathed a sigh of relief and said, "Thanks, guys," while smiling and nodding at their efforts. "It looks great."

And it really did.

There was no question the birthday guests would be gob smacked by both items, never mind the rest of the extravagant, over-the-top decor that matched the Mardi

Gras theme being created in the grand ballroom. Even Paula had to admit she was seriously impressed by how everything was coming together; and they weren't even finished yet.

The theatre team she'd hired to build the facade of Bourbon Street had far surpassed her hopes. The sets they'd created were so life-like, it was startling to pass through the doors of the pubs and restaurants they'd constructed only to discover there was nothing of substance behind the detailed fronts.

And then there was the street car!

Gleaming red and gold, and delivered into the venue piece by piece to be constructed like an oversized model toy, it wasn't just for show; Paula had come up with the perfect way for it to combine form and function by having it kitted out as a photo booth, all sorts of costumes at the ready. The party guests would have fun dressing up and being silly and would have a keepsake to take home with them at the end of the evening. Win-win. When she'd suggested the idea to Lanzo Bazzano, he'd endorsed the idea with great enthusiasm.

"Oh-my-stars, this is MAGNIFICENT!"

Paula spun around when the jarring sound of a woman's booming voice echoed across the ballroom and sent her heart racing. Who in the hell…. Oh, of course. It was the birthday girl's mother: missus Bazzano.

And how, one may ask, did Paula know it was her despite having never met the woman in person? Simple: she'd Googled her.

"Show time," Paula muttered, slapping on her professional grin and striding across the room, her tan colored high heels tapping sharply on the pale tile floor while she held her hand out in welcome. "Missus Bazzano, how lovely to meet you. I'm—"

"Paula Dempsey!" Missus Bazzano shrieked, before bypassing Paula's hand to pull her into a bear hug. "I know exactly who you are, I Googled you!"

Paula laughed as the petite, dark-haired woman squeezed her tightly and rocked her back and forth like a long-lost friend.

"And please, not so formal, you must call me Sophia!"

"Okay," Paula gasped, while Sophia gave another tight squeeze around her shoulders before releasing her. For such a tiny woman, she had a lot of strength.

"You are even more beautiful in person," Sophia complimented, stepping back to admire Paula in her red dress. "No wonder my Lanzo speaks so well of you! He always loves a beautiful woman. I'm going to have to tell him to watch his mouth."

"Oh, he's never said anything…." Paula sputtered, taken off guard by the comment. "That is, *we* … as in my *assistant* and I…."

"Look at all of this!" Sophia interrupted, gesturing with wild swings of her arms to the room around then, seeming oblivious to the awkwardness she'd created by her statement.

Paula couldn't help but think she and her mother would get along famously.

"It's a vision. An absolute vision. I feel as though I've been transported right onto Bourbon Street in New Orleans," she gushed, her eyes wide with child-like wonder. She clutched Paula's forearm and looked her straight in the eye. "I have to admit to you, I wasn't so confident when my Lanzo said you were going to create this party for our precious baby girl."

"Oh," Paula said, taken aback for a second time by not just the intensity of her grip, but her candor.

"It's true, I didn't know anything about you, so," she said, shrugging her shoulders. "But, *now*," she went on, releasing Paula's arm, "now, I see I was wrong. My Lanzo trusted you and he was right all along."

"I'm so glad you think so," Paula told her, surreptitiously rubbing her forearm when Sophia turned away to take in the splendor of the room a second time.

"How could I not?" she insisted, spinning on her heel so fast that Paula took a reflexive step backward. "I feel like I should go right into one of those pretend pubs ... they *are* pretend aren't they?"

"Absolutely!" Paula assured her, looking at the Bourbon Street facade. "And hand made by an incredible team of talented local artists."

"There you go," Sophia declared. "They look so real, I feel I should be able to push through those doors and order a round of Hurricanes. Brilliant!"

"All of the drinks at the party will be non-alcoholic as per your instructions, of course," Paula felt the need to clarify.

"Of course, of course!" Sophia replied, then leaned in as though she was sharing a secret. "And despite that being the case, our precious baby girl is going to love it. Love it!"

She laughed raucously at the idea of her daughter having to be happy even though her party would be a booze free affair and Paula felt it only polite to chuckle along with her. However, she'd barely uttered a few "ha, ha, ha's," when Sophie jabbed a finger at the ceiling and demanded, "What's going to happen here?"

Paula's chuckles lodged in her throat, making her cough while she followed the direction of Sophia's pointed digit to look up at the draping swaths of red, gold, green and purple cloth hung across the full length of the ballroom's ceiling. They looked good.

"There are lights hidden behind them," she explained, catching her breath. "Once they're turned on, the entire ceiling is going to glow with colors."

Sophia clapped and said, "Beautiful! Ambience, I love it," then turned and marched rapidly away, further into the room.

"Jeez," Paula muttered, quickly scrambling to keep up.

The woman was non-stop motion.

"Over here, on this currently empty table," she expounded, taking the reins before Sophia could demand further what it was she was seeing as she strode along. "We'll have all of the desserts - color coordinated to our purple and gold theme, of course."

"The ice sculpture?"

"It's amazing," Paula stated. "A four foot tall mask, just as you instructed, and the sculptor has added color to the ice - again as per your instructions - and it looks so real everyone will be in awe that it's made of frozen water. It's in the freezer in the back, if you want to see it."

"No, no!" Sophia waved her hands. "It sounds heavenly, but I want to see it for the first time with my daughter by my side. A memory, you understand?"

"Of course," Paula quickly agreed. "There *is* more decorating still to be done, do you want to stay and see it unfold, or...."

"No, no," she said, again, this time patting Paula's shoulder. "You're right, I've seen enough. I have to leave some surprises to have memories with my precious baby girl."

Paula nodded. Jackpot. It was the exact response she was hoping for. Having the client around as preparations were being done meant more work, period. She ended up in the awkward position of having to entertain them while simultaneously making sure everything was on schedule and crisis' were dealt with; a combination that inevitably caused her guts to churn.

"You are a wise woman, Paula Dempsey," Sophia complimented, as they walked back toward the ballroom entrance, weaving their way between the lavishly decorated tables and chairs. "I will go now to tell my husband he was right to put his faith in you and your company and he will, of course, tell me he was only following my instructions all along."

Paula grinned. "And I'm sure he's right."

Sophia threw her head back and laughed. Then she waved and said, "See you soon," as she exited the room, leaving a heady trail of sweet smelling lavender perfume in her wake.

Paula watched her wait for her assistant to open the main doors to the outside where, she was certain, a warm and comfortable limo awaited the woman's return.

"Right," she said, squaring her shoulders and returning her attention back to the ballroom. "On with the show."

The sound of the front door opening and closing alerted Donna and Declan, in the kitchen with Douglas, that someone was home. Before they could wonder if it was Paula or Amber, Paula came charging into the room, her face a picture of annoyance.

"Hey, babe," Declan said, smiling.

"The key to the house doesn't work. Do you know that?" she demanded, her hands on her hips.

Donna's eye's widened and she looked at Declan standing next to the island. His smile had dropped from his face to be replaced by guilt, so she tried to help out.

"Paula! You're home earlier than expected, everything okay?"

Douglas, seated at the table and munching on salt and vinegar chips from a bowl in front of him, looked up from the crossword puzzle he was working on, his brow furrowed. "What's this now? Paula, are you unwell?"

"No." She shook her head at her Dad then looked back at Declan. "I went over to the house and my key wouldn't work. I tried both doors and couldn't get inside."

"What about the big party?" Donna interrupted. "I thought you were needed there?"

"I *was* there, from the time it started until it ended a half hour ago. Erin is taking care of supervising the cleanup."

"Oh." She shrugged. "I guess I thought it would go later than ten o'clock."

"It was a sweet sixteen party," Paula told her.

"So?"

"*So*, they're still kids and the Bazzano's weren't going to be throwing an all-nighter."

"Mmm, I guess so," Donna reluctantly agreed, reaching a hand to take a chip from Douglas' bowl and popping it into her mouth. "Although, kids today…."

Paula put her focus back on Declan, hoping to move the conversation back to where she'd started. "So, any idea what's up with the locks?"

"Right, that," he stammered, clearing his throat. "After we left the house this morning, I got a call from Vince—"

"Who's Vince, again?" Donna asked, trying one more time to pull focus so Declan could get his bearings.

"Our contractor," Paula said, not taking her eyes from Declan. "Continue."

He nodded. "Right. Vince told me one of the workmen lost our key yesterday and he figured it would be a good idea to change out the locks, just to be safe."

"What was one of the workmen doing with our house key?"

Declan shrugged his shoulders. "Dunno. Didn't ask."

"Alright, well, can I have my new key please?"

"I don't have one for you yet."

Donna inadvertently flinched. *That* wasn't going to go over well.

"What? Why not?" Paula frowned at him and folded her arms across her chest.

Declan walked over to the table and pulled up a chair beside Donna, using the action to break eye contact. "I didn't have time to go and get multiples made. I'll get them done right away."

"See, problem solved," Donna piped up, now focusing her efforts on shifting the conversation away from getting access to the new house.

"Not really," Paula countered. "I still can't get into the house."

"Pishaw," she exhaled, waving her hand dismissively. "What *really* deserves attention are the Christmas party preparations."

Declan caught her eye and grinned at the segue. Show time. "Why's that? Is everything okay, Donna? You sound distressed."

"Oh, well...." she said, slumping her shoulders.

He reached out a hand to pat her arm. "Can *I* be of help?"

Douglas looked up from his puzzle again. "What's going on now? What's wrong?"

"Nothing, nothing," Donna replied, affecting a weary tone to give weight to her slumping.

"Oh, now," Declan cajoled, as he slid his chair closer to hers and began reading from the notepad in front of her on the tabletop. "What's this all about? Are these the Christmas party notes? Do you need our help?"

Donna brightened. "Well, yes, it would be great if *all* of you—"

"I'm going to take a bath, I'm exhausted," Paula announced, sharply cutting her mother off. "That birthday party took the cake. And, speaking of which, you should have seen the cake. I took a photo, I'll show you later."

"Ooh, that's an idea," Donna gushed. "Should we have a theme cake? Paula? What do you think?"

"*I* think," Declan declared, giving Paula a pointed look. "She should go take her bath and *we'll* work this out together."

Paula nodded and vacated the kitchen.

"Alrighty," he said, loudly, so she would overhear as she ascended the staircase to the second floor. "Let's have a look and see what we can do here."

Donna waited a beat then patted Declan on his shoulder when she was sure Paula was out of hearing range. "I think it worked," she whispered.

He nodded and replied, his voice hushed, "Now I can help you without her suspecting a thing. Win-win."

"And nice solution with the house, by the way," Donna praised, giggling.

He chuckled. "Yeah, it seemed like the only way to keep her out without her getting suspicious. Now I just have to figure out a believable way to make sure she doesn't get a new key for this week while we're setting up for the party."

Donna reached over to pat his hand. "No worries. I can help with that, no problem."

Douglas grinned at the pair of them. As long as they were happy, he was happy.

Liam stepped across the threshold of the *Tipsy Pigeon* then swiped briskly at the fresh snow coating the arms and collar of his jacket while he glanced around the room for his brothers.

"Li!" Emmet called out, lifting a hand to signal where he and Declan were seated, off to the left in one of the booths that lined the pub wall.

Liam nodded and began weaving his way through the patrons standing around the pub tables in the middle of the space, laughing and drinking with their friends. It was the typical Saturday night crush and he was impressed his brothers had managed to secure a booth.

"Hey," Declan said, when Liam sat down on the bench seat opposite him.

"Shit roads out there," Emmet offered, by way of greeting. "This better be important."

He was referring to the fact that Liam had called him, and Declan apparently, insisting he needed a sounding board for a situation he needed to talk about.

Liam raised an eyebrow at Emmet's so-called greeting and replied, "Good to see you, too."

Declan chucked. "So, what's this big deal you were going on about that made us risk out lives coming out in the cold and snow?"

"I'm going to get a drink," Liam declared, removing his jacket and letting it drop it onto the seat behind his back. "What can I get you?"

"Beer's good," Declan said, while Emmet stated, "Whiskey, neat."

He nodded and stood up. "Right. Be right back."

Emmet folded his arms across his chest and leaned back in his seat, watching him as he threaded his way through the crowd to the bar. "This better be as serious as he made it out to be, or I'm never letting him live it down."

Declan yawned then said, "I'm sure he thinks it is. Just hear him out."

Emmet shot him a wry grin. "You'd think *you* were the older brother instead of the other way around. Sure you're only thirty three there, bro, and not eighty three?"

"Yeah, yeah," Declan said, brushing his words away. "So that makes you eighty five then?"

Emmet chortled and scanned the room for viable women. "If I see someone worth pursuing, you're going to be my wingman, right?"

Declan rolled his eyes. "What do you think?"

"You've become such a drag since you became a senior," he teased, shifting in his seat and zeroing in on a blonde woman near the pool tables. "You know you don't have to actually *do* anything if she's got a friend, right? Just be sociable until I've sealed the deal."

Declan was spared from having to respond when Liam emerged from the crowd, drinks in hand. Thank god. He'd had the conversation with Emmet too many times and didn't want to have it again.

"Whiskey, neat," Liam reported, placing the glass he was holding in one hand down onto the table in front of Emmet then sliding back into the seat opposite them and setting down two bottles of beer he had clutched in his other hand.

"Thanks," Declan said, reaching for one of the bottles.

"Alright, forget about the pleasantries," Emmet said, cutting to the chase. "What's up?"

Liam picked up his beer, tipped the bottle to his lips and took a long swallow then set it back down on the table. "It's about Amber."

Declan held up a hand. "Wait."

"What?"

"What does 'it's about Amber' mean exactly? 'Cause if you're going to start talking about sex stuff, I'm out."

Emmet raised an eyebrow. "When'd you get to be such a prude?"

"I'm not. But he's talking about my sister-in-law, for Christ's sake, a person I currently see *every day*. Being a prude has nothing to do with it. *And*," Declan added, jerking his chin in the direction of the blonde girl, "she's too young for you. She looks like she's barely legal. Have some bloody pride."

Liam snickered at the dressing down while Emmet cut his eyes at Declan for the comment.

Declan ignored his glare and took a swig of beer while he waited for Liam to continue.

Liam cleared his throat then shook his head and confirmed, "No. I'm not talking about sex stuff or anything like that."

"Okay, good," Declan stated, drinking more of his beer.

"So, *what* then?" Emmet pressed, still blatantly checking out the girl in open defiance of Declan's jab.

Liam took a breath and released it. "I'm thinking of asking her to move in."

"Seriously?" Declan put his bottle down on the table.

"Whoa, there, quick draw," Emmet cautioned, the news diverting his attention from the blonde. "Moving things along pretty damned fast, wouldn't you say?"

Liam snorted derisively. He could have been dating Amber for two years, instead of two months, and Emmet would have declared her moving in to be too fast.

"What prompted this decision?" Declan asked, ignoring Emmet's comment.

Their brother was a bona fide commitaphobe and could be trusted for one thing: to be completely freaked out by anything that looked or sounded like fidelity.

"I've never felt this way before," Liam admitted. "I can't stop thinking about her and I hate when I have to drop her off at home at the end of the day. I want to go to sleep beside her and wake up beside her and look around my place and see evidence that she's there. Even now, I hate the idea of going home and she won't be there."

"Wow." Declan nodded, impressed. He'd never heard Liam talk that way.

Emmet pulled a face. "God. That sounds fucking awful. I'm getting claustrophobia just thinking about it."

Declan turned and delivered a sharp punch to his shoulder.

"Hey!" he blurted, glaring at him. "What the hell was that for?"

"Guess," Declan replied, blandly.

Liam picked up his beer and took another swig from the bottle. "Don't worry about it," he said, shaking his head at Declan. "I'm used to it. Whatever he says is like water off a duck's back."

"Jeez," Emmet exhaled, grabbing his drink and sliding out of the booth. "I'm going over to meet the blonde before you two start pulling out your knitting needles."

Declan smirked while he watched him stalk away. "I gotta give him credit, the way he's acting you'd never know he was in the wrong."

Liam chuckled and placed his beer back on the table. "He's had lots of practice."

"So, it's serious then with Amber?"

Liam nodded.

Declan leaned forward in his seat and rested his elbows on the table. "And not a rebound thing from Trina?"

Liam frowned and Declan held up his hands in mock surrender.

"Hey," he said, "just asking the questions that need asking and you know it."

Liam's face softened. "Yeah, alright. And, no, definitely not a rebound from Trina. In fact," he divulged, leaning into the table, mirroring Declan. "I'd go so far as to say Trina was just a sort-of place holder for Amber. Not that I knew it at the time, of course, I'm not that much of a heartless bastard."

"So what does Amber think of all this?"

Liam cleared his throat then took a breath to say, "She doesn't know yet."

Declan leaned back in his seat and waited.

"And that's where you come in."

Declan lifted an eyebrow. "Meaning?"

Liam ran his fingers through his hair and fidgeted in his seat.

Again, Declan waited.

"I need you to find out for me if I'm jumping the gun."

Declan groaned and ran his fingers through his hair in a perfect imitation of his brother.

"I know, I know," Liam said, nodding. "It's a lot to ask—"

"There's an understatement," Declan cut him off, before putting on a voice that sounded as though he was reading from a script. "Hey Amber, sister-in-law of mine, quick question for you. Liam wants to move in with you, do you want to move in with him? Here's a paper with two boxes on it, one with 'yes' and the other with 'no'." He mimed holding out a piece of paper and said, "Check the box you think applies to you."

Liam sat back, an impassive expression on his face. When Declan stopped talking he asked, "Are you done?"

"Yeah." Declan reached for his beer, tipped the bottle to his mouth and swallowed the last of it.

"So, are you saying you won't help me out?"

Declan placed the bottle on the table next to the empty glass Emmet had left behind and sighed. "Of course I'll help you." When Liam's face lit up, he clarified, "I really don't want to, but I will because you're my brother."

Liam grinned, practically vibrating in his seat. "Thanks, Dec. I really appreciate it. Really. Just get a lay of the land, so I don't make an ass of myself if she's not on the same page as me."

"Don't worry about it," he said, then added, "but can I ask you one question?"

"Shoot."

Declan shifted in his seat so that he could see Emmet by the pool tables, chatting up the too-young-for-him blonde. "What the hell possessed you to ask Emmet to come out? He's the last guy you'd want to talk to about this sort of thing."

Liam chuckled. It was a valid question. "Yeah, I know, but I didn't actually ask him. I texted Cian to find out if he was free to meet up and when he didn't text back I called the massage studio. Instead of him answering—"

"Emmet did," Declan finished. "And when you told him what it was about, he invited himself along."

"Yup. Got it in one," Liam agreed. "And since I didn't want to argue about it and Cian was still working on a client, I gave in."

Declan laughed. "And that's why he's full of shit right now, acting like he's been put-upon when *he* was the one who insisted on coming out in the first place."

"Two for two." Liam picked up his beer and lifted it in a mock salute.

"God, what a guy. Good thing he's our brother and we have to love him." Declan shifted back to face the table. "So what about Cian? Is he coming out tonight as well?"

Liam drank from his bottle then shook his head. "No. Turns out he and Michael already had plans and I didn't want to get in the way of that. Truth be told, I'm just glad you were available, otherwise I would have had to bail out altogether and suffer Emmet's wrath."

"Yeah, no worries. Paula had a huge thing with work today, so she was bagged and went to bed early."

Liam put his bottle on the tabletop and leaned in. "Speaking of which, I heard she went to the new house and almost found out about the party and the kitchen being finished?"

Declan nodded. "Yeah, but I got her outta there without her seeing anything, so all good."

"How are you going to keep her away for the next week? Hearing Amber talk, it sounds like things are going to get seriously obvious insofar as the all of party paraphernalia goes. If she gets inside, everything goes belly up."

"I've got a plan."

Liam lifted an eyebrow. "Cryptic. All you need is the cat and a monocle."

Declan laughed. "Well, I've got the cat now, so I'm halfway there."

"You could substitute the monocle for a turkey, if Ernie wasn't leaving."

Declan grinned. Clearly all news that went on in the Hayes' household was reported by Amber. That alone, in his opinion, was enough proof she was on the same page as Liam. But, he'd said he'd talk to her and get a feel for things and he would.

"I take it you'll be around to pick up the pieces once he's gone to his new home?" Declan asked, sliding out of the booth to stand up and reach for his coat.

Liam followed his lead. "Yup. She said she needs my support when he leaves, so I'll be there."

They each slipped into their respective jackets then Declan pointed at the table. "You want to finish your beer?"

"Nah, I'm good." Liam jerked his head toward the pool tables. "Should we tell Emmet we're leaving?"

Declan turned and yelled "Emmet!" over the din in the pub, making him and the too-young blonde girl and a few of the patrons turn around. "We're outta here," he stated, then patted Liam on the back and said, "There. Done."

Liam laughed and followed him out the door.

Paula rolled over in bed and reached for Declan. His side of the mattress was empty. She leaned further across the empty space to look at the clock sitting on the nightstand, the bright red numbers making her squint in the darkness. Two o'clock in the morning? Could that be right? And if it was, where the hell was her husband?

Paula slid from beneath the warm cocoon of covers and walked across the chilly bedroom floor to retrieve her yellow robe from the back of the dressing table chair. A shiver ran up her spine as she slipped her arms into the soft fleece and wrapped it around her shoulders then moved over to the window to pull back the drapes and look down at the street below. It was a complete whiteout.

"Holy baloney," she exhaled, taking in the view.

Suddenly, she was seriously concerned about Declan's absence.

He should have been back hours ago from meeting with Liam and Emmet. She let the curtain drop back into place and quickly padded across the room to open the door and head downstairs.

Maybe her Mom knew more.

Sylvester, snuggled into the comforter, looked up as she disappeared. He listened, ears perked, to the sound of her descending the staircase then tucked his head back down and returned to sleep.

Paula strode purposefully into the kitchen, but stopped in her tracks when she saw her Mom, Amber and Declan all clustered around the table. They were talking and laughing and didn't even notice she'd come in. Granted, the two empty wine bottles and four empty beer bottles on the island could have been a clue as to why they'd failed to notice her arrival, so she loudly cleared her throat to alert them to her presence.

"Goodness," Donna said, swiveling around in her seat and holding a hand against her flowered robe, over her heart. "Paula. You startled me."

Declan followed that with, "Hey, Hon, why aren't you in bed?"

Paula walked further into the room. "I woke up and you weren't there and I got worried. It's after two in the morning."

"Is it?" Amber yawned and squinted her eyes to try and read the clock on the microwave across the kitchen. "That explains why I'm feeling so tired."

"Want to join us?" Declan offered, pushing out the chair next to him for her to sit down.

She shook her head. "No. I'm just glad you're home safe. What time did you get back?"

Declan looked at Donna as he said, "Umm, somewhere around midnight, I think? Does that sound about right?"

She nodded. "Uh-huh. I was just finishing baking the muffins when you came in."

"Right," he agreed, pointing at her. "The muffins."

"Did you get the key?" Paula asked.

Declan's eyebrows furrowed together. "What?"

"The key," she repeated. "To the house. You said you'd stop on your way to meet Liam and have the new key cut for me."

"Did I?" He looked again at Donna.

She immediately jumped in. "Did you hear about the turkey?"

Paula stared at her. "What? Is that a start of a joke, or are you being serious?"

Amber burst out laughing until her giggles turned into hiccups.

"No, I'm serious," Donna insisted, reaching over to pat Amber on the back.

"Do you want some water?" Paula offered, going over to the cabinet beside the kitchen window and retrieving a glass.

"Yes, please," Amber managed to utter, before more hiccups took over.

Paula poured a glass from the tap at the sink and carried it over to the table and set it down in front of her.

"Thanks," she gurgled, picking it up.

"So, what about the turkey?" Paula queried, tightening the sash on her robe.

"Right," Donna agreed. "Ernie's new family is coming tomorrow to pick him up."

"Are you sure about that?"

Donna frowned and looked at Declan. "Am I?"

"That's what you told me," he said.

"Yeah, but have you looked outside recently?" Paula walked to the backdoor and pointed at the window. "It's a total whiteout."

Donna waved a hand, dismissively. "Psshaw. It'll be fine. They're farm people. They're prepared for this sort of thing."

"Last time they didn't come in because of the weather," Paula reminded her.

"Because they were caught unaware," she countered. "Now, they're ready."

Paula shrugged her shoulders. "Okay, whatever. So, anyway, about the key—"

"Oh! I almost forgot!" Donna blurted, making them all startle. "We MUST get your feedback on this!"

Paula's eyes widened at the vehemence in her mother's tone. "Jeez, Mom. On what?"

"We're thinking of bringing in a magician to entertain the kids at the Christmas party! Who do you think would be good? You must know someone, right? That's your sort of thing, right? What kind of price would be looking at?" She leaped up from her chair then grabbed the back of it to steady herself.

"Whoa, you okay, Mom?" Amber asked.

Donna giggled. "Apparently the wine has gone to my head more than I thought."

Declan got up and offered her his hand. "Well, be careful, we don't need our number one party planner going down lame before the big event."

Donna let him help her back into her seat and surreptitiously gave him a wink when Paula was blocked from view by his shoulders.

"You go back to bed, Hon, we've got things here." Declan waggled his eyebrows up and down at Paula to signal she could escape before she got dragged into a party planning conversation.

"Oh, but, the magician…," Donna repeated, then tapered off to give Paula a chance to flee.

She took it.

"I'll see you when you come up," she said, to Declan, then backtracked from the kitchen and disappeared around the corner of the doorway.

"'Night, dear," Donna called out. "Talk tomorrow."

Hiccups finally gone, Amber pressed her lips together to keep her giggles to herself. When she heard Paula's rapid footsteps on the stairs she whispered, "Impressive. You two could have your own act at the party."

Donna snickered while Declan said, "Quick thinking, thanks. Clearly, I'm going to have to come up with a few excuses as to why I don't have a key for her."

"Only six more days," Donna soothed, patting his hand. "And bringing up the party planning is a fast way to get her off topic."

"Are you seriously thinking about hiring a magician?" Amber asked, picking up her glass and tipping the last of her wine into her mouth.

Donna nodded. "I actually do think it would be fun for the kids."

Declan sat back down in his chair. "I can ask Erin for her suggestions, tomorrow. I was planning on asking her if she might have any suggestions to keep

Paula distracted from getting a house key, so I'll ask her about a magician as well."

Donna smiled. Just six more days.

Chapter 23

Amber climbed the staircase that lead to Paula's office, strode purposefully along the carpeted hallway and gave a sharp rap on the door with *Certain Events* engraved on the frosted glass window. Before anyone could offer a reply to her knock, she twisted the knob and pushed open the door like she owned the place.

"Hello!" she sang, crossing the threshold with a flourish and closing the door smartly behind her. "I've arrived!"

Erin looked up from her computer and laughed. She adored Paula's sister.

"Hey, stranger," she said, getting up and walking over to give Amber a hug.

Paula swiveled around in her desk chair. "It's about time," she teased, by way of greeting.

Amber and Erin untangled themselves and Amber lifted her eyebrows at her sister. "Hey, I *said* I'd come by *after* lunch."

"Yes," Paula agreed, glancing up at the large clock on the wall then back again. "But normal people assume that means *less* than two hours afterward."

Amber waved her words away. "Whatever. I'm here, aren't I? That's what matters."

"So, I hear the turkey went off to his new family?" Erin queried, walking back to her desk.

"He did," Amber agreed, shucking her candy red, wool coat and hanging it on the coat rake, then stamping her thigh-high, black boots on the mat in front of the door to rid them of any moisture from the snow outside. "It was sad, but the family was so excited it was also really sweet. Our Dad even gave them Ernie's house to settle him into his new environment and they already sent me some pictures to show how well he's doing. Want to see them? I have them on my phone."

"First, before you do that," Paula interrupted, holding out a hand. "Can I have it, please?"

Amber carried her oversized purse to the sofa and sat down. She frowned at Paula's open palm and said, "Have what?" then her face cleared and she said, "Oh, right, that. Hang on a sec."

Paula watched her unzip the top of the bag, revealing a plethora of odds and ends within its depths.

"It's in here somewhere," she muttered, digging around inside the purse.

Paula's patience began to slip when the pawing continued and she lamented, "God, how do you carry that much crap around with you?"

Amber stopped searching and looked up from the bag. "It's not crap."

Paula took a breath and released it. "Fine. But, it seems that *not crap* is getting in the way of you finding it."

Amber rolled her eyes and went back to searching. "Hang on a minute."

Paula shifted her gaze to Erin at her desk, hoping to share an amused grin about the theatrics happening on their sofa, but she had her eyes firmly locked onto her computer screen. Too bad.

"Hmm," Amber grumbled, frowning.

"What?" Paula asked.

"Nothing," she said, then commenced removing items from the depths of her purse and placing them on the couch cushions.

Paula's face grew rigid. "Ohmygod, are you serious right now? Don't tell me you can't find it."

Amber looked up at her, exasperated. "Yes, I *can*. Hang on, for god's sake. I just need to get a few things out of the way."

Erin got up from her chair and said, "Excuse me, I have to use the bathroom," then walked speedily across the room to the office door.

Paula lifted her eyebrows in surprise at the abruptness of her statement and equally fast departure. The office door closed behind her and, suddenly, there was only her and her sister: still emptying her purse.

"Oh, for god's sake," Paula groused, when Amber added a pair of lime green socks to the pile on the sofa cushion that already included her cellphone, a toy pony, her wallet, a sizeable crystal ball, a folded up umbrella and a bag of salt and vinegar chips.

"Wait, wait!" she exclaimed, pulling a jangling item from the bag with a flourish.

Paula fixed her with a grave stare when they both realized the thing she held in her hand was a charm bracelet and *not* the keychain with the recently cut key for the new house.

"Oh, my bad," she said, shrugging her shoulders and dropping the bracelet onto the pile on the cushion.

"Oh, give it up," Paula said, between gritted teeth. "You've lost it, haven't you? Just admit it, already."

Amber sat up ramrod straight, affronted. "I will not!"

"Well, then, where the hell is it?" Paula demanded, gesturing to the items on the cushion. "'Cause, I don't see it in that crazy-ass jumble of crap you pulled from your clown bag, do you?"

Amber exhaled sharply and began stuffing her things back into her purse. "I don't have to take this," she said, ramming the socks into a side pocket. "I was just trying to help when Declan said he didn't have time to bring you your key and *this* is the thanks I get!"

"And I *do* appreciate that, but how am I supposed to thank you when you didn't actually bring me the key!"

"Oh, sure, rub my nose in it," Amber shot back, zipping her bag shut and standing up.

"What, so that's it?" Paula asked. "You're just going to leave?"

"Yup." She marched across the room, tugged her coat from the rack and swung open the office door. "And when I *do* find the key, *then* who'll be all smuggie smuggerson from smuggersville, huh?"

Paula blinked, speechless, as she watched Amber flounce out into the hallway and yank the door closed behind her: leaving her to sit alone in the silent office.

What the hell?

Amber pulled her jacket across her shoulders while she retraced her steps away from the office, beetling speedily down the staircase in case Paula decided to follow her. She stopped at the second floor bathroom and tapped on the door. It slowly opened and Erin poked her head out.

"All clear?"

"Yes, and your idea worked perfectly," Amber said, grinning. "Thank you so much."

She was referring, of course, to Erin's brilliant suggestion to Declan when he'd called and asked for her help in keeping Paula distracted from getting a key for the changed locks at the new house. Have someone lose the key, she'd said. So simple, but it would do the trick. And, of course, the perfect person for that job was Amber as she was famous in the family for losing and finding things.

Erin returned her smile. "Excellent. I'm so glad."

"Now I'll just claim I'm still looking for it for the rest of the week and then find it on Saturday in time for the party."

"Was she angry?"

Amber wrinkled her nose. "And then some. Sorry. You'll probably have to hear her bitch about it for the rest of the afternoon."

Erin shrugged. "No worries. I just had to get out of there in case she tried to pull me into the conversation and I gave things away with my face. I'd make a terrible poker player."

Amber laughed.

"Anyway, now I'll just keep my head down and murmur sympathetic noises if she rants. She won't even notice if I don't say anything."

"You're a doll," Amber said, giving her a quick hug. "I should get out of here before she comes looking for you and finds me still here. I'll see you on Saturday at the party."

Erin waved her off.

Declan yawned widely and raked his fingers through his hair, massaging his scalp. To put it mildly, he was beat. The past few evenings spent working out the final tweaks for the party had dragged out way past the stroke of midnight and, combined with the accompanying bottles of wine, he felt he hadn't slept in a week.

"Wow, you look rough."

Declan shifted around in his seat at the table and shot Amber a wry grin as she entered the house through the kitchen door, bringing a blast of cold, damp air along with her.

"Seriously," she said, shutting the door behind her, "you look like you could use some sleep, brother."

"Where are you coming from this late?" he asked, rubbing his eyes. "Don't you have work in the morning?"

Amber shucked her coat from her shoulders and hung it on a hook then unzipped her boots and pulled them off of her feet. "They're good to me at the flower shop and they'll cut me some slack if I'm a bit late. I'm going to make some tea, want some?"

He shook his head. "No, thanks."

She left her boots on the mat and padded across the kitchen to pick up the kettle from its base on the countertop. "Where's Paula, in bed?"

"Yeah," he said, while she filled the kettle from the tap then set it back on the base and flipped the switch to turn it on. "She and the cat went up about an hour ago."

Amber chose a cup from the wooden mug-tree next to the coffee pot then reached into the container on the countertop to retrieve a bag of Chamomile tea to drop into her cup. "What about Mom and Dad?"

"They went up around the same time, your Mom said something about taking a bath."

"So, did you manage to get everything finished?"

"Yup." He yawned and stretched his arms up over his head. "Your Mom will make the final couple of calls to confirm things and the party is good to go."

"Wow. And all without Paula's help. It's like a new dawn."

"Yeah, well, it's not one I want to revisit anytime soon," he remarked, dropping his arms back down and leaning back in his chair. "I don't know how Paula does it, day in and day out."

Amber picked up the kettle when it clicked off and poured the boiled water into her mug. "She's a master multi-tasker, that's for sure. That's why I'm going to be doing my best to keep out of her sight for the rest of the week, so she isn't reminded to nag me about finding the key to your house."

Declan regarded her, a small smile playing at his lips.

"What?" she demanded, putting the kettle back on its base. "What's with the look?"

"I'm just thinking how much I appreciate your helping out."

Amber blushed and picked up her mug to carry over to the table. "Forget it. And, besides, you're my best brother-in-law and I wanted to help."

Declan's small smile turned into a large grin. He wasn't sure how Jaimie would feel hearing that Trent was second-best brother-in-law, but it sure made him feel good.

"But don't tell Jaime I said that," she said, reading his mind while she set her mug on the wooden tabletop and pulled out a chair across from him to sit down.

"My lips are sealed," he confirmed, getting up from his chair. "And thanks."

"Before you go up," she said, eyes shining, "I have some big news."

He sat back down.

"I haven't told anyone else in the family yet, but I've finally settled on what I want to do with my life."

"You mean like career-wise?"

"Uh-huh," she agreed, lifting the teabag in her cup up and down.

"Wow, that's big news. Congratulations."

Amber nodded and stopped dunking the teabag. "Yup, I'm pretty pumped."

"*So*," he pressed, "are you going to tell me what it is, or do I have to guess?"

She sat up straight in her chair to deliver the news. "A Marine Biologist."

Declan's face went blank.

Amber relaxed her posture and started giggling. "God, your face! You should see it!"

"Well, come on," he chucked, defending himself. "You knew damned well I wasn't expecting to hear that."

"I know, I know," she admitted. "And I can't wait to tell everyone else. They'll be worse than you."

"So, seriously, you want to study Marine Biology?"

"Uh-huh. And I've even applied to a school on the coast."

"Wow," Declan said, digesting the information.

"And … I've been accepted!"

"What? Seriously?"

"Yes!" she squealed, then clamped her hand across her mouth. "But don't say anything! Promise you'll keep this to yourself. I'm going to wait until after the party and tell everyone then. I don't want to take anything away from all of the effort that's gone into it."

"Wow," Declan repeated himself, rubbing his hand across the stubble on his chin. "This is huge, Amber."

"I know! I'm so excited, I had to tell someone."

Declan thought of his brother and their conversation at the pub where he'd agreed to try and get an idea of where her head was at. Clearly, without even having to try, he has his answer. Which posed another question: did he share it with Liam? That was the real quandary.

"What?" she asked, puzzled by the unreadable expression on his face.

He shook his head. "It's nothing, just … stuff. It doesn't matter because what *does* matter is your news! I'm sure you're going to be a great success."

She beamed and scrambled out of her chair when he opened his arms for a congratulatory hug.

After a quick squeeze, he released her and shook his head at her.

"What?"

"Talk about a dark horse. None of us had any idea about your aspirations and now you're about to start a whole new adventure."

Amber blushed.

"Seriously, I'm both proud of you and a bit jealous."

"Jealous?" she parroted, confused.

"Sure. You're going to be starting something brand new. All new experiences, new people, it's very cool and I envy you, little sis."

"Oh. Okay." She sat back down and picked up her mug. Her tea was finally cool enough to drink. "I'm actually a bit nervous, truth be told. It's been a long time since I've been inside a classroom."

"You'll do great," he assured her, then cleared his throat and nonchalantly asked, "So, does this mean Liam doesn't know yet?"

She took a sip of tea then shook her head. "Nope. As I said, you're the first to know."

"Right," he said, not wanting to press further. It definitely was between her and Liam. "Well, again, I'm proud of you." He yawned for a third time and stretched his neck. "And now I really have to get some sleep."

"Go," Amber said, waving him out of the kitchen. "And remember, I want this kept quiet until after the party and you guys are moved into your house. I don't want to spoil the big surprise."

"Mum's the word," he agreed, walking out of the room.

"Mmm, gotta be honest with you, that feels sinfully good," Paula exhaled, as the tension left her shoulders.

It was late morning and she'd slipped out of the office to a hair appointment at *A Cut Above*. Now, reclining at one of the washing stations while her brother-in-law, Michael, massaged conditioner into her hair and scalp, she wished she could stay there for the rest of the day.

"You'll have to tell Cian," he admitted, before turning on the tap and checking the temperature of the water. "He's the one who insisted on teaching me the *proper* way to do a scalp massage. He'll be delighted to know his tutorials haven't been in vain."

"No, they haven't," Paula told him. "Can he teach Declan?"

Michael chortled while he rinsed the conditioner out of her hair. "He'd probably love that, he's such a control freak sometimes. They could call it the Dempsey scalp massage and make a video of it to promote the massage studio."

Paula grinned at the idea while he turned off the tap and wrapped a black towel around her head.

"Come on back to my chair," he instructed, "and let's get this cut back into shape."

Paula walked over to his station, the fourth in a row of eight workstations that ran the length of the wall, and made herself comfortable in the padded, chocolate brown leather chair that faced the oversized mirror. She sighed, loving the vibe of the salon. With its dark, distressed hardwood floors, walls painted a cool butter yellow and accented by wide panels of chunky rock that matched the front desk, it was the perfect blend of modern sleekness paired with an easygoing, lived-in feel.

"Comfy?" Michael asked, fussing around her, making sure her black cape was draped over both her and the back of chair.

"Perfect," she stated. "Couldn't ask for better."

"You're easy to please. Lucky Declan."

Paula smirked when she caught the glint of mischief in his brown eyes in the reflection of the mirror. He was such a flirt. Not to mention, he looked so much like Cian and the rest of the Dempsey men that if she didn't know better, she would have assumed he was another brother, instead of Cian's husband.

"I don't know, I'd say you and Cian are lucky," she bantered back. "How nice is it to have two wardrobes to choose from, instead of one?"

He removed the towel wrapped around her hair. "Yeah, *now*, but not when we first met. My husband, lord love him, had zero fashion sense when we met five years ago. Trust me, I saved him from himself. The man of style you know today is not the man I met all those moons ago."

Paula giggled while she looked at his reflection in the mirror. His pants were faded denim, rolled at the ankle, and his black and white patterned dress shirt was casually loose at the collar, sleeves zhooshed to his elbows. There was no denying he was the picture of unaffected style.

"Speaking of which, you and Cian are going to Jaimie's Christmas party on Saturday, right?"

"Of course!" he enthused, while focusing upon running his fingers through her layers as an excuse to break eye contact in the mirror.

Michael was a terrible liar and he knew it. Pretending he had no idea that the *supposed* Christmas party was, in fact, a surprise housewarming party for her and Declan was pushing him to his limit.

"That's good," Paula said. "Declan has been such a prince, running interference with my mother. He deserves to have everyone there to praise his efforts."

"I'm sure it's going to be great," he said, then swiftly shifted gears, all business. "But now we have to focus on making a choice. The color's done and looks sensational, are we sticking with the same cut or changing it up a bit?"

Paula regarded her reflection in the mirror. Maybe a new look would be a good thing.

Michael monitored her facial expression closely then asked, "Change it up a bit, yes?"

"Do you have any suggestions?"

His eyes lit up. "As a matter of fact, I do!"

Paula grinned at his transparency. "I'm getting a vibe here that you've had an idea for a bit and have just been waiting for me to come in so you can present it, am I right?"

He ran his fingers through her layers again. "Well, since you've left it for a while, it has some more length to play with. Hold tight for a minute while I get my phone. I saved a picture of a cut I thought would suite you. You're going to love it."

Paula settled herself more comfortably in the leather chair while he strode away to the back of the salon to disappear through the doorway to the staff room. Trust Michael, she thought, to have not just an idea, but a photo as well to back it up.

The bell above the salon entrance pinged and Paula looked over to see who'd entered the shop. It was Jessica, the owner of *A Cut Above*.

"Hey, Paula," she called out, lifting a hand in greeting then stopping to talk to the receptionist at the front desk.

Paula gave a small wave back. They'd become friendly when Jessica had hired *Certain Events* to put together the previous year's staff Christmas party. She'd spared no expense for the party, believing that a happy staff was a productive and successful staff.

"It's been a while since you've been in," Jessica said, once she'd finished with the receptionist and made her way over to Michael's station.

"I've been swamped at work," Paula admitted, admiring her long, copper red and bronzed brown curls.

Truth was, when she'd first met Jessica, she'd been a bit overwhelmed by how pretty she was. With her waterfall of hair and shapely, statuesque figure, she looked like a fairytale princess come to life. Paula had felt she would barely be noticed in the face of such beauty. Turned out, she couldn't have been more wrong. Jessica's personality matched her looks and as lovely as she was on the outside, she was equally - if not more so - on the inside. Kind, generous, welcoming: she embodied all of those qualities and more.

"Christmas party stuff?" she asked, cocking her head.

"No, a huge, splashy birthday party for a sixteen year old girl whose parents have more money than God."

"Yikes. Sounds like a lot of work."

"It was. And that's the reason its taken me so long to find the time to get in here."

"Are you and your husband moved into your new house yet?"

Paula looked at her with surprise. "How did you know we're moving?"

"Your sister was in a while ago," she said. "She mentioned it."

"Here we go!" Michael called out, as he emerged from the staff room and strolled back to his station: his movements like that of a lanky, self-assured cat.

Jessica reached out to give him a hug and when they were done, he leaned back and lifted some of the curled strands of her hair, nodding approvingly. "Very nice. The color is perfect on you."

She met Paula's eye. "He's complimenting himself, of course, since *he* did the color."

Paula giggled. If there was one thing Michael was confident about, it was his abilities as a stylist and colorist. He made no apologies about it.

"Okay," he announced, to Jessica. "Now leave us, you gorgeous thing, and let me work my magic on my lovely sister-in-law."

"Yes, sir," she replied, then touched Paula's shoulder and added, "We can catch up before you leave."

"Sounds good," she agreed, while Michael made grand shooing motions with his hands.

"Okay, okay, I'm going," she responded, pretending to be harried as she left them to it and walked away toward the back of the salon.

"Love you," Michael called after her.

"Yes, you do," she sang back.

"Alrighty, Aphrodite," he said, plunking his phone onto Paula's lap then picking up the blue water bottle from his black trolley beside the chair. "What do you think? Should we go for it?"

Paula looked at the picture then nodded. "Absolutely."

"I knew you'd like it!" he enthused, then confirmed, "Do you really like it?"

She nodded again. "I really do. You have a great eye."

He squeezed her shoulder, pleased, then said, "It still has that easy going vibe, but a bit edgier and sexier in its messiness. Just like you."

"Well, what are we waiting for?" she said, sitting up straight beneath her cape and placing the phone on the wide ledge beneath the mirror.

Needing no further encouragement, Michael began spraying her hair with water from the bottle. "Now, tell me *everything* about the glamorous birthday party you created and leave nothing out! The closest Cian and I have been to glamour lately is lighting some candles when we have our takeaway, I need to live vicariously. I want details, I *need* details."

Paula chuckled at his exaggeration. "Got it. *So…*"

Chapter 24

Donna raced through the house, check list clutched in her hand, and nearly knocked Paula off her feet as she blazed by her into the kitchen.

"Geez!" Paula exclaimed, gripping the top of the island to steady herself.

"Sorry, dear!" she sang, waving the paper in the air. "Only a few hours to go until the party!"

"And, somehow, that means you have to charge around like an over-zealous puppy?"

Donna laughed and dropped the list onto the countertop then retrieved a glass from the cupboard to pour herself some water from the tap. "Oh, my dear, if you had *any* idea of how much goes into planning an event like the one we have planned: well, you'd be charging, too! Five hours to you may seem like forever, but not to me!"

Paula's jaw tensed. If *she* had any idea? Really? Instead of offering a retort, she picked up a cracker from the plate in front of her, popped it into her mouth and focused her attention on chewing. She would not allow herself to be baited by the comment.

"Do you want to see what's left on the list?"

Paula shook her head. "Nope. Sounds like you've got everything in order."

Donna lifted the glass of water to her lips and took a long swallow then placed it on the countertop next to the piece of paper. "Well, I don't know about that—"

"I do," Paula interrupted, brushing cracker crumbs from her fingertips onto the plate. "Declan told me you guys are working like a well-oiled machine. Even Jaimie has said Trent is full of good words about everything."

"Still," she said, before being interrupted by Douglas loudly bellowing, "STORM'S A-COMIN'!" from the living room.

Paula and Donna raised their eyebrows at one another while he strode purposefully into the kitchen and asked, "Did you hear?"

Donna shifted her gaze to her husband. "Well of course we did! You were so loud I think it's safe to say the entire crescent may have, too. What are you going on about at the top of your lungs?"

"Ah-ha, so you *didn't* hear," he insisted, nodding.

"Yes, we did. I'm just asking you to elaborate, that's all."

"A winter squall is headed this way," he reported, rubbing his hands together.

Paula frowned. "A squall? Isn't that usually associated with water?"

Douglas looked taken aback. "So? What's your point?"

"Well, for starters, it's winter out there, Dad." She gestured toward the windows and, more accurately, what lay beyond them. "No water of any kind to be seen."

"Now, you see, dear," he said, pulling up a chair at the table, "that's where you're misinformed. Snow, also known as *frozen* water, can produce a squall. If you don't believe me, look it up."

Paula raised her hands in surrender. "I'll take your word for it."

"When?"

Douglas turned to Donna. "When? What when?"

"*When* is this so-called *squall* supposed to arrive?"

"Soon," he said, leaning back in his chair. "Maybe a day."

She laid a hand on her blouse, over her heart. "Oh, thank goodness."

"Or possibly sooner."

"What? NO! It can't come sooner!" Donna snatched up the list from the countertop and rattled it at them, so violently she almost knocked over her glass of water. "The party!"

Comprehension dawned on Douglas' face and he quickly stood up and crossed over to where she stood; clutching her chest with her free hand.

"How will it affect our plans?" she demanded, her voice taking on a frantic tone.

"It won't," he declared, placing a steadying hand on her shoulder.

"It won't?"

"No."

"You're sure?"

Paula watched their exchange, back and forth, back and forth, as though they were engaged in a conversational tennis match.

"I'm sure," he stated again, his voice firm and decisive.

Donna took a deep breath and nodded.

Paula wished someone else was in the room with them, so she could share the incredulous look she was wearing. Did her mother really believe that simply stating 'it won't' and 'I'm sure' would make her father's word come true? As though he had some sort of powers to control the weather?

"Whew!" Amber exhaled loudly, as she pushed open the kitchen door and let a gust of frigid wind blow her forward across the threshold into the house.

"Eeek!" Donna blurted, clutching at her list as though, at any moment, it was going to fly away. "Close that right now! Before something bad happens!"

Paula let her eyes roll this time. God, the drama. It was too much.

Amber pushed the door closed while Douglas wrapped a protective arm around Donna.

"What's going to happen from an open door?" Paula insisted, tightly. "Seriously, what? The winter boogieman is going to dart inside?"

No one paid her any mind. In fact, it was as though she was invisible the way they all started chattering at once.

"Snow squall is coming," Douglas stated.

"What does that mean?" Amber asked, shucking her coat from her shoulders.

"We have to hold on tight and be ready for anything," Donna proclaimed, pressing her precious list to her chest.

"Will the power go out? Should we get the candles and flashlights ready? Should I call Liam and warn him?" Amber's eyes grew round like saucers. "Ohmygod, what about the party? Will it affect the party?"

Donna grimaced and Douglas tightened his arm around her in a show of support.

"Oh, for the love of heaven," Paula exhaled, not that anyone noticed.

She shoveled the last of the crackers into her mouth and exited the room, acutely aware she would not be missed. If she had the darned key that Amber still hadn't found, she'd head over to the new house and make sure it was battened down for the, *supposed*, squall. Anything was better than the amateur theatre going on in the kitchen.

Declan held tight to the string of Christmas lights he was holding, lest they get carried away in the strong wind blowing in from the north. Donna had gotten it into her head that putting another string of lights on the house would keep him out of the way of Paula nagging for the house key, but, privately, he believed the real truth was she was eager for more lights and was using the situation to get him outside to do it.

"Jeez," he complained, as yet another gust of icy wind slammed against his jacket.

At this rate, his best option was looking to be wrapping the lights around the porch rails alongside the set already there and calling it a day.

"Hey!" Amber called out, her voice nearly carried away on the wind as she rounded the corner of the house and crossed the driveway toward Declan. "How's it going?"

"Brutal!" he hollered back.

She laughed and shuffled along through the snow that had blown across the pathway to the house.

"How are things inside?"

"Don't ask," she replied, stopping beside him and stamping her boots to clear them of snow.

Declan began executing his plan, starting at one end of the bannister.

Amber cocked her head while she watched him thread the string of lights through the rails. "So, you're just going to wrap them beside the lights already there?"

"Yup."

She nodded. "Good idea. Mom will never notice anyway. She's in such a tizzy over everything being just so, she's probably forgotten she even went batshit crazy over the idea of more lights."

Declan continued wrapping. "You know, I have to admit I was enjoying the process of planning everything, but now that the day is here, I honestly just want to get it done and finally sleep in my own bed."

Amber pulled a sympathetic face. "Yeah. I'm sure it will be fun once everyone is at the house, but I'm starting to look forward to it being a memory, am I right?"

Declan wound the last of the lights around the opposite end of the bannister. "Exactly. Perfectly said."

"Is there going to be enough cord to light those up?" she asked, pointing at the plug end of the lights.

"Nope."

She snickered at his blunt reply.

"Like you said, your Mom's not going to notice anyway. And I did what I said I'd do: added the lights. No one said anything about turning them on."

She held her mittened hands in the air as though she was showing she had nothing to hide. "No arguments here. As far as I'm concerned, I saw nothing."

"Agreed." Declan shivered in his jacket as another blast of bone-chilling air washed over them. "Now let's get the hell back inside before we freeze to death."

Amber glanced at the thick clouds darkening the sky then followed him up the porch steps toward the house. "Looks like Dad's squall prediction might be right after all."

Paula darted through the kitchen door into the house; wind swirling snow around her heels. She'd had the idea that taking a walk in the fresh air might be a good idea, but soon changed her mind and returned to the house when the wind started biting at her cheeks.

"Holy hell," she exhaled, shoving the door closed behind her. "You can't see anything out there."

"Snow squall," Douglas stated, gravely, by way of agreement.

"Dad!" Amber blurted, making her father startle. "*Pleeease* stop saying that."

Paula pulled her knitted pat from her head and hung it and her coat on a hook by the door. "Where's Declan?"

"In the living room," Douglas replied, turning his back so she wouldn't catch him casting a meaningful glance at Amber.

She got the message and opened the kitchen junk drawer, then made a show of exclaiming, "Ohmygod, look!"

Paula turned away from the hooks on the wall. "What?"

"Your house key!" Amber announced, reaching into the drawer and pulling out the key with a flourish. "It was right here all this time. I KNEW I'd find it!"

Paula crossed the kitchen and took the key from her outstretched hand.

"*See*," she said, smugly. "I *told* you I'd find it. I must have put it there for safe keeping and you have to admit, I kept it safe."

Paula stared at her levelly.

She lifted an eyebrow and stared back.

"Okay, fine," Paula agreed, giving in. "Yes, you did. You kept it safe."

"Ha," Amber said, then traipsed out of the room while throwing over her shoulder, "now you guys can go over and see the house."

Paula looked at the key then at her Dad. "Seriously? Does she think we're going to go there in this weather when it's the opposite direction from Jaimie and Trent's?"

"Oh, I don't know," Douglas offered, shrugging his shoulders. "Might not be such a bad idea."

"What might not be such a bad idea?" Donna asked, breezing into the kitchen.

"Paula and Declan popping over to the new house before they go to Jaimie and Trent's for the party."

Donna's face lit up and she nodded at Douglas. "That's a wonderful idea! Does that mean Amber finally found the key?"

"Amber finally found the key?" Declan repeated, striding into the room. "Excellent. So we can go over to the house and check everything's okay?"

Paula shook her head. "No."

His face fell. "She didn't find it?"

"No, that's not what I meant," she clarified. "I meant she did find the key, BUT there's no way we should consider going there *and* all the way back to Jaimie and Trent's for the party in this weather. That much driving around is just asking for trouble."

"Oh, please," Declan said, dismissively. "It'll be fine."

"Absolutely," Douglas agreed. "We'll all probably be the only ones on the roads."

"Okay, so it's settled." Declan rubbed his hands together. "Why don't we leave in…."

"About an hour should be good," Donna stated, meeting his eye.

"Perfect." Declan nodded and smiled at Paula.

She gave up. "Okay, fine. I know when I'm out-numbered. We'll leave in an hour."

Declan drove the car at a snail's pace down the street toward the new house. The snow was falling fast against the windshield and, try as they might, the wipers were having one heck of a time keeping the glass clear.

Despite the weather, Paula couldn't help but smile as they crept along. The slow pace was allowing her to take in the glowing Christmas lights that all of their new neighbors had strung on their houses and through their trees. She sighed. Beautiful.

"Okay?" Declan asked, keeping his eyes on the road ahead.

"It's all so pretty," she replied. "I just wish we could have put up decorations, too, so our place doesn't seem so…. Oh!"

Declan grinned. He knew why she'd gasped. He and Liam had gone over and strung lights around the entire house and it was glowing just as cheerfully as the rest of the homes on the block.

"How did you do this?" she asked, staring out her window like a child as they pulled up to the house. "I thought we couldn't get inside?"

"Liam and I did it before Amber misplaced the key," he explained, stretching the truth. "They're on a timer, inside."

Paula turned to him, her smiling face lit up by the glow coming off the house. "It's perfect. Thank you."

He pulled the car into the driveway and cut the engine. "Let's get inside, before we can't find the front porch."

She laughed and unclipped her seatbelt. "Ready when you are."

He put his hand on the door handle and said, "Break for it," as they exited the vehicle in tandem.

"Whoa!" Paula yelped, laughing as they dashed from the car and slipped and slid their way through the snow to the cover of the front porch of the house. "We may have a hard time finding the car when we go back."

Declan, on her heels, shielded her from the snow falling onto the steps by tucking her between him and the entrance door. "Do you have the key?"

Paula reached into her pocket and pulled out the key Amber had given her. "Yup. Ready?"

"Wait."

Paula paused and turned around to face him. "What?"

"Before we go in, I just want to say that I love you."

Her face softened. "I love you, too, Sweetie."

"And," he continued, "even though we've had a long haul getting here, not to mention a lot of *adventures* with the family…."

She raised an eyebrow. "That's an understatement."

"I still wouldn't trade any of it, because it's been *our* journey and *our* story and it's made this part of things all the better."

Paula leaned into him and planted a kiss on his lips. "Ditto," she said, when they pulled apart. "But can we continue this inside, so we don't turn into popsicles?"

He chuckled. "Go for it."

She turned around, inserted the key into the lock and twisted the doorknob.

"Tadaaa!" she sang, pushing open the door: only to be greeted by a chorus of voices yelling "SURPRISE!" that drowned out her both her words and shriek of shock.

Declan burst out laughing at the wide-eyed expression on her face, no longer wishing for the night to be over, but reveling in the fact it had just begun; just like the life they had ahead. It was all beginning right then in that moment and he was feeling like the luckiest man alive to be a part of it. It was time to celebrate.

Paula sighed and a slow, contented grin curved her lips as she stood in the comfort of her kitchen. HER kitchen. Bliss. She was finally home.

Declan strode into the room, all smiles as well. "How's everything in here?"

"Good. Although I think I'm still a bit shell-shocked. Just a couple of hours ago we were going - supposedly - to a party at my sister's and Trent's, and now I'm here in our new home and we don't have to go back to my parent's house!"

Declan felt the same thrill run through him. They were finally home. He walked around the kitchen island and swept her up into his embrace, tilting his face toward hers so they were nose to nose, looking into each other's eyes.

"And you're happy?"

She giggled. "Happy? That's an understatement. I feel like I'm in a perfect dream. Don't wake me up!"

Declan kissed her then said, "That's exactly how I wanted you to feel."

She shifted back slightly, so she could see his entire face. "And I know I've said it already, but thank you so much for this amazing surprise party."

He released her from his embrace and shook his head. "Don't thank me, remember. It was all your Mom's idea."

"Yes, but you helped. You and Amber and Dad and Jaimie and Liam and your Mom, all of you."

"Only because she had such a time-crunch to pull things off," he clarified. "She wanted it to be perfect for you, so you would realize how much she wants your relationship to change for the better."

Paula nodded. She knew that. Her Mom had taken her aside and bared her soul once the initial surprise was over and everyone had started digging into the food. It had been a lot to take in and Paula hoped it wasn't a fleeting thing and over time everything would slowly slip back to how they'd been.

Declan watched the emotions flit across her face and reached out to take her hand. "It's real, Hon. You can let yourself be happy about it. Your relationship with your Mom is finally going to be something positive in your life."

She looked into his eyes. "I hope so. I really do."

"I *know* so," he countered. "And, sure, she's still going to be wacky: a leopard doesn't change its spots entirely. But she's done some serious soul searching and *she's* the one who came to the understanding she needed to change. No one forced her. Give it some time, keep an open mind and you'll see, okay?"

She nodded. "Okay. Besides, what have I got to lose, right?"

He gave her a wry grin. "I suppose that's one way of looking at it."

"Hey!" Donna cheered, charging into the room, a sparkling smile plastered on her face. "Here you both are!"

"There they are!" Douglas echoed, following close on Donna's heels, Sylvester draped in his arms.

"You two need to come into the living room," Donna told them, while picking up a bottle of white wine and topping off the glass in her hand.

Declan and Paula exchanged a look, then he asked, "What's going on?"

"Your brother asked us to come get you," Douglas stated, holding out his glass for Donna to pour more wine into as well. "That's all we know."

"Which brother?" Paula queried, watching her mother pour the wine while trying to make sure Sylvester didn't stick his nose into the glass at the same time.

Donna placed the emptied bottle back on the island. "Liam. And bring your drinks. I think he's going to make a toast."

"Right behind you," Declan said, as she, Douglas and Sylvester left the kitchen. He looked at Paula and asked, "Shall we?"

"Right behind you," she echoed.

Liam took a deep breath and exhaled it slowly when Declan and Paula came into the living room. Perfect. They were all here. He stood up and walked over to stand in front of the large hearth adorned with Donna's homemade stockings; the perfect spot for everyone to see and hear him.

"Everyone," he called, raising his voice. "Could I have your attention?"

The room quieted and all of his family, Paula's family, and their friends turned to face him.

Liam cleared his throat. "Thanks. I just wanted to say a few words, so I hope you don't mind my interrupting your visiting."

"What's with the ceremony?" Emmet quipped, not being able to resist giving him a bit of heckling.

Liam met Amber's eye and grinned. She lifted her eyebrows in question, he hadn't told her he was going to say anything.

"I'm getting to it," he replied, then threw in the retort, "God, just as impatient as always."

Emmet couldn't help but smirk when his family all chuckled at the dig. It was true, there was no use denying it. He was impatient as hell.

"So, get on with it then," he bantered back, good-naturedly.

"I want to make a toast to Declan and Paula," Liam stated. "If I can get a word in edgewise."

Everyone immediately readied their glass while Bonnie sharply nudged Emmet to keep quiet.

Liam saw the reprimand, but kept his amusement in check as he continued. "I wish them nothing but happiness in their new home and even though it took a while for them to finally get moved in, now that they have I hope life treats them kindly ... and we all get invited to a lot more parties. Cheers!"

Everyone lifted their glasses and created a chorus of, "Cheers!" in return.

"*And*," Liam started to add, but was interrupted by Travis, Paula and Declan's realtor, singing,

"One more *THIIING!*" before jumping up from his seat on the sofa and dashing forward toward the hearth.

Liam took a step to the side when Travis bumped his shoulder against him, nearly knocking him over in his enthusiasm.

"Oh! Sorry about that!" Travis apologized. "You okay?"

"Fine," Liam assured him, while Emmet loudly remarked, "Another toast? I'm going to need another drink," earning himself a few chuckles and yet another sound jab in the ribs from Bonnie.

Travis chortled and batted a hand in Emmet's direction. "No! Not a toast. But you can get another drink anyway, once I'm done."

Gerry, seated next to the space Travis had just vacated on the couch, tittered.

"Okay, so," Travis began, "as you all know, my wonderful Gerry and I were the fortunate ones to help Paula and Declan find this beautiful home."

He paused to let the room offer their collective murmur of appreciation, then continued.

"However, what you don't know is, we haven't yet had the opportunity to give them their housewarming gift!"

Declan and Paula exchanged smiles, then Declan said, "You got us the house, Trav, that was your gift."

"Oh, so sweet," he called back to him. "But we have one more little thing for you."

At that, Gerry got up and raised a finger to indicate Paula and Declan should wait one moment.

They exchanged puzzled glances, instead of smiles, as Gerry dashed from the room.

"Patience, patience," Travis counselled, when he noticed the rest of the guests also raising their eyebrows and beginning to natter quietly.

Gerry strode back into the room a moment later and this time he wasn't holding the wine glass he'd left with but, instead, cuddling a....

"Puppy!" Amber blurted, excitedly.

"You've gotta be kidding me," Declan muttered, under his breath, not that he needed to be all that quiet as Travis and Amber were emitting matching cooing noises while their guest's nattering had turned up a notch from under-breath commentary to louder, "ohmygod, it's a puppy," sort of commentary.

Gerry carried the puppy - an eight week old, black and tan, wire-haired dachshund - to Paula and gently offered it to her.

While she took it from him, Travis clapped excitedly from his place at the hearth and gushed, "*Now* you see why we had to wait on our gift, it wasn't ready yet!"

Some of the guests chuckled at the comment, while he further revealed, "When we ran into you at the coffee shop and you told us you weren't even in the house yet, well count us pleased! Not about you having to wait so long to move in, of course, just that we were relieved to know we didn't have to keep fretting about being so late on giving you your gift!"

Against her better judgement, Paula could feel her heart softening as she cradled the small, warm puppy bundle against her stomach. Then, while her mother, Jaimie, Linda, Amber, Bonnie and Erin all crowded around her to get a better look, she lifted her eyes to peek at Declan.

He grinned at the smitten expression on her face.

He knew that look.

Like it or not, they now had a dog added into their family.

First the cat, now a dog. What was next, a bird?

"Is it a boy, or girl?" Bonnie asked, reaching out to gently stroke its little head.

"A boy," Gerry replied.

"Aww, a furry little grand-dog," she teased, grinning at Craig, making him chuckle.

Linda and Angus' boys managed to squeeze themselves between the women's legs and plastered themselves up against Paula.

"Can we play with him when he's a bigger?" Ethan asked.

Paula smiled at him and appreciated his ten year old wisdom to recognize the puppy was still so small and fragile.

"Absolutely," she agreed.

"We could even babysit him for you, if you ever need us to," Finn informed her, then turned to Linda and said, "Right, Mom?"

Paula had to bite her lip to keep from laughing at the expression on Linda's face.

"Umm," she said, trying to find a non-committal answer.

"Don't worry," Paula whispered to her. "I'm sure Amber will be all over the *babysitting* idea. It'll probably never happen."

Linda's shoulders relaxed and she smiled at Paula before saying to Finn, "I'm sure, if Auntie Paula and Uncle Declan need a sitter, we'd be able to help out."

"Yay!" Finn cheered.

"Not if I get there first," Amber declared, under her breath, but still loudly enough for both Paula and Linda to overhear.

"See?" Paula said. "Told you."

Linda snickered and patted her shoulder.

"Speaking of which, where's Sylvester?" Amber asked, turning to look at her Dad.

"He's upstairs," Douglas told her. "When I put him down, he scampered up the staircase and that's the last I've seen of him."

"Oh, don't worry about the cat," Travis assured, going over to Amber. "Dachshunds are known for getting along famously with cats. They'll be fast friends in no time."

Declan managed to extract himself from the group of women and sidled over to Liam, now leaning up against the wall next to the fireplace.

"Congrats on the new addition to the family," Liam chuckled, knowing full well the dog had come as a complete surprise.

Declan gave him a wry grin. "Yeah, thanks."

"Guess you'll be needing that dog door after all, huh?" he teased, then drank the last of the wine in his glass.

"Jeez, talk about foreshadowing, right?" Declan joked, before asking, "So, were you done there? 'Cause it looked like you had something else to say before Travis took over."

Liam shrugged. "Yeah, but it's fine, just—"

"Everyone," Declan said, loudly, interrupting Liam much as Travis had done. "Liam still has something else he'd like to say."

All heads swiveled in their direction.

Declan patted him on the back. "There you go. Have at it."

"Thanks," Liam replied, putting his glass on the mantle and refocusing on what he'd wanted to say.

"Okay, this one had better be good to top the dog," Emmet ribbed, brazenly, as his mother was well enough away from him still fawning over the puppy.

Liam laughed and shook his head at his brother. "Okay, sorry, I know the puppy deserves his spotlight, but this won't take long. This next bit is about Amber."

A flush crept up Amber's neck when all of the people in the room shifted their focus from the puppy to her.

"Me?" she said, wide-eyed in the face of their attention.

Liam smiled at her and began to elaborate. "Okay, so here's the thing, my lovely girlfriend has shared with me a wonderful piece of news this evening." He took a breath then met Bonnie's eye as he added, "And no, before you go there, she's not pregnant, Mom."

The room filled with the sound of good natured chuckling as Bonnie giggled and took the teasing with grace.

"So what was the news?" Emmet badgered, ever impatient.

"The news," Liam went on, "is that not only has Amber secretly applied to go to school to become a Marine Biologist…."

There was a gasp from Paula, Donna, Douglas and Jaimie.

"But that she's been accepted!"

"Oh!" Donna screeched, reaching out to pull Amber into a tight hug.

"Wait, there's more," Liam declared.

Donna released Amber, her eye's shining with proud mother tears. "More? Are you trying to do me in?" she demanded.

He chuckled then said, "Amber, Hon, could you come over here?"

"Okay," she said, looking at her sisters and shrugging her shoulders, then walking over to join him in front of the fireplace.

Liam looked into her eyes once she stood beside him. "So, here's the thing, your news is some of the best I've heard in a long while. I know you've been trying to find your path and I think it's wonderful you finally have."

"Here, here," Douglas said, lifting his glass.

Amber grinned at Liam, slightly embarrassed by his very public admission, but also a bit pleased by it as well.

"And, with that in mind, now I'm hoping - in front of our entire family and friends - you'll agree you want to move forward on your new path as a duo, instead of solo."

Amber's brow furrowed with confusion. However, when Liam reached into his pocket and pulled out a small box then lowered himself down onto one knee, she sputtered, "Wait, what are you doing? What's happening?"

"Amber Jade Hayes, will you do me the immense honor of being my wife?"

A heavy silence settled over the room as everyone took in what Liam had said. As though they'd all been flash frozen and were waiting for her reply to free them.

Amber blinked rapidly, looked at Liam, then at the small box he'd opened to reveal a ring with a single, perfectly round jade stone surrounded by tiny swirls of glittering diamonds. It was the last thing she'd expected.

"Well?" he asked, so nervous he was barely able to get enough oxygen into his lungs to get the word out.

Amber shifted her gaze from the box back to his eyes. Her lips curved and her mouth bloomed into the warmest smile she'd ever worn in her life as she said, simply, "Yes."

Freed from their breathless state, the party guests all cheered in unison: immediately surging forward to congratulate them. Declan pulled Paula aside, wanting a moment before she got swept away into her sister's good news.

She let him lead her into the kitchen room, away from the din, then asked, "What's wrong?"

He shook his head. "Nothing. In fact, everything is perfect. I just wanted a moment to tell you that I love you and I love this life we're creating."

She cuddled the puppy close to her chest and stretched upward to plant a solid kiss on his lips. When they came up for air, she said, "Me, too. And with that crew in there, never-mind this new addition and the feline upstairs, I have a feeling the chaos will continue undaunted."

Before he could answer, Jaimie came rushing in, all gesturing hands and wide-eyed insistence.

"Come on! Trent's got Hazel and I need your muscle to help me shove everyone aside to get to Amber!"

Declan chortled while Paula slipped from his embrace.

"Go," he said, opening his arms to invite her to give him the puppy. "Help your sister."

She giggled, handed over the dog, then let Jaimie drag her from the room.

Declan watched them disappear then lifted the little animal higher to better see his face. The puppy leaned forward to gently sniff his nose and Declan grinned.

"She's right, you know," he told him, philosophically. "It won't be boring. Not even a little. It'll be just the opposite, which means it'll be perfect."

THE END

About the Author

Kathleen began storytelling in grade school and has many fond memories of passing summer afternoons, out on the swings in her backyard, creating tales that entertained her neighborhood friends.

Many years later, too many to talk about without seeming rude and nosey, Kathleen has channeled her imagination to the pages of her novels. She hopes you enjoy her tales and encourages you to feel free to read her stories on the swing set in your own backyard.

Kathleen now spends time in her backyard with her beloved husband, adored son and silly dog. They let her tell them stories and always laugh in all of the correct places. She's lucky, and she knows it.

Connect with Kathleen Online

Website: kathleenkole.com

Facebook: facebook.com/KathleenKoleAuthor

Twitter: twitter.com/kathleenkole